TRICKS A

MW01140383

A Mystery Writers of America Classic Anthology

JEAN L. BACKUS   ANTHONY BOUCHER

BETTY BUCHANAN   JOHN DICKSON CARR

WILLIAM CHAMBERS   STANLEY ELLIN

RICHARD ELLINGTON   HARLAN ELLISON

JOE GORES   LEN GRAY   JOE L. HENSLEY

EDWARD D. HOCH   JAMES HOLDING   JOHN LUTZ

ELIZABETH A. LYNN   JOHN D. MACDONALD

DAN J. MARLOWE   ARTHUR MOORE

WILLIAM F. NOLAN   STEPHEN R. NOWAK

ALBERT F. NUSSBAUM

BILL PRONZINI & BARRY N. MALZBERG

ELLERY QUEEN   S. S. RAFFERTY   JACK RITCHIE

HENRY SLESAR   PAULINE C. SMITH

EDWARD WELLEN   JESSAMYN WEST

DONALD E. WESTLAKE

Edited by
JOE GORES AND BILL PRONZINI

TRICKS AND TREATS

Copyright © 1976, 2019 by Mystery Writers of America.

A Mystery Writers of America Presents: MWA Classics Book published by arrangement with the authors

Cover art image by Ilkin Zeferli
Cover design by David Allan Kerber
Editorial and layout by Stonehenge Editorial

PRINTING HISTORY

Mystery Writers of America Presents: MWA Classics edition / February 2019

For information contact: Mystery Writers of America, 1140 Broadway, Suite 1507, New York, NY 10001

Contents

Foreword   ix

Introduction   xi

THE DONOR   1
Dan J. Marlowe

THE PILL PROBLEM   8
Pauline C. Smith

I ALWAYS GET THE CUTIES   22
John D. MacDonald

THE CROOKED PICTURE   30
John Lutz

NIGHT PIECE FOR JULIA   37
Jessamyn West

NO MORE QUESTIONS   42
Stephen R. Novak

VIOLATION   55
William F. Nolan

HOLLYWOOD FOOTPRINTS   61
Betty Buchanan

THE TIME OF THE EYE   67
Harlan Ellison

FACE VALUE   76
Edward Wellen

THE LEOPOLD LOCKED ROOM   82
Edward D. Hoch

IF I QUENCH THEE...   99
William E. Chambers

THE SPOILS SYSTEM   105
Donald E. Westlake

ROPE ENOUGH   111
Joe Gores

ROBERT   119
Stanley Ellin

MY MOTHER, THE GHOST   135
Henry Slesar

MURDER BY SCALPING   142
S. S. Rafferty

We All Have to Go   150

THE LITTLE OLD LADY OF CRICKET CREEK   161
Len Gray

YOU CAN GET USED TO ANYTHING   166
Anthony Boucher

MISER'S GOLD   182
Ellery Queen

THE GIRL WHO JUMPED IN THE RIVER   189
Arthur Moore

HAND IN GLOVE   197
James Holding

THE SILVER CURTAIN   201
John Dickson Carr

SHUT THE FINAL DOOR   217
Joe L. Hensley

THE COUNTERFEIT CONMAN   225
Albert F. Nussbaum

MY SISTER AND I   233
Jean L. Backus

GOODBYE, CORA   241
Richard Ellington

MULTIPLES   254
Bill Pronzini and Barry N. Malzberg

THE DEVERAUX MONSTER   259
Jack Ritchie

Afterword   277
The Mystery Writers of America Presents Classic   279
Anthology Series

For the Memory of LEO MARGULIES (1900-1975)

*Editor, Publisher, Gentleman, and Friend and Benefactor to Countless MWA
Members and Other Writers for Nearly Fifty Years*

*His life was gentle, and the elements
So mix'd in him that Nature might stand up And say to all the world,
"This was a man!"*

*JULIUS CAESAR, ACT V, SCENE V
—WILLIAM SHAKESPEARE*

Foreword

Joe Gores (1931-2011) and Bill Pronzini (1943-) had both been active in the mystery field less than a decade or so when *Tricks and Treats* was published in 1976, but they were already major names. Joe had won two Edgar awards, and Bill had turned out more novels and short stories than many of us (me, for example, born the same year) would accomplish in a lifetime. While Joe is gone, Bill, recipient of the MWA Grand Master Award in 2008, is still going strong and prolific as ever.

The theme of their anthology was McGuffins (more commonly spelled MacGuffins), a term sort of like *noir*, that has a very specific meaning for purists, but is generally used to mean just about anything you want it to mean. The Hitchcock anecdote in their introduction hints at without spelling out both the narrow and the broad definitions. According to Wikipedia, the MacGuffin is "a plot device in the form of some goal, desired object, or another motivator that the protagonist pursues, often with little or no narrative explanation. The MacGuffin's importance to the plot is not the object itself, but rather its effect on the characters and their motivations." The Meriam-Webster definition, more inclusive if a bit vaguer: "an object, event, or character in a film or story that serves to set and keep the plot in motion despite usually lacking intrinsic importance." It's easiest to think of in terms of an object (sources differ on whether it should be something really important like the formula for world peace or trivial but tantalizing like the meaning of "Rosebud") that the protagonist and other characters are after. Some examples: the Maltese Falcon, the Ark of the Covenant in the *Raiders of the Lost Arc*, the NOC list of informants in the first *Mission Impossible* feature, the Holy Grail, military plans, weapons designs, or other vital papers. Readers of this anthology are invited to consider in each of these stories whether there is really a MacGuffin and if so, what it is.

Mystery Writers of America anthologies have changed since their mid-1940s launch. Early volumes in the series consisted entirely of reprints, all donated by their authors for the good of the organization. Recent volumes have been comprised entirely of new stories, either commissioned by the editor or selected by a panel of judges from anonymous submissions, and now contributors are paid rather well. *Tricks and Treats* belongs in a transitional period: the stories were still donated, but some originals were included. Both editors of the volume offer new stories, Pronzini in collaboration with Barry N. Malzberg, along with previously unpublished work by Betty Buchanan, William E. Chambers, Elizabeth A. Lynn, and Jean L. Backus. The reprints represent Golden Age old-timers (Ellery Queen, Anthony Boucher, John Dickson Carr), stalwarts of the magazine market (Edward D. Hoch, Henry Slesar, James Holding, Jack Ritchie), novel-writing royalty (John D. MacDonald), and one surprise from the mainstream (Jessamyn West). The introductions to each story by Joe or Bill show that they were conscientious editors. Forty plus years after its first publication, their anthology stands the test of time.

–Jon L. Breen

Introduction

Since this anthology depends on tricks and treats, surprise endings, twists, gimmicks—in a word, McGuffins—we had best define for you, Gentle Reader, just what a McGuffin is. The best, in fact to our knowledge the *only,* definition was given by the Master himself, Alfred Hitchcock, during a discussion of his films. We can only paraphrase his remarks, of course, but they went something like this...

It seems that an American in London got on a train which was bound for the Scottish Highlands. He found himself sharing a compartment with a grizzled British sportsman of the sort who consistently drops his "g's"; a sportsman loaded down with huntin' and fishin' gear who was obviously heading north for a bit of a shoot.

On the overhead rack, however, this gentleman had placed a rather strange-looking box. The American, unable to contain his curiosity, finally leaned forward and said, "I beg your pardon, but could you possibly tell me what that odd-looking box is?"

The sportsman looked at the American, transferred his gaze to the box, and then fixed it again on the American.

"That's a McGuffin," he said.

"A...McGuffin? Ah...what purpose does a McGuffin serve? What is it *used for?*"

"Why, a McGuffin is indispensable when one is hunting lions and tigers. Since I am going to the Scottish Highlands to hunt tigers..." He stopped there, as if he had explained sufficiently.

After a moment, the American felt impelled to lean forward again. "I don't know how to tell you this, sir, but there aren't any tigers in the Scottish Highlands."

"You don't say." The grizzled sportsman stared at him for several seconds in surprise, then looked up at the box again. Contemplatively he said, "Then that can't be a McGuffin, can it?"

Now that we—and Mr. Hitchcock—have explained to you *exactly* what a McGuffin is, you know all about the stories in this anthology. But if some whisp of confusion lingers in your mind, let us assure you that *we* know a McGuffin when we see one. And all of the wonderful and talented writers who appear herein, who have donated this use of their work to Mystery Writers of America without pay or recompense, *they* know what a McGuffin is.

After all, they've collectively written a *whole book* about the bloody things.

Haven't they?

—Bill Pronzini and Joe Gores
San Francisco
December 1975

The Donor

Dan J. Marlowe

SURPRISE!

We chose "The Donor" to lead off this anthology because it is the very essence of the McGuffin, with an understated symmetry and a whiplash ending which leaves the reader breathless as a roller-coaster ride. Great McGuffins demand great artistry, a quality not always in evidence in the paperback original novels which are Mr. Marlowe's chosen arena. But the growing talent he displayed in 1962 with the unforgettable The Name of the Game is Death *was confirmed in 1970, when his* Operation Flashpoint *was awarded the Edgar. Today his Earl Drake series enjoys booming sales and reprinting in over a dozen foreign countries. So any would-be or want-to-be writers reading these words take heart: Dan Marlowe is an ex-professional gambler who didn't write a word for money until he was pushing fifty! - J.G.*

I WENT to reform school when I was twelve, prison when I was eighteen, and I've spent most of my life in one penitentiary or another. I've stolen cars, cashed bad checks, burglarized stores, and committed armed robberies. During any given ten-year period, I was seldom outside the walls of an institution for more than a few months at a time.

Then I took a trip west to change my luck. It changed it for the worse. I took another fall, and then in prison one day I was standing alongside another con when he was knifed in the back. I was tried for his murder. It didn't matter that for once I was innocent; the judge pronounced the mandatory death sentence. I couldn't help thinking that it seemed to be what I had unconsciously been preparing myself for all my life.

So, at forty-eight, with the handwriting on the wall, I made up my mind to leave life with more style than I'd lived it. When the automatic appeal had been denied, I told my court-appointed lawyer I wouldn't need him anymore. I settled down to the death row routine of tearing pages from a calendar and waiting for the big day.

I thought the warden would be happy to have a prisoner who wasn't always bugging him for some privilege, but he wasn't. For some reason my attitude seemed to concern him.

"It's not natural for a man in your position to show so little concern," said Warden Raymond.

"How would you know what's natural, warden?" I asked. "You're young. All you know about prison you got out of books. You've only had your appointment for about a year. You've got a lot to learn."

He shook his head. He looked like a tired David Niven except that his hair was reddish-brown. He had dark circles under his eyes most of the time. There was a prison joke about the dark circles. Warden Raymond had a young wife. I'd never seen her, but the men who had said she had an unconsciously sexual appeal.

The chaplain came to see me a few times, but I always ran him off. "It's got to be better the second time around, Pilot," I told him. The men called him the Sky Pilot. He couldn't cope with my theories on reincarnation, but he didn't stop coming.

My only other visitor was Warden Raymond. He would have himself admitted by the ever-present guard, and I'd set down the book I'd been reading. The warden made more frequent trips from his office to my cell as the big day grew closer. Each time I saw him he looked worse. It was going to be the first execution for each of us, but to look at him you'd think he was the one who was going to ride the lightning.

"You know that the-uh-execution is only a short time away," he said to me one day.

"I know."

"Have you decided upon which-uh-which method you want us to use?"

I stared at him. "Which method? I don't get it."

"There are two approved methods of execution in this state, hanging and the firing squad." I must have looked blank. "I thought you knew."

I tried to sound flippant. "Is that what happens when there's no more cheap power? I thought it would be electrocution."

"You have a choice, as I indicated," he answered. He didn't sound happy even telling me about it.

"It's not going to be hanging, warden," I said positively. "Have the firing squad oil up the rifles."

The warden spoke urgently. "Doesn't this bother you at all? Don't you feel-uh-odd, having to choose the way you're going to die?"

"Why, no. If I've got to go, and I don't seem to have much say about that, what's so hard about selecting the method?"

He grimaced and left the cell.

During the next couple of weeks I ate well and got plenty of rest. I gained five pounds and the warden lost ten. He obviously spent more time thinking about my execution than I did. The man had too much empathy for his own good. He even tried to get the governor to commute my sentence to life imprisonment. He came to my cell almost in tears when he failed. He was really getting on my nerves a little bit, although it's difficult to dislike a man because he doesn't want to kill you.

THE WARDEN SHOWED up in front of my cell with a stranger when the execution was a week away. His usual uneasiness seemed to have been replaced by embarrassment. "This is Dr. Sansom," he said to me. "He'd like to talk to you."

I looked Dr. Sansom over. He had to have some kind of clout. Not every doctor makes it onto death row. The guard came over and unlocked the cell door, but only the doctor came inside.

"I'll leave you two alone," Warden Raymond said quickly, and hurried away.

"Come to see if I'm healthy enough to kill, Doc?" I asked as he sat down. His mouth smiled, but his eyes didn't. He was young, but he had the coldest-looking eyes I'd ever seen on a human being.

"You don't want to mind him," I went on, nodding in the direction of the warden's departure. "He's taking all this pretty hard."

"And you're not?"

"That's right."

"That's what they told me, and that's why I'm here." He crossed his legs leisurely. "I'm chief of neurosurgery at Mercy Hospital in town. I want you to donate your body to science. Specifically, I want you to donate it to me."

There was certainly nothing bashful about the doctor. Just like that, he wanted my body. "How come, Doc?"

"You've read about the organ transplants performed recently—kidneys, livers, hearts?"

"I can read the big print in the newspapers."

Irony was wasted on him. He was all business. "Techniques have been developed that would have seemed miraculous a short time ago. You might be able to save several lives."

"Several?" I had a mental picture of myself being cut and dealt like a deck of cards. I wanted to discourage him. "Look, I'm not a kid any longer. I'm pushing fifty. I always thought you people wanted young meat. Besides, when the bullets get through with me, my ticker won't be any good to me or to anyone else."

But Dr. Sansom had an answer for everything. "The prison physician tells me you're in remarkable condition for a man your age. He attributes this to your being sheltered so often and so long from the vices prevalent outside prison. I'm sure your organs are just what I want. As for the wasteful method of execution you've chosen, though, I wish you'd reconsider."

"Not a chance, Doc."

"Well, what about your body?"

I still didn't care for the idea of being used for spare parts, but with the new image I'd been building for myself it proved hard to be ungracious. "I'm not about to change my mind about the firing squad," I told him, "but you're welcome to what's left."

"I'll make do with that," he said, and rose to his feet. He pulled a large envelope from his inside breast pocket and handed me a crackling legal paper to sign. He was taking no chances on my changing my mind. I signed the paper, and Dr. Sansom departed.

After that I was glad the execution date was so near. It had been difficult enough on some days to seem unconcerned, and the doctor had added a mental burden. When I had thought of myself as dead, I had always pictured myself sleeping peacefully with my hands folded across my chest. Now I didn't care to dwell upon the final scene.

ON THE MORNING of the execution, though, Warden Raymond was still far more disturbed about it than I was. He looked as though he'd been up all night, and his whiskey breath made no secret about how he'd spent his time. I followed him out into the prison yard with the chaplain by my side. The prison guards I'd come to know waved or nodded as I passed. A few murmured reassurances. The ones who weren't following on my heels, that is, to make sure I didn't change my mind about going peaceably.

The prison yard was cool. The first rays of the sun were striking the wall. A heavy wooden chair with leather straps attached to it sat facing a small wood-and-canvas structure fifty yards away. I knew the firing squad was already inside the structure, concealed from view by the canvas awning. When the time came, the awning would be raised, and —*BOOM!*

A large, white tractor-trailer was parked twenty yards to the left of the chair. Dr. Sansom stood beside it with a number of other men. They were all wearing light-green hospital gowns. The only sound in the prison yard was the hum of a diesel generator mounted on top of the trailer. I figured out finally that it was needed to keep my organs from spoiling during the run into town.

I went directly to the chair and sat down. I could hear the collective sigh of relief from the guards, happy that they didn't have to wrestle me into it. The warden read a paper—mumbled would be more accurate—to the official observers, and then a pair of guards fastened my arms and legs with the leather straps. The prison physician pinned a target to the front of my shirt, and then a hood was dropped over my head.

In the dead silence that followed nothing happened for a few seconds. I was trying to think of something clever to say when I felt as though I'd been struck in the chest by a sledgehammer.

Immediately after that I heard the roar of the rifles. The echo rebounded from the stone walls. Blood gushed into my throat, and I remember thinking that Dr. Sansom wouldn't be able to use my lungs, either.

Then I couldn't think anything...

I COULD SEE light and movement when I opened my eyes, but I had difficulty in focusing upon it. I felt weaker than I had ever felt in my life.

"Call Dr. Sansom in here at once!" a female voice said urgently.

"He's regained consciousness again, and this time he seems rational!" There was a flurry of activity around me. Shadowy figures gradually became more distinct. Then I was looking up at Dr. Sansom. There was a flicker of something other than the usual impassivity in his cold-eyed stare. Excitement? The situation became clear to me at once. Dr. Sansom had taken me from the firing squad chair and given me a new heart. I raised a trembling hand as I tried to complain to him, but all I could utter was gibberish.

Then I saw freckles on the back of my hand.

My hand?

I'd never had a freckle in my life!

I sank back upon the pillow, exhausted. Dr. Sansom. that diabolical surgical magician, hadn't given me a new heart. He had implanted my brain in someone else's head. I wondered where the rest of me was. God only knew into how many parts I'd been divided.

"Don't try to talk yet, Tom," Dr. Sansom said soothingly. "You've been in a coma for a long time. Relax and get your bearings." I became conscious of bandages on my face. "You're making a fine recovery. We'll have you up and moving around in a few days now. When we remove the bandages, you'll look almost the same as you did before you tried to mix drinking and driving and went through the window of your car. Most of the scars will be hidden by your hair."

Not so much as by the flicker of an eyelash did he indicate—and no one could know more surely—that I wasn't "Tom."

I hadn't noticed previously, but there were tubes connected to my other arm and my side. Dr. Sansom directed the nurses as they disconnected them, and my own life cycle took over the function of keeping me breathing. My own? I closed my eyes and stopped thinking about it. They took away all the machinery that had kept me alive while I was in the coma.

Tom's wife was allowed to visit me for five minutes a day. She was a tall, buxom girl with an anxious expression that in ensuing days changed to one of hope. She sat and held my hand and stared at my bandaged face with tear-stained eyes. "I thought I'd lost you," she said repeatedly.

Another complication, I thought wearily.

But life takes over. I worked at gaining control of my new body in the days that followed. Speech was the most difficult. At first I had to concentrate hard to form each word, but soon I was speaking simple sentences. Dr. Sansom permitted me to get out of bed and move carefully around the hospital room. He watched me with a gleam in his eye. I found that it was like trying to drive a car after a long prison stretch. I had to develop judgment and a new depth perception.

I gained strength every day. That was when I first became aware that my new body was a young body. I felt better than I had for years. I felt a chill, though, when Dr. Sansom said something one day about getting me back on the job. Surely he realized there was no job to which I could return? I was still a middle-aged convict who'd spent more than thirty years behind bars. I had no skills, no training, no education that hadn't come from reading two or three books a week no matter what prison I happened to be calling home. The only thing prison had prepared me for was more prison.

The more I saw of Tom's wife the more I wished I could really be him, but there was no possible way. I didn't know what Tom's job had been, but whether it was lawyer, engineer, architect, or street cleaner, I didn't try to fool myself into thinking I could step into it as easily as I had taken over his body.

Then Dr. Sansom appeared in my room one day with an armful of clothing. "Get dressed," he said. "We're going to take a ride to your office." I tried to protest, but he ignored me. "It will be just a short visit. When we get back, we'll take your bandages off."

One of the nurses drove the car. I sat in the middle with Dr. Sansom beside me. I stared at the dashboard, trying to keep the blur of rapidly passing scenery from confusing me further. Then the car stopped, and I looked up. I drew a long, unbelieving breath.

They helped me out of the car. The concrete walk was lined with people. Smiling people. All the way to my office I accepted greetings from uniformed guards, many of whom I knew well. Very well.

"Welcome back, Warden Raymond," they said.

The Pill Problem

Pauline C. Smith

"ARSENIC AND OLD LACE"

The one word which perhaps best describes Joseph Kesselring's classic 1940s farce, Arsenic and Old Lace, *is "romp"—and the same word applies to Pauline C. Smith's "The Pill Problem." Like the play, this story has a dizzying, quietly mad plot, a good deal of rather macabre humor, and a memorable and wacky cast of characters; and it is a dandy McGuffin in the bargain. Mrs. Smith, a gentle lady who lives in Southern California, has to her credit an impressive list of sometimes bloodthirsty, uniformly excellent short stories, one of which was nominated for an Edgar in 1972 and several of which have been included in the annual Best Detective Stories of the Year. - B.P.*

PHYLLIS CRENSHAW WAS A SLOB. In an ordinary dining chair, her fat lopped over the seat and puffed against the back. However, Phyllis no longer sat in a dining chair, up to a table; not since the doctor had told her in no uncertain terms and with a concerned click of his tongue, "Mrs. Crenshaw, you are in terrible shape."

That was obvious. She knew her shape was terrible.

Then the doctor added not only a word of advice, but an awful prognostication: "If you don't take off some of that weight, you are going to drop dead."

A brutal statement, but effective.

Phyllis went on an immediate diet, not the high-protein, low-carbohydrate diet the doctor had ordered and carefully written out, but one she herself devised, solidly liquid and sweetly noncaloric, consisting of tea loaded with saccharin. She drank this diet all day long, sometimes even at night when she awakened famished.

Horace Crenshaw, Phyllis' husband, was toothpick thin and nervous as a cat. He leaped at sudden sounds and breathed fast when he walked more than ten steps. He looked miserable.

The doctor told him so. "Mr. Crenshaw," he said, "you've got to take care of yourself," and wrote out a prescription for nitroglycerin tablets, explaining how, at the first sign of tightness in his chest, Horace was to pop one of those tablets under his tongue.

The doctor's diagnosis in each case was absolutely correct. Phyllis *was* appallingly obese and Horace's heart posed a fluttering problem. His diagnoses, however, had embraced only the effect and not the cause of the Crenshaws' condition, which had begun twenty-five years before when Phyllis, slim as a reed, married Horace, sturdy as an oak.

They were a handsome couple then, not too young and not too old for marriage, so everything might have been fine when they set up housekeeping in the Crenshaw family home except that they began to get on each other's nerves.

Phyllis turned out to be coy beyond Horace's belief, and Horace came up as a fuddy-dud, which was really too bad because they had everything going for them—the Crenshaw Lumber Company, the palatial house and the very first seven-inch television set in town that Phyllis named "Rover."

She named things: the car, the rosebushes and the fireside chairs. She bounced and ducked her head when she chattered. She squealed and giggled. Horace took unsmiling refuge behind his cold pipe, beginning to hate her.

Early in their marriage, Phyllis shed her cutesy ways and settled down to a total involvement with food. She spent half her time in the kitchen turning out souffles, dumplings, chocolate chiffon pies, noodles, and sponge cake, and the other half eating what she had prepared. Every time she opened her mouth to stuff something into it, Horace's heart murmured.

She ate through the next twenty years, growing so fat that Gertrude, who used to come two days a week to do the heavy cleaning, finally was needed six days a week to do everything, and Horace retired from the business (being only a figurehead anyway) to rest his jumping heart in his Morris chair in the den.

From then on, Horace emerged only occasionally at a slow walk to see if Phyllis might be in her usual place, overflowing the big fanback chair in the back parlor. She generally was—with a food tray fitted across the arms. He then walked slowly back to the den to sink down in the Morris chair and feel his heart hammer out an uneven hostility.

With Horace forever home, Phyllis chewed him up with her steaks and swallowed him with barbecue sauce.

Even Gertrude, somewhat slow-witted, noticed that this was a house divided against itself, and discussed it with her equally slow-witted husband in the evenings.

"I don't know," she said.

"Don't know what?" he asked.

"About them!"

"What about them?" he coaxed. "They sure are funny."

It was after the doctor's visit that Phyllis took her last waddle up the stairs to her bedroom to instruct Gertrude to cart down all her bedroom furniture and put it into the back parlor and cart all the back parlor furniture up to her bedroom (all except the fanback chair), then she went downstairs and stayed there.

Gertrude was still gasping from her labors when Horace decided that he too must never again tax his heart by climbing the stairs, and instructed her to exchange his bedroom furniture for that in the den (leaving the Morris chair where it was, of course).

"I never," breathed Gertrude to her husband that night.

"You never what?" he asked.

"I never seen the like. All that hauling and pulling. They must think I'm a horse."

"What hauling and pulling?"

"The furniture. Upstairs and downstairs."

"How come?"

"She wants to sleep downstairs now—in the back parlor. He wants to sleep downstairs too—in the den."

"Maybe they want to be close to each other."

"YOU kidding?"

THE GROCERY STORE delivered a case of tea and the drugstore delivered a bottle of 1000 quarter-grain tablets of soluble saccharin, and Phyllis took off on her diet, immediately establishing a pattern of twenty to twenty-five cups of tea a day, each loaded with so much sweetener that the drugstore made an automatic once-a-week delivery, packing the orders so that the prescription bottle of nitroglycerin tablets and the bottle of saccharin tablets could be sent on the same day.

"You wouldn't believe it," Gertrude told her husband.

"I wouldn't believe what?" he asked.

"Now they keep their pills in little saucers."

"Who?"

"Both her and him. She has me dump 'em out of the bottle into this saucer and has the saucer right there in the back parlor so she can grab a handful for her tea. She says it's easier. He does the same thing. He's got a saucerful of his right next to him in the den all the time. He says that way he don't have to unscrew the cap while he's maybe having a heart attack and he might be dead before he gets it unscrewed."

Phyllis' diet told on her almost immediately, not that there was much noticeable difference in her weight, the puffy fat simply changing to droopy fat—but it was her strength that lessened, her only exercise being a weak totter from the back parlor to the downstairs bathroom at the end of the hall, a trip she was forced to make frequently because of all the tea she consumed.

Now and then she met Horace in the hallway, usually on his way to the dining room for a fulsome low-fat meal. At these times, she glared in resentful envy and he glared back with contemptuous hatred. It was after one of these silent glare-filled meetings that Phyllis, on her way to the bathroom, thought of killing Horace, and he, on his way to the dining room, thought how nice it would be if Phyllis were dead.

"THEY LOOK JUST ALIKE," Gertrude said to her husband when she got home.

"Who?" he asked.

"The pills."

"You mean her and him?"

"No. The pills they take. Hers for her tea and his for his heart. One of the bottles is littler than the other, but I always forget which is which because the pills look exactly the same. So I stop and look while I'm still out in the hall to see whose name is on what bottle, and then I put his little bottle in my left hand and her bigger bottle in my right hand so they'll be all ready for when I go into the back parlor and empty hers out in her saucer and then on into the den to empty his out in his saucer."

It was Gertrude's weekly anxiety that she would, somehow, get those pills mixed. She soothed herself, however, with the comforting knowledge that should she confuse them and her employers found out, she could quickly correct her mistake by using the spares, since Mr. Crenshaw had two extra bottles of nitroglycerin tablets in his desk drawer in the den and Mrs. Crenshaw had two extra bottles of saccharin tablets in her dresser drawer in the back parlor.

Phyllis did not realize that the shape, size and weight of her saccharin tablets were identical to Horace's nitroglycerin tablets until one delivery day when she happened to be tottering up the hall from the bathroom at the same time the doorbell rang. She opened the door, accepted the two bottles, closed the door and leaned against it, her eyes widening in the droopy folds of her cheeks.

"They look just alike," she told Gertrude who appeared in the hall to answer the doorbell.

"Yes, ma'am," Gertrude said, then she added, to indicate her astute alertness, "but one bottle is bigger than the other," and hoped Mrs. Crenshaw would not ask her which bottle was which. "And they got your names on each one, see."

The quarter-grain saccharin tablets in the larger bottle were about one-tenth the size of an aspirin and probably two-thirds the thickness. Phyllis held both bottles close to her eyes and studied their contents. The 0.6 mg 1/100 grain nitroglycerin tablets in the smaller bottle were exactly the same size, shape, and thickness as the saccharin tablets. The pills could be switched, Phyllis decided, and she would not know the difference outside the bottle, so if she would not know the difference, neither would Horace, and certainly not dumb Gertrude.

She handed Gertrude the smaller bottle with a warning, "You be careful now," and tottered off to the back parlor with her bottle of saccharin tablets to think things over.

"Now I'm worried," Gertrude confessed to her husband.

"What are you worried about?" he asked.

"She's got me so nervous about the pills I almost forget, even before I get to the back parlor, which one's in my left hand and which one's in my right, and which one is the big one and which is the little one. Even reading the names, the writing gets so blurred with my nervousness I'm not sure which is Mr. and which is Mrs."

"Maybe if they look all that much alike, it don't make any difference," soothed Gertrude's husband, who wasn't very smart.

"Maybe it don't," answered Gertrude, a little on the dull side herself. Then she added later, after profound contemplation, "But I think maybe it does."

She continued to worry, particularly after Mr. Crenshaw answered the doorbell on a pill delivery day while she was out in the back yard hanging up clothes, and greeted her with essentially the same expression of dawning inspiration on his face as had been on his wife's, and the same cautionary tone in his voice she had used. "Gertrude," he said, "the pills in these bottles look exactly the same. I want you to be careful."

"I know, sir. I will, sir," she answered, trembling, and pointed out the difference in bottle size and the individual names on the bottles, to which he did not appear to be listening. Instead, as he walked toward the den with his smaller bottle of nitroglycerin tablets, he seemed to be greatly absorbed in his own thoughts.

"I just hope," Gertrude said to her husband, "that I don't get rushed when I have to dump out those pills someday."

"What would rush you?" her husband asked.

"Well, I don't know," she said, distracted. Then, calmer and after due reflection, "Nothing, I guess."

But something did.

The drugstore always delivered the Crenshaw order late in the morning or during the early afternoon; but on a damp spring day with half the town down with the flu, including one of the pharmacists and the store's only delivery boy, the Crenshaw order was necessarily late. So late, in fact, that Gertrude, anxious to be off and home before the brewing storm set in, leaped timidly in startled recollection of her fearsome duty when the doorbell rang, almost dropping the coffee service she was carrying into the dining room to Mr. Crenshaw.

She set down the tray, streaked up the hall just as Mrs. Crenshaw tottered down it toward the bathroom, opened the front door, snatched the two bottles and stood in the twilight-shadowed hallway in an agony of indecision, the Mr. and Mrs. labels of identification a blur before her nervous eyes.

Coming to a sudden, irresolute compromise, she switched the small bottle to her right hand, clutched the larger one in her left, scurried into the back parlor, dumped the nitroglycerin tablets into Mrs. Crenshaw's saucer, scampered across the hall to dump the saccharin tablets into Mr. Crenshaw's saucer and was back in the kitchen before Mr. Crenshaw had barely sipped at his first cup of after-dinner coffee in the dining room.

Phyllis tottered from the bathroom, feeling the immediate need of a sweet cup of tea. Remembering the ring of the doorbell, she glanced through into the dining room, glared at Horace's back as he sat at the table polishing off a satisfying meal, gnashed her teeth, tottered to the back parlor, whisked up the saucerful of fresh nitroglycerin tablets placed there through Gertrude's error, tottered to the den, switched the saucers, thus mistakenly correcting Gertrude's error, tottered to the bathroom, flushed the saccharin tablets from Horace's bedside down the toilet and emerged with the empty saucer clasped to her drooping bosom.

Phyllis then tottered to the back parlor, emptied a spare bottleful of saccharin tablets from her dresser drawer into the den saucer, poured a steaming cupful of tea, laced it liberally with saccharin, and enjoyed the sweetness of her labors.

Gertrude tidied up the kitchen, called a good night to Mr. Crenshaw, who was still at the table, called nothing to Mrs. Crenshaw,

supposing her to be in the bathroom, and gave no further thought to
the pills until after she had plowed through the rain and reached home.

"My gracious!" she exclaimed to her husband.

"My gracious what?" he asked.

"I was in such a hurry when they came."

"Her and him?"

"Their pills. I think I got it all straight, though."

"Got what straight?"

"The pills. The ones that go to her and the ones that go to him." She
pondered, attempting to recapture her thoughts and actions during
those crucial moments with the pill bottles in her hands after they were
delivered.

"At least I *think* I got it straight," she qualified.

PHYLLIS LAY BACK, warmed and energized by her over-sweetened tea,
allowing pleasant pictures to flicker through her mind...all of Horace.
As soon as all the coffee had begun to swell the food in his stomach,
tightening up his chest, he would push from the table, stagger to the
den and reach in desperation for a pill from his saucer, place it under
his tongue and get no relief. She pictured his panic, his passionate and
futile snatch at pill after pill, reaching out for his ebbing life as he
gagged and clutched at his heart.

The pictures were as sweetly bitter as the taste of saccharin still on
her tongue, and she drifted into dreamless sleep as they faded out.

"BUT WHAT IF I DIDN'T?" Gertrude worried later that evening.

"What if you didn't what?" asked her husband.

"What if I didn't get those pills straight? What if I gave her his and
him hers?"

"If they look alike," he explained, "they probably taste alike. So it'll
be all right."

Gertrude was not sure; but, then, Gertrude was unsure about
everything.

RESTLESS, unable to sleep, Horace was acutely aware of Phyllis' heavy breathing. It resounded from the back parlor, beat against the walls of the hall and entered the den in an explosion of cacophonous sound that triggered his fingers for the saucer and the *correct* pill, since Phyllis mistakenly had corrected Gertrude's error. As the nitroglycerin tablet dissolved under his tongue, easing his erratic heart to a slow and steady hammer of hatred, Horace remembered his inspirational thought the day he discovered his heart-steadying tablets to be identical to those that Phyllis packed in her teacup—in size, shape, and weight.

The snore thundered as Horace rose with determination and, shuffling on bare feet, carefully picked up his saucer-filled nitroglycerin just-alike pills. It was raining and dark, the hall patterned with small far-apart circles of night lights marking a path for his slim, white, groping feet.

The back parlor was a well of darkness filled with sound. He made his way around the fanback chair and the bed, holding his elbows close to his pajama'd sides, cupping the saucer in two hands as if it were the Holy Grail—or a Borgia cup.

The snoring intake of breath in the darkness and the whistling outpour, sent his heart to a crescendo accompaniment. He paused, felt in the saucer with delicate thumb and forefinger, lifted a tiny pill and popped it under his tongue, smiled in the dark, and reached for the saucer by the side of the sleeper.

He set down his own saucer and picked up the other. The snoring halted, quivered on the air, and resumed a fine, rich *obbligato*.

Almost youthfully, nearly healthfully, Horace left the room nimbly and on his toes. He walked the faint light-circled hallway quickly, entered the bathroom and flushed the saccharin pills that Phyllis had so carefully supplied from her dresser drawer bottle, down the toilet. Then he returned to the den, opened his desk drawer, plucked out one of his spare bottles of nitroglycerin, filled the saucer, and lay down slowly to think about Phyllis.

Immediately upon waking she would, he knew, reach for the teakettle, put it on the hot plate and pour herself a cup of tea, tossing in a handful of death. He curled in a fetal position, hugging his chest and his knees, his heart steady and strong against his arms as he thought of what would happen then.

First, her fat face and padded neck would flush, she would feel the heat like fire. Then would come the headache, during which she would probably cry out...to no one, for he would be asleep and would not hear. She would flounce and flounder, attempting to rise, to reach the hall—and him, which would do her no good—or the medicine cabinet in the bathroom, which would do her no good either. Dizziness would then send her reeling back to the bed or crashing to the floor in a faint—and no one would hear the crash, for he would sleep soundly, and Gertrude would not yet have arrived. The pupils of her eyes would dilate finally—blue eyes staring black just before cyanosis, collapse, and death.

Horace slept, a smile on his face.

GERTRUDE POKED her husband in the darkness just before dawn. "Huh?" He half woke, dazed.

"I've been thinking. I woke up thinking," Gertrude said.

"Huh?"

"I'm pretty sure I got them mixed."

Her husband pulled himself forth. "Who?" he asked. "Him and her?"

"Their pills. I remember now." Her voice reached a high note of guilty hysteria. "I put the little bottle in my right hand and the big bottle in my left hand. But the little bottle was supposed to be in my left hand and the big bottle was supposed to be in my right." She leaped from the bed.

Gertrude's husband sat up in an attempt to sort out such an intricate statement.

DAMP LIGHT STREAKED the sky as Gertrude, her raincoat crackling with movement, scampered through the alley, up the back walk and nervously fitted the key in the Crenshaw back door.

She dropped her raincoat on the kitchen floor and stood, frozen, listening to what was either a two-hour-earlier silence in the house or a several-hours-later death caused by her.

She began to whimper and crept from the kitchen through the shadowed dining room. Her frightened eyes took in the coffee service on the table, the coffee cup stained darkly, the chair pushed back... So Mr. Crenshaw lived through his coffee at least...

She had reached the hall when she heard the first sound. She jerked to attention. A familiar sound, the sound of the teakettle dragged from the hot plate in the back parlor.

She ran, and reached the room just as Mrs. Crenshaw scooped up a handful of nitroglycerin tablets placed there by Horace in the night.

Mrs. Crenshaw dropped the pills into the cup.

"Mrs. Crenshaw!" cried Gertrude.

She looked fine, just as unhealthily fat and diet-drooped as usual, still sleepy, ready for her first cup of tea.

"Mrs. Crenshaw?"

Gertrude shrank in the doorway in a torment of perplexity—how in the world could she get those little white pellets of death away from her employer without letting her know that she had committed an awful error? Her hands fluttered, tears sprang to her eyes as she watched Mrs. Crenshaw stir the tea, holding the string of the teabag from tangling.

Phyllis looked up in surprise at Gertrude's dawn-early appearance, then in astonishment at her agitatedly twitching nose and the fingers that danced a perturbed tremolo—what in the name of heaven was the matter with that fool girl? Then she dropped the teabag string and clattered her spoon in her cup, remembering slowly, coming awake gradually after her fine deep sleep following her switch of the pills which she fondly hoped would give only sweet conclusion, not remedy, to Horace's ailing heart.

"Mr. Crenshaw?" she cried and rolled from the bed with fantastic agility. "He's dead?" she caroled with optimism, and tottered energetically past Gertrude, who had flattened herself against the wall.

Gertrude pounced. She dumped the pills into her apron pocket, those very nitroglycerin tablets Horace had so quietly deposited in the night which had reversed Phyllis' mistaken correction of Gertrude's original error. She yanked open the dresser drawer, took out the remaining bottle of saccharin tablets, dumped them into the saucer, and flew from the room, forgetting entirely the dissolved danger in the tea, and bumped into *Mrs.* Crenshaw in the hall.

"He isn't dead," Mrs. Crenshaw gritted through her teeth; then in awe, "He's just as alive as you and me," and finally in wonder, "What in the world went wrong?" and flounced, tottering, into the back parlor and reached for her teacup.

Gertrude, her mind still on the pills in her pocket, scurried down the hall to the bathroom and flushed them down the toilet, her corrective mission now half accomplished. Then she thought of Mrs. Crenshaw's remark, not why she had made it, but that it had been made, and selected the one phrase that gave her comfort—Mr. Crenshaw was still alive, so she had not killed him. She rushed for the den to keep him alive and found him in a state.

"Mr. Crenshaw," she cried just as he popped a pill under his tongue. "Mr. Crenshaw," as he muttered an incredible something about the "constitution of an ox," and a garbled query of bewilderment as to what in hell went wrong? "*Mr.* Crenshaw," as he pushed past her and shambled rapidly down the hall.

The bathroom door slammed, and a muffled crash sounded from the back parlor.

Gertrude raced across the den for the saucer pills she supposed to be the saccharin tablets she had so stupidly dumped there the day before, but which were, instead, the nitroglycerin tablets from Horace's desk drawer that he had replaced for the nitroglycerin tablets Phyllis had exchanged for the saccharin tablets Gertrude had so stupidly dumped there in the beginning. Gertrude dumped the nitroglycerin tablets from the saucer into her apron pocket, yanked open the desk drawer and took out the remaining bottle of nitroglycerin tablets, dumped them into the now empty saucer, heard Mrs. Crenshaw's plaintive call following the crash, closed the drawer, smoothed her apron, took several long, righteous breaths of rectification and marched down the hall to the back parlor.

IT HAD BEEN a long day for Gertrude. She described it to her husband that night.

"It was a real long day," she said.

"Sure," he agreed. "It started early."

"But I got them all fixed up."

"Him and her?"

"Their pills. It was a good thing I went so early. She was fixing a cup of tea when I got there. With the pills in it. The wrong pills."

"You mean his pills in her saucer?"

"I was lucky. As soon as she saw me, she got up to go to the den to look at him. She's never done that before, but maybe she does it early in the morning before I get there. And this morning I got there early enough so I saw her do it. But while she was gone, I got rid of those wrong pills in her saucer, put them into my apron pocket and dumped in some right pills from a bottle in her dresser drawer. Then I went to the bathroom and flushed the wrong pills from my pocket down the toilet.

"I went to the den after that to see if he was alive and he was. I was lucky again, because he went charging off to the bathroom. He seemed to be mad about something. Anyway, while he was gone, I put his wrong pills from his saucer into my pocket and got his extra bottle of right pills out of the desk drawer to put in his saucer. Then I went back to the back parlor..." Gertrude paused to breathe heavily.

"Was she dead yet?" her husband asked.

"Was who dead?"

"Her. She had that cup of tea with the wrong pills in it. That's what you said. You said you dumped out the wrong saucer pills. But you didn't say anything about dumping out the wrong cup pills, see?"

Gertrude stared at her husband blankly. Then she clapped a hand over her mouth, her eyes horrified. "My goodness!" she mumbled behind her hand, remembering at last how, in her eagerness to dispose of the killing saucer pills, she had completely forgotten the lethal cup of tea.

She jerked up from her chair, thinking she should go back to the Crenshaws and do something about that cup of tea, her mind pinpointed, caught at dawn as she realized her one sin of omission during the rectification of her original error. Then she sank back, slowly and limply, further remembering how it had been.

"She broke it," she said with sudden thanksgiving, not knowing, until now, that she had this extra blessing to be thankful for.

"The pills?" asked her husband.

"The cup. The cup with the wrong pills in it. She broke it. That was the crash, and that's why she called me. It was all over the floor in pieces, the cup and the tea with the pills in it. She was nervous—her hands were shaking about as bad as mine..." Gertrude held out her quivering hands and began to laugh, a laugh that quivered along with her hands. "She broke it with the pills in *it,* the wrong pills."

"Well, now you can start all over," said Gertrude's husband. "And

I'm sure not going to mix up those pills again. I'm going to keep every-thing straight from now on."

"Sure you will."

Gertrude heaved a sigh and hauled herself up out of her chair. "Shall I heat up some coffee?" she suggested, feeling the need of strength after her day-long ordeal and her just-realized, freshly-escaped burden.

"Sure thing," said her husband.

She started for the kitchen.

"You flushed all them pills down the toilet all right?" asked her husband. "So her and him won't get hold of the wrong ones?"

Gertrude paused and ground her brain into action. "Yes," she said, thinking back. Then she felt the bulge in her apron pocket. "Oh, no," she cried out contritely. "Oh, no. I forgot the last bunch. They were those wrong ones of Mr. Crenshaw's. He was in the bathroom, and I went to clean up her broken cup with her wrong ones in it. I forgot— and here they are."

"Which ones are those?"

"They're the ones I got out of his saucer. The mixed-up ones. The ones that should have gone to her and went to him." She looked criti-cally at her husband, then patted her own ample hips. "We're both putting on a little weight. What do you say we use these in our coffee, instead of sugar?"

"You're sure they're all right?" questioned her husband. "You sure they're the right ones?"

"Of course I'm sure," Gertrude said. "These are Mr. Crenshaw's that were supposed to be Mrs. Crenshaw's. Didn't I tell you I'm *never* going to get mixed up again?"

Gertrude and her husband sat down to drink their coffee.

I Always Get the Cuties

John D. MacDonald

THE "HOWDUNIT"

Back about the time that Monsignor Ronald Knox was laying down impossible rules for the detective story to follow, the "whodunit" was the rage. This was followed by the "howdunit" and the currently popular "whydunit"—each merely a shorthand term to indicate whether a story turned on plot, method of murder, or character. "I Always Get the Cuties" depends as much on character as on methodology, but it still is vitally concerned with numerous "hows" both spoken and unspoken. After sixty novels and five hundred published short stories, John D. MacDonald is finally achieving the recognition his work so richly deserves. Two years ago, MWA made him a Grand Master; and last year his Travis McGee caper titled The Dreadful Lemon Sky, *a heady mixture of non-stop action and trenchant comment on American mores, topped the bestseller charts for several months. - J.G.*

KEEGAN CAME INTO MY APARTMENT, frosted with winter, topcoat open, hat jammed on the back of his hard skull, bringing a noisy smell of the dark city night. He stood in front of my birch fire, his great legs planted, clapping and rubbing hard palms in the heat.

He grinned at me and winked one narrow gray eye. "I'm off duty, Doc. I wrapped up a package. A pretty package."

"Will bourbon do?"

"If you haven't got any of that brandy left. This is a brandy night."

When I came back with the bottle and the glasses, he had stripped off his topcoat and tossed it on the couch. The crumpled hat was on the floor, near the discarded coat. Keegan had yanked a chair closer to the fire. He sprawled on the end of his spine, thick ankles crossed, the soles of his shoes steaming.

I poured his brandy and mine, and moved my chair and the long coffee table so we could share either end of it. It was bursting in him. I knew that. I've only had the vaguest hints about his home life. A house crowded with teenage daughters, cluttered with their swains. Obviously no place to talk of his dark victories. And Keegan is not the sort of man to regale his co-workers with talk of his prowess. So I am, among other things, his sounding board. He bounces successes off the politeness of my listening, growing big in the echo of them.

"Ever try to haggle with a car dealer, Doc?" he asked.

"In a mild way."

"You are a mild guy. I tried once. Know what he told me? He said, 'Lieutenant, you try to make a car deal maybe once every two years. Me, I make ten a day. So what chance have you got?'"

This was a more oblique approach than Keegan generally used. I became attentive.

"It's the same with the cuties, Doc—the amateurs who think they can bring off one nice clean safe murder. Give me a cutie every time. I eat 'em alive. The pros are trouble. The cuties leave holes you can drive diesels through. This one was that woman back in October. At that cabin at Bear Paw Lake. What do you remember about it, Doc?"

I am always forced to summarize. It has got me into the habit of reading the crime news. I never used to.

"As I remember, they thought she had been killed by a prowler. Her husband returned from a business trip and found the body. She had been dead approximately two weeks. Because it was the off-season, the neighboring camps weren't occupied, and the people in the village thought she had gone back to the city. She had been strangled, I believe."

"Okay. So I'll fill you in on it. Then you'll see the problem I had. The name is Grosswalk. Cynthia and Harold. He met her ten years ago when he was in med school. He was twenty-four and she was thirty. She was loaded. He married her and he never went back to med school. He didn't do anything for maybe five, six years. Then he gets a job selling medical supplies, surgical instruments, that kind of stuff. Whenever a wife is dead, Doc, the first thing I do is check on how they were getting along. I guess you know that."

"Your standard procedure," I said.

"Sure. So I check. They got a nice house here in the city. Not many friends. But they got neighbors with ears. There are lots of brawls. I get the idea it is about money. The money is hers—was hers, I should say. I put it up to this Grosswalk. He says okay, so they weren't getting along so good, so what? I'm supposed to be finding out who killed her, sort of coordinating with the State Police, not digging into his home life. I tell him he is a nice suspect. He already knows that. He says he didn't kill her. Then he adds one thing too many. He says he couldn't have killed her. That's all he will say. Playing it cute. You understand. I eat those cuties alive."

He waved his empty glass. I went over and refilled it.

"You see what he's doing to me, Doc. He's leaving it up to me to prove how it was he couldn't have killed her. A reverse twist. That isn't too tough. I get in touch with the sales manager of the company. Like I thought, the salesmen have to make reports. He was making a western swing. It would be no big trick to fly back and sneak into the camp and kill her, take some money and junk to make it look good, and then fly back out there and pick up where he left off. She was killed on maybe the tenth of October, the medical examiner says. Then he finds her on the twenty-fourth. But the sales manager tells me something that needs a lot of checking. He says that Grosswalk took sick out west on the eighth and went into a hospital, and he was in that hospital from the eighth to the fifteenth, a full seven days. He gave me the name of the hospital. Now you see how the cutie made his mistake. He could have told me that easy enough. No, he has to be cute. I figure that if he's innocent he would have told me. But he's so proud of whatever gimmick he rigged for me that he's got to let me find out the hard way."

"I suppose you went out there," I said.

"It took a lot of talk. They don't like spending money for things like that. They kept telling me I should ask the L. A. cops to check because that's a good force out there. Finally, I have to go by bus, or pay the difference. So I go by bus. I found the doctor. Plural—doctors. It is a clinic deal, sort of, that Grosswalk went to. He gives them his symptoms. They say it looks to them like the edge of a nervous breakdown just beginning to show. With maybe some organic complications. So they run him through the course. Seven days of tests and checks and observations. They tell me he was there, that he didn't leave, that he *couldn't* have left. But naturally, I check the hospital. They reserve part of one floor for patients from the clinic. I talked to the head nurse on that floor, and to the nurse that had the most to do with Grosswalk. She showed me the schedule and charts. Every day, every night, they were fooling around with the guy, giving him injections of this and that. He couldn't have got out. The people at the clinic told me the results. He was okay. The rest had helped him a lot. They told him to slow down. They gave him a prescription for a mild sedative. Nothing organically wrong, even though the symptoms seemed to point that way."

"So the trip was wasted?"

"Not entirely. Because on a hunch I ask if he had visitors. They keep a register. A girl came to see him as often as the rules permitted. They said she was pretty. Her name was Mary MacCarney. The address is there. So I go and see her. She lives with her folks. A real tasty kid. Nineteen. Her folks think Grosswalk is too old for her. She is tall Irish, all black and white and blue. It was warm and we sat on the porch. I soon find out this Grosswalk has been feeding her a line, telling her that his wife is an incurable invalid not long for this world, that he can't stand hurting her by asking for a divorce, that it is better to wait, and anyway, she says, her parents might approve of a widower, but never a guy who has been divorced. She has heard from Grosswalk that his wife has been murdered by a prowler, and he will be out to see her as soon as he can. He has known her for a year. But of course I have told him not to leave town. I tell her not to get her hopes too high because it begins to look to me like Grosswalk has knocked off his wife. Things get pretty hysterical, and her old lady gets in on it, and even driving away in the cab I can hear the old lady yelling at her.

"The first thing I do on getting back is check with the doctor who took care of Mrs. Grosswalk, and he says, as I thought he would, that she was as healthy as a horse. So I go back up to that camp and unlock it again. It is a snug place, Doc. Built so you could spend the winter there if you wanted to. Insulated and sealed, with a big fuel-oil furnace, and modem kitchen equipment, and so on. It was aired out a lot better than the first time I was in it. Grosswalk stated that he hadn't touched a thing. He said it was unlocked. He saw her and backed right out and went to report it. And the only thing touched had been the body.

"I poked around. This time I took my time. She was a tidy woman. There are twin beds. One is turned down. There is a very fancy night-gown laid out. That is a thing which bothered me. I looked at her other stuff. She has pajamas which are the right thing for October at the lake. They are made from that flannel stuff. There is only one other fancy nightgown, way in the back of a drawer. I have found out here in the city that she is not the type to fool around. So how come a woman who is alone wants to sleep so pretty? Because the husband is coming back from a trip. But he couldn't have come back from the trip. I find another thing. I find deep ruts off in the brush beside the camp. The first time I went there, her car was parked in back. Now it is gone. If the car was run off where those ruts were, anybody coming to the door wouldn't see it. If the door was locked they wouldn't even knock maybe, knowing she wouldn't be home. That puzzles me. She might do it if she didn't want company. I prowl some more. I look in the deep freeze. It is well stocked. No need to buy stuff for a hell of a while. The refrigerator is the same way. And the electric is still on."

He leaned back and looked at me expectantly.

"Is that all you had to go on?" I asked.

"A murder happens here and the murderer is in Los Angeles at the time. I got him because he tried to be a cutie. Want to take a try, Doc?"

I knew I had to make an attempt. "Some sort of device?"

"To strangle a woman? Mechanical hands? You're getting too fancy, Doc."

"Then he hired somebody to do it?"

"There are guys you can hire, but they like guns. Or a piece of pipe in an alley. I don't know where you'd go to hire a strangler. He did *it* himself, Doc."

"Frankly, I don't see how he could have."

"Well, I'll tell you how I went after it. I went to the medical exam-iner and we had a little talk. Cop logic, Doc. If the geography is wrong, then maybe you got the wrong idea on timing. But the medico checks it out. He says definitely the woman has been dead twelve days to two weeks when he makes the examination. I ask him how he knows. He says because of the extent of decomposition of the body. I ask him if that is a constant. He says no—you use a formula. A sort of rule-of-thumb formula. I ask him the factors. He says cause of death, temperature, humidity, physical characteristics of the body, how it was clothed, whether or not insects could have got to it, and so on.

"By then I had it, Doc. It was cute. I went back to the camp and looked around. It took me some time to find them. You never find a camp without them. Candles. They were in a drawer in the kitchen. Funny-looking candles, Doc. Melted down, sort of. A flat side against the bottom of the drawer, and all hardened again. Then I had another idea. I checked the stove burners. I found some pieces of burned flaked metal down under the beating elements.

"Then it was easy. I had this Grosswalk brought in again. I let him sit in a cell for four hours and get nervous before I took the rookie cop in. I'd coached that rookie for an hour, so he did it right. I had him dressed in a leather jacket and work pants. I make him repeat his story in front of Grosswalk. 'I brought a chain saw last year,' he says, acting sort of confused, 'and I was going around to the camps where there are any people and I was trying to get some work cutting up fireplace wood. So I called on Mrs. Grosswalk. She didn't want any wood, but she was nice about it.' I ask the rookie when that was. He scratches his head and says, 'Sometime around the seventeenth, I think it was.' That's where I had to be careful. I couldn't let him be positive about the date. I say she was supposed to be dead a week by then, and was he sure it was her. 'She wasn't dead then. I know her. I'd seen her in the village. A kind of heavy-set woman with blonde hair. It was her all right, Lieutenant.' I asked him was he sure of the date and he said yes, around the seventeenth like he said, but he could check his records and find the exact day.

"I told him to take off. I just watched that cutie and saw him come apart. Then he gave it to me. He killed her on the sixteenth, the day he got out of the hospital. He flew into Omaha. By then I've got the stenographer taking it down. Grosswalk talks, staring at the floor, like he was talking to himself. It was going to be a dry run. He wasn't going to do it if she'd been here in the city or into the village in the previous seven days. But once she got in the camp she seldom went out, and the odds were all against any callers. On his previous trip to Omaha he had bought a jalopy that would run. It would make the fifty miles to the lake all right. He took the car off the lot where he'd left it and drove to the lake. She was surprised to see him back ahead of schedule. He explained the company car was being fixed. He questioned her. Finally she said she hadn't seen or talked to a living soul in ten days. Then he knew he was set to take the risk.

"He grabbed her neck and hung on until she was dead. He had his shoulders hunched right up around his ears when he said that. It was evening when he killed her, nearly bedtime. First he closed every window. Then he turned on the furnace as high as it would go. There was plenty of oil in the tank. He left the oven door open and oven turned as high as it would go. He even built a fire in the fireplace, knowing it would be burned out by morning and there wouldn't be any smoke. He filled the biggest pans of water he could find and left them on the top of the stove. He took the money and some of her jewelry, turned out the lights and locked the doors. He ran her car off in the brush where nobody would be likely to see it. He said by the time he left the house it was like an oven in there.

"He drove the jalopy back to Omaha, parked it back in the lot, and caught an 11:15 flight to Los Angeles. The next morning he was making calls. And keeping his fingers crossed. He worked his way east. He got to the camp on the twenty-fourth—about 10 in the morning. He said he went in and turned things off and opened up every window, and then went out and was sick. He waited nearly an hour before going back in. It was nearly down to normal temperature. He checked the house. He noticed she had turned down both beds before he killed her. He remade his. The water had boiled out of the pans and the bottoms had burned through. He scaled the pans out into the lake. He said he tried not to look at her, but he couldn't help it. He had enough medical background to know that it had worked, and also to fake his own illness in L. A. He went out and was sick again, and then he got her car back where it belonged. He closed most of the windows. He made another inspection trip and then drove into the village. He's a cutie, Doc, and I ate him alive."

There was a long silence. I knew what was expected of me. But I had my usual curious reluctance to please him.

He held the glass cradled in his hand, gazing with a half-smile into the dying fire. His face looked like stone.

"That was very intelligent, Keegan," I said.

"The pros give you real trouble, Doc. The cuties always leave holes. I couldn't bust geography, so I had to bust time." He yawned massively and stood up. "Read all about it in the morning paper, Doc."

"I'll certainly do that."

I held his coat for him. He's a big man. I had to reach up to get it properly onto his shoulders. He mashed the hat onto his head as I walked to the door with him. He put his big hand on the knob, turned, and smiled down at me without mirth.

"I always get the cuties, Doc. Always."

"You certainly seem to," I said.

"They are my favorite meat."

"So I understand."

He balled one big fist and bumped it lightly against my chin, still grinning at me. "And I'm going to get you too, Doc. You know that. You were cute. You're just taking longer than most. But you know how it's going to come out, don't you?"

I don't answer that any more. There's nothing to say. There hasn't been anything to say for a long time now.

He left, walking hard into the wild night. I sat and looked into my fire. I could hear the wind. I reached for the bottle. The wind raged over the city, as monstrous and inevitable as Keegan. It seemed as though it was looking for food—the way Keegan is always doing.

But I no longer permit myself the luxury of imagination.

The Crooked Picture

John Lutz

THE LOCKED ROOM

That classic of detective-story types, the locked-room "miracle problem," is one of the most challenging of all in conception. The gimmick (method of commission) must be fresh and plausible, and that is no simple task for the writer. There are a limited number of ways in which a person may be murdered, or appear to be murdered, in such circumstances; and the acknowledged experts at the lockedroom story, John Dickson Carr and Ellery Queen, have already exhausted a good percentage of the possibilities. John Lutz has met the challenge admirably in "The Crooked Picture," and given us a clever variation on the theme. Mr. Lutz is one of today's best practitioners of the mystery short story, having published well over a hundred in the past decade; be is also the author of one fine novel, The Truth of the Matter, *published in 1971. - B.P.*

THE ROOM WAS A MESS. The three of them, Paul Eastmont, his wife, Laura, and his brother, Cuthbert, were sitting rigidly and morosely. They were waiting for Louis Bratten.

"But just who is this Bratten?" Laura Eastmont asked in a shaking voice. She was a very beautiful woman, on the edge of middle age.

Cuthbert, recently of several large eastern universities, said, "A drunken, insolent sot."

"And he's a genius," Paul Eastmont added, "in his own peculiar way. More importantly, he's my friend." He placed a hand on his wife's wrist. "Bratten is the most discreet man I know."

Laura shivered. "I hope so, Paul."

Cuthbert rolled his king-size cigarette between thumb and forefinger, an annoyed look on his young, aquiline face. "I don't see why you put such stock in the man, Paul. He's run the gamut of alcoholic degeneration. From chief of homicide to—what? If I remember correctly, you told me some time ago that they'd taken away his private investigator's license."

He saw that he was upsetting his sister-in-law even more and shrugged his thin shoulders. "My point is that he's hardly the sort of man to be confided in concerning *this.*" He looked thoughtful. "On the other hand, half of what he says is known to be untrue anyway."

The butler knocked lightly, pushed one of the den's double doors open, and Louie Bratten entered. He was a blocky, paunchy little man of about forty, with a perpetual squint in one eye. His coarse, dark hair was mussed, his suit was rumpled, and his unclasped tie hung crookedly outside one lapel. He looked as if he'd just stepped out of a hurricane.

"Bratten!" Paul Eastmont said in warm greeting. "You don't know how glad I am to have you in on this!"

Cuthbert nodded coldly. "Mr. Bratten."

Laura stared intently at her hands, which were folded in her lap.

"Give me a drink," Bratten said.

Paul crossed to the portable bar and poured him a straight scotch, no ice.

Bratten sipped the scotch, smacked his lips in satisfaction, and then slouched in the most comfortable leather armchair in the den.

"Now, what's bugging you, Paul?" he asked.

Cuthbert stood and leaned on the mantel. "It's hardly a matter to be taken lightly," he said coldly.

"How in the hell can I take it lightly," Bratten asked, "when I don't even know what the matter is?"

Paul raised a hand for silence. "Let me explain briefly. Several years ago, before Laura and I had met, a picture was taken of her in a very—uncompromising pose. This photo fell into the hands of a blackmailer named Hays, who has been milking us for two hundred dollars a month for the past four years. Recently Hays needed some cash badly. He offered to give me the photo for five thousand dollars."

Paul Eastmont glanced protectively at his embarrassed wife. "Naturally I agreed, and the deal was made. The negative, incidentally, was destroyed long ago, and I happen to know that the photo wasn't reproduced at any time since by taking a picture of it That was part of the original blackmail arrangement. It's the only picture in existence, an eight-by-ten glossy."

"Interesting," Bratten said.

"But Hays turned out to be a stubborn sort," Paul went on. "He gave me the photograph yesterday, and like a fool I didn't destroy it. He saw me put it in my wall safe. Last night he broke in here and tried to steal it back."

"And did he?"

"We don't know. Clark, the butler, sleeps in that part of the house, and he heard Hays tinkering about. He surprised him as he ran in here."

"Terrific scotch," Bratten said. "Did he have the photo?"

"Yes. It wasn't in the wall safe. As you can see, he hurriedly rummaged about in this room, lifting cushions, knocking over the lamp, we think looking for a place to hide the photo. Then he leaped out the window."

"Caught?"

"Hurt himself when he landed and couldn't run fast enough. Shot dead by the police just outside the gate. And he didn't have the photo on his body, nor was it on the grounds."

"Hays was a smart blackmailer," Bratten said. He squinted at Paul. "You left the room as it was?"

Paul nodded. "I know your peculiar way of working. But the photo must be in this room. We looked everywhere, but we didn't disturb anything, put everything back exactly the way we found it."

"Ah, that's good," Bratten said, either of the scotch or of the Eastmonts' actions. "Another drink, if you please." He handed the empty glass up to Cuthbert, who was the only one standing.

"Really," Cuthbert said, grabbing the glass. "If I had my way, we wouldn't have confided this to you."

"We never did hit it off, did we?" Bratten laughed. "That's probably because you have too much education. Ruins a man sometimes. Restricts his thinking."

Cuthbert reluctantly gave Bratten his fresh drink. "You should be an expert on ruination."

"Touch. That means *touché* in English." Bratten leaned back and ran his tongue over his lips. "This puts me in mind of another case. One about ten years ago. There was this locked-room-type murder—"

"What on earth does a locked room murder have to do with this case?" Cuthbert interrupted in agitation.

"Everything, you idiot."

Paul motioned for Cuthbert *to* be silent, and Bratten continued. "Like they say," Bratten said, "there's a parallel here." He took a sip of scotch and nonchalantly hung one leg over an arm of his chair. "There were these four brothers, rich, well-bred-like Cuthbert here, only with savvy. They'd made their pile on some cheap real estate development out West. The point is, the business was set up so one of the brothers controlled most of the money, and they didn't get along too well to start off with."

He raised his glass and made a mock bow to Cuthbert. "In language you'd understand, it was a classic sibling rivalry intensified by economic inequality. What it all meant was that if this one brother was dead, the other three would profit a hell of a lot. And lo and behold, this one brother did somehow get dead. That's when I was called into the case by a friend of mine, a local sheriff in Illinois."

"Seems one of the brothers had bought a big old house up in a remote wooded area, and six months later the four of them met up there for a business conference or something. The three surviving brothers' story was simply that their brother had gone into this room, locked the door, and never came out. Naturally not, lying in the middle of the floor with a knife in his chest."

"I fail to see any parallel whatever so far," Cuthbert said.

"The thing of it was, this room was locked from the inside with a sliding bolt and a key still in the keyhole. The one window that opened was locked and there wasn't a mark on the sill. It was summer, and the ground was hard, but I don't think we would have found anything outside anyway."

"Secret panel, no doubt," Cuthbert said.

"Nope. It did happen to be a paneled room, though. We went over that room from wall to wall, ceiling to floor. There was no way out but the door or the window. And to make the thing really confusing, the knife was wiped clean of prints, and there was nothing nearby the dying man could have used to do that, even if he'd been crazy enough to want to for some reason. There was no sign of a struggle, or of any blood other than what had soaked into the rug around the body.

"Without question the corpse was lying where it fell. On the seat of a chair was an open book, and on an end table was a half-empty cup of coffee with the dead man's prints on it. But there was one other thing in the room that caught my attention."

"Well, get it over with and get to the business at hand," Cuthbert said, trying to conceal his interest. "Who was it and how was it done?"

"Another drink," Bratten said, handing up his glass. "Now here was the situation: dead man in a locked room, three suspects with good motives who were in the same house at the time of the murder, and a knife without prints. The coroner's inquest could come to no conclusion but suicide unless the way the murderer left the room was explained. Without that explanation, no jury could convict."

Bratten paused to take a long pull of scotch. "The authorities thought they were licked, and my sheriff friend and I were walking around the outside of the house, talking about how hopeless things were, when I found it."

"The solution?" Cuthbert asked.

"No. A nail. And a shiny one."

"Good Lord," Cuthbert said.

"Doesn't that suggest something to you?"

"It suggests that somebody dropped a nail," Cuthbert said furiously.

"Well, I tied that in with what had caught my attention inside the room," Bratten said, "and like they say, everything fell into place. We contacted the former owners of the house, who were in Europe, snooped around a bit, and that was that. We got a confession right away."

Cuthbert was incredulous. "Because of a nail?"

"Not entirely," Bratten said. "How about another drink, while you're up?"

Cuthbert turned to Paul. "How do you expect this sot to help us if he's dead drunk?"

"Give him another," Paul said, "and let him finish."

His face livid, Cuthbert poured Bratten another glass of scotch.

"What was it you saw in the room that you connected with the nail you found?"

"A picture," Bratten said. "It was hanging crooked, though everything else *in* the room was in order. It's things like that that bring first daylight to a case." He looked at Cuthbert as if he were observing some kind of odd animal life. "You still don't get it?"

"No," Cuthbert said, controlling himself. "And as I first suspected, there is no parallel whatsoever with our problem."

Bratten shrugged. "What the brothers did was this: through their business, they gathered the materials secretly over a period of time and got things ready. When the time was right, they got their victim to go out there with them and stabbed him on the spot, then wiped the knife handle clean. They had the concrete block foundation, the floor, the roof, and all but one of the walls up. They built in an L of the big house so there were only two walls to bother with. They even had the rug and furniture down and ready."

"After the victim was dead, they quickly put up the last wall, already paneled like the rest on the inside and shingled with matching shingles on the outside, and called the police. In short, the locked room was prefabricated and built around the body."

Cuthbert's mouth was open. "Unbelievable!"

"Not really," Bratten said. "No one would think to check and see how many rooms the house had, and they did a real good job on the one they built. Of course, on close examination you could tell. The heating duct was a dummy, and the half of the molding that fitted against the last wall had dummy nail heads in it."

"But from the outside, the room was perfect. The shingles matched, and the metal corner flashing was a worn piece taken from another part of the house. The trouble was they didn't think to use old nails, and they didn't want to leave the inside of that last wall bare when they fit it in place."

"An amusing story, I admit," Cuthbert said. "True or not. Now if you'll be so kind as to point out this damned parallel you keep talking about..."

Bratten looked surprised. "Why, the picture, you imbecile! The crooked picture on the last wall!" He pointed to a cheap oil painting that hung on the Eastmonts' wall.

"But that picture is straight!" Cuthbert yelled in frustration. "It is immaculately straight!"

"Exactly, you learned jackass. It's the only thing in this fouled-up room besides my drink that is immaculately straight. And I suspect if you look between the painting and the cardboard backing, you'll find your photograph."

They did.

Night Piece for Julia

Jessamyn West

CHARACTER STUDY

I have read this story at least a dozen times, yet its ultimate revelations raise the hairs on the back of my neck every time. It ineluctably reminds me that a great many murders have little to do with literal dying—a fact which makes them only the more horrible. The resounding success of such novels as The Friendly Persuasion *has done a disservice to this clear-eyed and clear-minded writer; far too many readers connect the name Jessamyn West with gentle Quaker folks thee-ing and thou-ing amid the bright eternal springtime years of this nation's infancy. But "Night Piece for Julia," which probes the depths of contemporary human experience, shows the true scope of this remarkable writer's talent. - J.G.*

TO BE ALONE in the night, to be cold, to be homeless, fleeing, perhaps: Julia had always feared these things.

Where was she? She couldn't be sure at first. Just outside Bentonville, perhaps. It was there she tried walking with her shoes off. Her pumps had cut into her heels until they were bleeding. But the icy gravel of the unpaved road hurt her feet more than the shoes. She stood still for a while without courage either to take another step forward or to force her cut feet back into her shoes. *I always heard coldness numbed,* she thought, *but it doesn't; it hurts, too, and it makes the other hurt more.* She could have walked in the half-frozen slush at the side of the road, but she still had a concern for her appearance that would not let her splash, stocking-footed, through the mud. Suddenly, almost spasmodically, she shoved her feet down into the shoes. The pain twisted her face. "I will think of them as outside myself," she said, "as if they were two animals, pets of mine that suffer." She laughed a little hysterically. *My dogs,* she thought. *Why, other people have played this game. That's what soldiers say, and policemen, when they think they can't take another step. They say, "My dogs hurt," and walk right on.* She looked down at her narrow feet in the rain-soaked, round-toed suede pumps, her ankles and insteps red through the gauzy stockings. "Poor dogs, *hundschen,*" she said, "it is almost night. We'll rest soon."

She managed a few short stiff steps, then, with teeth grating, she swung into an approximation of her usual stride. The rain was turning to sleet, but the wind had veered so it was no longer in her face. She was so cold she could not tell whether the clothes under her coat were wet or not. She got her hand out of her glove and put it inside her coat, but it was so numb she couldn't tell wet from dry. *Well,* she thought, *if I can't tell whether I'm wet or dry, what difference does it make?*

It had been so dark all afternoon that the added darkness of nightfall was scarcely noticed. It only seemed to her that she could see less clearly than she had, as if her sight were tiring, too. She rubbed the back of her wet glove across her wet face, but still the sodden corn shocks that lined the road were gray and indistinct. In her effort to concentrate on something outside herself, she saw a bird perched on the snake fence beside the road. She was almost as surprised as if it had been a child. "What are you doing *out* in weather like *this?*" she said.

She thought she'd been through the town before, but always quickly, in an auto. Two or three sentences would be said, and then, while their dust still lingered in the single block of stores that made up the town, they would have passed beyond it, onto the road between the cornfields. But walking, limping, whipped (words she had no knowledge of before now had meaning so intense she thought their look alone would always in the future hurt her) by the wind-driven sleet, she measured out the short distance by a scale that added infinity to them. She limped from sign to sign, from gas station to gas station. Without these means of marking her progress she could never have gone on. "I will just walk to the next station," she would say, and when she had reached it, she would hobble on to one more. The road was empty of cars, the service stations tight shut, their glass opaque with condensed moisture. Their swinging signs rattled in the wind with a sound of chains.

By the time she reached the town it was full night. Lights were on in most of the stores and houses. She skirted the main highway, taking a back street that paralleled it through town. She passed three or four shops, all closed; a dry-cleaning plant, a plumber's, a secondhand furniture store. The furniture store had one window set up as a bedroom, with a bird's-eye maple dresser, dressing table, and bed of a kind fashionable in the early nineteen hundreds. She leaned against the window, where she was somewhat protected from the sleet, and looked at the bed. It had a cheap factory-made patchwork quilt on it and two pillows in lavender slips. It looked like heaven to Julia, a bed, something she had taken for granted every night of her life before.

I'll have to ask someplace, she thought. *I can't go on in this cold. I'll have to risk it. I'll die if I don't.* She held her hands against the glass. The yellow light behind it made it look warm, but to her icy hands it was only an extension of ice.

She saw herself in the mirror of the dressing table and instinctively tried to tidy herself. Her face looked as hard and white as a stone, like something already frozen. In the mirror her gray eyes were black, her wet yellow hair gray. Her fingers were almost too numb to push the fallen strands of her hair back under her dark cap. She got her lipstick out of her pocket and tried to put lips onto the blue scar the cold had made of her mouth, but her fingers were too stiff for that precise work. She thought she looked sick and water-soaked, but still neat. Now that she was ready to go on, she became aware again of her heels, throbbing with a pulse of pain that seemed to beat even in her eyes.

I'll stop at the first place, she thought. *Everyone has to sleep. No one would refuse me on a night like this.* She walked on painfully, unable to joke any longer about her feet. The sleet bit into her face like fire.

She went up the steps of the first house where she saw a woman behind the undrawn blinds. From the street she had looked motherly, a plump, aproned woman with gray hair. She came to the door at once when Julia knocked.

"Well?" she asked in a harsh accusing voice.

"I haven't any money," Julia said. "I'm sick. I've been walking all afternoon. Will you let me have a bed for the night?"

"I'll call the authorities," the woman said. "There's a place for girls like you." She turned as if to go to a phone.

"No, no," Julia cried. "I won't bother you. I'll get to where I was going. Thank you."

The woman shut the door before she could turn around. "I didn't think she would," Julia said to console herself. "I didn't really expect it."

She got out of town as she had come into it, only more painfully, with more frequent stops. *I always heard it was easy to freeze to death,* she thought. She was shuddering all over, uncontrollably, so that the shuddering racked and hurt her. All of her body ached, as her hand had ached when, as a child, she had held a piece of ice as long as she could for a dare. "If there were only a snowbank, a bed of white snow where I could lie down and die. I would rest myself in it. I would pull it over me. I would press my cheek to it." But with this wet, ice-splintered ground, she would have to go on until she fell.

She was about to climb the curve of a small stone bridge when she saw the flicker of a red light beneath it, a fire, a windbreak, something to protect her from the sleet. She stumbled off the road and tried to run down the incline toward the fire. It was small, but really burning. She cupped her numb hands over it. Not until some of the heat had penetrated her skin did she look up, see the face of the man who sat with his back braced against the opposite side of the culvert.

She would have screamed, but a tide of slow cold horror rose in her throat, choking her.

JULIA STRETCHED her legs out along the warm smooth sheets and opened her eyes, saw the silver lights on the green ruffled curtains, the acacia spilling over the round bowl. "You almost overdid it tonight," she told herself. "You almost screamed then." She put her warm hand on the soft satin over her heart. It was jarred by her heartbeat. She had almost overdone it, but it had worked again.

Remembering that imagined suffering, that formless face, she was able to turn, once again, toward her husband, lying beside her in the warm sweet-smelling bed.

"So," he said in the tone of one who has been waiting. When he moved his hands slowly over her shallow breasts, she scarcely winced.

No More Questions

Stephen R. Novak

COURTROOM DRAMA

One of the most difficult ways in which to tell any story, let alone a McGuffin, is solely through dialogue; the dialogue in such a tale must not only be crisp and realistic, it must convey characterization and nuance of feeling, plant clues if and where necessary, and of course carry the entire weight of the plot. In "No More Questions," which does not contain a single narrative sentence until the story's powerful last line, Stephen Novak has written a memorable example of the dialogue-only type-and has created as well both a lovely McGuffin and a piece of courtroom drama to match the master himself, Erle Stanley Gardner. Mr. Novak, in addition to writing short stories, is also a playwright: he recently won a prize in a one-act playwriting contest held by the Paulist Players of New York, who will produce his play. B.P.

"THE DEFENSE CALLS as its last witness, the defendant, William Dempsey."

"The defendant will advance to be sworn."

"Do you solemnly swear that the testimony you are about to give is the truth, the whole truth and nothing but the truth, so help you God?"

"I do."

"State your full name and occupation."

"William Tunney Dempsey. I own an appliance store in town."

"You may be seated."

"How old are you, Bill?"

"Forty-six."

"That's a fighting name you have."

"It was my mother's idea."

"Are you married, Bill?"

"Yes, for over twenty years."

"Any children?"

"No, sir."

"And where do you live?"

"In Jersey, just over the line."

"That's about fifty miles away? Do you commute every day?"

"Yes, including Saturdays. Six days a week."

"And how long have you had your appliance business here in Wickham?"

"Close to four years."

"And what made you open a business in Wickham?"

"My father died, and I inherited a small estate. I've always wanted a business of my own."

"And how has business been?"

"Fair. But not as well as expected. It's difficult for a newcomer to be accepted here. And now this..."

"Yes...well now, Bill, the prosecution is going to try to make a big deal about that television set you gave to Maryann, so I'd like to clear that matter up right from the start. I ask you to identify that television set, which is marked Exhibit Sixteen. Is that the one you gave to Maryann?"

"Yes, sir. It is."

"What make set is it?"

"None, sir. I made it myself. I wanted to experiment with the new circuitry."

"The chassis says Magnavox."

"I used an old portable shell, because the components fit into it so neatly and polished it up."

"And about how much did it cost you to make?"

"Not counting my time, about two hundred dollars for the parts."

"So all you actually gave Maryann was about two hundred dollars?"

"If you put it that way, yes, sir. But I didn't think about the money. She liked the set, so I gave it to her."

"She saw you working on it?"

"Oh yes. She'd come in the store, and, when I wasn't needed on the floor, I'd be in my office working on this."

"She'd often come into your office?"

"Maybe every two or three days."

"Tell us, if you will, about when you first met Maryann."

"Well, sir, she was in her last year of high school, and she'd stop in every so often and buy records, you know, like most of the kids do, on their way home from school."

"And?"

"I don't know exactly how to explain it, but we got to talking to each other, she to me and me to her, and we were soon sort of confiding in each other. She always seemed so much older mentally than the other high school kids."

"And very pretty?"

"Oh yes. Very. But she never seemed to have any boyfriends in the high school crowd. She was too much of a loner. After a while I found out why, and I think I understood why she sort of liked to talk to me."

"We'd like to get to understand her character better, Bill, so would you tell the court why she liked to talk to you?"

"I guess I must of been something like a father or uncle that she'd never really had, but always wished she'd had."

"What do you mean?"

"Well, she never knew her real father. She grew up with a stepfather who was very nasty, drunk all the time. Even made passes at her once. He had lots of kids from a former wife who'd deserted him, and she was always neglected and left alone with all the dirty work and none of the love. As soon as she could, she left home and went on her own."

"And how old was she then?"

"Maybe thirteen, fourteen." "And what did she do?"

"Lived with an older married sister for a while. Then found various places to stay. Girlfriends mostly. A month here, a few weeks there. You know."

"Did she ever tell you if she lived with any men?"

"No, sir. She never said that."

"Did you ever get the impression that she...how shall I put it... played around?"

"No, sir. Not when she was in high school. At least as far as I know. As I say, she always seemed so much older, but then she was so naïve and trusting too."

"To you?"

"Yes, sir. She was always the kind of person you felt sorry for, without ever knowing exactly why. But, yes, sir. She trusted me, I think. That's why she always talked to me so much. But she never mentioned boyfriends. Just how lousy her family had been to her. And how she wanted to hurry and finish school, get a job, and be on her own. But, it seemed, she never could get what she wanted."

"Why do you say that?"

"Well, first of all, she flunked and didn't finish high school. Instead, she managed to get sent to some charity school with a bunch of other girls, where she was supposed to learn a trade she could work at. She used to write me and tell me how rotten the place was, how brutal and cheap and dirty the other girls were. And the dope and drugs! She stayed only a couple of months, then left and came back here, where she *did* get a job and was able to rent the room where she...where she was killed."

"Tell me truthfully, Bill, do you think Maryann was in love with you?"

"I...I...guess so, maybe, in a special sort of way, as I said. She used to tell me that all she wanted out of life was someone to love her."

"But you never encouraged her?"

"With me? No, sir."

"Why not?"

"Why not? Why not. I don't know how to answer. Maybe because I felt so sorry for her. Because I was so much older. Because I love my wife. But, I don't wanna lie to you, Mr. Buchanan, I loved Maryann all right, but not in the way people might think, just in my own mind...in a special way...maybe not like a daughter, but more like a protective kind of thing, where I just couldn't stand her being hurt by anyone after all she'd been through at such a young age."

"And you never told her?"

"I didn't have to tell her. She could see that, and that's why she used to tell me everything. Even when she found out she was gonna have a baby."

"She told you about her affair with another man?"

"Right away. The next day, in fact. And then later, when she found out she was pregnant, she was so scared. She didn't know how to tell me. She was afraid she'd lose my friendship, I think."

"And how did you react?"

"How could I? I knew right from the start this guy she was seeing was going to be trouble for her. She'd met him at a diner only a few months before...and she was so in love. I never liked it, but I yessed her and agreed with her because she was so happy about having found someone, even though he was married, and she said he'd leave his wife for her. I just thought to myself, 'Oh, yeah? Well, let's wait and see!' Then she found out about the baby."

"What happened?"

"She really broke down when she told me. She said the guy was no good. He was such a big shot, she said, but with her, he was nothing. He always took her to the most out-of-the-way places round here, where nobody would see them together. And when he found out about the baby, he really got angry with her. He blamed her for being careless, and he said he never wanted to see her again, unless she took the money he offered and got rid of the kid."

"He paid her to have an abortion?"

"Yes, sir. He gave her five hundred dollars."

"And she told all this to you?"

"Yes, sir. She told me."

"And what then?"

"She didn't know what to do. I suggested that she go see a priest or a minister, but she'd have none of that, and she sort of questioned me like I was her spiritual adviser, asking me what to do about the baby."

"And what did you advise?"

"I told her that if she had the abortion and if fate was cruel to her in the future and never gave her another child, she might not want to live with the terrible thought of having gotten rid of the only child she ever had. I also tried to make her see that, if she had the baby, for the first time in her life she would really have someone to love. And I also said that she might consider having the baby and placing it out for adoption as soon as it was born. There were agencies that handled that right from the hospital."

"How did she take these suggestions of yours?"

"I'm sure she was happier when she left than when she came in."

"But you don't know what she resolved to do?"

"No, sir. I don't."

"Did she ever tell you who her lover was, his name?"

"No, sir. Just that he'd told her not to tell anyone."

"Can you guess who he might be?"

"Your honor, I object. Defense counsel knows better than trying to get his witness to implicate someone by innuendo. Indeed, if there is someone."

"Mr. Buchanan, you are leading your witness."

"I'm sorry, your honor. I thought the witness might have some clue as to his identity."

"Rephrase your question then."

"Bill, did Maryann ever give you any specific indication of who her lover might be?"

"No, sir. She did not."

"And how long ago was this that she told you about the baby and getting the money from her lover?"

"About a month before she was killed."

"Now, Bill, and this is very important, as I know you realize, I want you to tell the court as best you can remember the details of the day Maryann was murdered."

"Well, sir, it was about five-fifteen in the afternoon. She must have just gotten home from work when she called me."

"She telephoned you?"

"Yes, sir. Said she had turned on the TV set and wasn't getting any picture and could I do anything about it after I finished work. Well, I close the store at six, so I said I'd stop by and check the set. Probably just a cold solder joint. I know how much she loved the TV set, because she always kept it on when she was home, always, from the time she got up, until going to sleep. She never had anything, you see. Never got a gift like it before from anyone. So...I closed the store about six-ten, got my tool caddy, got into my car, and drove the twenty blocks or so to her apartment."

"You'd been there before?"

"Several times outside, when I'd give her a lift home. Only once inside, and then only for a minute or so, when I carried the set inside the room for her and set it up. That was the only time."

"And when was that?"

"Just the week before. I guess I gave it to her to cheer her up."

"And that was the only time you were in her apartment?"

"Yes, sir. Except it wasn't really a whole apartment, just one room in this old private house, one room on the street side with its own side entrance."

"So, after you closed the store, you drove to her flat?"

"Yes, sir. It was dark out already. When I got there, I could see her lights were on and I could hear the TV set playing. So, I knocked at her side door entrance. There was no answer. I tried the doorknob and it opened. At first, I didn't see her, 'cause the couch faced the other way. First thing I noticed was the TV set, sounding off with one of the children's programs, but absolutely no picture—gray blank. I called her. 'Maryann?' Thought she might be next door or in the bathroom, but no answer. Then I saw her on the floor in front of the couch. Her face was all bruised and she was just lying there, all crumpled up. I touched her and I saw she was dead."

"Then what?"

"Then what? Oh, I think I cried, 'cause I remember hearing myself sobbing. I think I shut the TV off."

"How long was it before you called the police?"

"I don't know. Maybe ten minutes. Maybe fifteen."

"And they arrested you for her murder?"

"Yes, sir."

"And did you, William Tunney Dempsey, kill Maryann Ravelle?"

"No, sir. I swear I did not kill her."

"And now, Bill, with his honor's permission, I am going to turn you over to Mr. Whitaker, the district attorney, for cross-examination. I will have more questions to ask you on redirect."

"Yes, sir."

"Well, William Tunney Dempsey, your attorney has tried to portray you as sort of a generous poor slob, with a kind heart and a father's protective instinct over this poor little innocent girl who you say was killed by a person unknown, by a lover unknown who fathered her unborn child, paid her to have an abortion, then in a murderous rage beat this poor girl to death, killing not only her, but, if you are right, his unborn child also? Am I correct? Is that the gist of your testimony?"

"I object, your honor."

"Objection overruled. You may continue, Mr. Whitaker."

"If I offend learned counsel, I apologize, but I see his client as a vicious, calculating, heartless murderer, who, to exonerate himself, having had an affair with this child not half his age, has concocted this absurd story of another lover to draw suspicion from himself by trying to create a sympathetic doubt in the jury's minds. Well, I for one don't believe this jury will overlook the cold, hard facts of this crime, based on the testimony of all the witnesses we've had who have sworn to the relationship existing between the defendant and the victim."

"Is the district attorney making his summation at this point?"

"I'm sorry, your honor."

"Confine your remarks to questions of the defendant."

"Mr. Dempsey. Do you deny the testimony given by your employees...that they would see Maryann come in time and time again and go right into your office, where you'd close the door, and she'd stay for hours? Do you deny their testimony that they saw you drive away with her many evenings on closing the store?"

"No, sir. I don't deny any of that. But they have all read something into our relationship which just wasn't there."

"Oh, really? You mean to tell me that a man of your age, a good-looking middle-aged man, I might add, a handsome, mature-looking man—you mean to tell me you were not flattered by the affection shown you by this young girl? That you did not in the slightest return her affection?"

"I was flattered, yes. But I did not return her affection—not in the way you mean."

"And just what do I mean? I haven't asked that question yet."

"You're implying an affair which didn't exist."

"All right, do you deny having had sexual relations with Maryann Ravelle?"

"Yes. I deny it. I certainly do deny it!"

"And can you prove you *did not* have an affair with her?"

"I object, your honor."

"Objection sustained."

"Do you deny having the *opportunity* for an affair?"

"I object."

"Objection overruled. Answer the question, Mr. Dempsey."

"How can I deny having the opportunity? Certainly. I drove her home many times. I can't get witnesses to prove we went straight from the office to her home, or witnesses to say I stayed only a minute or two outside, or that I never went in, or that I didn't meet her somewhere on the sly."

"Thank you, Mr. Dempsey. Let's turn now to the gifts. Are you normally a generous person?"

"What do you mean by normally?"

"Well...do you give things to *all* your employees...*all* your customers?"

"Of course not."

"Do you give gifts to *some* of your customers?"

"Sometimes. Yes."

"Give me some examples."

"I can't think of any special examples. Certainly, when I liked a person, I gave small gifts, like records or books or things like that."

"But never television sets?"

"No, sir."

"But you gave Maryann a color television set. Did you give her any other gifts?"

"Just for Christmas and her birthday. You know."

"That's all? You never gave her money?"

"Oh, money. Yes, I guess I did. Occasionally."

"How much and how occasionally?"

"You know, ten dollars here, five there. Just to keep her going when things were tough."

"And you expect this jury to believe there was nothing more than platonic friendship between you and the girl?"

"Just friendship."

"Did you ever tell your wife about Maryann?"

"I object to this line of questioning, your honor. I don't see that it's relevant in view of the fact that the defendant's wife has already testified to the fact that she did not know of her husband's friendship for Maryann. District attorney is trying to prejudice the character of the defendant."

"Your honor. Learned defense counsel is correct in that I am trying to show that the character of the defendant is indeed on trial here."

"Objection overruled."

"No. I never mentioned it to my wife."

"But Maryann knew you were married?"

"Yes. She did."

"You saw nothing wrong with this young girl establishing a relationship with *you*—a married man, but yet you want this court to believe this fictitious story of another man she'd supposedly known for four months? The defense has not produced one shred of evidence to prove the existence of another man. I submit, your honor, that there never was such a third party. I submit, ladies and gentlemen of the jury, that the defendant has fabricated this story to cover his own sins, that he is the father of—"

"Mr. Whitaker! How long must I pound this gavel to get your attention? The jury will disregard the district attorney's statements. Mr. Whitaker, you will kindly save your emotional outbursts for your summation to the jury."

"Yes, your honor. I'm sorry. Now, Mr. Dempsey, if such a third party existed, and I emphasize the word 'if,' why do you think he would have killed Maryann? If he was so concerned about protecting his reputation?"

"I think she must have refused to have the abortion. That she told him so. And, in a fit of anger, he hit her, probably accidentally killing her."

"That's your guess?"

"Yes, sir."

"Mr. Dempsey. You admit having a relationship with the girl. You expect us to believe in your virtue. You admit to giving her gifts. You expect us to believe you are merely a generous person, without motives. You were at the scene of the crime when the police arrived. You expect us to believe that you did not run, but called the police because it was your duty to do so. You expect us to believe that you were in her apartment only once before; yet so many witnesses saw you drive her from your store time and time again. You expect us to believe in the existence of another man, when no one, not one single witness has corroborated your testimony? You expect us to believe all this?"

"Yes. Because it's true."

"Then what happened to the five hundred dollars this lover supposedly gave her? The police didn't find it. No bank accounts. No evidence of large purchases. Where is it? What did she do with it, Mr. Dempsey?"

"I don't know."

"No more questions, your honor."

"Mr. Buchanan, do you wish to redirect at this time?"

"Your honor, I would prefer adjourning until the day after tomorrow, so that I might study all the testimony given."

"Very well. Any objections from the district attorney?"

"No objection."

"This court stands adjourned until ten o'clock on Thursday."

"This court is now in session, the Honorable James R. Flanigan presiding."

"The defendant is reminded that he is still under oath. Mr. Buchanan, you may proceed with your redirect."

"Before I begin, your honor, may I ask the court's permission to have my clerk come forward with an electrical extension and connect the power to the television set, State's Exhibit Sixteen?"

"For what purpose, Mr. Buchanan?"

"The defendant has testified that the set was in need of repair. I wish to corroborate that testimony."

"Does the district attorney have any objection?"

"None, your honor."

"Proceed then."

"Jack, will you connect that extension please? Thank you. Now, Bill, you claimed that Maryann had called you to repair the television set and that when you arrived, one of the first things you noticed was that the sound was playing, but there was no picture. Is that correct?"

"Yes, sir."

"Would you now leave the stand and turn on the switch of the TV set?"

"Yes, sir."

"Fine. That's it. Is it on? I see nothing but a dark screen, no picture at all, no lines, nothing, the same as if the set were turned off. Am I correct, Bill?"

"Yes, sir."

"Nevertheless, I do hear people talking on what I think is the Channel 7 A.M. New York show. Is that correct?"

"Yes, it is. It's tuned to Channel 7."

"May I ask your honor for permission for this witness to step down temporarily, so that I may recall Sergeant Capilan of the Wickham police department to the stand?"

"Very well. Sergeant Capilan will take the stand, please."

"Now, Sergeant. I ask you to recall the scene of the death. When you arrived, was this television playing or not?"

"It was not playing, sir."

"And did you or anyone else, during the entire time this set has been in the custody of the police department, turn this set on to test it?"

"No, sir. We did not. We merely dusted it for fingerprints."

"And, of course, as you've already sworn to, you found the prints of both the defendant and the victim on it...and no other prints?"

"That's correct, sir."

"And the set has been in your custody all this time?"

"Yes, sir."

"And once more, did anyone, to your knowledge, turn this set on at any time since the crime?"

"No, sir."

"Thank you, Sergeant. Will the defendant please resume the stand?... Now, Bill, I would like to ask you more about this television set. You said you made this set?"

"Yes, sir, I did."

"I'm going to ask you, Bill, with the court's permission, to see if you can't repair that set for us right here and now."

"Your honor. I object to this display of showmanship by the defense counsel!"

"Do you have a purpose, Mr. Buchanan?"

"Yes, your honor. My client's guilt or innocence may very well depend on this exhibit, and I don't want him denied that chance."

"Very well. Proceed."

"Bill, would you then take your tool caddy, State's Exhibit Twenty-Four, and proceed to repair the set, if you can?"

"This shouldn't take too long."

"I call your attention, your honor, for the record, to the fact that the defendant is now turning the set over, loosening some screws, sliding the component tray out and checking the wire circuitry beneath. Have you spotted the trouble, Bill?"

"Just as I thought. Looks like a loose connection. Just a moment while this soldering iron gets hot...there, now we should have a picture. Yes, there it is."

"I was right, your honor. It is the AM. New York show, in living color. Thank you, Bill. You may turn the set off and take the stand. Now, Bill, that cabinet, the outside wood, where did that come from?"

"That was an old Magnavox portable. I took the old works out of that set and put the new works inside this box. It was lightweight and cut just right for the controls you see there."

"You mean the tuning knob, the volume, tone, et cetera?"

"Yes, sir."

"And tell me, Bill, is there any indication whatsoever...any marking on the cabinet or on the controls to indicate whether this is a black and white set or a color set?"

"No, sir, there is not."

"And tell me, did you, at any time during your testimony, or did I, in any of my questioning, indicate whether this was a color set?"

"No, sir, we did not."

"And exactly why did neither you nor I mention that this was a color set?"

"Because we knew that the only one else who could possibly know it would be Maryann's lover."

"And did we know who her lover was?"

"Yes, sir. We knew. But we couldn't prove it."

"And how did we know?"

"Because Maryann told me who her lover was."

"Then you lied when you were asked if you knew?"

"Yes, sir, I lied."

"And you were willing to commit perjury?"

"Yes, sir. He was too powerful. Who'd have believed me? But I knew sooner or later he'd have to say something, ask something which would give us the proof."

"He could have guessed it was color. Most sets are today."

"Yes, but only he could have known about the exact time he first met Maryann...four months before. I was careful not to mention that either."

"No more questions. Your witness, Mr. Whitaker."

But the district attorney was weeping.

Violation

William F. Nolan

"POLICE STORY"

The currently popular TV drama Police Story is a mosaic which presents a generally realistic picture of America's big city cops and, by extension, of the society which gives them sanction. Since "Violation" speaks in the future tense, we cannot judge its realism; but it has an inexorable logic about it which suggests it is an only too accurate reflection of both future police work and the society which gives it legitimacy. William F. Nolan is a novelist, short-story writer, dramatist, biographer, and literary critic who first won notice in the science-fiction field. Currently he is in great demand as a movie and TV scenarist. His Dashiell Hammett, A Casebook (McNally & Loftin, 1969), was awarded a special Edgar by MWA and provides seminal scholarship to any student of the author of The Maltese Falcon and The Thin Man. - J.G.

It is 2 A.M. and he waits. In the cool morning stillness of a side street, under the screen of trees, the rider waits quietly. At ease upon the wide leather seat of his cycle, gloved fingers resting idly on the bars, goggles up, eyes palely reflecting the leaf-filtered glow of the moon.

Helmeted. Uniformed. Waiting.

In the breathing dark the cycle metal cools; the motor is silent, power contained.

The faint stirrings of a still-sleeping city reach him at his vigil. But he is not concerned with these; he mentally dismisses them. He is only concerned with the broad river of smooth concrete facing him through the trees-and the great winking red eye suspended icicle-like above it.

He waits.

And tenses to a sound upon the river. An engine sound, mosquito-dim with distance, rising to a hum. A rushing sound under the stars. The rider's hands contract like the claws of a bird. He rises slowly on the bucket seat, right foot poised near the starter. A coiled spring.

Waiting.

Twin pencil beams of light move toward him, toward the street on which he waits hidden. Closer.

The hum builds in volume; the lights are very close now, flaring chalk-whiteness along the concrete boulevard.

The rider's goggles are down and he is ready to move out, move onto the river. Another second, perhaps two...

But no. The vehicle slows, makes a full stop. A service vehicle with two men inside, laughing, joking. The rider listens to them, mouth set, eyes hard. The vehicle begins to move once more. The sound is eaten by the night.

There is no violation.

Now...the relaxing, the easing back. The ebb tide of tension receding. Gone. The rider quiet again under the moon.

Waiting.

The red eye winking at the empty boulevard.

"How much farther, Dave?" asks the girl.

"Ten miles maybe. Once we hit Westwood it's a quick run to my place. Relax. You're nervous."

"We should have stayed on the mainway. Used the grid. I don't like surface streets. A grid would have taken us in."

The man smiles, looping an arm around her.

"There's nothing to be afraid of so long as you're careful," he said. "I used to drive surface streets all the time when I was a boy. Lots of people did."

The girl swallows, touches at her hair nervously. "But they don't anymore. People use the grids. I didn't even know cars still came equipped for manual driving."

"They don't. I had this set up by a mechanic I know. He does jobs like this for road buffs. It's still legal, driving your own car—it's just that most people have lost the habit."

The girl peers out the window into the silent street, shakes her head. "It's not...natural. Look out there. Nobody! Not another car for miles. I feel as if we're...trespassing."

The man is annoyed. "That's damn nonsense. I have friends who do this all the time. Just relax and enjoy it. And don't talk like an idiot."

"I want out," says the girl. "I'll take a walkway back to the grid."

"The hell you will," flares the man. "You're with me tonight. We're going to my place."

She resists, strikes at his face. The man grapples to subdue her and does not see the blinking light. The car passes under it swiftly.

"No!" says the man. "I went through that light! You made me miss the stop. I've broken one of the surface laws." He says this numbly.

"So what does that mean?" the girl asks. "What could happen?"

"Never mind. Nothing will happen. Never mind about what could happen."

The girl peers out into the darkness. "I still want to leave this car."

"Just shut up," says the man.

And keeps driving.

SOMETHING in the sound tells the rider that this one will not stop, that it will continue to move along the river of concrete despite the blinking eye.

He smiles in the darkness, lips stretched back, silently. Poised there on the cycle, with the hum steady and rising on the river, he feels the power within him about to be released.

The car is almost upon the light, moving swiftly; there is no hint of slackened speed.

The rider watches intently. Man and a girl inside. Struggling.

Fighting with one another.

The car passes under the light.

Violation.

Now!

He spurs the cycle to metal life; the motor crackles, roars, explodes the black machine into motion, and the rider is away, rolling in muted thunder along the street. Around the corner, swaying, onto the long, moon-painted river of the boulevard.

The rider feels the wind in his face, feels the throb and power-pulse of the metal thing he rides, feels the smooth concrete rushing backward under his wheels.

Ahead: the firefly glow of tail beams.

And now his cycle voice cries out after them, a siren moan through the still spaces of the hive-city. A voice that rises and falls in spirals of sound. And his cycle eyes, mounted left and right, blink crimson, red as blood in their wake.

The car will stop. The man will see him, hear him. The eyes and the voice will reach the violator.

And he will stop.

"Good Lord!" the man says coldly. "We picked up a rider at that light."

"*You* picked him up, I didn't," says the girl. "It's your problem."

"But I've never been stopped on a surface street," the man says, a note of desperation in his voice. "In all these years, never *once!*"

The girl glares at him. "Dave, you make me sick. Look at you, shaking like a pup. You're a damned poor excuse for a man."

He does not react to these words. He speaks in a numbed monotone. "I can talk my way out. I know I can. He'll listen to me. I have my rights as a citizen of the city—"

"He's catching up fast. You'd better pull over."

"I'll do the talking. You just keep quiet. I'll handle this."

The rider sees that the car is slowing, braking, pulling to the curb.

Stopping.

He cuts the siren voice, lets it die, glides the cycle in behind the car.

Cuts the engine. Sits there for a long moment on the leather seat, pulling off his gloves. Slowly.

He sees the car door slide open. A man steps out, comes toward him. The rider swings a booted leg over the cycle, steps free, advancing to meet this lawbreaker, fitting the gloves carefully into his black leather belt.

They face each other, the man smaller, paunching, balding, face flushed. The rider's polite smile eases the man's tenseness.

"You in a hurry, sir?"

"Me? No, I'm not in a hurry. Not at all. It was just...I didn't see the light up there until...I was past it. The high trees and all. I swear to you I didn't see it. I'd never knowingly break a surface law, officer. You have my sworn word."

Nervous. Shaken and nervous, this man. The rider can feel the man's guilt, a physical force. He extends a hand.

"May I see your operator's license, please?"

The man fumbles in his coat. "I have it right here. It's all in order, up to date and all."

"Just let me see it, please."

The man continues to talk. "Been driving for years, officer, and this is my first violation. Perfect record up to now. I'm a responsible citizen. I obey the laws. After all, I'm not a fool."

The rider says nothing; he examines the man's license, taps it thoughtfully against his wrist. The rider's goggles are opaque and the man cannot see his eyes as he studies the face of the violator.

"The woman in the car...is she your wife?"

"No. No, sir. She's...a friend. Just a friend."

"Then why were you fighting? I saw the two of you fighting inside the car when it passed the light. That isn't friendly, is it?"

The man attempts to smile. "Personal. We had a small personal disagreement. It's all over now, believe me."

The rider walks to the car, leans to peer in at the woman. She is pale, as nervous as the man.

"You having trouble?" the rider asks.

She hesitates, shakes her head mutely. The rider leaves her, returns to the man, who is leaning against the cycle.

"Don't touch that," says the rider coldly, and the man draws back his hand, mumbling an apology.

"I have no further use for this," says the rider, handing back the man's license. "You are guilty of a surface-street violation."

The man quakes; his hands tremble. "But...it was not *deliberate*. I know the law. You're empowered to make exceptions if a violation is not deliberate. The full penalty is not invoked in such cases. Instead, you are allowed to—"

The rider cuts the. flow of desperate words. "You forfeited your Citizen's Right of Exception when you allowed a primary emotion—anger, in this instance—to affect your control of a surface vehicle. Thus, my duty is clear."

The man's eyes widen in shock as the rider brings up a belt weapon. "You can't possibly—"

"I'm hereby authorized to perform this action per the 1990 Overpopulation Statute with regard to surface violators. Your case is closed."

And he presses the trigger.

Again and again and again. Three long, probing blue jets of star-hot flame leap from the weapon in the rider's hand.

The man is gone. The woman is gone. The car is gone.

The street is empty and silent. A charred smell of distant suns lingers in the morning air.

The rider stands by his cycle, unmoving for a long moment. Then he carefully holsters the weapon and pulls on his leather gloves. He mounts the cycle as it comes to life under his foot.

He is again upon the moon-flowing boulevard, gliding back toward the blinking red eye.

The rider returns to his vigil on the small, tree-shadowed side street, thinking *How stupid they are! To be subject to indecision, to quarrels and erratic behavior. Weak, all of them, soft and weak.*

He smiles into the darkness.

The eye blinks over the river.

And now it is 4 A.M. and now 6 and 8 and 10 and 1 P.M. and now it is 3, 4, 5, the hours turning like spoked wheels, the days spinning away.

And he waits. Through nights without sleep, days without food, a flawless metal enforcer at his vigil, watching, sure of himself and of his duty.

Waiting.

Hollywood Footprints

Betty Buchanan

NOSTALGIA

Everyone these days seems fascinated with the past: places, events, things; what people did, what they read, how they were entertained. And the greatest of our fascinations is unquestionably Hollywood. What was it like in the old days, the Golden Era of Bogart and Gable and Cagney? Well, Sam Swanson and Herman Greenfield, the protagonists of Betty Buchanan's "Hollywood Footprints," know exactly what it was like. And so does Betty herself: she comes from a theatrical family, grew up in Hollywood, has worked for such studios as RKO, MGM, Universal, and Disney Productions, and has written for Billboard and Daytime TV (the latter of which she is presently for as their Hollywood Editor). She is also the author of two well-received mystery novels under the pseudonym of Joan Shepherd. - B.P.

SAM SWANSON HAD GONE to the funeral of the old movie star Jason Towers, and a sudden attack of nostalgia made him head over the Pass to Hollywood instead of driving west to Woodland Hills. It had been years since he'd walked down Hollywood Boulevard. Without realizing it, he hoped to find some of the old magic still there. As a young press agent, he'd arrived in 1939 fresh from a grubby midwestern newspaper, and found Hollywood was all he had ever dreamed. Somewhere, in the back of his mind, it still existed as he'd first seen it, an illusion he'd managed to preserve by staying west of Doheny.

It was still early in the day, so he was able to park on Sycamore.

At the corner, he turned east on Hollywood Boulevard and walked down to Grauman's Chinese Theatre, his spirit dimming somewhat as he passed the featureless new buildings and the raffish new population. In the old days, he reflected, the cops would have hustled most of these cuckoos out of town, tossing them across Alvarado, going east. From whence, no doubt, they had arrived.

He was happy to see that the Chinese still looked impressive, though Sid Grauman's name had been taken off the theater he had built. Sam strolled about the forecourt, looking at the prints of all the stars who had plunked their hands and feet into wet cement for Sid and posterity. Sam had been to a hundred premieres (pronounced pree-meers in his time), but always as a working press agent. He'd never really taken the time to stroll over the pavement and look at all the prints and signatures. Publicity men were always too busy checking lists, hand-holding, getting the right people in front of the mikes and cameras. If they goofed off, they faced the wrath of Herman Greenfield.

In Sam's day, the studios had been run by the tycoons and their families, a system which had seemed to be a law of nature. And the tycoon at the head of the dream factory where Sam had worked was a wild man named Herman Greenfield. In all the other studios, the impact of publicity was only an echo that reached the head man when something went terrifically right or terribly wrong. Not with Herman, Sam recalled. Herman knew everyone in the department, and he wasn't above striding over to the offices and raising hell in person when he felt like it.

As he wandered over the irregular pavement of the famous fore-court, Sam remembered some of the exciting—and some of the deadly —nights in which he had participated, only slightly less starry-eyed than the fans beyond the barricades. He almost laughed aloud, thinking of Herman and the three-ring circus on premiere occasions. The lights sweeping the skies, the near disasters, the drunks, the fans, the confusion...then, the last fulsome gush into the microphone...the house lights down...the hush...the crackling sound track...and "*Herman Greenfield Presents...*" And, of course, the applause.

Suddenly, Sam was stopped in mid-reverie by activity in the far corner of the forecourt. Wooden forms. Buckets. Protective canvas draped over sawhorses. Someone important had just had his or her footprints saved for the future. Sam went over to see if the new name would be at all familiar. He made a small bet with himself that it wouldn't be. It wasn't. But he was fascinated to see that the cement square next to it contained the prints and signature of Dorina Belle.

He'd almost forgotten her. Oh, how adored she had been. He was happy to see that her bit of pavement was one of the larger ones, though from her prints, she must have had the feet of a ten-year-old girl. Her time had been brief. Sam had been here the night of her triumphant appearance at the premiere of her best-known film, *This Gilded Planet*. He tried to remember that night. Dorina interviewed by the emcee...Dorina pressing her hands into the wet cement...Dorina standing with one foot extended prettily while an attendant made the impression, and she held on to Herman Greenfield's arm to keep her balance...Dorina triumphant! And then she had walked out of the wet cement, out of the forecourt of Grauman's Chinese—and disappeared forever.

Now it looked as if they were getting ready to dispense with even this last remembrance of Dorina; the grout around her prints had been partly chiseled away. Sam hadn't realized that they took out the old, forgotten footprints. He supposed they must be running out of space; it had been fifty years since Norma Talmadge had walked into the wet cement by mistake and started the tradition.

A young usher was standing at the entrance, talking to the ticket taker, and Sam went over and asked about the cement work in the corner. "I don't know, exactly," said the usher. "They started it last night before I came on. Could be they're going to move the box office over there."

"That's not it," said the ticket taker. "They've just put in the new one. I think they're going to take out an old one and put it someplace else."

Sam went back to the sidewalk in front of the theater and stood looking out at the traffic and thinking about Dorina, the disappearing star. The rumors—she had eloped, and would return. She had run away, frightened by the sudden fame. She had contracted a rare disease and was confined in a sanitarium, her great beauty destroyed.

There had not been time to know her very well, Sam reflected. All he recalled now was a mobile face, sad eyes, and a surprising liveliness on the screen. He also remembered one tough little cookie. Sam had written her bio and given her a background to go with her face and screen personality—army officer father, socialite mother, European education. In reality, she was a child from a vaudeville act who had known only work, discipline, and ambition. Beyond that—nothing.

Sam remembered how Herman Greenfield had gone into action as the rumor of Dorina's disappearance spread. Frantic stories to the press. Midnight conferences. Detectives in the offices, even on the sets. Rumors of pay-offs. The hints in the columns that Dorina would return. The story was rehashed in the magazines from time to time. But Dorina never reappeared. And now, everyone who cared was gone. Or almost everyone. *I'm still here,* Sam said to himself. *And so is old Herman.*

Greenfield, the ex-terror and ex-tycoon, was now an old man who lived with his son's family in a Spanish castle in a no-longer-fashionable section of Hollywood. Poor Herman! Without Marge, the peppery little wife who had believed in Herman and his studio as fiercely as he himself did, he had gradually withdrawn from the business. Her death had also brought a halt to the famed Greenfield parties. After a time, people forgot that he was still around. Sam had exchanged phone numbers with him at last year's Christmas party at the Masquers, and though Sam had promised to call, he never had.

He found the number in his address book and called from the booth in front of the theater. Herman's voice sounded the same. And that was reassuring. "I'm here in the forecourt of Grauman's Chinese," Sam explained, "and I suddenly found myself thinking about you, Herman. I thought I'd just call and see how things are going."

"How things are going, for Christ sake?" Herman barked. "How the hell do you think they're going? I'm older than God, and I've got a houseful of grandchildren playing guitars. And a daughter-in-law from New York with an I.Q. of two hundred who hates movies. So things are just great. What about you, Swanson?"

"I went to the Towers funeral this morning," Sam said. "Then I drove over to Hollywood to look around."

"Damned place looked like a toilet the last time I was down there."

"They're still putting new footprints in the forecourt at Grauman's, anyway. Oh, by the way, I think they're removing Dorina Belle's cement square. They're going to move the box office or something."

"What?" Herman barked.

"Dorina Belle," Sam repeated. "Don't tell me you've forgotten *that* night?"

"Jee-sus! Forgotten? Listen. I'll meet you at Radlick's in twenty minutes." Bang. He'd hung up.

Radlick's? It took Sam a moment to remember that there had been a little cafe of that name in a corner of the theater property—but it hadn't been there for at least twenty years. Sam went over and stood in front of the souvenir shop that had replaced it.

Fifteen minutes later, a Mercedes driven by an angry-looking, dark-haired woman pulled up in front of the theater, and Herman Greenfield hopped out. He stuck his head back into the car, had a few words with the woman and then stood and watched the car zoom off. He looked around for a moment, spotted Sam, and said, "Hello, Swanson. What happened to Radlick's?"

Sam explained. "Doesn't matter," Herman said. "What I want to see is what the hell they're doing with Dorina's footprints."

He must be seventy, Sam thought in amazement, *and he hasn't changed at all.* Sam felt a little sorry for the smart daughter-in-law.

Herman strode over to the comer where the new footprints were slowly drying, and where the edges of Dorina's square had been partly chipped away. He stepped onto Dorina's piece of cement with an air of ownership. As he did so, the usher and the ticket taker approached. "Watch out for the wet cement, fella," the usher said.

"Where's the manager?" Herman barked. "Tell him Herman Greenfield wants to see him."

The ticket taker recognized the name and immediately became respectful. The two young men went off to find the manager.

When the manager appeared, he also seemed suitably impressed by Greenfield. "No, no, sir," he said, "we are certainly not removing any of the old footprints, and we're not relocating the box office. Nothing will be changed. After the ceremony, we decided to renew the grout around some of the older sections. Just chisel it down slightly and smooth the surface. Merely cosmetic. We can't change anything. This is a historical site."

"You're damned right," said Herman. The two shook hands, and the manager left, barely concealing a sigh of relief. Herman Greenfield still had that effect on people.

Sam had sensed a thread to be picked up. "You must have had a bad time when Dorina disappeared that night."

"Bad time is hardly the expression. I went through *hell*. God, it's great to talk to someone with a memory. I've been alone with so much, Sam." Herman paused, studying Sam as if trying to reach a difficult decision. An indecisive Greenfield? Finally, he took a deep breath and continued. "I've been alone with the truth *too* long. When you get older, a secret eats at your mind, and sooner or later you've got to get rid of it. You're afraid to take a drink—you might tell the wrong people. So I'm going to trust you, Sam. But it goes no further. Swear?"

"On the memory of D. W. Griffith," Sam said, frowning.

"That's good enough for me. Well—you know me, Sam; no casting couch crap, ever. Right? But somehow, I'd gotten involved with Dorina. She was so clever and ambitious, and I guess I was flattered. Anyway, Dorina's big night arrived, and I figured that was the end of the affair. It was a relief. And she'd gotten what she wanted. So, after the premiere, when everyone was still milling around, my wife and I and Dorina got into the car..."

But I thought she'd gone off alone," Sam said.

Herman shook his head. "There was so much confusion that no one remembered we'd left together. Then that legend about Dorina walking away alone got started. Fortunately. Anyhow, we drove back toward Bel Air, and on the ride home, Dorina decides this is it. The whole enchilada! She tells Marge that we're in love and that we're going to get married. Marge knew something was going on, but *that* was a bombshell. Marge was prepared, though. People always underestimate wives. Marge whipped out the little gun she'd carried ever since the last Hollywood kidnap scare and shot Dorina right through her gorgeous head."

Sam was so astounded that it took him a couple of beats to recover. "What—what did you do?"

"Buried her. What else? Poor Dorina! We did it late that night. It was one hell of a job, and we had to be very careful. And very neat. But we managed."

"But where? Where did you bury her?"

Herman Greenfield gave him a studio mogul stare. "Where?" he repeated. "What the hell do you think you're standing on?"

Sam looked down. He was standing on Dorina Belle's footprints.

The Time of the Eye

Harlan Ellison

THE MACABRE

In 1773 Reverend Paul Lorraine, prison chaplain at London's infamous Newgate Gaol, began publishing highly colored pamphlet versions of the prisoners' confessions. Crime stories from inside institutions have never lost their popularity since, perhaps because they echo some atavistic fear of ourselves being "put away." But what happens to the protagonist of "The Time of the Eye" inside the Place could as well happen on any big city street today. Or in some rural byway. Harlan Ellison has won five Hugos, two SFWA Nebulas, and an MWA Edgar. Three times his work has been chosen as Most Outstanding Teleplay of the Year by the Writers Guild of America. His most recent collection of short fiction is Deathbird Stories. *- J.G.*

IN THE THIRD year of my death, I met Piretta. Purely by chance, for she occupied a room on the second floor, while I was given free walk of the first floor and the sunny gardens. And it seemed so strange, that first and most important time, that we met at all, for she had been there since she had gone blind in 1945, while I was one of the old men with young faces who had dissolved after Korea.

The Place wasn't too unpleasant, of course, despite the high, flat-stone walls and the patronizing air of Mrs. Goody, for I knew one day my fog would pass, and I would feel the need to speak to someone again, and then I could leave the Place.

But that was in the future.

I neither looked forward to that day, nor sought refuge in my stable life at the Place. I was in a limbo life between caring and exertion. I was sick; I had been told that; and no matter what I knew—I was dead. So what sense was there in caring?

But Piretta was something else.

Her delicate little face was porcelain, with eyes the flat blue of shallow waters, and hands that were quick to do nothing important. I met her—as I say—by chance. She had grown restless, during what she called "the time of the eye," and had managed to give her Miss Hazelet the slip.

I was walking with head bowed and hands locked behind my bathrobe, through the lower corridor, when she came down the great winding stairway.

On many an occasion I had stopped at that stairway, watching the drab-faced women who scrubbed down each level, each riser. It was like watching them go to hell. They started at the top and washed their way down. Their hair was always white, always lank, always like old hay. They scrubbed with methodical ferocity, for this was the last occupation for them before the grave, and they clung to it with soap and suds. And I had watched them go down to hell, step by step.

But this time there were no drudges on their knees.

I heard her walking close to the wall, her fingertips brushing the wainscoting as she descended, and I realized immediately that she was blind.

That blindness deeper than lack of sight.

There was something to her; something ephemeral that struck instantly to the dead heart in me. I watched her come down with stately slowness, as though she tripped to silent music, until I was drawn to her in spirit.

"May I be of service?" I heard myself politely inquiring, from a distance. She paused there and her head came up with field mouse awareness.

"No, thank you," she said, most congenially. "I am quite able to care for myself, thank you. Something that *person*—" she twitched her head in the direction of upstairs, "—cannot seem to fathom."

She came the remainder of the steps to the napless wine-colored carpet. She stood there and exhaled deeply, as though she had just put a satisfactory *finis* to an immense project.

"My name is—" I began, but she cut me off with a sharp snort and, "Name's the same." She giggled.

"Names ring of little consequence, don't you agree?" and there was such conviction in her voice, I could hardly disagree. So I said, "I suppose that's so." She snickered softly and patted her auburn hair, bed-disarrayed. "Indeed," she said with finality, "that is so; very much so."

This was peculiar to me, for several reasons.

First, she was talking with a rather complicated incoherence that seemed perfectly rational at the time, and second, she was the first person I had spoken to since I had been admitted to the Place, two years and three months before.

I felt an affinity for this woman, and hastened to strengthen our flimsy tie.

"And yet," I ventured, "one must have something by which to know another person." I grew bold and went on, "Besides—if one *likes* someone."

She considered this for a long second, one hand still on the wall, the other at her white throat. "If you insist," she replied, after deliberation, and added, "you may call me Piretta."

"Is that your name?" I asked.

"No," she answered, so I knew we were to be friends.

"Then you can call me Sidney Carton."

"That is a fine name, should any name be considered fine," she said, and I nodded. Then, realizing she could not hear a nod, I added a monosyllable to indicate her pleasure was mine also.

"Would you care to see the gardens?" I asked.

"That would be most kind of you," she said, adding with a touch of irony, "as you see...I'm quite blind."

Since it was a game we were playing I said, "Oh, truly? I really hadn't noticed."

Then she took my arm, and we went down the corridor toward the garden French doors. I heard someone coming down the staircase, and she stiffened on my arm. "Miss Hazelet. Oh, please!"

I knew what she was trying to say. Her attendant. I knew then that she was not allowed downstairs, that she was now being sought by her nurse. But I could not allow her to be returned to her room, after I had just found her.

"Trust me," I whispered, leading her into a side corridor.

I found the mop closet, and gently ushered her before me, into its cool, dark recess. I closed the door softly, and stood there, very close to her. I could hear her breathing, and it was shallow, quick. It made me remember those hours before dawn in Korea, even when we were full asleep; when we sensed what was coming, with fear and trepidation.

She was frightened. I held her close, without meaning to do so, and her one arm went around my waist. We were very near, and for the first time in over two years I felt emotions stirring in me; how foolish of me to consider love. But I waited there with her, adrift in a sargasso of conflicting feelings, while her Miss Hazelet paced by outside.

Finally, after what seemed a time too short, we heard those same precise steps mounting the stairs—annoyed, prissy, flustered.

"She's gone. Now we can see the gardens," I said, and wanted to bite my tongue. She could *see* nothing; but I did not rectify my error. Let her think I took her infirmity casually. It was far better that way.

I opened the door cautiously, and peered out. No one but old Bauer, shuffling along down the hall, his back to us. I led her out, and as though nothing had happened, she took my arm once more.

"How sweet of you," she said, and squeezed my bicep.

We walked back to the French doors, and went outside.

The air was musky with the scent of Fall, and the crackling of leaves underfoot was a constant thing. It was not too chilly, and yet she clung to me with a soft desperation more need than inclination. I didn't think it was because of her blindness; I was certain she could walk through the garden without any help if she so desired.

We moved down the walk, winding out of sight of the Place in a few seconds, shielded and screened by the high, neatly-pruned hedges. Oddly enough, for that time of day, no attendants were slithering through the chinaberry and hedges, no other "guests" were taking their blank-eyed pleasure on the turf or on the bypaths.

I glanced sidewise at her profile, and was pleased by her chiseled features. Her chin was a bit too sharp and thrust-forward, but it was offset by high cheekbones and long eyelashes that gave her a rather

Asiatic expression. Her lips were full, and her nose was a classic yet short sweep.

I had the strangest feeling I had seen her somewhere before, though that was patently impossible.

Yet the feeling persisted.

I remembered another girl...but that had been before Korea... before the sound of a metallic shriek down the night sky...and someone standing beside my bed at Walter Reed. That had been in another life, before I had died, and been sent to this Place.

"Is the sky dark?" she asked. I guided her to a bench, hidden, set within a box of hedges.

"Not very," I replied. "There are a few clouds in the North, but they don't look like rain clouds. I think it'll be a nice day."

"It doesn't matter," she said resignedly. "The weather doesn't really matter. Do you know how long it's been since I've seen sunlight through the trees?" Then she sighed, and laid her head back against the bench. "No. The weather doesn't really matter. Not at this Time, anyhow."

I didn't know what that meant, but I didn't care, either.

There was a new life surging through me. I was surprised to hear it beating in my ears. I was surprised to find myself thinking minutes into the future. No one who has not experienced it can understand what it is to be dead, and not think of the future, and then to have something worthwhile, and begin to live all over again. I don't mean just hope, nothing that simple and uncomplicated. I mean to be dead, and then to be alive. It had come to be like that in just a few minutes since I had met Piretta. I had ignored the very next instant for the past two years and three months, and now suddenly, I was looking to the future. Not much at first, for it had become an atrophied talent in me, but I was expecting from minute to minute, caring, and I could feel my life ranging back to pick me up, to continue its journey.

I was looking ahead, and wasn't that the first step to regaining my lost life?

"Why are you here?" she said, placing a cool, slim-fingered hand on my bare arm.

I placed my hand over it, and she started, so I withdrew it self-consciously. Then she searched about, found it, and put it over hers again.

"I was in Korea. There was a mortar and I was hit, and they sent me here. I—I didn't want to—maybe I wasn't able to—I don't know—I didn't want to talk to anyone for a long time.

"But I'm all right now," I finished, at peace with myself abruptly.

"Yes," she said, as though that decided it.

Then she went on speaking, in the strangest tone of voice: "Do you sense the Time of the Eye, too, or are you one of *them?*" She asked it with ruthlessness in her voice.

"Who do you mean by *them?* The nurses and attendants? No, I'm not one of them. I'm as annoyed by them as you seem to be. Didn't I hide you?"

"Would you find me a stick?" she asked.

I looked around, and seeing none, broke a branch from the box hedge.

I handed it to her.

"Thank you," she said.

She began stripping it, plucking the leaves and twigs from it. I watched her dexterous hands flitting, and thought *How terrible for such a lovely and clever girl to be thrown in here with these sick people, these madmen.*

"You probably wonder what *I'm* doing here, don't you?" she asked, peeling the thin, green bark from the stick. I didn't answer her, because I didn't want to know; I had found something, someone, and my life had begun again.

"No, I hadn't thought about it."

"Well, I'm here because *they* know I'm aware of them."

"*They?*"

"Yes, of course. You *said* you weren't one of them. Are you lying to me? Are you making fun of me, trying to confuse me?" Her hand slipped out from under mine.

I hastened to regain ground. "No, no, of course not; but don't you see, I don't understand? I just don't know. I—I've been here so long." I tried not to sound pathetic.

She was pulling at the end of the stick, drawing off the bark, making a sharp little point there. "You must forgive me. I sometimes forget everyone is not aware of the Time of the Eye as am I."

"The Time of the Eye?" She had said it several times. "I don't understand."

Piretta turned to me, her dead blue eyes seeing directly over my right shoulder, and she put her legs close together. The stick was laid carelessly by her side, as though a toy it had been, but now the time for toys was gone. "I'll tell you," she said.

She sat very still for an instant, and I waited. Then: "Have you ever seen a woman with vermilion hair?"

I was startled. I had expected a story from her, some deep insight into her past that would enable me to love her the more...and in its place she had asked a nonsense question.

"Why...no...I can't say that I—"

"*Think!*" she commanded me.

So I thought, and oddly enough, a woman with vermilion hair *did* come to mind. Several years before I had been drafted, the rage in all the women's fashion magazines had been a woman named—my God! Was it? Yes, now that I looked closely and my memory prodded, it was —Piretta. A fashion model of exquisite features, lustrous blue eyes, and an affected vermilion-tinted hairdo. She had been so famous her glamour had lapped over from the fashion magazines, had become one of those household names everyone bandies about.

"I remember you," I said, startled beyond words of more meaning.

"No!" she snapped. "No. You don't remember *me*. You remember a woman named Piretta. A beautiful woman who cupped life in her hands and drank deeply of it. That was someone else. I'm a poor blind thing. You don't know *me,* do you?"

"No, I don't. I'm sorry. For a moment—" She went on, as though I had never spoken.

"The woman named Piretta was known to everyone. No fashionable salon gathering was fashionable without her; no cocktail party was meaningful with her absence. But she loved experience; she was a nihilist, and more. She would do *anything*. She climbed K.99 with the Pestroff group, she sailed with two men around the Cape of Good Hope in an outrigger, she taught herself the rudiments of drumming and recorded a novelty with Santana.

"That kind of life can jade a person. She grew bored with it. With the charities, with the modelling, with the brief fling at pictures, and with the men. The wealthy men, the talented men, the pretty men who were attracted to her, and who were at the same time held at bay by her beauty. She sought new experience...and eventually found it."

I wondered why she was telling me this. I had decided by now that the life I was anxious to have return was here, in her. I was living again, and it had come so quickly, so stealthily, that it could only be a result of her presence.

Whatever indefinable quality she had possessed as a world-renowned mannequin, she still retained it, even as a slightly-haggard, still-lovely, blind-eyed woman of indeterminate age. In her white hospital gown she was shapeless, but the magnetic wonder of her was there, and I was alive.

I was in love.

She was still speaking. "After her experiences with the urban folk singers and the artist's colony on Fire Island, she returned to the City, and sought more and different experience.

"Eventually she came upon them. The Men of the Eye. They were a religious sect, unto themselves. They worshipped sight and experience. This was what she had been born for. She fell into their ways at once, worshipping in the dawn hours at their many-eyed idol and living life to its hilt.

"Their ways were dark ways, and the things they did were not always clean things. Yet she persisted with them.

"Then, one night, during what they called the Time of the Eye, they demanded a sacrifice, and she was the one so chosen.

"They took her eyes."

I SAT VERY STILL. I wasn't quite sure I'd heard what I'd heard. A weird religious sect, almost devil worship of a sort, there in the heart of New York City; and they had cut out the eyes of the most famous fashion model of all time, in a ceremony? It was too fantastic for belief. Surprising myself, I found old emotions flooding back into me. I could feel disbelief, horror, astonishment. This girl who called herself Piretta, who *was* that Piretta, had brought me to life again, only to fill me with a story so ludicrous I could do nothing but pass it on as dream-fantasy and the results of a persecution complex.

After all, didn't she have those shallow blue eyes?

They were unseeing, but they were there. How could they have been stolen? I was confused and dismayed.

I turned to her suddenly, and my arms went about her. I don't know what it was that possessed me, for I had always been shy when women were involved, even before Korea, but now my heart leaped into my throat, and I kissed her full on the mouth.

Her lips opened like two petals before me, and there was ardor returned. My hand found her breast.

We sat that way in passion for several minutes, and finally, when we were satisfied that the moment had lived its existence fully, we separated, and I began to prattle about getting well, and marrying, and moving to the country, where I could care for her.

Then I ran my hands across her face; feeling the beauty of her, letting my fingertips soak up the wonder of her. My smallest finger's tip happened to encounter her eye.

It was not moist.

I paused, and a gleam of smile broke at the edge of her wondrous mouth. "True," she said, and popped her eyes into the palm of her hand.

My fist went to my mouth, and the sound of a small animal being crushed underfoot came from me.

Then I noticed she had the sharpened stick in her hand, point upward, as though it were a driving spike.

"You didn't ask if Piretta accepted the religion," she said softly, as though I was a child who did not understand.

"What do you mean?"

"*This* is the Time of the Eye, don't you know?"

And she came at me with the stick. I fell back, but she wound herself around me, and we fell to the ground together, and her blindness did not matter at all.

"But *don't!*" I shrieked. "I love you. I want to make you mine, to marry you!"

"How foolish," she chided me gently, "I can't marry you; you're sick in the mind."

Then there was the stick, and for so long now, the Time of the Eye has been blindly with me.

Face Value

Edward Wellen

THE "WHYDUNIT"

Why would a man come into a crowded, expensive restaurant and promptly offer large sums of money to the other patrons if they will agree to certain outlandish requests, such as a woman cutting off some of her hair or a distinguished husband and wife throwing a pie one into the face of the other? Edward Wellen neatly answers this question in "Face Value," a tricky, twisty "whydunit" McGuffin. At home in both the mystery and fantasy/science-fiction genres, Mr. Wellen is a prolific and multitalented East Coast writer whose work is consistently fresh and enjoyable, and therefore anthologized with enviable regularity. B.P.

HE LOOKED LIKE MONEY, but that can fool you. He sported the tie and dinner jacket the Penguin Club lent an otherwise welcome patron who hadn't had a chance to change into the proper attire. He sat at the table the head waiter reserved for the hundred-dollar tipper. But, watching the guy, I had reservations of my own.

He spoke to his waiter, handed him a clutch of banknotes, and looked on with a faintly amused expression as the waiter wound through the room to whisper into the ear of every brunette. Each in tum looked up in shock and outrage, then around to where the waiter indicated, and received a pleasant nod. And the guy got two takers; ignoring scowling escorts, two women took off their shoes, handed them to the waiter, and got a hundred bucks in exchange.

I smiled. Publicity stunt. A brassy redhead volunteered her green alligator pumps, but the guy regretfully told her he had all he needed— and paid her to cut off all her hair with a pair of pastry shears. A top-heavy blonde, her voice loud and clear in a trough of hush, said, "You'd think a person would have more pride," and the guy strode over and paid her a hundred bucks to give him her bra. I still felt it wasn't for real —the setup, I mean.

When he came back to his table, I got up and went over there. He was frowning at his wristwatch and looked up quickly. I put my hand on the back of an empty chair.

"Mind?"

His voice was cheerful, but he didn't smile. "Matter of fact, I do."

I sat down anyway. "Know who I am?"

He gazed at me. "No."

"A columnist for the *Telegraph-Adams*."

"I'm not hunting publicity."

"I see. You're trying to hide your light under a bushel."

"I'm not trying to hide anything."

"What *are* you trying to do?"

"Prove something."

"That you collect fetishes?"

He glanced at the shoes, the hair, the bra, and smiled. His lean face had the lines of a man pushing thirty, but they were laugh lines and the smile gave him sudden warmth and youth. "No, that everyone has a price." He toyed with his Gibson.

"What are you really buying?"

"Face." His eyes lit up and he gestured with his head. I turned and saw a waiter captain conveying a fiftyish couple to their table, the orchid corsage on the woman's bosom like the figurehead on a stately prow, the polished gray head of the man raked back like the funnel of a liner.

The guy leaned toward me. "Ever see such a dignified pair?"

I had to admit they looked, studying the menu together, like a heraldic lion and lioness supporting a coat of arms. The pearl onion was a third eye holding on them as the guy finished his Gibson. He rose without saying anything else to me and headed for their table. He was sweating, and I wondered why this one bit seemed more important to him than the others. But then, some people sweat when they drink.

The gray-haired man heard the abrupt hush, looked around, saw all gazes on him. He reddened slightly, once-overed himself and his companion, drew reassurance. He spotted the guy bearing down on them, and put on a waiting, inquiring expression.

The guy stood smiling down at the gray-haired man. "Good evening. Too bad you missed the floor show."

The man was a throat-clearer. "Oh? I did not know there was a floor show."

"Stick around. There's more coming, and you're in it."

The note of challenge—light, but there—got through to the gray-haired man, but he kept his composure. "I'm afraid there's a misunderstanding. We're Mr. and Mrs. Harvey Shelby."

The guy gave a polite tilt of acknowledgment, then a deprecating smile. "And I'm Neil Purley."

"Sorry, but that name doesn't mean anything to me."

"It could mean thousands of dollars."

"How's that?"

Purley turned to the waiter at his elbow. "Think you can round up a custard pie and deliver it to this table?"

"Yes *sir,* Mr. Purley."

Shelby's pale blue eyes grew hostile. "We don't want custard pie." He turned to his wife. "Do we, dear?" He turned back. "We've made up our minds what we're having. We certainly don't want custard pie."

Purley gave him a friendly, confident wink. "You will."

"Oh?" Shelby's voice was calm, but his face hardened. "See here, young fellow, you're spoiling what was to have been a happy occasion—an anniversary celebration."

"Say I offered you a thousand dollars. Would you take the custard pie?"

"Oh, come now."

"Would you?"

"I certainly don't need a thousand dollars. The whole thing is absurd. Kindly leave us alone."

"Would you for two thousand?"

"You must be joking. No one would pay two thousand dollars to see someone else eat a custard pie."

The waiter returned and set a custard pie on the table. Purley nodded and handed him a C-note.

"Thank *you,* Mr. Purley."

Shelby stared at the pie, then at his wife. "No, sir. I do not wish to eat this. Take it away."

"Four thousand?"

"Why are you doing this?"

"Say I'm being illogical. But illogic is what distinguishes humans from machines, isn't it? Among other factors."

Shelby glanced at his wife. She fanned herself with the menu. Shelby licked his lips. "Well, now. You're sure there's nothing wrong with this pie? This is no trick?"

"Nothing wrong with the pie."

"No, *sir,*" the waiter said.

"Well, now." Shelby laughed hollowly, a laugh that didn't stick to the ribs. "I don't see that a bite of custard pie ever hurt anyone. Looks delicious, in fact." He glanced up sharply. "You said four thousand dollars."

"I did."

"You *have* four thousand dollars?"

Purley plucked four G-notes from his wallet and stroked them into the waiter's convulsive palm.

Shelby studied the bills, then the pie. "Do you mean that we eat it now, or as dessert?"

"I didn't say you should eat it. I mean you should throw it."

Shelby flushed. "Ridiculous. Waiter, take this thing away. And you, sir, leave this table." He looked around. "Where's the manager?"

"Five thousand."

Shelby turned to his wife. "Shall we leave, dear?"

Mrs. Shelby slowly picked up her gloves and bag. Shelby squeaked his chair back.

"Six thousand."

Shelby sat still. He watched his wife, turned to Purley. "And what would I throw the pie at?"

Purley shrugged and said pleasantly, "Either she throws it in your face or you throw it in hers. Decide between you."

Shelby shook his head and half rose. "Seven thousand."

Shelby's brow took on a gloss. He spoke to himself. "After all, a wipe with a damp cloth and it would be as if nothing had happened."

"That's right." Purley nodded encouragingly.

Shelby sat down. He took a deep drag on a nonexistent cigarette. He looked at his wife. Mrs. Shelby sat tight-lipped, fanning herself more and more rapidly with the menu.

Then she stopped fanning, smiled. "Why not. dear?"

Shelby sighed a sigh of release. "Why not. All in fun. Make this a real celebration." He turned to Purley. "Seven thousand dollars?"

"Make it ten," Purley said. He cheerfully added six G-notes to those in the waiter's palm. "Let's say I'm betting you ten thousand you won't do it."

Shelby slid the pie nearer his wife and took off his glasses. "You, dear." He fitted his napkin around his neck.

Mrs. Shelby gently put down the menu, stood up, lifted the pie, hefted it, took a stance. With a strained smile Shelby stared at her, braced himself, closed his eyes. Mrs. Shelby threw the pie in his face. When they led him out to the men's room, the ten grand in his clutch and applause echoing in his wake, she had already gone out and was having the doorman whistle up a taxi.

Purley came back to his table. He looked happy but spent. He asked the waiter for his check.

"Yes *sir,* Mr. Purley."

I was still disbelieving this whole thing. "The party's over?"

He looked at me as if wondering about my price range, and I felt a bit uneasy. But he smiled slightly and said, "The party's over."

"When's the next one?"

"Won't be a next one."

"Why not?"

"No publicity, remember? And you're a columnist."

"Off the record. That's a promise."

His smile widened suddenly. "All right. Know who Harvey Shelby is?"

"No."

"My boss. My ex-boss, I should say."

"After what you just did, I would think so."

"Before that. I got my two weeks' notice this morning."

"You worked for him and he didn't know you?"

"That's just it," Purley said. "It's a big firm, and I was only a faceless guy—one who's now being replaced by a new computer. I waited in his outer office, but he wouldn't see me. I heard his secretary on the phone, reserving his table here. So I returned to my desk for the last time and processed a ten-thousand-dollar check through the machine—made it out to cash and charged it to Shelby's expense account."

"You mean that was his own ten grand you used to make a fool out of him?"

"Yes." He shrugged. "Or the stockholders."

"Technically, it's still stealing. How can you be sure they won't catch you for it?"

"Shelby won't raise a fuss. That would draw attention to the way he got the money back—and to the fact that his anniversary celebration also went on his expense account. The computer is trained not to ask embarrassing questions about his expense account."

I shook my head. "The whole thing strikes me as a pretty bizarre form of revenge."

"Not at all. Don't you see the irony?" Purley smiled down as if into his reflection in a drink. "A more efficient electronic brain replaced me, a computer that can do anything a human brain can do. Except *scheme*. There's just no way a computer can beat a man at thinking up a way like mine to steal money for the purpose of returning it."

"Maybe not, but where does that leave you now?"

"Somewhat flatter. The other expenses—" he gestured to the shoes, the hair, the bra, "—came out of my savings and severance. I'm not hurting financially, and besides, it was worth it." He frowned slightly. "But I'm hardly in Shelby's bracket. I'll have to look for another job soon: operating computers, I think. If you can't lick 'em, join 'em." His eyes lit up and I swear I almost heard a whir. "If a man and a computer put their brains together in the right way..."

I couldn't read his face, much less his mind, but I had the feeling I could be in at the birth of something big. A man could program a computer to steal money for the *purpose* of stealing. The right man might be able to program a computer to steal the world...

The Leopold Locked Room

Edward D. Hoch

THE IMPOSSIBLE CRIME

"When you have eliminated the impossible," Holmes tells Watson in "The Sign of the Four," "whatever remains, however improbable, must be the truth." What happens during the deadly confrontation between Captain Leopold and his ex-wife is obviously impossible; it is also the truth. The solution is fairly presented, is absolutely logical and possible, and is impeccably devious. But then Edward D. Hoch is used to dealing with much more impossible things than mere locked-room murders; for many years he has been practicing the Impossible Profession. He has made his living as a short-story writer. I doubt that even Mr. Hoch can any longer give an accurate tally of his published stories. Five hundred might be a good guess. One of them, the unforgettable "The Oblong Room," won an Edgar in 1968. - J.G.

CAPTAIN LEOPOLD HAD NEVER SPOKEN to anyone about his divorce, and it was a distinct surprise to Lieutenant Fletcher when he suddenly said, "Did I ever tell you about my wife, Fletcher?"

They were just coming up from the police pistol range in the basement of headquarters after their monthly target practice, and it hardly seemed a likely time to be discussing past marital troubles. Fletcher glanced at him sideways and answered, "No, I guess you never did, Captain."

"She's coming back," Leopold said simply, and it took Fletcher an instant to grasp the meaning of his words.

"Your wife is coming back?"

"My ex-wife."

"Here? What for?"

Leopold sighed. "Her niece is getting married. Our niece."

"I never knew you had one."

"She's been away at college. Her name is Vicki Nelson, and she's marrying a young lawyer named Moore. And Monica is coming back east for the wedding."

"I never even knew her name," Fletcher observed. "Haven't you seen her since the divorce?"

Leopold shook his head. "Not for fifteen years. It was a funny thing. She wanted to be a movie star, and I guess fifteen years ago lots of girls still thought about being movie stars. Monica was intelligent and very pretty—but probably no prettier than hundreds of other girls who used to turn up in Hollywood every year back in those days. I was just starting on the police force then, and the future looked pretty bright for me here. It would have been foolish of me to toss up everything just to chase her wild dream out to California. Well, pretty soon it got to be an obsession with her, really bad. She'd spend her afternoons in movie theaters and her evenings watching old films on television. Finally, when I still refused to go west with her, she just left me."

"Just walked out?"

Leopold nodded. "It was a blessing, really, that we didn't have children. I heard she got a few minor jobs out there—as an extra, and some technical stuff behind the scenes. Then apparently she had a nervous breakdown. About a year later, I received the official word that she'd divorced me. I heard that she recovered and was back working, and I think she had another marriage that didn't work out."

"Why would she come back for the wedding?"

"Vicki is her niece and also her godchild. We were just married when Vicki was born, and I suppose Monica might consider her the child we never had. In any event, I know she still hates me, and blames me for everything that's gone wrong with her life. She told a friend once a few years ago she wished I were dead."

"Do you have to go to this wedding, too, Captain?"

"Of course. If I stayed away it would be only because of her. At least I have to drop by the reception for a few minutes." Leopold smiled ruefully. "I guess that's why I'm telling you all this, Fletcher. I want a favor from you."

"Anything, Captain. You know that."

"I know it seems like a childish thing to do, but I'd like you to come out there with me. I'll tell them I'm working, and that I can only stay for a few minutes. You can wait outside in the car if you want. At least they'll see you there and believe my excuse."

Fletcher could see the importance of it to Leopold, and the effort that had gone into the asking. "Sure," he said. "Be glad to. When is it?"

"This Saturday. The reception's in the afternoon, at Sunset Farms."

SUNSET FARMS WAS a low rambling place at the end of a paved driveway, overlooking a wooded valley and a gently flowing creek. If it had ever been a farm, that day was long past; but for wedding receptions and retirement parties it was the ideal place. The interior of the main building was, in reality, one huge square room, divided by accordion doors to make up to four smaller square rooms.

For the wedding of Vicki Nelson and Ted Moore three-quarters of the large room was in use, with only the last set of accordion doors pulled shut its entire width and locked. The wedding party occupied a head table along one wall, with smaller tables scattered around the room for the families and friends. When Leopold entered the place at five minutes of two on Saturday afternoon, the hired combo was just beginning to play music for dancing.

He watched for a moment while Vicki stood, radiant, and allowed her new husband to escort her to the center of the floor. Ted Moore was a bit older than Leopold had expected, but as the pair glided slowly across the floor, he could find no visible fault with the match. He helped himself to a glass of champagne punch and stood ready to intercept them as they left the dance floor.

"It's Captain Leopold, isn't it?" someone asked. A face from his past loomed up, a tired man with a gold tooth in the front of his smile. "I'm Immy Fontaine, Monica's stepbrother."

"Sure," Leopold said, as if he'd remembered the man all along. Monica had rarely mentioned Immy, and Leopold recalled meeting him once or twice at family gatherings.

"We're so glad you could come," someone else said, and he turned to greet the bride and groom as they came off the dance floor. Up close, Vicki was a truly beautiful girl.

"I wouldn't have missed it for anything," he said.

"This is Ted," she said, making the introductions. Leopold shook his hand, silently approving the firm grip and friendly eyes.

"I understand you're a lawyer," Leopold said, making conversation.

"That's right, sir. Mostly civil cases, though. I don't tangle much with criminals."

They chatted for a few more seconds before the pressure of guests broke them apart.

"I see the car waiting outside," Inuny Fontaine said, moving in again. "You got to go on duty?"

Leopold nodded. "Just this glass and I have to leave." "Monica's in from the west coast."

"So I heard."

A slim man with a mustache jostled against him in the crush of the crowd and hastily apologized. Fontaine seized the man by the arm and introduced him to Leopold. "This here's Dr. Felix Thursby. He came east with Monica. Doc, I want you to meet Captain Leopold, her ex-husband."

Leopold shook hands awkwardly, embarrassed for the man and for himself. "A fine wedding," he mumbled. "Your first trip east?"

Thursby shook his head. "I'm from New York. Long ago."

"I was on the police force there once," Leopold remarked. He managed to edge away through the crowd.

"Leaving so soon?" a harsh, unforgettable voice asked.

"Hello, Monica. It's been a long time."

He stared down at the handsome, middle-aged woman who now blocked his path to the door. She had gained a little weight, especially in the bosom, and her hair was graying. Only the eyes startled him, and frightened him just a bit. They bad an intense, wild look he'd seen before on the faces of deranged criminals.

"I didn't think you'd come. I thought you'd be afraid of me," she said.

"That's foolish. Why should I be afraid of you?"

She motioned toward the end of the room that had been cut off by the accordion doors.

"Come in here," she said, "where we can talk."

Leopold followed her.

She unlocked the doors and pulled them apart, just wide enough for them to enter the unused quarter of the large room. Then she closed and locked the doors behind them, and stood facing him. They were two people, alone in a bare unfurnished room.

They were in an area about thirty feet square, with the windows at the far end and the locked accordion doors at Leopold's back. He could see the afternoon sun cutting through the trees outside, and the gentle hum of the air conditioner came through above the subdued murmur of the wedding guests.

She walked to the middle window, running her fingers along the frame, perhaps looking for the latch to open it. But it stayed closed as she faced him again. "Our marriage was as drab and barren as this room. Lifeless, unused!"

"Heaven knows I always wanted children, Monica."

"You wanted nothing but your damned police work!" she shot back, eyes flashing as her anger built.

"Look, I have to go. I have a man waiting in the car."

"Go! That's what you did before, wasn't it? *Go, go!* Go out to your damned job and leave me to struggle for myself. Leave me to—"

"You walked out on me, Monica. Remember?" he reminded her softly.

"Sure I did! Because I had a career waiting for me! I had all the world waiting for me! And you know what happened because you wouldn't come along? You know what happened to me out there? They took my money and my self-respect and what virtue I had left. They made me into a tramp, and when they were done, they locked me up in a mental hospital for three years. Three years!"

"I'm sorry."

"Every day while I was there I thought about you. I thought about how it would be when I got out. Oh, I thought. And planned. And schemed. You're a big detective now. Sometimes your cases even get reported in the California papers." She was pacing back and forth, caged, dangerous. "Big detective. But I can still destroy you just as you destroyed me!"

He glanced over his shoulder at the locked accordion doors, seeking a way out. It was a thousand times worse than he'd imagined it would be.

Her eyes closed to mere slits.

"I came all the way east for this day, because I thought you'd be here. It's so much better than your apartment, or your office, or a city street. There are one hundred and fifty witnesses on the other side of those doors."

"What in hell are you talking about?"

Her mouth twisted. "You're going to know what I knew. Bars and cells and disgrace. You're going to know the despair I felt all those years."

"Monica—"

At that instant perhaps twenty feet separated them. She lifted one arm, as if to shield herself, then screamed in terror. "No! Oh, God, no!"

Leopold stood frozen, unable to move, as a sudden gunshot echoed through the room. He saw the bullet strike her in the chest, toppling her backward. Then somehow he had his own gun out of its belt holster and he swung around toward the doors.

They were still closed and locked. He was alone in the room with Monica.

He looked back to see her crumple on the floor, blood spreading in a widening circle around the tom black hole in her dress. His eyes went to the windows, but all three were still closed and unbroken. He shook his head, trying to focus his mind on what had happened.

There was noise from outside, and a pounding on the accordion doors. Someone opened the lock from the other side, and the gap between the doors widened as they were pulled open.

"What happened?" someone asked. A woman guest screamed as she saw the body. Another toppled in a faint.

Leopold stepped back, aware of the gun still in his hand, and saw Lieutenant Fletcher fighting his way through the mob of guests. "Captain, what is it?"

"She... Someone shot her."

Fletcher reached out and took the gun from Leopold's hand carefully, as one might take a broken toy from a child. He put it to his nose and sniffed, then opened the cylinder to inspect the bullets. "It's been fired recently, Captain. One shot." Then his eyes seemed to cloud over, almost to the point of tears. "Why the hell did you do it?" he asked. "Why?"

LEOPOLD SAW nothing of what happened then. He only had vague and splintered memories of someone examining her and saying she was still alive, of an ambulance and much confusion. Fletcher drove him down to headquarters, to the Commissioner's office, and he sat there and waited.

He was not surprised when they told him she had died on the way to Southside Hospital.

"You have nothing more to tell us, Captain?" the Commissioner asked. "I'm making it as easy for you as I can."

"I didn't kill her," Leopold insisted again. "It was someone else."

"Who? How?"

He could only shake his head. "I wish I knew. I think in some mad way she killed herself, to get revenge on me."

"She shot herself with *your* gun, while it was in *your* holster, and while *you* were standing twenty feet away?"

Leopold ran a hand over his forehead. "It couldn't have been my gun. Ballistics will prove that."

"But your gun had been fired recently, and there was an empty cartridge in the chamber."

"I can't explain that. I haven't fired it since the other day at target practice, and I reloaded it afterward."

"Could she have hated you that much, Captain?" Fletcher asked. "To frame you for her murder?"

"She could have. I think she was a very sick woman. If I did that to her—if I was the one who made her sick—I suppose I deserve what's happening to me now."

"The hell you do," Fletcher growled. "If you say you're innocent, Captain, I'm sticking by you."

Leopold nodded. "Wait for the ballistics report," he said. "That'll clear me."

So they waited. It was another forty-five minutes before the phone rang and the Commissioner spoke to the ballistics man. He listened, and grunted, and asked one or two questions. Then he hung up and faced Leopold across the desk.

"The bullet was fired from your gun," he said simply. "There's no possibility of error. I'm afraid we'll have to charge you with homicide."

THE ROUTINES he knew so well went on into Saturday evening, and when they were finished Leopold was escorted from the courtroom to find young Ted Moore waiting for him.

"You should be on your honeymoon," Leopold told him.

"Vicki couldn't leave till I'd seen you and tried to help. I don't know much about criminal law, but perhaps I could arrange bail."

"That's already been taken care of," Leopold said. "The grand jury will get the case next week."

"I—I don't know what to say. Vicki and I are both terribly sorry."

"So am I." He started to walk away, then turned back. "Enjoy your honeymoon."

"We'll be in town overnight, at the Towers, if there's anything I can do."

Leopold nodded and kept on walking. He could see the reflection of his guilt in young Moore's eyes. As he got to his car, one of the patrolmen he knew glanced his way and then quickly in the other direction. On a Saturday night no one talked to wife murderers. Even Fletcher had disappeared.

The eleven o'clock news on television had it as the lead item, illustrated with a black-and-white photo of him taken during a case last year. He shut off the television in his little apartment, without listening to their comments and went back outside, walking down to the comer for an early edition of the Sunday paper. The front-page headline was as bad as he'd expected: *Detective Captain Held in Slaying of Ex-Wife.*

On the way back to his apartment, walking slowly, he tried to remember what she'd been like—not that afternoon, but before the divorce. He tried to remember her face on their wedding day, her soft laughter on their honeymoon. But all he could remember were those mad, vengeful eyes. And the bullet ripping into her chest.

"Hello, Captain."

"I—Fletcher! What are you doing here?"

"Waiting for you. Can I come in?"

"Well..."

"I've got a six-pack of beer. I thought you might want to talk about it."

Leopold unlocked his apartment door. "What's there to talk about?"

"If you say you didn't kill her, Captain, I'm willing to listen to you."

Fletcher followed him into the tiny kitchen and popped open two of the beer cans. Leopold accepted one of them and dropped into the nearest chair. He felt utterly exhausted, drained of even the strength to fight back.

"She framed me, Fletcher," he said quietly. "She framed me as neatly as anything I've ever seen. The thing's impossible, but she did it"

"Let's go over it step by step, Captain. Look, the way I see it there are only three possibilities: either you shot her, she shot herself, or someone else shot her. I think we can rule out the last one. The three windows were locked on the outside and unbroken, the room was bare of any hiding place, and the only entrance was through the accordion doors. These were closed and locked, and although they could have been opened from the other side you certainly would have seen or heard it happen. Besides, there were one hundred and fifty wedding guests on the other side of those doors. No one could have unlocked and opened them and then fired the shot, all without being seen."

Leopold shook his head. "But it's just as impossible that she could have shot herself. I was watching her every minute. I never looked away once. There was nothing in her hands, not even a purse. And the gun that shot her was in my holster, on my belt. I never drew it till *after* the shot was fired."

Fletcher finished his beer and reached for another can. "I didn't look at her close, Captain, but the size of the hole in her dress and the powder burns point to a contact wound. The Medical Examiner agrees, too. She was shot from no more than an inch or two away. There were grains of powder in the wound itself, though the bleeding had washed most of them away."

"But she had nothing in her hand," Leopold repeated. "And there was nobody standing in front of her with a gun. Even I was twenty feet away."

"The thing's impossible, Captain."

Leopold grunted. "Impossible—unless I killed her."

Fletcher stared at his beer. "How much time do we have?"

"If the grand jury indicts me for first-degree murder, I'll be in a cell by next week."

Fletcher frowned at him. "What's with you, Captain? You almost act resigned to it! Hell, I've seen more fight in you on a routine holdup!"

"I guess that's it, Fletcher. The fight is gone out of me. She's drained every drop of it. She's had her revenge."

Fletcher sighed and stood up. "Then I guess there's really nothing I can do for you, Captain. Good night."

Leopold didn't see him to the door. He simply sat there, hunched over the table. For the first time in his life he felt like an old man.

LEOPOLD SLEPT LATE SUNDAY MORNING. He got up and showered and dressed, reaching for his holster out of habit before he remembered he no longer had a gun. Then he sat at the kitchen table staring at the empty beer cans, wondering what he would do with his day. With his life.

The doorbell rang, and it was Fletcher. "I didn't think I'd be seeing you again," Leopold mumbled, letting him in.

Fletcher was excited, and the words tumbled out of him almost before he was through the door. "I think I've got something, Captain! It's not much, but it's a start. I was down at headquarters first thing this morning, and I got hold of the dress Monica was wearing when she was shot."

Leopold looked blank. "The dress?"

Fletcher was busy unwrapping the package he'd brought. "The Commissioner would have my neck if he knew I brought this to you, but look at this hole!"

Leopold studied the jagged, blood-caked rent in the fabric. "It's large," he observed, "but with a near-contact wound, the powder burns would cause that."

"Captain, I've seen plenty of entrance wounds made by a .38 slug. I've even caused a few of them. But I never saw one that looked like this. Hell, it's not even round!"

"What are you trying to tell me, Fletcher?" Suddenly something stirred inside him. The juices were beginning to flow again.

"The hole in her dress is much larger and more jagged than the corresponding wound in her chest, Captain. That's what I'm telling you.

The bullet that killed her couldn't have made this hole. No way! And that means maybe she wasn't killed when we thought she was." Leopold grabbed the phone and dialed the familiar number of the Towers Hotel. "I hope they slept late this morning."

"Who?"

"The honeymooners." He spoke sharply into the phone, giving the switchboard operator the name he wanted, and then waited. It was a full minute before he heard Ted Moore's sleepy voice answering on the other end. "Ted, this is Leopold. Sorry to bother you."

The voice came alert at once. "That's all right, Captain. I told you to call if there was anything—"

"I think there is. You and Vicki between you must have a pretty good idea of who was invited to the wedding. Check with her and tell me how many doctors were on the invitation list."

Ted Moore was gone for a few moments and then he returned. "Vicki says you're the second person who asked her that."

"Oh? Who was the first?"

"Monica. The night before the wedding, when she arrived in town with Dr. Thursby. She casually asked if he'd get to meet any other doctors at the reception. But Vicki told her he was the only one. Of course we hadn't invited him, but as a courtesy to Monica we urged him to come."

"Then after the shooting, it was Thursby who examined her? No one else?"

"He was the only doctor. He told us to call an ambulance and rode to the hospital with her."

"Thank you, Ted. You've been a big help." "I hope so, Captain."

Leopold hung up and faced Fletcher. "That's it. She worked it with this guy Thursby. Cao you put out an alarm for him?"

"Sure can," Fletcher said. He took the telephone and dialed the unlisted squadroom number. "Dr. Felix Thursby? Is that his name?"

"That's it. The only doctor there, the only one who could help Monica with her crazy plan of revenge."

Fletcher completed issuing orders and hung up the phone. "They'll check his hotel and call me back."

"Get the Commissioner on the phone, too. Tell him what we've got."

Fletcher started to dial and then stopped, his finger in mid-air. "What *have* we got, Captain?"

THE COMMISSIONER SAT behind his desk and listened bleakly to what Leopold and Fletcher had to tell him.

"The mere fact that this Dr. Thursby seems to have left town is hardly proof of his guilt, Captain. What you're saying is that the woman wasn't killed until later—that Thursby killed her in the ambulance. But how could he have done that with a pistol that was already in Lieutenant Fletcher's possession, tagged as evidence? And how could he have fired the fatal shot without the ambulance attendants hearing it?"

"I don't know," Leopold admitted.

"Heaven knows, Captain, I'm willing to give you every reasonable chance to prove your innocence. But you have to bring me more than a dress with a hole in it."

"All right," Leopold said. "I'll bring you more."

"The grand jury gets the case this week, Captain."

"I know," Leopold said. He turned and left the office, with Fletcher tailing behind.

"What now?" Fletcher asked.

"We go talk to lmmy Fontaine, my ex-wife's stepbrother."

THOUGH HE'D NEVER BEEN friendly with Fontaine, Leopold knew where to find him. The tired man with the gold tooth lived in a big old house overlooking the Sound, where on this summer Sunday they found him in the back yard, cooking hot dogs over a charcoal fire.

He squinted into the sun and said, "I thought you'd be in jail, after what happened."

"I didn't kill her," Leopold said quietly.

"Sure you didn't."

"For a stepbrother, you seem to be taking her death right in stride," Leopold observed, motioning toward the fire.

"I stopped worrying about Monica fifteen years ago."

"What about this man she was with? Dr. Thursby?"

Immy Fontaine chuckled. "If he's a doctor I'm a plumber! He has the fingers of a surgeon, I'll admit, but when I asked him about my son's radius that he broke skiing, Thursby thought it was a leg bone. What the hell, though, I was never one to judge Monica's love life. Remember, I didn't even object when she married you."

"Nice of you. Where's Thursby staying while he's in town?"

"He was at the Towers with Monica."

"He's not there anymore."

"Then I don't know where he's at. Maybe he's not even staying for her funeral."

"What if I told you Thursby killed Monica?"

He shrugged. "I wouldn't believe you, but then I wouldn't particularly care. If you were smart, you'd have killed her fifteen years ago when she walked out on you. That's what I'd have done."

LEOPOLD DROVE SLOWLY BACK DOWNTOWN, with Fletcher grumbling beside him. "Where are we, Captain? It seems we're just going in circles."

"Perhaps we are, Fletcher, but right now there are still too many questions to be answered. If we can't find Thursby, I'll have to tackle it from another direction. The bullet, for instance."

"What about the bullet?"

"We're agreed it could not have been fired by my gun, either while it was in my holster or later, while Thursby was in the ambulance with Monica. Therefore, it must have been fired earlier. The last time I fired it was at target practice. Is there any possibility—any chance at all—that Thursby or Monica could have gotten one of the slugs I fired into that target?"

Fletcher put a damper on it. "Captain, we were both firing at the same target. No one could sort out those bullets and say which came from your pistol and which from mine. Besides, how would either of them gain access to the basement target range at police headquarters?"

"I could have an enemy in the department," Leopold said.

"Nuts! We've all got enemies, but the thing is still impossible. If you believe people in the department are plotting against you, you might as well believe that the entire ballistics evidence was faked."

"It was, somehow. Do you have the comparison photos?"

"They're back at the office. But with the narrow depth of field you can probably tell more from looking through the microscope yourself."

Fletcher drove him to the lab, where they persuaded the Sunday duty officer to let them have a look at the bullets. While Fletcher and the officer stood by in the interests of propriety, Leopold squinted through the microscope at the twin chunks of lead.

"The death bullet is pretty battered," he observed, but he had to admit that the rifling marks were the same. He glanced at the identification tag attached to the test bullet: *Test slug fired from Smith & Wesson .38 Revolver, serial number 2420547.*

Leopold turned away with a sigh, then turned back.

2420547.

He fished into his wallet and found his pistol permit. *Smith & Wesson 2421622.*

"I remembered those twos on the end," he told Fletcher. "That's not my gun."

"It's the one I took from you, Captain. I'll swear to it!"

"And I believe you, Fletcher. But it's the one fact I needed. It tells me how Dr. Thursby managed to kill Monica in a locked room before my very eyes, with a gun that was in my holster at the time. And it just might tell us where to find the elusive Dr. Thursby."

By Monday morning, Leopold had made six long-distance calls to California, working from his desk telephone while Fletcher used the squad room phone. Then, a little before noon, Leopold, Fletcher, the Commissioner, and a man from the District Attorney's office took a car and drove up to Boston.

"You're sure you've got it figured?" the Commissioner asked Leopold for the third time. "You know we shouldn't allow you to cross the state line while awaiting grand jury action."

"Look, either you trust me or you don't," Leopold snapped. Behind the wheel, Fletcher allowed himself a slight smile, but the man from the D.A.'s office was deadly serious.

"The whole thing is so damned complicated," the Commissioner grumbled.

"My ex-wife was a complicated woman. And remember, she had fifteen years to plan it."

"Run over it for us again," the D.A.'s man said.

Leopold sighed and started talking. "The murder gun wasn't mine.

The gun I pulled after the shot was fired, the one Fletcher took from me, had been planted on me some time before."

"How?"

"I'll get to that. Monica was the key to it all, of course. She hated me so much that her twisted brain planned her own murder in order to get revenge on me. She planned it in such a way that it would have been impossible for anyone but me to have killed her. She set up the entire plan for the afternoon of the wedding reception, but I'm sure they had an alternate in case I hadn't gone to it. She wanted some place where there'd be lots of witnesses."

"Tell them how she worked the bullet hitting her," Fletcher urged.

"Well, that was the toughest part for me. I actually saw her shot before my eyes. I saw the bullet hit her, and I saw the blood. Yet I was alone in a locked room with her. There was no hiding place, no opening from which a person or even a mechanical device could have fired the bullet at her. To you people it seemed I must be guilty, especially when the bullet came from the gun I was carrying.

"But I looked at it from a different angle—once Fletcher forced me to look at it at all! I *knew* I hadn't shot her, and since no one else physically could have, I knew no one did! If Monica was killed by a .38 slug, it must have been fired *after* she was taken from that locked room. Since she was dead on arrival at the hospital, the most likely time for her murder—to me, at least—became the time of the ambulance ride, when Dr. Thursby must have hunched over her with careful solicitousness."

"But you *saw* her get shot!"

"That's one of the two reasons Fletcher and I were on the phones to Hollywood this morning. My ex-wife worked in pictures, at times in the technical end of movie-making. On the screen there are a number of ways to simulate a person being shot. An early method was a sort of compressed-air gun fired at the actor from just off-camera. These days, especially in the bloodiest of the Western and war films, they use a tiny explosive charge fitted under the actor's clothes. Of course the body is protected from burns, and the force of it is directed outward. A pouch of fake blood is released by the explosion, adding to the realism of it."

"And this is what Monica did?"

Leopold nodded. "A call to her Hollywood studio confirmed the fact that she worked on a film using this device. I noticed when I met her that she'd gained weight around the bosom, but I never thought to attribute it to the padding and the explosive device. She triggered it when she raised her arm as she screamed at me."

"Any proof?"

"The hole in her dress was just too big to be an entrance hole from a .38, even fired at close range—too big and too ragged. I can thank Fletcher for spotting that. This morning the lab technicians ran a test on the bloodstains. Some of it was her blood, the rest was chicken blood."

"She was a good actress to fool all those people."

"She knew Dr. Thursby would be the first to examine her. All she had to do was fall over when the explosive charge ripped out the front of her dress."

"What if there had been another doctor at the wedding?"

Leopold shrugged. "Then they would have postponed it. They couldn't take that chance."

"And the gun?"

"I remembered Thursby bumping against me when I first met him. He took my gun and substituted an identical weapon—identical, that is, except for the serial number. He'd fired it just a short time earlier, to complete the illusion. When I drew it, I simply played into their hands. There I was, the only person in the room with an apparently dying woman, and a gun that had just been fired."

"But what about the bullet that killed her?"

"Rifling marks on slugs are made by the lands in the rifled barrel of a gun causing grooves in the lead of a bullet. A bullet fired through a smooth tube has no rifling marks."

"What in hell kind of gun has a smooth tube for a barrel?" the Commissioner asked.

"A home-made one, like a zip gun. Highly inaccurate, but quite effective when the gun is almost touching the skin of the victim. Thursby fired a shot from the pistol he was to plant on me, probably into a pillow or some other place where he could retrieve the undamaged slug. Then he reused the rifled slug on another cartridge and fired it with his homemade zip gun, right into Monica's heart. The original rifling marks were still visible, and no new ones were added."

"The ambulance driver and attendant didn't hear the shot?"

"They would have stayed up front, since he was a doctor riding with a patient. It gave him a chance to get the padded explosive mechanism off her chest, too. Once that was away, I imagine he leaned over her, muffling the zip gun as best he could, and fired the single shot that killed her. Remember, an ambulance on its way to a hospital is a pretty noisy place—it has a siren going all the time."

They were entering downtown Boston now, and Leopold directed Fletcher to a hotel near the Common. "I still don't believe the part about switching the guns," the D.A.'s man objected. "You mean to tell me he undid the strap over your gun, got out the gun, and substituted another one—all without your knowing it?"

Leopold smiled. "I mean to tell you only one type of person could have managed it—an expert, professional pickpocket. The type you see occasionally doing an act in night clubs and on television. That's how I knew where to find him. We called all over Southern California till we came up with someone who knew Monica and knew she'd dated a man named Thompson who had a pickpocket act. We called Thompson's agent and discovered he's playing a split week at a Boston lounge, and is staying at this hotel."

"What if he couldn't have managed it without your catching on? Or what if you hadn't been wearing your gun?"

"Most detectives wear their guns off-duty. If I hadn't been, or if he couldn't get it, they'd simply have changed their plan. He must have signaled her when he'd safely made the switch."

The Boston police had two men waiting to meet them, and they went up in the elevator to the room registered in the name of Max Thompson. Fletcher knocked on the door, and when it opened the familiar face of Felix Thursby appeared. He no longer wore the mustache, but he had the same slim surgeon-like fingers that Immy Fontaine had noticed. Not a doctor's fingers, but a pickpocket's.

"We're taking you in for questioning," Fletcher said, and the Boston detectives issued the standard warnings of his legal rights.

Thursby blinked his tired eyes at them, and grinned a bit when he recognized Leopold. "She said you were smart. She said you were a smart cop."

"Did you have to kill her?" Leopold asked.

"I didn't. I just held the gun there, and she pulled the trigger herself. She did it all herself, except for switching the guns. She hated you that much."

"I know," Leopold said quietly, staring at something far away. "But I guess she must have hated herself just as much."

If I Quench Thee...

William E. Chambers

MOMENT OF TRUTH

"If I Quench Thee..." is a strong, disturbing story which deals with an important social issue of our times—and which offers, in the "moment of truth" faced by its protagonist, Arthur Stern, a significant lesson for us all. The title may seem to have little relation to the tale itself, but in fact is both appropriate and tragically ironic, as may be seen by an examination of its source: Shakespeare's Othello, Act V, Scene II. (The reader should not look it up until after completion of the story, however, because the exact quote gives away the basic plot.) William E. Chambers is one of the new young writers in the field of crime fiction, a graduate of MWA's Writing Course, and is currently and ambitiously working on his first two novels for 1976 publication by Popular Library. - B.P.

ARTHUR STERN LOOKED past his denim-clad daughter at the apartment she had taken in one of Manhattan's ghettos. It was the first time he had seen it and he frowned critically. A rickety wicker settee served as a couch. The top of an ancient and probably unworkable combination TV-radio cabinet was used as a bar, and held two bottles of cheap rye.

The lifelike poster of Communist rebel Che Guevara that decorated the otherwise plain wall behind the bar deepened the hue of Stern's pink complexion.

Closing the door behind him, he handed her his coat and said, "For God's sake, Monica, put on a bra. There's not much to that blouse you're wearing."

Monica stood on her toes and kissed his cheek. "Don't be so old-fashioned. If God wanted these things bound, I would have been born with a Playtex living—"

"Damn it! That isn't funny!"

"Okay! Okay!" Raising her hands like a holdup victim, Monica retreated backward through beaded curtains to her bedroom. She shouted from inside, "Hey, I'm glad you came to visit, Dad."

"Thought I'd surprise you, since you never visit me."

"I was going to get in touch with you—"

"I'll bet."

"I was. I've got a surprise of my own."

"Nothing you might say or do would surprise me any more."

Monica returned, mixed two highballs, and sat on the settee next to Stern. They clinked glasses. He said, "Happy birthday."

"Whoa. I'm not twenty-four until next week. Don't rush it."

"I didn't know what to give you as a present, Monica, so I thought I'd find out what you needed and write a check."

"Well, I don't really *need* anything—"

"Seems to me you could use everything."

"Like what? I have my home, my job—"

"Some home."

"The location's convenient for work."

"Toiling for peanuts among a bunch of savages—"

"Daddy—please! I do social work because I have a conscience."

"What kind of conscience prods a daughter to leave her own flesh and blood for a band of slum dwellers?"

"You don't need me. These people do."

"Need you? Do you think your mother—God rest her soul—and I slaved to build that mink farm upstate just for ourselves?"

When Monica failed to answer, Stern continued, "We did it to get *you* away from the city—the slums—and the kind of people who dwell in them."

"These *kind* of people are good people, Dad. All they need is some help—"

"Bull! All they need is to get off their butts and help themselves like I did."

Monica gulped her drink, took a deep breath and said, "You've always been strong, Dad. That's why you can't understand people who are weak."

The shrill buzz of the doorbell interrupted them, and Monica looked a little uncomfortable. Stem said, "Expecting company?"

"No. Not really." She fumbled with the buttons on her blouse. "It— well—it might be Tod Humbert."

"Another social worker?"

"Much more than that."

A second, more insistent buzz made Stem wince.

"Buzz him back, will you?"

The sound of a man coming up the stairs was followed by a vigorous tapping on the door. Monica opened it and said, "Oh—hi, Tod—"

A tall, thin black man wearing a short leather jacket and blue jeans wrapped his arms around her waist, kissed her on both cheeks and said, "You're looking bad, baby. Superbad!"

Monica gently withdrew from his embrace and turned sheepishly toward her father.

"Tod—I—I want you to meet Arthur Stern, my father."

A bright smile flashed across the black man's face. He walked forward, hand extended and said, "Mr. Stern, this is a pleasure, sir."

Ignoring Tod completely, Stern rose. "Monica, my coat please."

The girl looked pleadingly at him, then went wordlessly into the bedroom. Tod sat down on the settee and stared silently at his outstretched legs and crossed ankles. Stern wrote out a check and handed it to Monica when she returned with his coat.

"Fill in whatever you need."

"May I borrow your pen?"

"Of course. Here."

Monica blinked steadily as she filled out the check and handed it back to him. The amount read: *Nothing!*

THE ODOR of rancid food that pervaded the hall disappeared as Stem stepped into the cold night air. He crumpled the rejected check in his fist, threw it into the gutter and ordered himself to be calm. However, his stomach churned, and his temples throbbed as he envisioned the black man with his daughter, the black man's arms around Monica...

Stem strode around the block, trying to decide what to do. He could disown Monica and wash his hands of all responsibility toward her. But the very thought made him shudder. He could go home, and hope time would heal the wounds. But what if that failed? Finally, he decided he could return to her apartment, make apologies and an effort to tolerate Humbert, and start rebuilding their damaged relationship.

Choice number three was most logical, of course, so Stern swallowed his pride and marched back to his daughter's building. An elderly man who was leaving held the inner door open as Stem entered, making it unnecessary for him to ring the bell. A shaft of yellow light slanting from the recessed hall at the top of the stairs indicated a partially opened apartment door.

The sound of familiar voices made him hesitate at the foot of the landing. He heard Tod Humbert say, "Don't feel bad, honey. It's good to be snubbed occasionally. Humbles the ego."

"Thanks for being so understanding, Tod."

"You're extra-special. Marrying you will be the greatest thrill of my life."

A sudden upsurge of blood pressure made Stem grip the bannister rail for support. He had visions of friends and business associates sporting lewd grins and knowing leers. Damn it! He could stand her seeing Humbert, but not this—not marriage, a black son-in-law.

Fists clenched, teeth grating, he left the building again and ducked into the doorway of an abandoned house diagonally across the street. The burning hatred he was feeling now conjured up remembrances a quarter-century old. His mind filled with reflections of Korea, of another people different in skin color, an alien race that had threatened him and his fellow commandoes. A threat he had eliminated with bullets, piano wire, and bare hands.

Once again, after twenty-five years, he felt threatened. But this type of threat was different, wasn't it? New York wasn't a jungle-or was it? You couldn't react here the way you could in Korea-or could you...?

If the sight of Tod Humbert emerging several minutes later from Monica's hallway stimulated Stern's adrenal glands, he showed no sign of it. He remained still until the black man disappeared around the comer, then he followed. After walking a deserted block, he called out, "Mr. Humbert!" Tod Humbert glanced warily over his shoulder. "It's me, Arthur Stern."

Stem broke into a trot to catch up, then feigned breathlessness. He said, "I hope you can forgive my rude behavior. Monica and I had angry words before you arrived, and I let my emotions get the best of me. I was just returning to apologize when I happened to see you."

The black man chuckled, extended his hand and said, "We all have our faults, don't—"

He never finished his sentence. Stem gripped his outstretched hand, jerked him forward and kneed him in the groin. As Tod's legs buckled, he clawed wildly. Stem felt a burning sensation on one side of his face and beard cloth tear. Both men collapsed against a row of foul-smelling garbage cans lined up before a run-down tenement. The clatter of metal and the screech of an exasperated cat shattered the night.

Stern crawled on top of Humbert, gripped his hair with both hands and pounded his head against the sidewalk. An edge-of-the-hand chop across the black man's throat ended the conflict.

Stem lumbered to his feet, glanced about, then twisted his tie and tore his shirt. The facial cut he had received before falling bled enough to satisfy him. He knew muggings occurred with startling regularity in this section of New York City. He imagined how Monica would feel when her own father was victimized. It would be The Lesson that would teach her to despise the ghetto dwellers for the depths to which most of them sunk, and bring her home again to her own kind. Especially when be proved his attacker was Tod Humbert!

Yellow squares of light began flashing in various tenements, and somewhere nearby a window rattled open. Stern clutched his wounded face with one hand and staggered into the gutter, shouting for the police.

ARTHUR STERN GESTURED in disbelief as he spoke to the bored, flat-faced detective sitting across the desk from him. "As I told the patrolmen, I was just walking along when this man attacked me. I came back to the neighborhood because I wanted to talk to my daughter again.

You can imagine my shock—my—my horror when the mugger turned out to be the man my daughter had introduced me to only an hour earlier. The man—my God—the man she was going to marry—"

A detective put his head through the door. "His daughter's here."

"Send her in."

Monica, complexion drained, entered listlessly. Stem went to her and gently squeezed her shoulders, saying, "Thanks for coming, baby."

She stood stiffly, not returning the embrace. Instead, she said coldly, "I thought they handcuffed murderers."

Stem felt a sudden chill on his back. He clutched her harder. "It was self-defense," he said. "Humbert tried to mug me."

"Tod could never raise his hand in violence to anyone. It would be against his principles, his way of life. If there was violence, *you* caused it. And I'll tell that to a jury. You murdered someone very dear to me."

"It isn't murder when...someone like that..." Stem looked at the flat-faced detective, who was watching him closely. Then he shook his head, hissed air in through clenched teeth and said, "Damn it! How could you even *think* of marrying him, Monica!"

"Marry him? What are you talking about?"

"Don't pretend! I came back to apologize tonight and overheard your conversation from the hall. He said marrying you would be the greatest thrill of his life."

Monica stared at him for a long moment. Then she shrugged his hands from her shoulders, fumbled through her purse and produced a snapshot of a blond man in an army medical uniform. "This is the surprise I had for you, Dad. Next month, when he gets discharged, I'm going to marry *this* man."

Stem's eyes grew wide as they rested on the picture. He tried to speak, but his voice failed him. For the first time in his life, Arthur Stem knew fear as Monica's tear-stained face moved from side to side and he heard her say, "Tod was going to marry me, all right. He—he was an ordained minister..."

The Spoils System

Donald E. Westlake

"THE GENTLE GRAFTER"

Jeff Peters of O. Henry's "The Gentle Grafter" remarks at one point, "It was beautiful and simple, as all truly great swindles are." Perhaps the swindle in "The Spoils System" is not truly great—but only because Donald E. Westlake's gentle grafter is merely working a door-to-door scam while waiting for a major score. But no con man should ever forget that a person looking to score is already halfway to becoming a mark himself. Mr. Westlake knows his marks; in 1968 one of them (God Save the Mark) won him an Edgar. As for the humor in his sixty novels (published under half a dozen names), it just sort of creeps in despite itself. To wit, a note Mr. Westlake recently left me when I borrowed his apartment: "Joe—Welcome. Don't use these leather chairs, they were oiled the other day. Come to think of it, so was I." *- J.G.*

IT WAS in the catacombish club car of the Phoebe Snow, that crack passenger express that roars across the Southern Tier of the Empire State with the speed of an income tax refund, that I most recently met Judd Dooley, a man with a strong sense of family. He is named for his infamous grandfather, the Judd Dooley celebrated in song and wanted poster, the man who, with the aid of patent medicine, gold watch, and lost silver mine stock, opened the great Midwest to the rapid patter, the fast shuffle, and the quick getaway back around the tum of the century, a man sadly neglected by the television industry, which owes him a great deal.

The contemporary Judd Dooley is continuing the family tradition in a ceaseless barrage of non-violent outrages from Kennebunkport to Mexicali, and is usually good for a reminiscence or two on his latest depredations against a public which has grown no less puerile since Grandpa's time.

Of course, there have been subtle differences in both the customer and the approach since Grandpa Dooley last foisted a genuine gold brick on a fatuous farmer in the bunco belt of the great Midwest. Judd tells me that today's farmer is a much different cookie from the bucolic boob who supported his grandfather, and a much tougher cookie to crumble. But, says Judd, with a light of reverence in his eye, Grandpa would have felt right at home in today's suburbia, where the modern housewife controls the income and the modern con man controls the outgo.

"I have just come from Cleveland," Judd told me, as we sat over Scotch on the rocks while the Phoebe Snow struggled out of Binghamton, "a town with suburbs that would have made Grandpa cry with delight. I was plying the Free Home Demonstration gizmo through a split-level development when—"

"Free Home Demonstration gizmo? I don't think I know it."

"You don't? It's a little gem—the quickest fast-fin dodge since the invention of Something For Nothing. All it requires is a pocketful of forms, an identification card, an ingratiating smile and ten minutes of rapid chatter. The brand name involved is Electro-Tex Limited, and if the name sounds familiar, you're half hooked already. The merchandise is a combination washer-dryer-television-radio-popup toaster-oven that retails for a stratospheric sum I won't even mention. But the company is about to commence an intensive advertising campaign, built around the inane concept of the satisfied customer. Therefore, I have been sent around by the company to selected housewives to offer them a Free Home Demonstration, for a trial six week period, during which time they may have the Electro-Tex PushButton Dew-It-Awl Wonder Whiz in their home, *absolutely free,* on the condition that we may use their name and a statement of satisfaction from them in our advertising."

"I imagine Mrs. America is normally interested by this time," I said.

"Interested? She couldn't be more excited if I were giving her a season pass to the Garry Moore show and a two-week vacation for two in Saskatchewan. She is frothing at the mouth."

"You've got her hooked, all right. But where does the swindle come in?"

"With all the wonders I am offering," said Judd, "could anyone in the world quibble over a measly five-dollar damage deposit?"

"In advance, of course."

"If I had to wait until after the merchandise showed up, I'd be riding on top of the train, not inside here in the warm. But, as I was saying, I was working this gizmo with great success and dodging the pedigreed hounds who infest suburbia like one of the plagues of Egypt, when I happened to spy a personable young man working the same side of the street and coming my way. His briefcase was black, bulging and polished to perfection. His eyes twinkled with bland sincerity behind a pair of black-rimmed spectacles, and his suit was so stark in its lines it's a wonder he didn't cut himself putting it on. Here, obviously, was another man in the same line of work.

"Not wanting either of us to create problems for the other, and since there were so many suburbs to choose from in the locality, I called to him, hoping we could work out an equitable distribution of the terrain.

"His name was Dan Miller, and he was perfectly agreeable to a division of spoils. Our occupations being what they are, we were both equipped with maps of the city, so we hunkered down on the sidewalk, surrounded by dogs, children and young men delivering ten cents-off coupons, and divided the city between us in the age-old manner of the conquering invader. We learned that we were staying at the same hotel, a second-class but clean 'hustlery' called the Warwick, and made a date to meet in the cocktail lounge to compare notes on our sectors for future use."

I got to my feet. "Another Scotch?"

"As a matter of fact," he said, "yes."

When I returned with the Scotch, swaying a bit (only an inveterate seafarer could feel really at borne on the Phoebe Snow) I asked, "Was this Dan Miller working the Free Home Demonstration gizmo, too?"

"Thank you," he said, reaching for the glass, a man with whom first things are always first. "No, he was collecting donations for the Citizen's Committee to Keep Our Neighborhood Beautiful, with some magazine contest for the most beautiful neighborhood in the country as a tie-in. The donation games are all right, in a way, but I only work one when I'm really desperate. He'd have to do more talking per housewife for maybe a dollar donation than I had to do for a five-dollar damage deposit. Dan Miller looked to me like a boy who was building a stake. I've already got a couple of permanent dodges that give me a steady trickle of income, mail order things and other gimmicks along the same line, so I haven't had to fall back on any of the smaller routines for a couple of years now.

"At any rate, I didn't see Dan Miller for about a week, not until I was finished with my half of the territory. I don't drink while I'm working, not even an after-dinner cocktail. It's one of the rules Grandpa instilled in me, and I've never known Grandpa to be wrong yet. So I didn't go to the cocktail lounge until a week later, when I had run out of territory and receipts."

"Receipts?"

Judd nodded. "Another of Grandpa's dictums," he said. "Never leave a sucker empty-handed. Always give him something for his money, some little memento he can press between the leaves of the family bible, even if it's just a little scrap of paper with Theodore Roosevelt's signature scrawled on it.

"Well, as I was saying, when I'd completed my tour of Cleveland, I counted my gains and discovered I had damaged the Cleveland deposits to the tune of four thousand dollars. It was time for a celebration. I donned my money belt, a legacy from Grandpa, and went down to the cocktail lounge for a quiet toot.

"Dan Miller was there, happy as an early-morning disc jockey, and it turned out that he had just finished beautifying his half of the city to the tune of twenty-five hundred iron men. We had a congratulatory toast, and then Dan turned serious. He said, 'Judd, what do you do with your admirable profits?'

"'Spend it or bank it,' I told him. 'But mainly spend it.'

"He shook his head. 'Bad business,' he told me. 'Think about your old age. You should invest it. A solid investment today will bring joy to your declining years.'

"For just a minute, I didn't know what to say. Did Dan Miller think my declining years had set in already? Was he really going to try to sell *me* gold mine stock? It didn't seem possible, so I said, 'Dan, just what do you have in mind?'

'Uranium mine stock,' he whispered. He leaned close to me, looking earnestly at me through his plain-glass spectacles. 'I've been putting all of my cash into uranium stock for over a year now,' he confided. 'I've got over nine thousand dollars worth of stock. And it's a reputable New York firm, one that's been in business since the eighteen-fifties. Uranium stock just can't go anywhere but up. The way I'm salting it away, I'll be able to buy Long Island for my country estate when I retire.'

"'Well,' I said cautiously, 'I've never put much faith in stock, since I've sold a share or two myself from time to time.'

'This is legit,' he insisted. 'On the up and up. Come on up to my room, and I'll show you their brochure.'

"More out of a professional interest in the competition than for any other reason, I joined Dan Miller successively in the lobby, an elevator and his room, where he bolted the door, drew the blinds, and slammed the transom before taking a whole sheaf of papers out of a battered suitcase.

"I looked it all over. The stock certificates were fancy things, all curlicues and whirligigs and gewgaws and whereases, and the brochure had been written by a man who could name his own price on Madison Avenue. The Navajo Squaw Uranium Development And Mining Company really did things right.

"Dan hovered around me while I leafed through the evidence. 'What do you think of it, Judd?' he asked me.

"'Well,' I said, 'I'll have to admit it does look pretty good.'

"'Can you think of a better or safer place for your money?' he wanted to know.

"I had to admit I couldn't.

"'Well, then,' he said, 'I was about to send them a telegram, telegraph my profits and tell them to send me a batch more shares. Why don't we double up on the same telegram, send your money too, and tell them to add you to the list of stockholders?'

"'Well,' I said, 'I suppose that is the thing to do. It certainly does look like a better deal than three and a quarter percent interest at a bank.'

"So we went down to the Western Union office in the lobby, and I reached into my shirt and pulled three thousand dollars worth of damage deposits out of my money belt. We spent about half an hour getting the message down to fifteen words, then went back to the cock-tail lounge to celebrate our good fortune, good sense and good security."

Judd sipped musingly at his Scotch, and the silence was broken only by the clatter of the Phoebe Snow bucketing down a Sullivan County mountainside. Finally, I said, "Did you get the stock certificates?"

"Came just before I left Cleveland," he said. He reached into his pocket and withdrew a bundle of stock certificates. He handed them over, and I studied them. To my unpracticed eye, they looked perfectly legitimate. But so did the Confederate money handed out in Wheaties boxes a few years back. I'm anything but a judge.

I gave the certificates back, saying, "Do you suppose they're all right?"

"No," he said. "They're as phony as Dotto."

"But—you pumped three thousand dollars into them!"

"There wasn't much else I could do," said Judd. He smiled rather sadly. "I couldn't very well tell Dan Miller that the Navajo Squaw Uranium Development And Mining Company was one of *my* little projects, now could I?"

Rope Enough

Joe Gores

INTRIGUE

This powerful short-short by my eminent co-editor has a great deal going for it, and all in only 2,100 words: political intrigue in a foreign setting, strong characterization, a deceptively straightforward style, and a stunning shocker in the last line. As everyone who reads crime fiction already knows, Joe Gores won back-to-back Edgars (an unprecedented feat) in 1970 for Best First Novel, A Time of Predators, and for Best Short Story, "Goodbye, Pops." His most recent novel is Hammett, published last year, which was extremely well received and which might be labeled a "biographical suspense novel"—a whole new genre?—since it features none other than Dashiell Hammett as the protagonist. - B.P.

YOU MUST UNDERSTAND that I am a Nationalist. If I have been an unwitting political agent of the reactionaries who govern this poor land in collusion with the Colonialists, I have not been a traitor. Not to my country, nor to The Band, nor to the cause of national freedom. Yes, even now I say this.

If I am so dedicated to national freedom, you might ask, then how...

Politics.

You probably consider us heroes, or spies, or terrorists—depending upon your own political sympathies—but I was none of these things when I joined The Band. I was a shopkeeper's assistant and a...what? Not a political activist. Say, rather, one who sought to reduce to a personal level the frightening modem technology the Colonialists have brought to our backward desert land in their ninety years of domination. To *this* bridge, to *that* supply dump, to *those* sentries.

Do you understand so far?

Then understand my bitter disappointment when I first heard Number One speak. I had expected a great, bearded fellow whose very words would be missiles hurled into the teeth of the enemy. Instead, I found a slight, brown-haired man of about thirty, telling us that clandestine guerrillas had to be prepared for hatred and persecution, had to beware of all men...

I was on my feet, for my temper matches my hair.

"Why is it *we* who should beware?" I cried. "Why shouldn't the Colonialists beware? Why do I hear nothing of liberating our country from their exploitation? Why—"

"I've come to bring the sword to this land, Sicarius." His intelligence reports even then were good; he knew my name. "But what will we accomplish if every man's hand is turned against us? Let us first be guileless as pigeons, as wise as snakes..."

Admit it. You too would have joined. And would have expected missions of tactical destruction under the direction of our CO, Captain Peters, and his Exec Officer, Lieutenant Jimmy Zeb. Each of us had his assigned task—mine was stores, since I'd been a shopkeeper before joining The Band. I also was entrusted with whatever money we liberated from the populace, but there was precious little of that. Because for three long, dreary years our task was subversion: fashioning key elements of the populace into a passive espionage and intelligence network, to forestall the authorities' counterinsurgency mobilization once the time had come to strike. But it was so long in coming! Everywhere across our land we found men impatient to throw off the shackles of Colonialism—yet never was the order given to attack.

I had come for wine, I was given water.

But then, last weekend, we entered the Capital openly, as it was preparing for one of the few National Holidays which hasn't been suppressed, and its normal hundred-thousand was nearly doubled by out-of-towners. Yes, the ideal revolutionary situation, with Nationalist sentiment inflamed and the streets crowded with tourists, government workers, and merchants idled by the holiday.

Ideal. And still we did nothing. Cowered in the Safe House.

On Wednesday, night before last, I said to hell with team discipline and took to the narrow, twisting streets of the Old Quarter. I rubbed shoulders with enlisted men from the garrison whose job it was to apprehend such as me. I watched the thieves and pickpockets at work, joked with the whores trying to tempt passers-by with hired sex.

It was in a nameless dive near Fountain Gate that I saw the girl again, as slender as a palm tree, her skirt showing flashes of rounded thighs like precious jewels as she moved. She confirmed my suspicion that she'd been following me by deserting her pair of Colonial troopers for my table.

"Don't tell me it's Sicarius!" she exclaimed loudly.

That's when I recognized her. Ruth...something. She'd lived next door when we'd been kids, a skinny, gawky, awkward girl then. Now, as she slipped into a chair at my table, her breasts pressed out against the cloth of her bodice like clusters of ripe grapes.

"The Ruth I once knew would spit in the teeth of such foreign dogs."

"Spoken like a true terrorist," she said contemptuously.

"Why don't you denounce me to your friends? I'm sure I would be worth a few silver *staters* to you."

She gave a peal of laughter and slapped my arm as if I had told her a dirty joke. "Do you really believe that rebels are the only patriots?" she demanded in a low voice. "What of us who gather intelligence for the Nationalist leaders in LEGCO?"

"Nationalist leaders such as who?"

"Harim," she said promptly. She added, "Laugh."

We laughed together, I slapped a hand upon the table as if in glee. Harim! That shook me. Harim once had been President of the Legislative Council. He'd been ousted years before in a supposed power struggle; but now it was his son-in-law, the current President, who faced the assassins' daggers. And Harim, subject to the "supervision" of the Governor-General and the Colonial Office, still seemed to dictate national policy.

"Doesn't Harim learn enough of the foreigners' plans as be licks their boots?" I demanded coldly.

"You are a fool." She gave a gay, bright laugh. "He has been negotiating with the Colonial Office for Home Rule for months. That's why he sent me to seek you out."

"Harim wants to see *me?*" I asked stupidly.

"He fears Number One might upset the negotiations." Her hand was like heated metal against my bare arm. "Please. Talk with him."

Talking does not make one a traitor to his Cause, does it? While his companions, except for clandestine sorties after dark in groups of three or four, cower in a Safe House? It was I, Sicarius, who dared step upon the shadow of the enemy.

At a certain dark entryway in the Lower City, Ruth's knock opened a door beyond which ill-lit passageways led to a room dazzling in the richness of its appointments.

I turned to Ruth, but she was gone. Then through a doorway in the far wall came a white-haired, eagle-beaked man, his face showing its admixture of Greek blood. He was Harim. He noted my reaction.

"You know me, Sicarius?" His voice was deep and powerful.

"I have seen Your Excellency on the way to LEGCO meetings."

All right, I admit it: he overawed me. But you must understand that to the swarthy races of the Syrian littoral, civil and religious authority are not separable. One has an inbred feeling of personal respect for such as Harim.

"Tell me, Sicarius, just as a hypothetical case: how long do you think autonomy would last if Number One were to succeed in overthrowing Colonial rule?"

"Last? Why, I... He... We would be free..."

His lip curled. "Free for what? Intrigues? Revolts? Assassinations?" He shook his magnificent eagle's head. "Within a few weeks the national struggle would be dissipated in factionalism. Then the Governor-General, who may be weak but is no fool, would send in the Colonialist troops..."

"What has any of this to do with me?"

He was suddenly furious. "You dare ask, when your mangy band of rebels has a cache of arms northeast of the city?"

"But..." I stopped. Of course! I should have seen it in Number One's nightly absences with Captain Peters and the two Zeb boys. I said lamely, "We operate on a need-to-know basis..."

"Doubtless, doubtless." The subject seemed to have lost his interest.

"But the fact is that you people play with fire while I lay the groundwork for a new treaty with the Colonial Office."

"You trust a scrap of paper with foreign dogs?" I sneered.

"The Governor-General knows that local stability looks good on his record. And he knows that I speak for the people, Sicarius." He slammed an open palm on his desk. "That's why your scruffy little band of radicals is dangerous right now! Any other time, we'd give your precious Number One enough rope—"

"If you truly speak for the people, why do you fear us?"

"Because the Governor-General could claim that any attempted revolt, no matter how abortive, had been planned by the Nationalists in LEGCO..." His eagle eyes glared. "Number One. Could you undertake to arrange a meeting between us? I could tell him—"

"He wouldn't come to any meeting with you."

"As I feared." Harim was on his feet, pacing in agitation. "And yet, Sicarius, we both know that I am the only one he would believe. There *must* be a face-to-face meeting..."

Well, where did my duty lie? With The Band, which did nothing? Or with Harim, who was negotiating the first Home Rule treaty for our Nation in ninety years? Number One would believe in it, too, if he once were convinced such a treaty could work...

What would *you* have done?

THE BAND MET last night at the Safe House in Old Town, for the traditional Holiday feast of roast lamb seasoned with bay leaf, thyme, marjoram, and basil. I was nervous, because the others would not understand what I had to do. So when I slopped horseradish sauce across Number One's hand as we dipped our meat into the common dish, I stood up hurriedly and wiped my mouth on my sleeve. If I remained there any longer my own tenseness would betray me.

"Where the devil are you off to?" demanded Captain Peters, his heavy features stupid with wine and meat.

"I forgot the traditional offering to the beggars." I did not add, of course, that the oversight had been deliberate, a means of getting me out of the room and down the stairs.

Peters looked over to Number One, who was deep in conversation with young Johnny Zeb. "Sir?"

Number One looked up, saw me on my feet with the offering money in my hand, and nodded. "Yes, of course. What you're doing, Sicarius, do it quickly."

Which sent me scurrying through the streets, once I had made sure no one was following me, to the Security Police barracks in New Town. What if they left before I returned with the police? Which is exactly what happened. We found the cenacle where The Band had dined deserted.

"I will find them," I told the police, with an assurance I didn't feel. I should have been more confident; The Band was indeed assembled in the park-like area northeast of the Capital where Harim believed our arms were cached. I pointed out Number One while keeping back to avoid a knife between the ribs. I needn't have worried. The Band, except for Captain Peters, melted away into the trees in the face of danger. He made a half-hearted lunge for me, but was easily restrained. Number One wasn't even armed.

After they took him off to meet Harim, I returned to my room, but it wasn't until six this morning that I dropped into an exhausted sleep.

I woke with a blinding headache at noon, dressed quickly, and went to Harim's residence as he had directed. He was with his son-inlaw, a lean, sly-faced man with darting eyes.

"Ah, Sicarius. Here. Now, we're very busy..."

I stared at what was in my hand. "What's this?"

"I have never believed in patriotism as its own reward."

Then he told me of the secret tribunal which, last night, was waiting to condemn Number One to death for sedition. At dawn, as I had slept, the man I had unwittingly betrayed had been rushed through the deserted streets to the Governor-General's office for the sentence to be confirmed.

"Number One is dead now, or soon will be," said Harim.

Staring into his eagle eyes, I knew there had never been a treaty. There had been only his fear of Number One's growing popularity. He had used me to betray innocent blood. I could hear my own blood singing in my ears.

I must have spoken, for Harim exclaimed, "Then the devil take you, man. Do what you want with it."

I hurled it on the polished floor at their feet. For an hour I wandered the streets, dazed, unseeing. Finally I returned to my room, and here I have remained, bound in the ever-tightening circle of my own thoughts.

What was...oh. Thunder. Three p. m. and clouding up for rain over the Hill of Gareb north of the city. That's fitting, really. Because in a moment I will go downstairs, and with that frayed old halter I saw in the stable will perform my final act of destruction. There's rope enough for that.

Here I am, about to die by my own hand, and I find myself compulsively wondering not about eternity, but about Harim—whom some men call Annas. What will he and his son-in-law Caiaphus do with the thirty pieces of silver they gave me for the life of the man called, by many, Jesus of Nazareth?

AUTHOR'S NOTE

The use of such British Empire terms as LEGCO (Legislative Council) for Sanhedrin, President for High Priest, and Governor-General for Procurator, was suggested by this passage from historian Henri Daniel-Rops' *Daily Life in the Time of Christ:*

> *"The high priest retained an authority that was...more than merely spiritual... His appointment was, in fact, subject to the politician masters of the country, (but)...a call by this spiritual leader could perfectly well begin an uprising, or calm it. The...(Romans) therefore preferred to be on good terms with this high personage..."*

A few of the many other clues pointing to "Number One" as Christ: He is thirty when Sicarius (of which Iscariot is a corruption) joins the band; he is executed three years later. Israel bad been a Roman satellite for ninety years, Jerusalem was 100,000 in population, Gethsemane lay northeast of the city, and Golgotha was on the Hill of Gareb. The *stater* was the standard Jewish silver coin of the day. Ananius, or Annas (a corruption of the Hebrew Harim) was deposed as high priest in A.D. 14, but remained in control through his son Elezear and then his son-in-law Caiaphus. Like most Jews (including the Apostles until the Resurrection), he believed Christ planned an armed revolt against Rome. The supper of herbed lamb, during which Christ and Judas dipped in the hot sauce together, is the traditional Passover feast. Legend says Judas was red-headed, Matthew says he hanged himself with a halter. Lines from Genesis (XVl:12), Psalms (VII:8-9), Matthew (X:16-17, 36 and XXVIl:3-9), and John (XIIl:27) are closely paraphrased or flatly quoted in the story.

Robert

Stanley Ellin

QUIET HORROR

Alfred Hitchcock once said that suspense is letting your audience know there is a live bomb under someone's chair, and then talking about baseball. To create supernatural terror, one must never let the reader actually meet the demon in the closet or the monster in the attic. As to quiet horror, this can only grow from a perversion of the commonplace, a distortion of the ordinary. A restaurant which specializes in a frightful entrée, for instance, as in Stanley Ellin's first published story. Or a classroom where angelic-faced children resort to obscene threats as in "Robert"—where the final paragraph gives its own sudden glimpse into unsuspected hells. Mr. Ellin is the recipient of three Edgars; his work, as epitomized by such connoisseurs' novels as The Eighth Circle *and* Mirror, Mirror on the Wall, *consistently blurs the line between popular entertainment and lasting literature. - J.G.*

THE WINDOWS of the sixth-grade classroom were wide open to the June afternoon, and through them came all the sounds of the departing school: the thunder of bus motors warming up, the hiss of gravel under running feet, the voices raised in cynical fervor.

"So we sing all hail to thee,
District Schoo-wull Number Three..."

Miss Gildea flinched a little at the last high, shrill note, and pressed her fingers to her aching forehead. She was tired, more tired than she could ever recall being in her thirty-eight years of teaching, and, as she told herself, she had reason to be. It had not been a good term, not good at all, what with the size of the class, and the Principal's insistence on new methods, and then her mother's shocking death coming right in the middle of everything.

Perhaps she had been too close to her mother, Miss Gildea thought; perhaps she had been wrong, never taking into account that someday the old lady would have to pass on and leave her alone in the world. Well, thinking about it all the time didn't make it any easier. She should try to forget.

And, of course, to add to her troubles, there had been during the past few weeks this maddening business of Robert. He had been a perfectly nice boy, and then, out of a clear sky, had become impossible. Not bothersome or noisy really, but sunk into an endless daydream from which Miss Gildea had to sharply jar him a dozen times a day.

She turned her attention to Robert, who sat alone in the room at the desk immediately before her, a thin boy with neatly combed, colorless hair bracketed between large ears; mild blue eyes in a pale face fixed solemnly on hers.

"Robert."

"Yes, Miss Gildea."

"Do you know why I told you to remain after school, Robert?"

He frowned thoughtfully at this, as if it were some lesson he was being called on for, but had failed to memorize properly.

"I suppose for being bad," he said at last.

Miss Gildea sighed.

"No, Robert, that's not it at all. I know a bad boy when I see one, Robert, and you aren't one like that. But I do know there's something troubling you, something on your mind, and I think I can help you."

"There's nothing bothering me, Miss Gildea. Honest, there isn't."

Miss Gildea found the silver pencil thrust into her hair and tapped it in a nervous rhythm on her desk.

"Oh, come, Robert. During the last month every time I looked at you your mind was a million miles away. Now, what is it? Just making plans for vacation, or, perhaps, some trouble with the boys?"

"I'm not having trouble with anybody, Miss Gildea."

"You don't seem to understand, Robert, that I'm not trying to punish you for anything. Your homework is good. You've managed to keep up with the class, but I do think your inattentiveness should be explained. What, for example, were you thinking this afternoon when I spoke to you directly for five minutes, and you didn't hear a word I said?"

"Nothing, Miss Gildea."

She brought the pencil down sharply on the desk. "There must have been *something,* Robert. Now, I must insist that you think back, and try to explain yourself."

Looking at his impassive face, she knew that somehow she herself had been put on the defensive, that if any means of graceful retreat were offered now, she would gladly take it. *Thirty-eight years,* she thought grimly, *and I'm still trying to play mother hen to ducklings.* Not that there wasn't a bright side to the picture. Thirty-eight years passed meant only two more to go before retirement, the half-salary pension, the chance to putter around the house, tend to the garden properly. The pension wouldn't buy you furs and diamonds, sure enough, but it could buy the right to enjoy your own home for the rest of your days instead of a dismal room in the County Home for Old Ladies. Miss Gildea had visited the County Home once, on an instructional visit, and preferred not to think about it.

"Well, Robert," she said wearily, "have you remembered what you were thinking?"

"Yes, Miss Gildea."

"What was it?"

"I'd rather not tell, Miss Gildea."

"I insist!"

"Well," Robert said gently, "I was thinking I wished you were dead, Miss Gildea. I was thinking I wished I could kill you."

Her first reaction was simply blank incomprehension. She had been standing not ten feet away when that car had skidded up on the sidewalk and crushed her mother's life from her, and Miss Gildea had neither screamed nor fainted. She had stood there dumbly, because of the very unreality of the thing. Just the way she stood in court where they explained that the man got a year in jail, but didn't have a dime to pay for the tragedy he had brought about. And now the orderly ranks of desks before her, the expanse of blackboard around her, and Robert's face in the midst of it all were no more real. She found herself rising from her chair, walking toward Robert, who shrank back, his eyes wide and panicky, his elbow half lifted, as if to ward off a blow.

"Do you understand what you've just said?" Miss Gildea demanded hoarsely.

"No, Miss Gildea! Honest, I didn't mean anything."

She shook her head unbelievingly. "Whatever made you say it? Whatever in the world could make a boy say a thing like that, such a wicked, terrible thing!"

"You wanted to know! You kept asking me!"

The sight of that protective elbow raised against her cut as deep as the incredible words had.

"Put that arm down!" Miss Gildea said shrilly, and then struggled to get her voice under control. "In all my years I've never struck a child, and I don't intend to start now!"

Robert dropped his arm and clasped his bands together on his desk, and Miss Gildea, looking at the pinched white knuckles, realized with surprise that her own hands were shaking uncontrollably. "But if you think this little matter ends here, young-feller-me-lad," she said, "you've got another thought coming. You get your things together, and we're marching right up to Mr. Harkness. He'll be very much interested in all this."

Mr. Harkness was the Principal. He had arrived only the term before, and but for his taste in eyeglasses (the large, black-rimmed kind which, Miss Gildea privately thought, looked actorish) and his predilection for the phrase "modern pedagogical methods" was, in her opinion, a rather engaging young man.

He looked at Robert's frightened face and then at Miss Gildea's pursed lips. "Well," he said pleasantly, "what seems to be the trouble here?"

"That," said Miss Gildea, "is something I think Robert should tell you about."

She placed a hand on Robert's shoulder, but he pulled away and backed slowly toward Mr. Harkness, his breath coming in loud, shuddering sobs, his eyes riveted on Miss Gildea as if she were the only thing in the room beside himself. Mr. Harkness put an arm around Robert and frowned at Miss Gildea.

"Now, what's behind all this, Miss Gildea? The boy seems frightened to death."

Miss Gildea found herself sick of it all, anxious to get out of the room, away from Robert. "That's enough, Robert," she commanded. "Just tell Mr. Harkness exactly what happened."

"I said the boy was frightened to death, Miss Gildea," Mr. Harkness said brusquely. "We'll talk about it as soon as he understands we're his friends. Won't we, Robert?"

Robert shook his head vehemently. "I didn't do anything bad! Miss Gildea said I didn't do anything bad!"

"Well, then!" said Mr. Harkness triumphantly. "There's nothing to be afraid of, is there?"

Robert shook his head again. "She said I had to stay in after school."

Mr. Harkness glanced sharply at Miss Gildea. "I suppose he missed the morning bus, is that it? And after I said in a directive that the staff was to make allowances—"

"Robert doesn't use a bus," Miss Gildea protested. "Perhaps I'd better explain all this, Mr. Harkness. You see—"

"I think Robert's doing very well," Mr. Harkness said, and tightened his arm around Robert, who nodded shakily.

"She kept me in," he said, "and then when we were alone, she came up close to me and she said, 'I know what you're thinking. You're thinking you'd like to see me dead! You're thinking you'd like to kill me, aren't you?'"

Robert's voice had dropped to an eerie whisper that bound Miss Gildea like a spell. It was broken only when she saw the expression on Mr. Harkness' face.

"Why, that's a lie!" she cried. "That's the most dreadful lie I ever heard any boy dare—"

Mr. Harkness cut in abruptly. "Miss Gildea! I *insist* you let the boy finish what he has to say."

Miss Gildea's voice fluttered. "It seems to me, Mr. Harkness, that he has been allowed to say quite enough already!"

"Has he?" Mr. Harkness asked.

"Robert has been inattentive lately, especially so this afternoon. After class I asked him what he had been thinking about, and he dared to say he was thinking how he wished I were dead! How he wanted to kill me!"

"Robert said that?"

"In almost those exact words. And I can tell you, Mr. Harkness, that I was shocked, terribly shocked, especially since Robert always seemed like such a nice boy."

"His record—?"

"His record is quite good. It's just—"

"And his social conduct?" asked Mr. Harkness in the same level voice.

"As far as I know, he gets along with the other children well enough."

"But for some reason," persisted Mr. Harkness, "you found him annoying you."

Robert raised his voice. "I didn't! Miss Gildea said I didn't do anything bad. And I always liked her. I like her better than *any* teacher!"

Miss Gildea fumbled blindly in her hair for the silver pencil, and failed to find it. She looked around the floor distractedly.

"Yes?" said Mr. Harkness.

"My pencil," said Miss Gildea on the verge of tears. "It's gone."

"Surely, Miss Gildea," said Mr. Harkness in a tone of mild exasperation, "this is not quite the moment—"

"It was very valuable," Miss Gildea tried to explain hopelessly. "It was my mother's."

In the face of Mr. Harkness' stony surveillance, she knew she must look a complete mess. Hems crooked, nose red, hair all disheveled. "I'm all upset, Mr. Harkness. It's been a long term and now all this right at the end of it. I don't know what *to* say."

Mr. Harkness' face fell into sympathetic lines.

"That's quite all right, Miss Gildea. I know how you feel. Now, if you want to leave, I think Robert and I should have a long, friendly talk."

"If you don't mind—"

"No, no," Mr. Harkness said heartily. "As a matter of fact, I think that would be the best thing all around."

After he had seen her out, he closed the door abruptly behind her, and Miss Gildea walked heavily up the stairway and down the corridor to the sixth-grade room. The silver pencil was there on the floor at Robert's desk, and she picked it up and carefully polished it with her handkerchief. Then she sat down at her desk with the handkerchief to her nose and wept soundlessly for ten minutes.

THAT NIGHT, when the bitter taste of humiliation had grown faint enough to permit it, Miss Gildea reviewed the episode with all the honesty at her command. Honesty with oneself had always been a major point in her credo, had, in fact, been passed on through succeeding classes during the required lesson on The Duties of an American Citizen, when Miss Gildea, to sum up the lesson, would recite: "This above all, To thine ownself be true..." while thumping her fist on her desk as an accompaniment to each syllable.

Hamlet, of course, was not in the syllabus of the Sixth Grade, whose reactions over the years never deviated from a mixed bewilderment and indifference. But Miss Gildea, after some prodding of the better minds into a discussion of the lines, would rest content with the knowledge that she had sown good seed on what, she prayed, was fertile ground.

Reviewing the case of Robert now, with her emotions under control, she came to the unhappy conclusion that it was she who had committed the injustice. The child had been ordered to stay after school, something that to him could mean only a punishment. He had been ordered to disclose some shadowy, childlike thoughts that had drifted through his mind hours before, and, unable to do so, either had to make up something out of the whole cloth, or blurt out the immediate thought in his immature mind.

It was hardly unusual, reflected Miss Gildea sadly, *for a child badgered by a teacher to think what Robert had*; she could well remember her own feelings toward a certain pompadoured harridan who still haunted her dreams. And the only conclusion to be drawn, unpleasant though it was, was that Robert, and not she, had truly put into practice those beautiful words from Shakespeare.

It was this, as well as the sight of his pale accusing face before her while she led the class through the morning session next day, which prompted her to put Robert in charge of refilling the water pitcher during recess. The duties of the water pitcher monitor were to leave the playground a little before the rest of the class and clean and refill the pitcher on her desk, but since the task was regarded as an honor by the class, her gesture, Miss Gildea felt with some self-approval, carried exactly the right note of conciliation.

She was erasing the blackboard at the front of the room near the end of the recess when she heard Robert approaching her desk, but much as she wanted to, she could not summon up courage enough to turn and face him. *As if,* she thought, *he were the teacher, and I were afraid of him.* And she could feel her cheeks grow warm at the thought.

He re-entered the room on the sound of the bell that marked the end of recess, and this time Miss Gildea plopped the eraser firmly into its place beneath the blackboard and turned to look at him. "Thank you very much, Robert," she said as he set the pitcher down and neatly capped it with her drinking glass.

"You're welcome, Miss Gildea," Robert said politely. He drew a handkerchief from his pocket, wiped his hands with it, then smiled gently at Miss Gildea. "I bet you think I put poison or something into that water," he said gravely, "but I wouldn't do anything like that, Miss Gildea. Honest, I wouldn't."

Miss Gildea gasped, then reached out a hand toward Robert's shoulder. She withdrew it hastily when he shrank away with the familiar panicky look in his eyes.

"Why did you say that, Robert?" Miss Gildea demanded in a terrible voice. "That was plain impudence, wasn't it? You thought you were being smart, didn't you?"

At that moment the rest of the class surged noisily into the room, but Miss Gildea froze them into silence with a commanding wave of the hand. Out of the corner of her eye she noted the cluster of shocked and righteous faces allied with her in condemnation, and she felt a quick little sense of triumph in her position.

"I was talking to you, Robert," she said. "What do you have to say for yourself?"

Robert took another step backward and almost tumbled over a schoolbag left carelessly in the aisle. He caught himself, then stood there helplessly, his eyes never leaving Miss Gildea's.

"Well, Robert?"

He shook his head wildly. "I didn't do it!" he cried. "I didn't put anything in your water, Miss Gildea! I told you I didn't!"

Without looking, Miss Gildea knew that the cluster of accusing faces had swung toward her now, felt her triumph turn to a sick bewilderment inside her. It was as if Robert, with his teary eyes and pale, frightened face and too-large ears, had turned into a strange jellylike creature that could not be pinned down and put in its place. As if he were retreating further and further down some dark, twisting path, and leading her on with him. And, she thought desperately, she had to pull herself free before she did something dreadful, something unforgivable.

She couldn't take the boy to Mr. Harkness again. Not only did the memory of that scene in his office the day before make her shudder, but a repeated visit would be an admission that after thirty-eight years of teaching she was not up to the mark as a disciplinarian.

But for her sake, if for nothing else, Robert had to be put in his place. With a gesture, Miss Gildea ordered the rest of the class to their seats and turned to Robert, who remained standing.

"Robert," said Miss Gildea, "I want an apology for what has just happened."

"I'm sorry, Miss Gildea," Robert said, and it looked as if his eyes would be brimming with tears in another moment.

Miss Gildea hardened her heart to this. *"I apologize, Miss Gildea, and it will not happen again,"* she prompted.

Miraculously, Robert contained his tears. "I apologize, Miss Gildea, and it will not happen again," he muttered and dropped limply into his seat.

"Well!" said Miss Gildea, drawing a deep breath as she looked around at the hushed class. "Perhaps that will be a lesson to us all." The classroom work did not go well after that, but, as Miss Gildea told herself, there were only a few days left to the end of the term, and after that, praise be, there was the garden, the comfortable front porch of the old house to share with neighbors in the summer evenings, and then next term a new set of faces in the classroom, with Robert's not among them.

Later, closing the windows of the room after the class had left, Miss Gildea was brought up short by the sight of a large group gathered on the sidewalk near the parked busses. It was Robert, she saw, surrounded by most of the Sixth Grade, and obviously the center of interest. He was nodding emphatically when she put her face to the window, and she drew back quickly at the sight, moved by some queer sense of guilt.

Only a child, she assured herself, *he's only a child,* but that thought did not in any way dissolve the anger against him that stuck like a lump in her throat.

THAT WAS ON THURSDAY. By Tuesday of the next week, the final week of
the term, Miss Gildea was acutely conscious of the oppressive
atmosphere lying over the classroom. Ordinarily, the awareness of
impending vacation acted on the class like a violent agent dropped into
some inert liquid. There would be ferment and seething beneath the
surface, manifested by uncontrollable giggling and whispering, and
this would grow more and more turbulent until all restraint and discipline was swept away in the general upheaval of excitement and good
spirits.

That, Miss Gildea thought, *was the way it always had been.* But it was
strangely different now. The Sixth Grade, down to the most irrepress-
ible spirits in it, acted as if it had been turned to a set of robots before
her startled eyes. Hands tightly clasped on desks, eyes turned toward
her with an almost frightening intensity, the class responded to her
mildest requests as if they were shouted commands. And when she
walked down the aisles between them, one and all seemed to have
adopted Robert's manner of shrinking away fearfully at her approach.

Miss Gildea did not like to think of what all this might mean, but
valiantly forced herself to do so. *Can it mean,* she asked herself, *that all
think as Robert does, are choosing this way of showing it? And, if they knew
how cruel it was, would they do it?*

Other teachers, Miss Gildea knew, sometimes took problems such
as this to the Teacher's Room, where they could be studied and
answered by those who saw them in an objective light. It might be that
the curious state of the Sixth Grade was being duplicated in other
classes. Perhaps she herself was imagining the whole thing, or, frightening thought, looking back, as people will when they grow old, on the
sort of past that never really did exist. Why, in that case—and Miss
Gildea had to laugh at herself with a faint merriment—he would just
find herself reminiscing about her thirty-eight years of teaching to
some bored young woman who didn't have the fraction of experience
she did.

But underneath the current of these thoughts, Miss Gildea knew
there was one honest reason for not going to the Teacher's Room this
last week of the term. She had received no gifts, not one. And the spoils
from each grade heaped high in a series of pyramids against the wall,
the boxes of fractured cookies, the clumsily wrapped jars of preserves,
the scarves, the stockings, the handkerchiefs, infinite, endless boxes of
handkerchiefs, all were there to mark the triumph of each teacher. And

Miss Gildea, who in all her years at District School Number Three had been blushingly proud of the way her pyramid was highest at the end of each term, had not yet received a single gift from the Sixth Grade class.

After the class was dismissed that afternoon, however, the spell was broken. Only a few of her pupils still loitered in the hallway near the door, Miss Gildea noted, but Robert remained in his seat. Then, as she gathered together her belongings, Robert approached her with a box outheld in his hand. It was, from its shape, a box of candy. Automatically, she reached a hand out, then stopped herself short. *He'll never make up to me for what he's done,* she told herself furiously; *I'll never let him.*

"Yes, Robert?" she said coolly.

"It's a present for you, Miss Gildea," Robert said, and then as Miss Gildea watched in fascination, he began to strip the wrappings from it. He laid the paper neatly on the desk and lifted the cover of the box to display the chocolates within. "My mother said that's the biggest box they had," he said wistfully. "Don't you even want them, Miss Gildea?"

Miss Gildea weakened despite herself. "Did you think I would, after what's happened, Robert?" she asked.

Robert reflected a moment. "Well," he said at last, "if you want me to, I'll eat one right in front of you, Miss Gildea."

Miss Gildea recoiled as if at a faraway warning. *Don't let him say any more,* something inside her cried; *he's only playing a trick, another horrible trick,* and then she was saying, "Why would I want you to do that, Robert?"

"So you'll see they're not poison or anything, Miss Gildea," Robert said. "Then you'll believe it, won't you, Miss Gildea?"

She had been prepared. Even before he said the words, she had felt her body drawing itself tighter and tighter against what she knew was coming. But the sound of the words themselves only served to release her like a spring coiled too tightly.

"You little monster!" sobbed Miss Gildea and struck wildly at the proffered box, which flew almost to the far wall, while chocolates cascaded stickily around the room. "How dare you!" she cried. "How dare you!" and her small bony fists beat at Robert's cowering shoulders and back as he tried to retreat.

He half-turned in the aisle, slipped on a piece of chocolate, and went down to his knees, but before he could recover himself Miss

Gildea was on him again, her lips drawn back, her fists pummeling him as if they were a pair of tireless mallets. Robert had started to scream at the top of his lungs from the first blow, but it was no more than a remote buzzing in Miss Gildea's ears.

"Miss Gildea!"

That was Mr. Harkness' voice, she knew, and those must be Mr. Harkness' hands which pulled her away so roughly that she had to keep herself from falling by clutching at her desk. She stood there weakly, feeling the wild fluttering of her heart, feeling the sick churning of shame and anguish in her while she tried to bring the room into focus again. There was the knot of small excited faces peering through the open doorway, they must have called Mr. Harkness, and Mr. Harkness himself listening to Robert, who talked and wept alternately, and there was a mess everywhere. *Of course,* thought Miss Gildea dazedly, *those must be chocolate stains. Chocolate stains all over my lovely clean room.*

Then Robert was gone, the faces at the door were gone, and the door itself was closed behind them. Only Mr. Harkness remained, and Miss Gildea watched him as he removed his glasses, cleaned them carefully, and then held them up at arm's length and studied them before settling them once more on his nose.

"Well, Miss Gildea," said Mr. Harkness as if he were speaking to the glasses rather than to her, "this is a serious business."

Miss Gildea nodded.

"I am sick," Mr. Harkness said quietly, "really sick at the thought that somewhere in this school, where I tried to introduce decent pedagogical standards, corporal punishment is still being practiced."

"That's not fair at all, Mr. Harkness," Miss Gildea said shakily. "I hit the boy, that's true, and I know I was wrong to do it, but that is the first time in all my life I raised a finger against any child. And if you knew my feelings—"

"Ah," said Mr. Harkness, "that's exactly what I would like to know, Miss Gildea." He nodded to her chair, and she sat down weakly. "Now, just go ahead and explain everything as you saw it."

It was a difficult task, made even more difficult by the fact that Mr. Harkness chose to stand facing the window. Forced to address his back this way, Miss Gildea found that she had the sensation of speaking in a vacuum, but she mustered the facts as well as she could, presented them with strong emotion, and then sank back in the chair, quite exhausted.

Mr. Harkness remained silent for a long while, then slowly turned to face Miss Gildea. "I am not a practicing psychiatrist," he said at last, "although as an educator I have, of course, taken a considerable interest in that field. But I do not think it needs a practitioner to tell what a clear-cut and obvious case I am facing here. Nor," he added sympathetically, "what a tragic one."

"It might simply be," suggested Miss Gildea, "that Robert—"

"I am not speaking about Robert," said Mr. Harkness soberly, quietly.

It took an instant for this to penetrate, and then Miss Gildea felt the blood run cold in her.

"Do you think I'm lying about all this?" she cried incredulously. "Can you possibly—"

"I am sure," Mr. Harkness replied soothingly, "that you were describing things exactly as you saw them, Miss Gildea. But—have you ever heard the phrase 'persecution complex'? Do you think you could recognize the symptoms of that condition if they were presented objectively? I can, Miss Gildea, I assure you, I can."

Miss Gildea struggled to speak, but the words seemed to choke her. "No," she managed to say, "you couldn't! Because some mischievous boy chooses to make trouble—"

"Miss Gildea, no child of eleven, however mischievous, could draw the experiences Robert has described to me out of his imagination. He has discussed these experiences with me at length; now I have heard your side of the case. And the conclusions to be drawn, I must say, are practically forced on me."

The room started to slip out of focus again, and Miss Gildea frantically tried to hold it steady.

"But that just means you're taking his word against mine!" she said fiercely.

"Unfortunately, Miss Gildea, not his word alone. Last week end, a delegation of parents met the School Board and made it quite plain that they were worried because of what their children told them of your recent actions. A dozen children in your class described graphically at that meeting how you had accused them of trying to poison your drinking water, and how you had threatened them because of this. And Robert, it may interest you to know, was not even one of them.

"The School Board voted for your dismissal then and there, Miss Gildea, but in view of your long years of service, it was left for me to override that decision if I wished to on my sole responsibility. After this episode, however, I cannot see that I have any choice. I must do what is best."

"Dismissal?" said Miss Gildea vaguely. "But they can't. I only have two more years to go. They can't do that, Mr. Harkness; all they're trying to do is trick me out of my pension!"

"Believe me," said Mr. Harkness gently, "they're not trying to do anything of the sort, Miss Gildea. Nobody in the world is trying to hurt you. I give you my solemn word that the only thing which has entered into consideration of this case from first to last has been the welfare of the children."

The room swam in sunlight, but under it Miss Gildea's face was gray and lifeless. She reached forward to fill her glass with water, stopped short, and seemed to gather herself together with a sudden brittle determination. "I'll just have to speak to the Board myself," she said in a high breathless voice. "That's the only thing to do, go there and explain the whole thing to them!"

"That would not help," said Mr. Harkness pityingly. "Believe me, Miss Gildea, it would not."

Miss Gildea left her chair and came to him, her eyes wide and frightened. She laid a trembling hand on his arm and spoke eagerly, quickly, trying to make him understand. "You see," she said, "that means I won't get my pension. I must have two more years for that, don't you see? There's the payment on the house, the garden—no, the garden is part of the house, really—but without the pension—"

She was pulling furiously at his arm with every phrase as if she could drag him bodily into a comprehension of her words, but he stood unyielding and only shook his head pityingly. "You must control yourself, Miss Gildea," he pleaded. "You're not yourself, and it's impossible—"

"No!" she cried in a strange voice. "No!"

When she pulled away, he knew almost simultaneously what she intended to do, but the thought froze him to the spot, and when he moved it was too late. He burst into the corridor through the door she had flung open, and almost threw himself down the stairway to the main hall.

The door to the street was just swinging shut and he ran toward it, one hand holding the rim of his glasses, a sharp little pain digging into his side, but before he could reach the door he heard the screech of brakes, the single agonized scream, and the horrified shout of a hundred shrill voices.

He put his hand on the door, but could not find the strength to open it. A few minutes later, a cleaning woman had to sidle around him to get outside and see what all the excitement was about.

MISS REARDON, the substitute, took the Sixth Grade the next day, and, everything considered, handled it very well. The single ripple in the even current of the session came at its very start, when Miss Reardon explained her presence by referring to the "sad accident that happened to dear Miss Gildea." The mild hubbub which followed this contained several voices, notably in the back of the room, which protested plaintively, "It was *not* an accident, Miss Reardon; she ran right in front of that bus," but Miss Reardon quickly brought order to the room with a few sharp raps of her ruler and after that, classwork was carried on in a pleasant and orderly fashion.

ROBERT WALKED HOME SLOWLY that afternoon, swinging his schoolbag placidly at his side, savoring the June warmth soaking into him, the fresh green smell in the air, the memory of Miss Reardon's understanding face so often turned toward his in eager and friendly interest. His home was identical with all the others on the block, square white boxes with small lawns before them, and its only distinction was that all its blinds were drawn down. After he had closed the front door very quietly behind him, he set his schoolbag down in the hallway, and went into the stuffy half-darkness of the living room.

Robert's father sat in the big armchair in his bathrobe, the way he always did, and Robert's mother was bent over him, holding a glass of water.

"No!" Robert's father said. "You just want to get rid of me, but I won't let you! I know what you put into it, and I won't drink it! I'll die before I drink it!"

"Please," Robert's mother said, "please take it. I swear it's only water. I'll drink some myself if you don't believe me." But when she drank a little and then held the glass to his lips, Robert's father only tossed his head from side to side.

Robert stood there watching the scene with fascination, his lips moving in silent mimicry of the familiar words. Then he cleared his throat

"I'm home, mama," Robert said softly. "Can I have some milk and cookies, please?"

My Mother, The Ghost

Henry Slesar

FANTASY

If there exists a royal class among the writers of short mystery fiction in general and the McGuffin in particular, Henry Slesar indisputably belongs to it. He has published more than five hundred stories since he began writing in the mid-1950s, the preponderance of them crime/suspense, and each and every one, in its own way, is a polished gem. "My Mother, the Ghost" is not only vintage Slesar—flawlessly crafted and constructed, with a surprise ending guaranteed to fool and delight almost any reader—it is also a complete home-study course in how to write the fantasy story, the short-short story, and (naturally) the McGuffin. - B.P.

HIS SHOW CLOSED, his mother died, and his hair started to fall out, a combination of events that led Raymond Schiff to think seriously about aiming a gun at the roof of his mouth. The show, called *Flapper,* was dubbed "Flopper" by the grips at the first rehearsal, a verdict confirmed on opening night. The mother, called Mama, had succumbed to a failing heart that had beaten solely for her Raymond's sake for the past 40 years. The hair came out in handfuls on the day he received word from the bank concerning an overdraft of $1,100. Eleven hundred hairs, Raymond estimated gloomily.

Because his rent was two months in arrears, his landlady locked him out of his room immediately after the reviews appeared. She had sat up half the night, like a theater buff, waiting for Kerr, Watts, and the rest of the critics to tell her if she had a solvent tenant. When Raymond returned from Lindy's, stuffed with cheesecake and remorse, he found his one shabby suitcase thoughtfully left outside. He checked into a hotel down the street.

He was lying on the bed in his underwear, thinking about his old Army .45, when the 60-watt bulb in the ceiling whooshed out like a candle in the wind. He *felt* the wind, too; it made ripples along his hairy calves. He received a frantic message from his brain telling him to be afraid. Yet he was calm, even expectant, when suddenly another light materialized at the foot of his bed and gradually took on a plump, familiar shape.

"Mama!" Raymond Schiff exclaimed.

"Raymond!" said his mother's ghost. "Look at you! Two months I'm away, and *this* is how you take care of yourself? Lying around naked in drafty hotel rooms?"

"Mama," Raymond said in a trembling voice, lifting himself from the bed, "is it really you?"

"So who else?" The spirit shrugged. "Listen, talk quick, this is a long-distance call. The only reason they let me come is on account of you need me so bad."

"Oh, Mama!" Raymond groaned, catching a sob. "Do I need you! I can't tell you how rotten things are. We had to close the show. One night, and we closed!"

Even in incorporeal form, his mother expressed a certain down-to-earth practicality. "All right, so it closed. You'll have another show, don't worry. Ideas you always had, Raymond, ever since you were a little boy."

"Ideas, ideas," Raymond groaned. "Who'd listen to my ideas now? The Japanese wrestlers I brought over—a failure! The Italian movie with the gladiators—a loss! The musical—a flopperino! I'm through, Mama, I'm washed up!"

She waggled a ghostly finger. "What did I always tell you, Raymond? Didn't I always tell you I'd take care of you? If it's a matter of a few dollars—"

"There's nothing you can do for me *now,* Mama."

"Name it! Name it!" she said, striking her breast. "What wouldn't a mother do? Alive, dead, what does it matter?"

Tears slid from Raymond's eyes. Then they narrowed, and generated a light of their own. The idea that exploded in his mind had a kilowatt power that was almost blinding.

"Mama!" he said. "Mama, could you do this again? Could you come back to earth again?"

"Well, maybe. Maybe once more they'll let me come, if you really need me."

"For *sure,* Mama, for positive sure?"

"If it's so important, all right. For sure."

"Could you come at a certain time—a certain place?"

"Why not?" said the ghost, lifting an insubstantial shoulder. "Didn't I come to this dirty, old hotel room? You tell me where you want me, I'll be there."

Raymond hastily consulted a pocket calendar. "Could you make it a theater, Mama? On the night of, say, the 10th of October? At nine o'clock?"

"For what?"

"For a show," Raymond whispered in delighted anticipation. "A show—starring you!"

"Raymond, Raymond," his mother clucked. "From your old mother you want to make a hoochy-koochy dancer? Who'd pay money to see *me?*"

"Thousands of people, Mama! Thousands! It'll be terrific—spectacular! Something nobody ever saw on stage before. *A real live ghost!*"

He waited breathlessly as the image wavered.

"So, all right," his mother sighed. "I told you I'd take care of you, Raymond. And if this is what you want me to do—all right. Only one thing!" The finger waggled again. "It's got to be decent, understand? No nakedness!"

"I swear!" Raymond Schiff shouted ecstatically.

SID SALMON, of course, thought he was crazy when Raymond described the enterprise he had in mind: a one-time performance in a large-capacity house, say, Madison Square Garden, Carnegie Hall, the Winter

Garden—$5 general admission, $10, $20 and more for a closer view of his mother, the ghost. Raymond didn't ask Sid to *believe* him, all he said was: "*If* I could do it, Sid, *if* is all I'm asking. Is it worth five bucks a head? Would I pack them in?"

Sid gave a cracked, high-pitched giggle. "And when the ghost doesn't come, Raymond? And they stamp their feet, break up the furniture and kill you? What then?"

"I'll give them a guarantee," Raymond said triumphantly. "The ghost shows or their money back. What can they lose?"

"*They* nothing. *You* plenty. The rental. The ushers. The stagehands. The orchestra. Union labor. Raymond, better to spend the money on a good psychiatrist."

But Raymond was unshakeable in his faith. "Mama wouldn't let me down," he said. "Mama always promised to take care of me. Sidney, this time God is on my side. Can you loan me five thou?"

"Go ask God," Sid answered. But that night he wrote him the check. Sid was his uncle.

Five thousand wasn't enough, of course, so Raymond sold a Lincoln Continental he didn't really own to his best friend, Earl Steckel.

He also wrote his ex-wife and told her he was seriously ill with a polluted kidney and could she send him a few bucks? She did, upon receipt of his I.O.U. for $2,500. He was still some $8,000 short of the total he needed, so he did something he had sworn never to do. He went to The Friend, a bulgy-necked hood who had absolutely no connection with Chase Manhattan, but whose loan business was thriving. (Those who patronized The Friend did so at their own risk, paying for any default with their well-being.)

At last he had the money, picked the date, chose the place and sent an earnest prayer up to his mother.

"Mama," he said on his knees beside the hotel bed, "you're booked for the 10th. The 10th, Mama. Don't fail me. The tickets go on sale this week."

The tickets went on sale-and the town chuckled.

RAYMOND SCHIFF PRESENTS
MY MOTHER, THE GHOST
FOR THE FIRST TIME IN HISTORY
ON STAGE—IN PERSON

A GENUINE MANIFESTATION PROM THE SPIRIT WORLD
NOT A FILM—NOT A RECORDING
THE GHOST OF MRS. HANNA SCHIFF
BORN 1897—DIED 1965
APPEARANCE GUARANTEED OR YOUR MONEY REFUNDED
WINTER GARDEN—ONE NIGHT ONLY
OCT. 10—9:00 P.M.

AT FIRST, people laughed. Then, they bought a few tickets. And a few more. The line at the box office was started by two or three sheepish-looking customers. But it began to grow. It lengthened and wound like a snake, down the block and around the comer. The ticket brokers caught the scent of money. Demand began to overtake supply. Suddenly, a full-scale panic was on. Two weeks before the performance date, the theater was SRO, and Raymond Schiff saw a balance-sheet total that rose to a dizzying height. Loans, expenses, and all—after the 10th of October, he would be a wealthy man.

There was one more expense: the hiring of a dress suit, for Raymond himself planned to introduce the star of the evening. He occupied the theater's best (meaning least objectionable) dressing room and meticulously prepared himself. In the grimy mirror, he saw a new look of optimism, even a new growth of hair.

"Mama, Mama," he whispered to the ceiling. "You're really taking care of me, just like you promised." No shadow of a doubt crossed his mind. In truth, he was the only one in the theater that night, on both sides of the velvet curtain, who believed that the show *could* go on.

AT 8:40, the orchestra struck up a jazzy version of "Ghost of a Chance." Raymond was humming the tune when Sid Salmon came in babbling. "Raymond, Raymond, what kind of madness is—I never thought you'd really—did you see the *people* out there?—Raymond, what have you done?"

"Relax," Raymond laughed. "Mama will be here, Sidney, no question about it."

Raymond left the dressing room shortly before nine. He went out on stage, in front of the single painted backdrop representing a star-filled universe. He took a quick house count and wished he hadn't. Sid was right. There were a lot of people out there.

But he thought of Mama, concentrated on her goodness and felt confident again. He walked to stage center and lifted his eyes heavenward. On the other side of the closed curtain, the orchestra had stopped. The audience murmur died away.

Raymond said, "Okay, Mama. You're on." Nothing happened.

Raymond's heart went *balump*.

"Okay, Mama," he said. "Come down."

At 9:13, the audience buzz was audible again and, wisely, the orchestra began to play once more.

By 9:30, Raymond's face was drenched. "Mama!" he pleaded. "Don't do this to me, Mama. You promised. You said you'd take care of me!"

At 9:42, the crowd began to stamp in unison, a threat to the fixtures. The theater manager rushed out to Raymond and said, "Do something, will you *do* something? Raise the curtain at least!"

Ready to listen to any advice, Raymond nodded dumbly. The curtain was lifted. When the audience saw him, they hooted but quieted down—hopefully. He lifted his arms and said, "Ladies and gentlemen, if you'll please be patient—"

It was the wrong opener. The rhythmic stamping began again, out of step with the orchestra's feeble version of "Got a Date with an Angel." Minutes later, the first flying object hit the starry backdrop. It was an orange-drink container—filled. It was followed by half a dozen more and Raymond, for his own protection, was hustled into the wings by the stagehands. The theater manager screamed for the curtain. Its lowering only infuriated the audience more.

"Mama, Mama!" Raymond wept. "How could you do this to me?" At 10 o'clock, the manager made a timid appearance from behind the curtain and delivered a short speech about an immediate refund at the box office. It started a stampede out front in which six people were trampled.

Raymond, of course, owned nothing. He was in debt some $20,000, mainly to The Friend, whose emissaries had been in the front row watching the investment.

Raymond managed to leave the theater without being stopped. He got back to the hotel room and shut the door on the world. In the bathroom, he looked into the mirror and said, "Mama, how could you? Only tell me that. How could you do it?"

He opened his suitcase and found his Army .45 under his pajamas. He checked to see if it was loaded. It was. Not everything would go wrong tonight.

He sat down, drank half a glass of whiskey and then made a mental recapitulation of his troubles. That convinced him. He put the gun to his temple and squeezed the trigger. At that very moment, he saw his mother sitting on the sofa opposite, an interested observer.

The gun went off.

"Now," his mother said with a contented smile. *"Now,* Raymond, I can really take care of you."

Murder by Scalping

S. S. Rafferty

PAST: TENSE

What more fitting for this Bicentennial Year than a story from the pre-Revolutionary era of our nation? A story with a locked-room murder, a new and fresh McGuffin, a period background impeccably researched, a nice approximation of the rhythms of authentic colonial speech, and in Captain Cork, perhaps (unless we count one of James Fenimore Cooper's characters) America's earliest fictional sleuth. S. S. Rafferty is the pen name of an ebullient Irish-American transplanted from his native New England to the crumbling purlieus of New York City. He has been a professional publicist and a lifelong amateur historian whose specialty is those halcyon days when the United States did not stretch from sea to shining sea, but merely gleamed in the collective eye of thirteen lusty British colonies along our eastern seaboard. - J.G.

IT WAS the first time in my remembrance that Captain Cork and I were abroad in these Colonies without it costing him money for expenses, food, and travel. Squire Norman Delaney had written several times, urging a visit to his "ranch," as he called it, in the Rhode Island Colony.

Cork accepted Delaney's bidding because he loves good food and a chance to talk to an expert in any field. The Squire was a jocose Irishman with a plump wife and seven brawny sons who operated the ranch. This gave the Squire the leisure he required for the gentlemanly arts, with time left over for such minor municipal duties as keeping the peace between the Indians beyond the tree line and the frontier farmers.

The last about Indian affairs reminds me that I have forgotten to mention Tunxis, which is not easy to do. Tunxis is a tamed Quinnipiac, whose main employment is to serve as the Captain's shadow, even when the sun is not out. He goes everywhere with us. On the few occasions he has spoken to me, it has been in perfect English, but he is always jabbering away to Cork in aborigine. This usually leaves me in the dark about many matters, but I have learned to live with it. Just as I have learned to accept the fact that Tunxis will not sleep indoors at any time and that he takes a daily swim, even in mid-winter, which is a sight to shiver your liver. Needless to say, Tunxis was also a guest at Delaney's ranch-an outdoor guest by choice.

It was our third evening of relaxation at the ranch. We had supped well on a delicious bear's paw sauced in cranberries, and had settled in for a cozy October night's conversation with pipes and bowl and glasses of *usquebaugh*, a Scotch-Irish corn liquor as potent as the Captain's own concoction, Apple Knock. I sat back and listened to these two fertile minds run the gamut of politics, enterprise, soldiering, women, and finally, as with all stout hearts well warmed by liquor, of philosophy.

"It is well to talk of good and evil," the Squire said, trickling the smoke from aside his clay stem, "but it's another thing to control it. Take crime, for example. Much of it in these Colonies is undetectable. I wouldn't hazard to guess how many culprits have committed foul deeds along this frontier and had them entered in life's ledger as accidents—people lost on the trail or taken by Indians. What stands in the criminal's way in these rude climes, I ask you, sir?"

"I do," Cork said. And he said it without pride or prejudice. "If all of us do in theory, some of us must do in practice."

I was thinking "practice and no profit" when Madame Delaney entered the parlour and announced a Mr. Goodman Stemple. It was prophetic that the discussion of the theory of crime should be interrupted by the reality of it. Stemple was a split rail of a man, made all the coarser by his buckskins and moccasins. But his back-country appearance was belied by his educated speech. Although he was obviously agitated, he had himself under control, and addressed himself to the Squire. His tone was cool, but his tale was horrifying.

"It's a scalping, Squire, right in my own home—my own future son-in-law. There's talk among the trappers and frontier folk about raising a punitive expedition against the Tedodas, and I'm afraid the talk is getting out of hand."

I must say I admired Delaney's ability to sustain a shock and to rebound from it in a logical state. Indian uprisings were considered a thing of the past in these parts, a dark, bloody thing long forgotten.

"Let's have the details," the Squire said, bidding Stemple to a chair. He first introduced the Captain and myself, and the flicker in the frontiersman's eyes at Cork's name was an unspoken awareness of my employer's reputation.

As it turned out, Goodman Stemple was no light under a bushel in his own right. He was the owner of Stemple's Redoubt, a prosperous trading post that serviced upcountry trappers and farmers in barter, or truck, as it is called.

Although the Redoubt flourished and Stemple's family grew, his children were all female. Eight daughters and not one son. It was this dilemma that had led to the scalping.

Stemple's eldest daughter, Faith, was, at 18, beyond average marrying age, but her father had steadfastly refused offers for her hand from local farmers and woodsmen. Since he was without a male heir and was likely to remain so, he wanted his affairs to pass to a son-in-law of some brainpower.

His wishes seemed hopeless, however, until the arrival of Donald Greenspawn, the son of a distant cousin who had settled and fared well in the Maryland Colony. Greenspawn brought with him a letter from his father, which explained in vague terms that the young man had gotten into a bit of trouble in the South, and that a new start in the North was advisable.

As Stemple saw it, one father's misfortune was another's gain, for Stemple planned to marry off Faith to the newcomer. The trader admitted to us that Greenspawn indeed had some faults. Like many of his kind, he was a dandy, with a superior attitude which did not sit well with Stemple's customers, but Stemple felt that time would temper the situation.

In the two months that Greenspawn had been at the Redoubt, there had been several problems with the Tedoda tribe, whose medicine man, Shellon, had accused the Southerner of short-counting pelts. This Stemple ignored, since he too had had run-ins with Shellon from time to time.

With this background, the trader brought us to the night of the tragedy, which proved to be more mysterious than we first had suspected. Greenspawn had been killed and scalped in a closed room, and the only person who could have done it was Faith Stemple herself —or an Indian who could walk through walls. Either conclusion was patently ridiculous, but no other was in the offing.

Just two days before his death, Greenspawn had agreed to take Faith in marriage. As is the custom, a period of courtship was begun, which, of course, included bundling. Now I must interpolate here that bundling is often misunderstood at home in England. Lascivious minds might smirk at the idea of an unmarried couple sharing a bed, with only a wide wooden board between them. However, the custom is quite practical and innocent.

Since the couples are occupied at chores all day, there is left only nightfall for private conversation. Cabins on the frontier usually have only one fireplace, in the main room, and that is reserved for the parents. Small children are tucked into unheated attics, and the only place left for an affianced couple was an unheated side room. Thus, on these cold winter nights, it was logical to send Faith and Greenspawn to bundle, fully clothed and protected from temptation by the bundling board and by Providence.

On the eve of the tragedy, the trader went on, a certain Vicar Johnson was visiting the Stemples and was asked to spend the night before continuing his journey north. He accepted, and was bedded down in the main room on a pallet just outside the room where Faith and Greenspawn had bundled. The Vicar, it so happened, was stricken with gumboils, and, unable to sleep, spent the night reading a volume of Cotton Mather's sermons by the light of the dying embers in the fireplace. This good man of the cloth could answer that no one entered or left the side room all night save Faith and Donald.

"And yet, by Moses, gentlemen, when my daughter woke, there was Donald Greenspawn dead in his side of the bed, his head stove in, and his scalp gone." Stemple's composure failed as he spoke, and Delaney quickly poured another *usquebaugh* and bid him to quaff it. "Thank you, sir," he said, tossing it back to his gullet. "There he was, all bloody pated and covered with gold dust."

"Gold dust!" Cork sprang from his chair.

"Yes, Captain, gold dust. All over his chest, the bed, and across the floor to the north wall. It was as if some spirit from the nether world had entered, done the foul deed, then left a trail of lucre behind him. It could only have been Indian magic, I swear. My little Faith would not harm a flea, much less scalp the man she was betrothed to."

"Astounding, eh, Cork?" the Squire said, relighting his pipe. "What passes for astounding is often merely curious."

"You parry in the adjectival, Captain. If it's Indian trouble, I don't like it."

THE COMFORTABLE APPOINTMENTS of the Delaney domicile were but a memory after twelve hours in the saddle. From long before sunup to almost dusk we had ridden through a panorama of this American country. We had left the beach and pushed inland, past well plotted farms and villages and beyond into rude woods pocked with oasis-like clearings where hearty tillers of soil had thrown down the gauntlet to Nature.

As our journey had progressed, the woods thickened, the trails thinned, and I bad the ominous feeling that I was riding closer and closer to the unknown. Finally, we broke through a cluster of elms to find ourselves in touch again with humankind. Ahead was the Redoubt, enclosed by a 12-foot-high stockade. Over its huge gate was a weather-worn, hand-painted sign that read:

STEMPLE'S
GOODS AND WARES
FOR CASH OR TRUCK
THAT WILL ANSWER

WITHIN THE MAIN enclosure was a large building and several smaller ones, all of log and mud-chinking construction. The large building, which served as Stemple's home, was a one-and-a-half-story house with a sloped roof wing attached. The wing was windowless, and I assumed it was behind these solid walls where Donald Greenspawn had met his Maker.

As we rode into the enclosure of the stockade, we saw a cluster of thirty or forty men milling around one of the outbuildings which served as the trading post. They were woodsmen and farmers, all armed to the teeth with steel muskets and powder horns. The sight of Squire Delaney brought them forward as we dismounted.

"It was the militia you shoulda brung, Squire," said one of them, a bearded man with a tomahawk at his belt. "Them Tedodas don't need a talkin' to, just a good lickin'." His statement brought grunts of approval from the group.

"Let's not get a lather up before we see what the trouble is, Delly Tremont, and that goes for the lot of you." The Squire continued with his chiding which was proving to be a fine piece of diplomacy, when I noticed Cork disappear through the door of the main house. Withdrawing from the group as inconspicuously as I could, I followed him and entered what was the main room of the Stemple abode.

It was not unlike the rooms in other backwoods cabins. To the left there was a dining board, and to the right several chairs were scattered near the fire. Two women sat holding each other's hands, while a man read to them from the Good Book. I had no trouble deducing that these were Goodwife Stemple, her daughter Faith, and the Vicar Johnson, although the latter startled me. I had expected a wizened old clergyman, infirm from gumboils, and yet here was a strikingly handsome youth no more than two or three years out of Divinity School. Goodwife Stemple's head was bowed at the holy words, but Faith looked straight into the Vicar's face, as if drawing warmth from his aesthetic countenance.

An open door to the far right led us into the murder chamber, where Cork became busy examining the body, and Tunxis prowled around on all fours, like a bloodhound.

The sight of Donald Greenspawn in death was not pleasant. But even had he been lying there alive and unwounded, I would have been taken aback.

Where Stemple had led us, or at least me, to believe that Greenspawn was a lad, such was not the case. Despite his disfiguration,

I could see that he was a grown man in his late thirties. His body, now rigid in death, had in life been dissipated and flaccid.

While I stood mutely in the background, Cork directed his attention to the gold dust on the earthen floor. He fingered it for a few seconds and then said something to Tunxis in aborigine. The Indian nodded and left the room. I swear by heaven I am going to learn Indian talk one of these days and surprise the two of them. But Indian talk or not, I had some suspicions of my own.

"Perhaps we had better examine someone to see if he really has gumboils," I said slyly to the Captain.

"Excellent idea, Oaks," he responded. "Perhaps I could get the Vicar to sing us a psalm or two while you peek into his mouth."

I knew he was jibbing me, but I let it pass. I thought at the moment that he was a bit ruffled that his own yeoman had so quickly come to the heart of the matter.

Cork left the bundling chamber and strode across the main room without stopping, until he was outside the house. And as always, I was right behind him.

The Squire's early diplomacy was eroding into anger as he held off the verbal attacks of the countrymen. The mob quieted, however, as Cork walked into its midst. Most groups do, because a six-foot-six giant with a grandee's barba and a plumed Cavalier's hat always commands attention.

"Goodman Stemple," he asked the trader in a loud voice, "who among these gathered here has ever asked for your daughter's hand?"

There were groans and a giggle or two from the group. "Practically every man Jack of them, Captain. Jeb Howard there, and his brother Pete, Win Goulding and Tappins here. Just about everyone, even old Delly Tremont." As Stemple pointed to the bearded man, hoots were heard from the rest. Tremont did not like it and gripped his musket as if to menace one and all.

"Seems to be you're all turned mighty merry when we got murderin' Injuns about," he said.

"You are right, Mr. Tremont," said the Captain. "This is no time for jollity. You look like a man who knows his way with the redman, Tremont."

"He should," Stemple said. "That's how he got his name. Lived with the Delawares for five years, didn't you, Delly? Best trapper in these parts."

The bearded man relaxed a bit under the flattery and Cork went on, "The Delawares! Well, my compliments, sir. You learned a great deal along that great river's banks, did you not? I'll wager you are quite a fisherman, Tremont."

It all happened so quickly that it still boggles my mind to reconstruct the scene. As Cork talked, I didn't notice Tremont's trigger finger, but as he swung to fire on the Captain, Tunxis's knife smashed into Tremont's chest, deflecting the muzzle blast to the ground. I later estimated that the Indian had hit his target from at least twenty feet away.

"TREMONT'S METHOD was obvious from the first," Cork told us later that day as Goodwife Stemple served us a piping-hot corn pudding and generous cups of hard cider. "He was enraged at the thought of being spurned by Faith, and sought vengeance on Greenspawn."

"But such an elaborate plan for a crude backwoodsman!"

"I don't think it was a plan, Squire. It was luck and everyone's ignorance that brought the Indian scalping into it. Tremont lurked about that night, and when all was quiet, he removed some of the dry mud chinking from between the logs of the north wall. It could easily be replaced and be dry by morning. Using an arrow attached to a tag line, he killed his victim as the Delawares catch fish, harpoon fashion.

"But when he tugged his line to retrieve the arrow from Greenspawn's head, he found he had caught more than death. You see, a close examination of Greenspawn showed me that this vain man was somewhat bald, and wore a wig piece, as is fashionable on the Continent. When the arrow was retrieved, the wig came with it, hence, the look of a scalping."

"And the gold dust, Captain?" Stemple asked.

"I suggest that you examine your strongbox, Stemple. I think you'll find that your coins have been cleverly shaved since Greenspawn's arrival. And what better place to hide his ill-gotten gains than in the lining of a wig nobody even suspected he wore."

We All Have to Go

ELIZABETH A. LYNN

FUTURE SHOCK

Nothing gives us more pleasure than reading a good piece of work by a promising new writer, and Elizabeth Lynn's "We All Have to Go" is just that —and then some. Among other things, it is a suspense tale told with feeling and efficacy, an in-depth character study, and a wholly chilling and plausible extrapolation of what might be in store for the television viewer of tomorrow. Ms. Lynn lives in San Francisco, where she is currently devoting her full time to writing mystery and science fiction. You'll be reading more of her work soon: we guarantee it. - B.P.

EIGHT A.M. FRIDAY, September 4, 1998, Chicago: Jordan Granelli sat at his desk, reading the Corpse Roster. High above the street, on the two hundredth floor of Daley Tower, he escaped the noise of city sirens and chatter of voices: here there was only rustling paper and the click of computers, and a blue, silent sky.

He read the printouts slowly and carefully, making little piles on the desk top. On Sheridan Road, in the heart of the Gold Coast, there was a crippled girl whose rich family bankrupted itself to keep her alive; she died at four this morning. On Kedzie, the hard-working mother of three just died of DDT poisoning... Good, heartbreaking stories. In Evanston, a widower's only son was just killed swinging on a monorail pylon, ten last night... He frowned and tossed that one aside. They'd done a dead child Tuesday.

He flipped back, pulled a sheet out of the pile, and buzzed for a messenger.

NOON, on a Friday in Chicago: it's 1:00 in New York, 11:00 in Denver, 10:00 in Los Angeles. In L.A. the housewives turn off their vacuums and turn on the TVs, and the secretaries in San Francisco and in Denver take their morning half-hour breaks in a crowded lounge. In New York, clerks and tellers and factory workers take a late lunch, and the men in the bars, checking their watches, order one last quick one.

And in Chicago, the entire city settles into appreciative stillness. On lunch counters and in restaurants, up on the beams of rising buildings jutting through dust clouds and smog, like Babel, even inside the ghastly painted cheerfulness of hospitals, mental homes, and morgues, TV sets glow.

JORDAN GRANELLI LOOKED out at them all through the camera. "It is a sad thing," he said, his voice graceful and deep, "when the very young are called. Who of us has not, would not, mourn for the death of a child? But it is doubly sad when young and old join in mourning for one they loved, and miss. Today, my friends, we talk with Ms. Emily Maddy, who has lost her only daughter, Jennifer. Jennifer was a woman in her prime, with three young children of her own, and now they and her own mother have lost her."

The camera swung slowly around a shack-like house, and stopped at the face of a bent, tired woman looking dully up at Jordan Granelli. "The kids don't understand it yet," she said. "They think she's coming back. I wish it had been me. It should have been me."

A WOMAN in a factory in Atlanta rubs her eyes. "She looks like my mother. I'm voting my money to her."

"Look at that hole she's living in!" comments a city planner in San Diego, watching the miniature Japanese set on his secretary's desk. "Mary and I just bought our voting card last week. I wonder if we'll get to see the kids?"

A man on a road construction crew in Cleveland says: "I'm voting for her."

"You said Tuesday you were gonna vote for the guy whose son was killed by the fire engine," his neighbor reminds him.

"Well, this old lady needs *it* more; she's got those kids to look after."

On their big wall screen in Chicago, the network executives watch the woman's tears with pleasure.

"That son-of-a-bitch sure knows how to play it," says a vice-president. "I'm damned if I know why no one ever thought of it before. It's a great gimmick, death. He'll top last week's ratings."

"Shh!" says his boss. "I want to hear what he says."

The woman's sobs were at last quieting. She bent her head away from the bright lights, and they touched the white streaks in her hair with silver. One shaky hand shaded her eyes. Jordan Granelli took hold of the other with tender insistence. The camera moved in closer; the button mike on Granelli's collar caught each meticulous word, and resonated it out to eighty million people.

"Let your grief happen," he said softly. It was one of his favorite remarks. "Ms. Maddy, you've told us that your daughter was a good person."

"Yes," said her mother, "oh, yes, she was. Good with the kids, and always laughing and sunny—"

"There's nothing to be ashamed of in tears for youth and grace and goodness. In all your pain, remember—" he paused histrionically, and she looked up at him as if he might, indeed, comfort her, with his precisely rounded sentences, "—remember, my friends, that we are all in debt, and we pay it with our sorrow. Ms. Maddy, there are millions of people feeling for you at this very moment. We live by chance, and Dame Fortune, who smiles on us today, cuts the thread of our lives tomorrow. Mourn for those you love—for you may not mourn for yourself—and think kindly of those that death has left behind. In life—we are in death—and we all have to go."

Poetic, smooth, Christy Holland thought. She moved her camera closer in, catching his craggy expressive hand holding the old woman's, the dirty, dark furniture, the crinkled photograph of the dead daughter on the table, the stains on the floor—*push that poverty, girl, it brings in the money every time*—and, as the light booms drew back, the play of moving shadows across white hair. *That ought to do it.*

The sound crew had cut out at Granelli's final echoing syllable. She cut out and stepped back; simultaneously, Leo, the set director, standing to her left, sliced his long fingers through the air. The crew relaxed.

Granelli stood briskly up, dropping the old woman's hand. He brushed some dirt off his trousers and walked towards the door. As he passed Christy he inclined his head: "Thank you, Ms. Holland."

She ignored his thanks. She would have turned her back, except that would have been too pointedly rude, and even she, his chief camerawoman, could not be rude with impunity to Jordan Granelli. One word from him and the network would break her down to children's shows. She concentrated on storing her camera in its case. Her arms ached. Ms. Maddy, she saw, was looking after Granelli as if he had left a hole in the air.

Zenan, the second cameraman, strolled over to her from his leaning place against the wall. She smelled the alcohol on his breath. He stayed drunk most of the time now.

"You okay?" she asked him.

"Another day, another death, right, Chris?" he said.

"Shut up, Zen."

"Tell me, Christy, how much do you think the great-hearted American public will pay the lady for her sterling performance? Friday's death has an edge, they say, on the ones at the beginning of the week. If ten million people vote a dollar a week, take away the network cut, and Mr. Granelli's handsome salary, and what you and I need to pay our bills—hell, I was never very good at arithmetic at school. But it's a lot of money. Weep your heart out for Mr. Death, and win a million!" he proclaimed.

"Zen, for pity's sake!" She could see Jake leaning toward them from his post near the door, listening.

"For pity's sake?" Zen repeated. He looked down at her from his greater height. "Here I am, a sodden voice crying in the wilderness, crying that when Jordan Granelli walks, on the dark nights when the moon is full, the deathlight shines around him!"

And Jake was there, one big hand holding Zenan's arm. "Come on, Zen, come outside."

Christy watched them go. *Have I really only been doing this for two years?*

She lugged her case over to Willy, manager of Stores. "See you Monday," he said cheerily. He'd been there eight years, longer than anybody. Nothing seemed to touch him.

She ducked out of the house to get a breath of air. Granelli's limousine, pearl-white with a black crest on the side, sat parked at the curb. Around the house, in a big semicircle, kept back by a line of police, a crowd had gathered to watch.

Jake came around the corner. "What'd you do with Zenan?" she asked him.

"Locked him in the crew trailer with Gus," Jake said. He looked worried. "Christy, you a friend of Zenan's? Tell him to shut up about Mr. Granelli. If he starts upsetting people, Mr. Granelli won't like it, and the network won't either."

"I don't know what he has to complain about—Zenan, I mean," Christy said. "Any TV show that gets eighty million people watching it every day can't be wrong."

He started to answer, and then the car motor rumbled and he ran for his seat, riding shotgun next to Cary, who drove. Stew sat in the back next to Jordan Granelli. *Does he ever talk to them?* Christy wondered. *Does he know that Jake used to be a skyhook, and Cary paints old houses for fun? Or are they merely pieces of furniture for him—part of the landscape-conveniences bought for him by the grateful network, like the cameras, and the car?*

Leo came walking out of the house as the white car pulled away. "Another week gone," he said.

"Jake stuck Zenan in the crew trailer," Christy said.

Leo wiped his big hand across his eyes and shrugged. "I don't want to deal with it," he said. "I think I'll just go home. It's Friday. Want to walk to the subway?"

"I'd love to."

"Good. I'll tell Gus to go without us." He strolled down the sidewalk to the crew trailer and leaned his head in to talk to the driver.

They walked down Kedzie Street to Lake, and turned east. The sun was hot; Chris felt her shirt starting to stick to her back. She hummed. The show was behind her now, and with all her will she would forget it;

today was Friday, and she was going home, home to two days with Paul. Leo's head was down, as if he were counting the cracks in the broken pavement. He looked tired and bothered. Maybe he was worried about Zenan.

He surprised her. "Do you ever think about Dacca?"

I never forget it, she thought.

Once she had tried to tell Paul about it, what it had been like for her, for them all, that summer in Bangladesh. For him it was barely remembered history: he had been fourteen. He had stopped her after five minutes, because of what it did to her eyes and mouth and hands. *But Leo remembers it just the way I do.*

Scenes unreeled in the back of her mind. Babies, crawling over one another on slimy floors, dying as they crawled, and bodies like skeletons with grotesque, distended bellies, piled along dirt roads; the skitter of rats in the gutters like the drift of falling leaves, and flies, numerous as grains of rice—and no rice. No food. The Famine Year: it had killed fifty million people in Bangladesh. And she and Leo had met there, on the network news team in Dacca. "I remember it. I dream about it sometimes."

He nodded. "Me, too. Thirteen years, and I still have nightmares. The gods like irony, Christy. When I came home, I *asked* for daytime TV, asked to work on soap operas and children's shows and giveaways. And here I am working for Jordan Granelli." He stopped. "I sound like Zenan, don't I? I know why he drinks. We're the modem equivalent of a Roman circus. Under the poetry and Granelli's decorum, the viewers can smell the blood—and they love it. It titillates them, being so close to it, and safe. Death is something that happens to other people. And when it happens—call an ambulance! Call a hospital! Tell the family gently. And bring the camera close, so we can watch. We all have to go."

"I have Paul," Christy said. "What do you do, Leo?"

"I take long walks," he said. "I read a lot of history. I try to figure out how long it will take us to run ourselves into the ground—like Babylon, and Tyre, and Nineveh, and Rome."

"Are we close?"

"I own a very unreliable crystal ball."

They had reached the subway line. Christy could feel beneath her feet the secret march of trains. "See you Monday," she said.

As she went down the stairs, Christy looked with curiosity at the people around her. Was there really such a thing as a mass mind? The faces bobbing by her—some content, some discontented, thin, fat, calm or harried, bored, or excited—what would they do, each of them, if she were to collapse at their owners' feet? Observe, in an interested circle? Ignore it? *Call the police or an ambulance, maybe; the professionals, who know how to deal with death. Death is something that happens to other people. All we, the survivors, have to do is mourn.*

She was riding on the city's main subway line. It ran from south to north, passing beneath the city's vital parts—City Hall, the business district, the towering apartment complexes of the rich, the university—like a notochord. East of it lay Lake Michigan, with its algae and seaweed beds, like green islands in a blue sea. West of it the bulk of the city sprawled, primitive and indolent in the summer heat, a lolling dinosaur.

And Paul was out there, high in the smoggy sky, a mite on the dinosaur's back. She'd first seen him through a camera's eye. She'd been shooting a documentary on new city buildings, six years back. He had been walking the beams of a building sixty stories up, dark against the sun, his hair blazing gold, his hooks swinging on his belt. She had asked one of the soundmen: "What are those hooks they carry?"

"Those are the skyhooks. They're protection. See the network of cables on the frame?" Through the lens she could see it, like a spiderweb in the sun. "If a worker up there falls, he can use those hooks to catch the cable and save himself. Experienced workers use the cables to get around. They swing on them, like monkeys, hand over hand. The hooks don't slip, and the cables are rough—they fit like two gears meshing." He made a gear with the interlocking fingers of his two hands.

"I thought the name for the *people* was skyhooks," she said.

"It is."

Human beings, she thought, *with hooks to hold down the sky...*

SHE OPENED the door to the apartment. Paul was sitting in a chair, waiting for her.

He jumped up and came to her across the room, fitting his hands against her backbone and his lips to hers with the precision of anticipation. His lips were salt-rimmed from a morning's sweating in the sun. She leaned into him. At last she tugged on his ears to free her mouth. "Nice you're home. How come?"

"Monday's Labor Day. Dale gave us the afternoon off. Said to get an early start on drinking, so we'd all get to work on Tuesday sober."

"That was smart of her." Dale was the crew boss on the building.

"So we have three and a half days!"

"No," she said sadly, "only two and a half."

"Why?" He pulled away.

"The show doesn't stop for Labor Day. Think of all those lucky folks who'll be home to watch it! Makes more money. Christmas, New Year's, yes. Labor Day, no."

He grunted, and came back to her arms abruptly. "Then let's go to bed *now*."

CHRISTY WOKE from the drowse first. Paul's head lay against her breasts. The camera eye inside her came alive: she saw him curled like a great baby against her, chunky and strong and satiated, his skin dark red-bronze where the sun had darkened it, fairer elsewhere, his hair red-gold... *How brown I am against him,* she thought. A thin beard rose rough on his cheeks and chin, his chest was hairless, well-muscled, his hands work-calloused...

He stirred, and opened his eyes. "What do you see?" he asked her.

"I see my love. What do *you* see?"

"I see *my* love."

"Thin brown woman."

"Beautiful woman."

It was an old ritual between them, six years old. It amazed Christy that, in their transient world, they had survived six years together. *I love you,* she thought at him.

Suddenly, as if someone had spliced it into her mind, she saw Jordan Granelli, holding the hand of Ms. Maddy. Angrily she thrust the show from her mind. Like a shadow on a wall it crept back at her.

"What is it?" Paul said.

"Ah. Come with me to work Monday," she said suddenly.

"Why?"

"So I can see you sooner." *So I can hold you in front of the shadow,* she thought, *like a bright and burnished shield.* "Please."

"I will," he said.

THEY WOKE LATE MONDAY MORNING. It was hard to dress at the same time: they kept running into one another on the way to the bathroom. Paul shaved, standing naked in front of the mirror. When he pulled on his pants, he stuck his skyhook sheaths on his belt, like a badge of office, and thrust the hooks into them.

Christy glared at him. "You are coming with me."

"I said so. But I want to make sure that nobody asks me to do *anything.* I won't look like a cameraman in these."

That's for sure, Christy thought. He looked like an extra from a movie set. She suspected, with envy, that he was going to visit his building, later, just for the fun of swinging around it. *Wish I could love my job like that.*

They were late to the studio. The equipment van, which carried the cameras and the lights, the cable wheels and the trailing sound booms, was parked outside on the roadway, its red lights flashing. The crew trailer sat behind it. Christy and Paul stepped up into it. "Sorry we're late," she said to Leo.

"Hello, Paul," Leo said. "O.K., Gus. Let's go."

Gus played race-car driver all the way to the South Side, flinging them happily against the sides of the van like peas in a can. He stopped at last. Jordan Granelli's limousine was parked up the street. He was standing outside it, his three guards around him.

Jake walked across the street to them as they came out of the trailer. "Mr. Granelli's getting impatient," he said. Leo shrugged. Jake looked at them uncertainly. He eyed Paul.

Christy said, "Jake, this is Paul, he's a friend of mine. Paul, this is Jake. He's one of Jordan Granelli's bodyguards."

They nodded at each other. "Skyhook," Jake said. "So was I."

Paul was interested. "Were you? Where'd you work?"

"Lots of buildings. Last year I was working on the new City Trust when a swinging beam bit me—so." He made a horizontal cut with the edge of his hand against his right side. "Knocked me off. I hooked the cable—but it cracked some ribs, and my back's been bad ever since. I had to quit."

"Tough luck," said Paul sympathetically.

They waited. Christy shivered suddenly. Paul put an arm around her shoulders. "Cold?"

"No—I don't know," she answered, irritated.

"Goose walking on your grave," commented Jake.

The equipment van finally came screeching round the comer. The driver pulled it up past them, and then backed with a roar of the engine. Paul caught Christy's arm. The doors of the van, jarred by the forceful jerky halt, came flying open, and something black came careening out.

For Christy the events resolved suddenly to a series of stills. She sprawled where a thrust of Paul's arm bad put her. The cable spool bounded high in the air, as it hit a projection in the ill-paved road. The thick cable unwound like a whip cracking. Paul seemed to leap to meet it. She heard the sound as it struck him, saw him fall—and saw the wheel roll past him, stringing cable out behind it, to hit the curb, where it shattered, and sat. Cable uncoiled like a snake around the jigsaw wreckage of wood.

She stood up slowly. Her palms and arms and knees and chin hurt, and the taste of gravel stung her lips. She walked to Paul. It took her a long time to reach him, and when she did her knees gave out, so that she sat thudding on the ground.

The cable had lashed him down; there was a black and purple bruise across his right cheek. His eyes were open but unseeing. She interposed her face between his eyes and the sky. Nothing changed. In one hand, his fingers clenched a skyhook. *He tried to hook the cable,* she thought. She touched his hand. The fingers lolled loose. The hook rolled free with a clatter. She reached for it and used it like a cane, to pry herself up off the street.

Leo came round in front of her, hiding Paul from her. He took hold of her shoulders. "Come away, Christy," he said. "We've called the ambulance."

"He doesn't need one," she said. "And I don't either." They circled her: Leo, Zenan, Jake, Gus.

"Christy," said another voice, a stranger's. The circle broke apart. Jordan Granelli extended his fine hands to her. "Christy, I'm so sorry."

"Yes," she said.

He stepped up to her and took her hand. "Don't be afraid to mourn for him, child," he said. "I know what grief is. We all do. Chance takes us all, and gives nothing back. There's no way to make the weight any lighter. We feel for you." He stepped back, spreading his arms in supplication and sympathy. Christy felt the first tears thicken in her eyes. She stared at him through their distorting film.

Behind his back, in macabre mime, Zenan cranked an ancient imaginary camera. From a distance came the high keening of the ambulance.

Granelli turned his back on her as one of the sound men approached him. The man asked him something, pointing at the loose cable. She heard his answer clearly.

"Of course we'll shoot!" he said. "Get someone to help you move that thing back. And wipe it clean first."

Leo turned, his face whitened with anger. Jake looked shocked.

"Mr. Granelli," Christy whispered, to herself, to Paul. "Mr. Death, who only happens to other people." She walked toward him. *Not this time, Reaper,* she thought.

The metal skyhook was cold and hard and heavy in her palm. She swung it: back, forth, back, forth—and up.

The Little Old Lady of Cricket Creek

Len Gray

TWIST ENDING I

The true twist-ending story depends for its effect on the same sort of misdirection a magician practices: our eye is distracted by a sudden movement, noise, or line of patter, so the vital and ultimately baffling bit of stage business can be worked unseen. Caveat lector—let the reader beware. Even though we were watching him like a hawk, Len Gray somehow made a switch which caught your editors totally by surprise. This is made even more embarrassing by the fact that it was the author's first published fiction when it originally appeared. Len Gray is the pseudonym of a prolific young Southern California writer who teaches college English, literature, and writing in the Los Angeles area, and who regularly reviews mysteries for a large-circulation daily newspaper. - J.G.

ART BOWEN and I were trying to analyze performance evaluations when Penny Thorpe, my secretary, walked into the office.

"Yeah, Penny. What's up?"

"Mr. Cummings, there's a woman out in the lobby. She's applying for the file clerk's job." Penny walked over and laid the application form on my desk.

"Good, good. I sure hope she's not one of those high school dropouts we've been getting—" I stopped, staring at the form. "Age fifty-five!" I roared. "What the hell are we running around here? A playground for Whistler's mother?"

Art put his Roman nose in it. "Now, Ralph, let's take it easy. Maybe the old gal's a good worker. We can't kick 'em out of the building just because they've been around a few years. How's the app?" Good old Art. The peacemaker. With about as much sense as a lost Cub Scout.

"Well," I said doubtfully, "it says her name is Mabel Jumpstone. That's right. Jumpstone. Good experience. Seems qualified. *If* she checks out. You game for an interview?"

"Sure. Why not? Let's do one together," which is against the company policy of Great Riveroak Insurance Company. All personnel interviewers are to conduct separate interviews and make individual decisions—at least that's what we're supposed to do. Usually we double up and save time.

Penny remained standing in front of my desk, tapping her pencil on the glass top. "Well?" she asked haughtily, which sums up her disposition perfectly.

"Okay, Penny. Send Mrs. Jumpstone in."

She came shuffling into the office, smiling and nodding her head like an old gray mare. Her black outfit looked like pre-World War I. She had on a purple hat with pink plastic flowers around the brim. She reminded me of Ida Crabtree, my housekeeper, whose one passion in life is running over stray cats in her yellow Packard.

She sat down in the wooden chair and said, "Hello there!" Her voice was almost a bellow.

I looked at Art who was leaning forward in his chair, his mouth open, his eyes round.

"Uh…Mrs. Jumpstone," I began.

"Mabel. Please."

"Okay, Mabel. This is Mr. Bowen, my associate." I waved a hand at Art, who mumbled something inappropriate.

"This is a very interesting application, Mabel. It says here you were born in Cricket Creek, California."

"That's right, young man. Home of John and Mary Jackson." She smiled at me, proud of the information.

Art bent over, scratching his wrist. "John and Mary Jackson?"

"Oh, yes," she replied, "the gladiola growers."

He tried to smile. I'll give him credit. "The—the—oh, yes, of course. It must have slipped my mind. Let me see that application, Ralph." He grabbed it from the desk and took a few minutes to study it thoroughly.

Mabel and I sat and watched each other. Every once in a while she'd wink. I tried looking at the ceiling.

Art glanced up and snapped, "You worked at Upstate California Insurance for ten years. Why did you quit?" Sharp-thinking Art. He made a career of trying to catch people off guard. I'd never see him do it yet.

Mabel shrugged her tiny shoulders. "Young man, have you ever lived up north? It's another world. Cold and foggy. I just had to leave. I told Harry—that's my husband who passed away recently, God rest his soul—that we had to come down here. Mr. Bowen, you wouldn't believe how much I enjoy the sun. Of course, you've never been in Cricket Creek," she added, which was true, of course. I doubted very much if Art had even *heard* of Cricket Creek.

Art looked as if he wanted to hide. Mabel smiled brightly at him, nodding pleasantly.

"Mabel," I said, "the job we have open entails keeping our personnel files up to date. Quite a bit of work, you know, in an office this size."

"Really?"

"Really. Even requires a bit of typing. You *can* type?"

"Oh, heavens, yes. Would you like me to take a test?"

"Uh...yes, that might be a good idea. Let's go find a typewriter. Coming, Art?"

He grinned. "Wouldn't miss it for the world."

We walked out of the office. Art whispered in my ear, "Maybe ten words a minute would be my guess."

It turned out to be more like ninety. I handed Mabel one of our surveys on employee retention and told her to have a go at it. She handled the typewriter like a machine gun. The carriage kept clicking back and forth so fast that Art almost got himself a sore neck watching the keys fly.

Our applicant handed me three pages. I couldn't find a single error. Art looked over each page as if he were examining the paper for fingerprints. He finally gave up, shaking his head.

Mabel went back to my office. Art and I walked over to a comer, Art holding the typed sheets.

"Well, what do you think?" he asked.

"She's the best typist in the building. Without a doubt."

"She's different. But you're right. Check her references."

"And if they check out?"

He shrugged. "Let's hire ourselves a little old lady from Cricket Creek."

ART POKED his head in my door the next day. "What about our type-writer whiz?"

"I just called her. Application checked out perfectly."

He laughed. "I bet she raises a few eyebrows," which wasn't a bad prediction at all.

Within two months, Mabel Jumpstone was the most popular employee in the building. Anytime someone had a birthday she brought in a cake and served it during the afternoon break. She never failed to make announcements over the company P.A. system when she learned about new benefits. People with problems started coming to Mabel. She arrived early each morning and stayed late. She never missed a day of work. Not one.

SIX MONTHS after we hired her, Art walked slowly into my office. His eyes were glassy and his mouth was slack. He plunked down heavily in a chair.

"What's the matter with you?" I asked.

"The cash mail," he groaned. We receive quite a lot of cash from our customers. Once a week, on Friday, we take it to the bank. It was Friday.

"What about the cash mail, Art? Come on, what's the matter?"

He looked at me, his eyes blinking. "Harvey was taking it to the bank. He called ten minutes ago. He was robbed. Conked. Knocked out. And guess who did it?"

"Who?"

"Mabel. Mabel Jumpstone. Our little old lady."

"You're kidding. You've got to be *kidding,* Art."

He shook his head. "Harvey said she wanted a lift to the bank. After they got going, she took a pistol out of her handbag and told him to pull over. Harvey said it looked like a cannon. The gun, I mean. He just woke up. The money and Harvey's car are gone. So's Mabel."

I stared at him. "I can't believe it!"

"It's true. Every word. What are we going to do?"

I snapped my fingers. "The application! Come on."

We ran to the file cabinets and opened the one labeled *Employees*.

The application was gone, of course. There was a single sheet inside her manila folder. It was typed very neatly. "*I resign. Sincerely yours, Mabel.*" The name had been typed, too. There was no handwritten signature. Mabel had never written anything. She always insisted on everything being typed.

Art stared at me. "Do you remember anything on the application? Anything? The references?" He was pleading.

"For Pete's sake, Art, it was six months ago!" I paused for a moment. "I can remember *one* thing. Just one."

"What?"

"She came from Cricket Creek. I wonder if there *is* a Cricket Creek?"

We checked.

There wasn't.

I FINALLY GOT HOME to my two-bedroom bachelor apartment late that evening. The police had been sympathetic. Real nice to us. They didn't even laugh when we told them they were after a little old lady of 55. They asked for a photograph or a sample of handwriting.

We didn't have either.

I opened a can of beer and then walked into one of the bedrooms.

Mabel was sitting on the bed, neatly counting the $78,000 into two separate piles.

I looked at her, smiled, and said, "Hi, Mom."

You Can Get Used to Anything

Anthony Boucher

THE "WHODUNIT"

When Tony Boucher passed away in 1968, at the age of fifty-seven, the world lost a true Renaissance Man. He was a constructive and incisive book reviewer, a fine writer, a creative editor and anthologist, an expert on the mystery and fantasy/science fiction genres, a dedicated opera lover and critic-and a great deal more, including a friend and an inspiration to the two of us personally and to dozens of other writers. Part of his legacy to us all is his fiction, of which most is quite well known; but there are a few short stories that over the years have surprisingly remained unanthologized. "You Can Get Used to Anything" is one of these—an atypical Boucher story in that it is tough and not a little gory, and yet a typical one, too, because it is the kind of "whodunit" he did so well and because it is so painstakingly plotted and written. We're proud and pleased to present it here. - B.P.

IT's hard to tell where to start this story. I could start it back in Iowa with the Wythe murder, if a common death by shooting is interesting enough. I could start it with Hagar, and the way her stubby fingers twitched when she thought of a killer. Or I could start it much further on, with the Pasadena police when they discovered that you can cut the head off a corpse, but you can't necessarily fit it back on.

But I think it's best to start in with Alonzo. It all revolves around Alonzo. Hagar and Willis and me…the whole picture would never have come into focus if it hadn't been for Alonzo and his profession.

They say you can get used to anything. Aunt Martha used to say, "You can get used to hanging if you hang long enough." I wouldn't know about that, though Willis might have. But I do know you can get used to a hangman.

At first there wasn't any telling Alonzo from the other retired Iowans playing checkers and horseshoes in the Arroyo. He chewed cigars like the rest of them; he had the same paunch and the same bald-ness. He played a fair game of checkers and a better than average game of horseshoes. And like the others, on a hot day he took off his coat and sat around in a shirt with a collar and tie and suspenders, which was to indicate that even though he was a voluntary exile from Iowa, he still hadn't given in to Southern California.

I used to wear a tie myself when I went down to the Arroyo. I fit in better that way. Maybe it seems a funny place for me to want to fit in—a bunch of men a generation ahead of me living out their retired lives with huffs and ringers.

But to retire you have to have money. That's sort of in the nature of things. And that makes a city like Pasadena, where being retired is a major occupation, a logical place for a man like me. Because when you have money you always want it to be a little more, and a gilt-edged proposition for doubling it in six months looks mighty attractive.

That's how I met Alonzo—on what you might call a scouting expe-dition down to the checker tables. I was soothing down a retired banker from Waterloo, explaining to him how a flock of new government regu-lations was hampering the quick return he'd expected, when I first heard Alonzo.

"It's a shame," he was saying, loud and sort of petulant, "it's a shame and a disgrace to the nation."

At first, I thought it was more of the straight damn-the-White House talk I was used to around there, like what my retired banker was giving me now. (He was willing to believe anything about government regulations.) Alonzo said something about "the American Way" and I almost stopped listening; I know that speech.

But then he said, "Only eleven states left, unless you count Utah, and you can't hardly do that. Only eleven states still following the American Way."

This sounded like a new approach. I listened while I kept telling my banker how right he was.

"California held out a long time," Alonzo went on, "but what've you got now? Murder, that's what you've got; plain cold-blooded legal murder. What does the Constitution say? I'll tell you what the Constitution says. The Constitution says..." He paused and held his breath. He let it out slowly, and then said, with a pause between every pair of words: "*Cruel and unusual punishments shall not be inflicted.* That's what the Constitution says."

Alonzo made pretty much of a speech of it. Even my banker began listening and pretty soon there was a little crowd around him. He had all the facts: Twenty-two states where they fry you in the chair, eight where they use the lethal gas chamber, six (and this seemed to hurt Alonzo the worst) where they don't even kill you at all.

I kind of liked Utah. There they give you a choice. You can select whether you want to get shot or hanged. And all the time that law's been in force, nobody's picked hanging yet.

That really got Alonzo. "What kind of murderers is that?" he argued. "Afraid to die the good old American Way? And what kind of legislators pass laws like that?"

Somebody said something about Communists, and somebody else said the only trouble with them was hanging'd be too good for them, and the conversation began to get away from Alonzo.

It's always a good time to hit a man, just when the conversation's getting away from him; so I slipped up next to Alonzo and listened to him for as long as he wanted to talk.

Finally, I said, "Just what makes you so hot about this, Mr. Fuss?" (We'd exchanged names by then.) "Sounds like maybe you had some kind of personal angle on it."

"Well," Alonzo said, "I guess for me it is kind of talking shop, like. You see, son... Well, there's no use being modest about it. I was the best darned hangman the state of Iowa ever had."

You know how you get ideas. You think of a hangman as gaunt and grisly, like the Thing that comes for Mr. Punch. And you sit in the hot Pasadena sunlight and you look at this plump little man with the white collar on the blue shirt and the sweat stains under the armpits, and he grins at you and says he's a retired hangman.

You think a hangman must be grisly in his mind too, like a war criminal or a mass murderer. And you sit and listen to him and the voice goes on flat and colorless and it's just another retired businessman talking shop, and his big executions have about as much thrill to them as a retired dentist's account of his trickiest impacted wisdom tooth.

It was a job and he worked at it. He took a certain pride in it; he was a craftsman. He wasn't just a hangman; he was the best darned hangman in Iowa history. But the fact that he'd killed people...

"Everybody kills a murderer," Alonzo said. "You elect the attorney that convicts him and the judge that sentences him. You pay for the detectives that track him down and the rope that hangs him. Why son, I haven't killed a man any more than you have."

I smiled at that one. It was certainly one way to put it. But it wasn't the way Hagar looked at it.

I met Hagar at a dinner party. The dinner was intended as another scouting expedition; but I didn't think about that much after I sat down next to Hagar.

Maybe you've read some of her stuff. Hagar Dix is the full name. Factual murder stories—not the true-detective kind of stuff, but pretty subtle probings into murderers and what makes them tick. I'd read some and liked them—I've got a certain interest in murder. And I guess I'd thought of her as one of these admirable research workers—the women that think in straight lines and wear their clothes the same way.

I was wrong. Hagar had straight lines strictly in the right places only. She had a face that should've been ugly, and black eyes looked out at you and you didn't see the face. You didn't see much else around you and you didn't taste your food; and you tried to decide whether you hated this woman or... Well, or not. And you could underline that *not*.

I don't talk much about the Wythe case. My connection with the Wythes wasn't one of my more triumphant episodes. Herman got some ideas about that Trans-Con bond issue that were as unfair and unjustified as they were accurate: and I kind of preferred to forget the whole episode.

But this night I wanted to make a pitch with Hagar; and murder being her business, you might say, I sort of offhand said I'd known a convicted murderer.

It was then I first noticed her hands. Her legs were long, her neck was high and slim; but her hands were the shortest and stubbiest I've ever seen. The three segments of her fingers added up to the length of the first two on most hands. They were strong, those stubs; and now the brief forefingers made sharp staccato stabs at the tablecloth, while the little fingers arched and twitched.

"You've known...a murderer?" It was a deeper voice than she'd used before, and yet it had the tone of a bobbysoxer addressing Frankie's valet.

But the fact that I'd exchanged maybe twenty sentences with Willis Wythe wasn't quite enough to keep her keyed up for long. Her fingers knocked off and rested, and she said, "I've never known a murderer. With all my work. Oh, I've talked to them through jail bars, I've seen them in court. I've met men who were acquitted...but always justly, I'm sure. If only once..." She turned the eyes on me, and I almost said something I'd've been sorry for.

But the girl on my other side wanted the salt, and when I turned back, Hagar asked me if I'd been to the Community Theater lately.

It was a few hours and a lot of drinks later that I was standing with Hagar on the balcony overlooking the Arroyo.

The white sand in the moonlight looked like bleached bones and I said so—which is not the sort of remark I usually make to girls on balconies, but there is no accounting for what happens to a man with Hagar.

One stubby finger twitched slightly. "Death..." Hagar said. "Death is the only power..." Then she faced me abruptly and announced, "I'm a fake."

I said, "So?" which seemed as plausible an answer as any.

"I write books. I pretend to try to explain why people commit murders. But I know that. You know that. It's only being human to know that. What I don't know is the other thing. Why *don't* people commit murders? Why are there so few? What is there about killers that makes them...I don't know...*free* from whatever hampers all the rest of us?"

It was looking down at the Arroyo that gave me the idea "I know a killer," I said slowly. "He's killed forty-nine men. You can meet him tomorrow."

The balcony rail throbbed under Hagar's twitching tattoo.

YOU DIDN'T REGULARLY SEE anything like Hagar around the checker tables. But her presence didn't seem to bother Alonzo any. Things didn't bother him much.

I'd got to know him pretty well the past few weeks. We kind of liked each other, I guess. And I knew most of his stories, and I couldn't share Hagar's excitement when he told about how the Mad Butcher of Clover Hill started singing a hymn just before the trap sprang, or how Mrs. Leroux (whose baby farm was a sort of after-the-fact method of birth control) went stark raving mad on the trap. It was hard to get excited about them anyway, the drab matter-of-fact way he told them. But Hagar sat there with her black eyes fixed on him, and the checkerboard next to us jumped with the thumps of her fingers.

"But I did have one...I guess you might call it a failure," Alonzo confessed. "Young Willis Wythe... Danged trap went down one inch, and then stuck. Left him standing there with no more damage than you'd suffer from a tight collar. So they take him off. I go to work and oil the trap and test it. Works fine. They put him back on and what do you know? Danged trap sticks again. Three times it happens—never did find out what was wrong."

"I remember," Hagar said softly. "The Governor commuted his sentence...then later pardoned him because the women's organizations made such a to-do."

"He was guilty," I said.

Hagar looked at me hastily as though she'd forgotten I was there. "That's right...you knew the Wythes." Then back to Alonzo, "And that was your one failure, Mr. Fuss?"

"Dang it," said Alonzo. "It was fine for him—pardoned and everything. But somehow I never have felt quite right about that."

He sounded a little guilty, like a doctor who'd lost a prize patient from causes he couldn't explain.

It was just then that my retired banker tapped me on the shoulder and I withdrew.

I didn't see either Alonzo or Hagar again for a year. My banker had been talking to his lawyer and to some stuffed shirt calling himself an Investment Counselor. I didn't much care for the shortsighted ideas they'd been planting in his mind, and it looked like a good notion to stay away from Pasadena for a while.

So it was in a Nebraska paper that I read about the marriage. *Hagar*

Dix, 35, it read, *noted criminologist, and Alonzo Fuss, 63, retired professional man.*

I spoke out loud in the hotel lobby. "This," I said, "I gotta see."

I WASN'T TAKING any chances on meeting my banker. I went to Alonzo's home. It was on North Orange Grove, which isn't South Orange Grove, but is still a pretty comfortable neighborhood. The house looked like it'd been done over recently, and I guessed Hagar was sinking her criminological income into this latest research.

They were glad to see me. There was a lot of talk about how I brought them together and wasn't it fate and stuff. The talk was more on Alonzo's level than on Hagar's.

Alonzo had changed. I thought in my mind that he looked haggard and then I thought what a lousy pun that was and then I thought pun hell! it's the exact truth. I never did understand just how the marriage was arranged. Hagar never talked about it, and I doubt if Alonzo understood himself. How much does a male spider understand?

Hagar? She looked a little...I don't know...richer, maybe. Fuller. She could listen to Alonzo now and her fingers stayed still. I couldn't figure if that was good or bad.

I learned after Alonzo went to bed. "I'm a man that needs his eight hours," he said, "and I've got a championship horseshoe match on in the morning."

Hagar and I looked at each other while his footsteps echoed off. I said, "Well? Did it work?"

Hagar said, "What do you think?"

I said, "I think it did at first and now it doesn't. Change your ideas about killing?"

Hagar said, "No. Just my ideas about Alonzo."

I said, "Because he isn't a killer after all, is he? He's just a poor old guy whose job happened to involve death. And maybe if you met Jack the Ripper, his shop talk wouldn't be so hot either."

Hagar said nothing.

I stood up for the next speech. I said, "Maybe you've been wrong all down the line. Maybe you ought to give a try to—"

She didn't let me finish. She said, "I met a man. Oh, not quite by chance. Let's say by premeditated coincidence..." Her fingers twitched on their imaginary drum. "You'll stay for the weekend, of course?"

"I could, I guess. Do you think I'd find it...rewarding?"

"I'm sure you would. This man is coming. I want you...but then you know him already, don't you?"

"Who is he?"

"Alonzo's one failure... Willis Wythe."

I REMEMBERED Willis Wythe as a towheaded kid who was sore at his uncle—pretty much like any other kid you ever knew, except Uncle doesn't usually wind up with three bullets from the kid's target pistol. (The Governor decided it was all purely circumstantial evidence when the pressure was turned on him for the pardon.)

I wouldn't have known this hard, dark man with the lined face and the edgy, bitter voice. But I liked him, and when he talked about the things he'd done in the past years (I guess he was what the Sunday supplements call an Adventurer) I even began to think of angles where maybe we might work together.

We got through Friday night somehow, but even then I was glad I wasn't Willis. There wasn't a moment in the evening when either Alonzo or Hagar wasn't looking at him, and they were looks that there aren't words for in any books I know.

What Hagar meant you can figure by now. Here is a man who has murdered and escaped. He knows. And he isn't sixty-three with a potbelly.

Alonzo's was harder to define. It was a kind of worry. It was like a writer staring at a paragraph that stinks and wondering how the hell to revise.

Willis didn't understand that look. For once there wasn't a word said about Alonzo's former profession; and Willis probably hadn't even seen him on the one occasion their paths had crossed before. For Willis this was just a weekend with an interesting woman and a dull husband, and he was an Adventurer.

I had a little trouble getting to sleep that night. That's how I heard the slippered footsteps and the bedroom doors.

Even Alonzo must have noticed the difference in Hagar the next morning. This richness, fullness that I was talking about—it was like it was coming to its final intensity.

I had one chance to speak to Hagar alone. I said, "So now you think you know?" and my mouth twisted as I said it.

Hagar said, "Not yet. Not *quite* yet..." and Willis came in and we talked about old acquaintances back in Iowa.

That was Saturday, and Saturday night Willis and Hagar went dancing at the Hotel Green.

Alonzo said, "I'm not much of a hand at dancing. Good for her to go out with somebody nearer her own age." And he meant it, the poor guy, and I sat there and played checkers with him and wondered why I was sticking around.

I was just figuring that it was, in a way, just a standard method of mine in my other line—if things look headed for a crack-up, stick around; there's no telling what a smart man may pick up out of the wreck—when Alonzo looked up from the checkerboard and said, "It's Willis that's come between Hagar and me."

I didn't say anything about slippers and doors. Instead I laughed and said, "They've only just met. You must think he's a pretty fast worker."

"It isn't that." He let that denial ride flat for three moves. Then he added, "Failure. You see, Hagar...I'm no kind of a man to be married to her. You know that, son. But she thought I was...I don't know...kind of powerful, I guess, on account of what I'd... But you see, I wasn't, because..."

It was the first time I'd ever heard Alonzo talk about anything emotional, and he couldn't make it. His phrases wouldn't come straight. He just said "Willis" a couple more times, and once he said, "One hundred percent..."

After the game he sat there until his regular bedtime, just staring at the brand-new radio-phonograph. I couldn't think why until after he'd gone to bed. Then I remembered. I'd been around when it was delivered the day before. It came in a hell of a big packing case, all bound round with good strong rope.

I WAITED for Willis in his bedroom. He didn't like it when he came in and found me there. We could both hear Hagar moving around in the next room. Her fingers drummed on the objects she passed.

Willis said, "Bedroom vigils yet? What gives?"

I said, "Do you know who your host is?"

"I hear he tosses a mean horseshoe."

So I told him. "And he's worried," I added. "You're the...well, the blot on an otherwise stainless life, you might say. It's kind of a reproach to Alonzo Fuss that you're walking around here alive."

His lean face was tauter than ever. "I'm getting out of here," he said. We were both silent, and we listened to Hagar's fingers. His lips softened and he added, "Tomorrow."

"It isn't worth it," I said. "Staying, I mean. I only warned you because...hell, I feel I owe you something."

He was hard again. "Owe me what?"

"I was out of the state at the time of your trial. I wasn't even reading newspapers. But I maybe could've cleared you and I didn't. You see, I know Alonzo Fuss's record *is* clear. He didn't need to hang you—you were innocent."

He loomed over me. "You could have cleared me? And you didn't?" His heavy fist was balled.

"We're even," I said. "I'm giving you your life now. Get out...before Alonzo's ideas go too far."

His voice was getting high and sharp. "How could you have cleared me? Why didn't you?"

I started to tell him how and why. It was then he jumped me. His taut face twisted into curious shapes. His hard lips mouthed ugly words, rising higher and higher.

WHEN I LEFT the silent room, Hagar was waiting for me in the hall. She was in a nightgown that looked as if you'd save it for a bridal night. She put her black eyes on me and said, "I heard a little of it... What happened?"

I told her, just the way I've told it above.

I never saw a face do what hers did then. It went blank. Dead blank. Even the eyes...their blackness seemed to go away. There was nothing on the face, nothing at all.

And that emptiness was the most terrible thing I have ever seen.

ALONZO WAS the first one up the next morning. He was on his way off to the horseshoes by the time I got down to breakfast. I was on my third cup of coffee and the second section of the *Times* when Hagar came in.

She said, "Have you seen that rope around anywhere?"

"What rope?"

"From the packing case. I thought I'd use part of it to tie up a parcel of books."

"No, I haven't seen it."

She took the first section of the *Times* with her coffee. She was wonderfully relaxed this morning—calm literally to her fingertips. It was a domestic sort of scene—coffee and newspapers and silence. I liked it.

It was an hour before I began wondering about Willis. Hagar seemed unperturbed when I mentioned him. I wasn't really perturbed myself until I got no answer to my knock and walked on into his room.

First it was the smell. The day was building to a scorcher and the blood permeated the air. A window was open, and word of the blood had gotten about among the neighborhood's flies.

I took some fast gulps out the open window before I went near the bed. I don't know why I touched him. I didn't have to know he felt cold on that hot day.

Most men do when their heads are missing.

LIEUTENANT FURMAN HAD LARYNGITIS. His voice never rose above a whisper all the time he questioned us.

They were shrewd, economical questions. It wasn't long before he had a pretty thorough diagram of the three of us and our relations to that headless corpse upstairs. It wasn't long before he had the cleaver, too. It had been neatly washed, but he spotted the minute stains and knew what the laboratory analysis would do with them.

"You're intelligent people," Lieutenant Furman whispered. "I can talk to you."

Alonzo looked at him with vacant old eyes. Hagar was still cool and poised, still in her casual how-tragic-but-after-all-we-barely-knew-the-man attitude.

"You're something of a criminologist yourself, Mrs. Fuss," he whispered. "And death's no stranger to you, Mr. Fuss." He turned to me as though wondering how to continue the parallel.

"I've been around," I said helpfully.

"Exactly," he breathed. "So you all understand that the key to an understanding of this crime lies in the removal of the head. The commonest reason—preventing identification—can hardly apply here; the man's fingerprints are on file in Iowa. There'd be no hope of, let us say, ringing in a substitute body if he himself wished to disappear."

Hagar observed coolly, "Clearly, Lieutenant, you are trying to erect logic on an illogical basis. What can you 'deduce' from the act of a wandering madman?"

The Lieutenant shrugged. "I do not doubt," he murmured, "that we will be hearing about that 'wandering madman' from the defense. But in the meantime—with all deference to your knowledge of crime, Mrs. Fuss—let us be honest with each other. In all likelihood, we must assume—"

It was just then that the Sergeant came in with something wrapped in bloody newspapers. "Found it just west of here, Lieutenant. Halfway down the slope of the Arroyo. Also found this." His other hand held a length of rope, such as comes around packing cases.

"You will excuse me," said the Lieutenant's confidential voice. He rose, took the package from the Sergeant, and hastened upstairs. The Sergeant stood there in the doorway, looking from the rope in his hands to Alonzo and back again. Conversation did not flourish under the circumstances.

When the Lieutenant returned, his voice came as near as possible to breaking the whispered monotony of his speech. It all but rose to excitement as he announced, "I have made a most interesting discovery. This will fascinate you as a student of murder, Mrs. Fuss." He paused. I've never seen a man in authority yet that didn't have a touch of ham in him. He held the pause, and finally said, "I have discovered that the head and the body do not fit."

I jumped. Hagar rose slowly to her feet. Alonzo stared at the rope in the Sergeant's hands.

"Does this mean, Lieutenant," said Hagar, "that there is some fraud after all, some confusion?"

"No fraud, Mrs. Fuss." The whisper was eager. "A little confusion, yes. But I'm sure you can think it through." He went on slowly, "They don't fit. Because there is only a body, and a head. How could they fit?"

I hated the man. He was enjoying this scene. But Hagar went calmly on, "Don't they usually? Heads and bodies? Isn't it the accepted thing?"

"Not quite. You see, Mrs. Fuss, most use a neck to connect them."

He let that one sink in. I tried to think fast. The neck was missing. The cleaver had been used twice. The Sergeant began drawing the rope through his fingers.

"Why?" came the whispered question. "The neck has been removed. Perhaps chopped in smaller pieces and...disposed of. But why? Surely there is one reason—because the neck would betray the murderer. Because something about that neck would prove the method of killing and point the directly accusing finger. Because..." Lieutenant Furman held his pause again. Then he whirled, carried away by his own words, and pointed the directly accusing finger. "Because the neck would prove that the corpse *was hanged!*"

On the last words his voice, for one instant, reached normal volume.

The effect was deafening.

Alonzo rose slowly to his feet. He still looked past the directly accusing finger at the rope. His voice was hardly louder than the Lieutenant's as he said, "One hundred percent..."

He said nothing else as they took him away.

WE WERE ALONE in the house now, Hagar and I. The stretcher had gone, and so had the wagon. The lawyer had been telephoned, the plans had been laid for the insanity defense. Suddenly there was nothing but an empty, hot day ahead.

It was the first time that we had ever been completely alone. I looked at Hagar as though I had never seen her before. As indeed I hadn't. Not this Hagar. Not this ripe, complete, fulfilled woman, with serene black eyes and passive fingers.

I said, "You did it all, you know."

Hagar bowed her head gracefully. She said, "I know. It was cruel to bring them together. To make Alonzo face what he called his 'failure.' I might have foreseen... But I had to *know*."

"And now you know?"

"More than you can dream."

"Not more than I can guess."

"Guessing is nothing. *Nothing*."

"I said you did it. That's more than guessing."

She looked at me without expression. "Am I to blame? Any more than you are to blame for introducing me to Alonzo? Every meeting starts ripples—some place those ripples intersect at murder. This was only more...direct than usual."

"I said you did it. Not caused it."

She said nothing, but her eyes became interested. Nothing more than that, but interested.

"The Lieutenant's a glib ham. His reasoning doesn't hold water for a second. Remove the neck to destroy the evidence of hanging? Nonsense. All removing the neck does is call attention to the neck. Bring to mind the idea of murder by the neck. Suggest hanging, in fact.

"And the mere fact of hanging would be no direct personal proof. Sure, it would point to Alonzo. But only as a lead, not as proof. There'd be no sense to the neck gimmick unless it removed *proof,* unless the neck positively had to be destroyed because the neck itself was irrefutable proof of the killer's identity."

"How?" asked Hagar calmly. "It's next to impossible to get finger-prints from flesh."

"You're on the track," I said. "He was strangled, wasn't he? That's why the neck had to be destroyed. Because you can't get prints, but you can get the size and shape of the fingers. And *yours are unique.*"

Hagar glanced down at her incredibly blunt and stubby hands, still restful and twitchless. "You're a clever man," she said. "But there's no point in making a Thing of it, is there? Poor Alonzo is obviously mad. I hadn't counted on the shock's doing that. But since he is... He has to be put in a place anyway; is there any reason why he shouldn't carry...this along with him?"

"None," I said. Hagar smiled and rose. I stopped her. "Wait a minute, Hagar."

"Yes?"

I don't usually grope for words. I did a little now. "Hagar. Ever since I met you. That dinner. I've wondered."

"Wondered?"

"Whether I hate you or love you."

"And now you know?" There was a smile on her lips. I'd never noticed her lips much before. I'll swear they were never full like that, never so warm-looking.

"Now I know."

"You hate me, of course."

"No."

I moved toward her. She stood still.

I said, "You found what you were looking for. In its damnable way, it's made you a woman. The twitches are gone. You're real and warm."

She didn't avoid my touch. She didn't respond either. She said, "And why should I care what you think?"

I said, "Because I'm what you want. I've almost said it before. And then I'd think, 'No boy. You don't want her enough—not for that.' But now I know. I know a lot of things. I know *why* you killed Willis Wythe. Because you thought you'd found it with him, and then you learned he was innocent. Not a murderer. And you hated him because you had been fooled.

"But you're not fooled now, Hagar. Because I'm what you want. I'm the Wythe murderer."

The words were coming easier now. They came almost too fast as I rushed on, "Uncle Herman was onto a racket of mine. It was too dangerous. I used the kid's gun—it was lying around the house—and cleared out fast. I worried some when he was convicted. But hell, a man's got to look out for himself. That's what I told Willis last night. That's why he jumped me, why I had to knock him out and leave him there where you found him.

"I'm it, Baby. I'm your thing, I've carried it in me all these years and now—"

Almost imperceptibly, Hagar moved away from me. She stood very straight and her body touched my arm, but it was cold and unyielding.

She said, "You're what I wanted. Past tense. I was a fool. I thought I could know through a man. I never thought, I never knew..."

The black eyes rested on me with something like pity.

"Goodbye," she said.

WHEN I ANSWERED THE DOORBELL, I found Lieutenant Furman. He said, "The alienists are working the old man over." His voice was normal now, and I guessed the whisper was a part of the whole ham set-up. "I've come back," he added, "for the murderer."

I deadpanned. "I thought you proved from the neck, Lieutenant—"

"Snap judgment," he said. "Sometimes it gets results. But once I thought it over...Look: All that removing the neck does is to call attention to the neck. It'd be worth doing only if some vital positive clue..."

I let him go on. It was my speech almost word for word, and I had to admit I'd underrated the guy.

When he was through, I said, "You'll find her in there. And no complications this time. I'm admitting that the prints on her neck are mine."

THEY ARGUED over me for a while, the sovereign states of California and Iowa. Finally, they decided that California had the stronger case if I should go and retract my confessions, and who trusts a murderer?

That was too bad in a way. It meant the cyanide chamber. Alonzo wouldn't have approved at all.

Miser's Gold

Ellery Queen

RATIOCINATION

I will surprise no one with the revelation that Ellery Queen is a pen name for the lifelong collaboration between Frederic Dannay and the late Manfred B. Lee. But it is surprisingly difficult to find something fresh and meaningful to say about this remarkable team. So I will only remark that the Edgar awarded to my "Goodbye, Pops" owes as much to Mr. Dannay's editorial suggestions, in his capacity as editor-in-chief of Ellery Queen's Mystery Magazine, as it does to my original conception. And I will add that Ellery Queen as editor has done more for the mystery story than anyone since Poe, and that Ellery Queen as writer has created brilliant puzzles and sparkling gems of ratiocination which are far more honestly mystifying than any of the Sherlock Holmes tales which first attracted Dannay and Lee to the mystery field. - J.G.

IT IS doubtful if the master who created Baghdad-on-the-Subway ever produced a more wonderful entertainment than the tale of Uncle Malachi. The atmosphere is rich and twisted, the subject likewise, and the story full of sentiment and irony. It even has a surprise ending.

Uncle Malachi was born, he lived, and he died under the rusty shadows of the Third Avenue "El." Because he was a pawnbroker and owned the rickety, peeling old building in which he worked and lived, he was said to be Wealthy. Because he was an old crosspatch who distrusted banks and lived like a mouse, he was said to be a Miser. And since his one notable passion was the collecting of books—not rare books, or first editions, or books in perfect condition, but any books in any condition—he was said to be Queer.

It was all true—he was rich, he was a miser, and he was queer; but there was more to it than that. His riches came from selling real estate —Manhattan real estate—which his great-grandfather had bought; he was a miser, because all pawnbrokers are born accumulators; and his queerness lay not in collecting books, but in reading them.

Books swarmed like honeybees over his pawnshop and living quarters upstairs, which consisted of two impossibly cluttered cubbyholes. Here under jackets of dust could be found the collected works of such as Dumas, Scott, Cooper, Dickens, Poe, Stevenson, Kipling, Conrad, Twain, O. Henry, Doyle, Wells, Jack London—wholesale reading in low-cost lots; and Malachi devoted every moment he could spare from his shop to peering through wavering gaslight at the written treasures of the world. As he aged and eyesight withered, the tempo of his reading increased; for old Malachi had set himself the fine labor of reading every famous book ever printed, beginning with the more exciting ones. A magnificent lunacy, which went with his spidery mind and mystifying sense of humor—he was always grinning, chuckling, or laughing, although no one ever knew what the joke was.

Uncle Malachi's clients were fond of saying that the old miser bad no heart, which was a slander. He had a heart—as Dr. Ben Bernard, whose shingle drooped two doors up the street, was prepared to testify —one of the worst hearts, Dr. Ben said, in his experience, a valvular monstrosity and black as the devil's. But Uncle Malachi only cackled. "You're a fool, Doctor!" Dr. Ben retorted with a sigh that if he were not a fool he would not be practicing medicine on Third Avenue, and he continued to treat the old pawnbroker as if his monthly bills were honored.

As for Eve Warren, she came into Uncle Malachi's life the way most people did. Eve was struggling to keep her little greeting-card shop and circulating library across the street from the hot clutch of her creditors, so she became one of Malachi's clients. When his eyes failed, she felt a stem duty; there were few enough book-lovers in the world. So she began dropping in on him after closing her shop, and she would read to him. At first he was suspicious; but when he saw that she was a fool like Dr. Ben, old Malachi grinned, and after that he would even offer her with antique ceremony a cup of strong hot water which he alleged was tea.

Uncle Malachi's black heart cut its last caper one evening while Eve was reading *Treasure Island* to him. She looked up from Black Dog's wound and Dr. Livesey's lancet to find the pawnbroker on the floor, his head between two heaps of books, eyes popping and face blue-twisted.

"Lawyer...witnesses...will..."

Frankie Pagluighi, who was serving his first clerkship in a Murray Hill law office, was holding forth on the stoop next door to a group of neighbors on the latest Supreme Court decision; Eve screamed to him what was wanted and raced up the street to Dr. Ben's. By the time she and the young doctor got back, Uncle Malachi's head was resting on a red buckram set of Richard Harding Davis and Attorney Pagluighi was kneeling by his side, writing frantically.

"...all my property, real and personal...including my hidden cash... equally between the only human beings...who have ever shown me Christian charity..."

Dr. Ben looked up at Eve and shook his head sadly. "...Eve Warren and Dr. Ben Bernard."

"Oh!" said Eve; and then she burst into tears.

Grocer Swendsen, Patrolman Pat Curlihy, and Joe Littman of the dry goods store signed as witnesses, and then Frankie Pagluighi bent over the gasping man and said loudly, "This hidden cash you specify. How much does it amount to?" Old Malachi worked his blue lips, but nothing came out. "Five thousand? Ten thousand?"

"Four million." He managed a whisper. "In ten-thousand-dollar bills."

"Million." The young lawyer swallowed. "Four *million*? Dollars? Where? Where is it? Where did you hide it? Mr. Malachi!"

Uncle Malachi tried to speak.

"Is it in this building?"

"Yes," said the old man in a suddenly clear voice. "Yes. It's in—"

But then he came to attention and looked far beyond them, and after a while Dr. Ben said he was dead.

ELLERY CAME into the case not only because puzzles were his caviar, but also because it was clear as an aspic that his two callers were hopelessly gone on each other. Love and buried treasure—who could resist such a dish?

"You're sure it's really $4,000,000 and not 400 figments of the old man's imagination, Dr. Bernard?"

But Dr. Ben reassured him. In the pawnshop safe had been found a ledger listing the serial numbers of the 10,000-dollar bills, which various banks had confirmed. And Eve said Uncle Malachi had often made slyly mysterious remarks to her about his "cache of cash"—he was fond of puns and tricks, she said—defying anyone to find it, even though he had hidden it "on the premises." And the fact was she and Dr. Ben had gone over the little building from basement to roof, inside and out, and had found nothing but cobwebs and vermin. It was not a total loss, Eve admitted with a blush, for they had become engaged while digging up the cellar, under the sponsorship of an indignant rat which had sent her howling into Dr. Ben's arms.

"Well, well, we'll see about this," said Ellery delightedly; and he went right back to Third Avenue with them.

SIXTEEN HOURS LATER, he sank into Uncle Malachi's only chair, a betas-seled red plush refugee from some Victorian town house, and nibbled his thumb. Eve perched disconsolately on Uncle Malachi's bed, and Dr. Ben sat on a pile of books, wedged between The Works of Bret Harte and The Complete Novels of Wilkie Collins. And the gas jet flamed and danced.

"It isn't as if," said Ellery about an hour later, "it isn't as if you could hide 400 banknotes in a...unless..."

"Unless he separated them. One here, one there," said Dr. Ben help-fully. "Four hundred different hiding places."

Eve shook her head. "No, Ben. From hints he dropped to me, I'm sure he put them in one place, in a roll."

"Hints," said Ellery. "Hints, Miss Warren?"

"Oh, I don't know—cryptic remarks. About clues and things—"

"Clues!"

"Clues," gasped Eve guiltily. "Oh, dear!"

"He left a *clue?*"

"Think, Eve!" implored Dr. Ben.

"It was right in this room. I was reading to him—"

"Reading what?" Ellery asked sharply.

"Something by Poe...oh, yes, *The Purloined Letter.* And Uncle Malachi laughed, and he said—"

"His exact words, if you can recall them!"

"He said: 'Clever rascal, that Dupin. The most obvious place, eh? Very good! Fact is, there's a clue to my hiding place, Evie, and it's in this very room—the clue, I mean, *not* the money.' And he held his sides laughing. 'In the most obvious place imaginable!' He laughed so hard I thought he'd have a heart attack."

"Clue in the most obvious place in this room... Books. He must have meant in one of these thousands of books. But which one!" Ellery stared at Eve. Then he sprang from the chair. "Puns and tricks, you'd said. Of course..." And he began hunting wildly among the mountains and valleys of books, toppling volumes like a landslide. "But he's *got* to be here... Why, Doctor. You're sitting on him!"

Dr. Ben leaped from the Uniform Edition on which he had been seated as if it had suddenly wiggled.

Ellery dropped to his knees, shuffling through the various books of the set. "Ah!" And he sat down on the floor with one of the volumes, clutching it like a roc's egg. First he explored the binding with the tip of his nose. Then he went through it page by page. Finally, he turned back to one of the front pages and read it to himself, mumbling.

When he looked up, Eve and Dr. Ben cried in one voice: "Well?"

"I'm going to ask some questions. Kindly refrain from hilarity and answer as if your future depended on it—which it does." Ellery consulted the page. "Is there a potted palm anywhere in or about the premises?"

"Potted palm?" said Dr. Ben feebly.

"No," said Eve, bewildered.

"No potted palm. How about a room with a skylight?"

"Skylight..."

"*No.*"

"In that art stuff downstairs—ceramics, statuettes, vases—do you recall any object in the shape of, or illustrated with the picture of a dog? A yellow dog?"

"Now there's a blue horse," began Dr. Ben, "with a chipped—"

"No, Mr. Queen!"

"Bows and arrows? Archery target? Picture or statue of an archer? Or a statue of Cupid? Or a door painted green?"

"Not one of those things, Mr. Queen!"

"Clocks," murmured Ellery, glancing again at the book.

"Say," said Dr. Ben. "Dozens of 'em!"

"And I've examined them all," said Ellery, "and none of them conceals the hoard. That being the case," and Ellery got to his feet, smiling, "and Uncle Malachi having been fond of his little joke, only one possibility remains. So that's where he stashed his treasure!"

CHALLENGE TO THE READER: *In which book was Malachi's clue, and how did it tell where he had hidden his money?*

"SWIPING A LEAF FROM MALACHI'S RULE-OF-THE-OBVIOUS," continued Ellery, "in which of these thousands of books could his clue be hidden? Well, what was the nature of his treasure? Four million dollars. Four million—book. And among these standard sets is the complete work of O. Henry. And one of O. Henry's most famous books is entitled...*The Four Million.*"

Ellery waved the volume. "I found nothing foreign in the book. Then the clue was in its contents. Obvious development: see Contents Page. And the titles of the various stories? 'Tobin's Palm'—so I asked about a potted palm. 'The Skylight Room'—but no skylight. 'Memoirs of a Yellow Dog'—no yellow dog. 'Mammon and the Archer'—'The Green Door'—'The Caliph-Cupid and the Clock': all fizzled. Only one other possibility among the stories, so that must be Malachi's clue to the hiding place of the cash. 'Between Rounds.'"

"'Between Rounds,'" said Dr. Ben, biting his nails. "How the deuce does that tell you anything? Malachi wasn't a prizefighter, or a—"

"But he was," smiled Ellery, "a punster and high priest of the obscurely obvious. Rounds... A round is anything that's circular or spherical in shape. What in a pawnshop—in any and every pawnshop! —is spherical, and large enough to conceal 400 banknotes?"

Eve gasped and ran to the front window. From its rusty arm, which pointed accusingly at the Third Avenue "El," hung the ancient emblem of Uncle Malachi's profession.

"If you'll please find me some tools, Doctor, we'll open those three gilt balls!"

The Girl Who Jumped in the River

Arthur Moore

MAN BITES DOG

Among the virtues of Art Moore's "The Girl Who Jumped in the River" is absolutely the best throwaway ending we've ever seen: a last paragraph that literally makes you blink. The story itself defies categorization and description—another virtue—and for that and other internal reasons, it qualifies as a genuine archetypal "man bites dog" tale (no pun intended). Mr. Moore is a full-time professional writer, and as such is a versatile practitioner of a variety of fiction and non-fiction types, including mysteries, Gothic suspense, Westerns, and magazine articles. He is also a past vice-president of the Southern California Chapter of MWA. - B.P.

It was after dark when I came along the Redding Bridge, going home from work. I was late. Usually I get out earlier, but if I had I wouldn't have met her. I only saw her because I was on the walkway right beside the railing.

She was on an iron crossbeam, just out of the water, and she was soaking wet. I figured she had tried to end it all and had got cold feet at the last minute. You see those things in the papers all the time. Anyway, it sure surprised me, seeing her. I got over the rail and down there in a second and grabbed her. There wasn't anybody around. A few cars passed, crossing the bridge as I hauled her over the railing, but nobody stopped.

When I had her safe, I said, "What'd you try that for?"

She glared at me like I had something to do with it. "I like swimming," she said with a lot of sarcasm. "What'd you think?"

So I shut up. I knew she hadn't gone in swimming. It was way too chilly for that.

My name is Ralph Callicut, and I work across the bridge at the Ender Hardware plant, which is a wholesale place. I don't have a car, so I walk back and forth across the bridge except when the weather is bad, then I take the bus.

Well, her teeth began to chatter, of course, because she was sopping and in a very bad way. I asked her where she lived, and she said in Minneapolis, which was a long way off, so I figured she meant she was a stranger in town.

What do you think? I ended up taking her to my apartment so she could get dry. By the time we got there she was a worse mess, hair all stringy and her disposition very edgy. I got the heater going; she shucked her clothes in the bedroom, put on my old bathrobe and stood in front of the beater with her clothes spread out to dry.

"Jeez, Ralph," she said, "can't you make this thing hotter?"

I said it only got so hot and that was it. It was, too. I had already told her my name. She said hers was Louise, and she was hungry. I said I could make her some soup, and she sighed like it would have to do.

She was looking at me very close. "I thought you were older."

"I'm twenty-three."

"Yeah? So am I. What d'you do?"

I told her I work for a hardware company. She wanted to know what I make, and I told her a hundred and four take-home every week, but with a chance of advancement.

She said, "Yeah?"

So I went in and fixed her the soup. I had already eaten at Joe's Place. While the soup was heating, she came in and looked around the kitchen. It is not big. I have a small pad; living room, bedroom and kitchen. The landlord is going to paint next year, he says.

She looked at the soup and the peanut butter on the shelves. "Is that all you eat, soup and peanut butter?"

"You want some? I got bread, too."

"No, thanks."

She had combed her hair a little. It was slightly curly with frizzy ends, a little darker than blonde. Her face was shiny and raw-looking, with lines because she was tired. With no makeup she was on the seedy side. I wondered if she had run off from a husband, but I didn't ask her. She had a snappy way of talking; she bit at you, sort of. I guessed she'd had a bad time, having to jump into the river and all.

Louise ate the soup. I made her some toast and she ate that too, even with peanut butter. She was hungrier than she thought. Then she smoked a cigarette and stared at me. "Don't you have any coffee?"

I said sure, and boiled some water and made instant

I wasn't used to having a girl around. I never did get married, and I don't have a steady girlfriend. Girls like me okay, but I'm not pushy, you know what I mean? When I ask them for a second date they usually say, "Oh gee, Ralph, why didn't you ask me sooner? I got something to do tonight." Like that.

While we bad coffee, Louise turned all her clothes over and let them dry on the other side. She smoked most of my pack and kept staring at me. I went into the bathroom once and combed my hair.

It was after eight o'clock when her shoes and clothes were all dry. They were pretty wrinkled, but she went into the bedroom and put them on. She was a very rumpled doll, but I didn't say so.

Then she told me she had a suitcase.

I asked, "Where?"

"It's at a guy's house. He's keeping it for me." "Where's the house?"

She told me. It was about a mile away. She wanted to go over and get it. She got up and said, "Why don't we go over and get it?"

I said, "OK," and we went. About halfway there I began to wonder why I was going with her, but I couldn't back out then.

We walked all the way and she found the house easy. It was a tall flat; we went in and up the stairs. She knocked at a door on the second floor. A guy opened it and frowned at her. He was about my size and had a pencil behind his ear.

She said, "I came for my bag, Charlie."

I was surprised, because he had it waiting for her right by the door. He just shoved it with his foot and she looked at me, so I stepped in and picked it up. Charlie stared at me too, but he didn't say anything at all, only I kind of thought he smiled a little bit. When I backed out, he slammed the door.

"He was just keeping it for me," Louise said as we went down to the street.

It was on my mind to ask her, "What next?" but she marched us right back to my pad like that was the only place to go. I didn't know what to say.

When we got inside, she went right into the bedroom and flopped on the bed. "Jeez, you made me walk the whole way. My feet're killing me."

I said, "You want to go to bed?" I guess I had ideas.

She looked at me then with a kind of funny stare. "Yeah, why don't you sleep on the couch, Ralph?"

So I said, "Sure, okay." Well, what the crackers—just for one night.

In the morning, instead of eating at Joe's again, I had to rush out for milk, eggs and some bacon. Louise said she liked bacon. "Get some marmalade too, Ralph."

While we were eating she asked me what my hours were and I told her, then I asked her, "What you going to do today?" I thought maybe she had someplace to go. "You going someplace?"

She said, "Nowhere. I guess I'll stay here."

I figured she had to think things over. I gave her a couple of bucks in case she needed to get something—you know. Then I slid out.

That night when I got off, I was sure surprised to see Louise coming across the bridge to meet me. It gave me a funny feeling having a sort of pretty girl interested in me. I guess I'm not a Don Juan or anything, really.

She was looking me over when we met. She said, "Don't slouch over that way, Ralph."

I said I wouldn't, and we walked back to the apartment. I hoped she had made dinner, but she hadn't. She said she thought we were going out somewhere, which was funny because I hadn't mentioned nothing. Anyhow, I took her to a beanery where they have pretty good stuff, but she didn't think too much of it. They used too much salt in everything, she said.

I asked her what she did all day, and she said she slept most of the time. "Except you can't sleep real good because of all that street racket under the window."

I said I was sorry.

When I turned on the TV set, she said, "How come you still got a black and white, huh?"

After a while I made some more coffee, and when it got late, I realized she was going to stay there that night, too.

So I slept on the couch again.

I THOUGHT a lot about it the next day, but when I got home that night the apartment was all changed around. Louise had gone out and bought new curtains and charged them to me at the neighborhood center where they know me. Also she got me a new pillow for the couch. "It's better for you than those two little ones."

She had a fifth of gin too, and a couple of boxes of cookies. Later, when I saw the bottle, it was down by half and the cookies were all gone.

The next time she came across the bridge to meet me after work, she said the stores were still open, and that she really needed a new dress because she only had one. So I took her shopping. She bought a dress, pantyhose, a pair of shoes and some underwear.

"I'll get the rest later," she said.

On the way back to the bridge she noticed Manny's Hofbrau Cafe, which is a kind of ritzy spot in the little park at the end of the bridge.

I had never been there. Louise said it looked a lot better than the beanery.

Dinner cost me eleven bucks; just the dinner alone. Her martinis cost a buck eighty.

That really started me thinking.

I am sort of an easygoing guy, not pushy at all. I've never been pushy with dames. But by this time, I was beginning to figure that if I was letting her sleep in my bed, with me on the old lumpy couch, and buying her expensive dinners and gin and cigarettes and clothes, especially underwear, that maybe I ought to have something going *my* way.

You know what I mean? It occurs to a guy. Things like that, they occur to a guy.

So, later on, when we got home and she was in the bed and I was on the old, lumpy couch-well, I got up and went into the bedroom.

Louise turned over and said, "Hey, what you doing in here?"

"I thought...er...it seemed to me—"

"Hey, Ralph, you just knock off with those ideas."

"But...b-but—"

"No buts. We don't hardly know each other."

So I went back to the couch and thought about that. It was sort of true. Only it did seem to me that we could speed up the learning.

I KEPT on thinking about it. In the morning I got up and made both breakfasts, then thought about it all the way to work. At lunch time I had to borrow a buck because I had given Louise all my dough.

When I got home, she was watching TV. She had bought another bottle of gin and more cookies. After I cooked dinner and was washing up, I asked her about the gin and she bit at me again, so I didn't say nothing more. The house was in a kind of mess, so I mopped and dusted a little and she complained that I was making her sneeze.

She said, "Why don't you do that on Saturdays?"

I said, "*You* could do a little something..."

She looked at me and snapped, "Hey, we're not married, Ralph." Yeah. That was true, all right.

THE NEXT DAY a new bed was delivered—some surprise when I got home! My old one was gone. The new one had a pinkish coverlet on it and some of those cute little rag dolls sitting at the comers. There were frilly yellow and pink curtains on the two bedroom windows.

"That old bed was saggy in the middle, Ralph."

"Oh?" I hadn't noticed that. I said I hadn't noticed it.

"You don't notice anything, Ralph. I had my hair done, too."

Then I saw it; and I also noticed the bills that were piling up. She had put them under my new pillow on the couch. They added up to a lot more than I make in a week; one bill was for two more bottles of gin.

ONE EVENING the apartment house manager stopped me in the hall and asked about something. I was edgy because I thought he'd want to raise the rent because Louise was there, but he didn't say nothing, which surprised me. He is the snappy-dresser kind of sport who plays the ponies and is very tight with a buck if the buck happens to be his. It sure surprised me, him not adding a little something to the rent. He asked me when I was going to work late next. That was all.

I happened to ask Louise if she had met him and she said, "Why don't you fix yourself up a little bit, Ralph? You don't always have to look like a grape picker."

I said, using her comeback, "Ha ha, we're not married."

"Ha ha, you bet. You sure are a smart aleck, Ralph."

Then the guy in the grocery store mentioned her the next time I went in, and when I left he said, "Say hello to Louise, pal. Tell her Freddie said hello."

I had been trading there a year and I didn't even know his name was Freddie.

The telephone bill was forty-seven bucks because of long-distance calls to Chicago. When I yelled, Louise said she didn't make them. She didn't know anybody in Chicago. I called the operator and she gave me a rundown when I complained.

"They were made to a party named Kostivich, sir."

I told her that was their trouble. They had made a mistake and got my phone calls mixed up with the manager's. *His* name was Kostivich, not mine. She gave me an argument, then called the supervisor who said they didn't make them kind of mistakes. I didn't get anywhere with them.

Louise said, "Jeez, don't make a big stink, Ralph."

So all this stuff was making me think more and more. I'm not dumb, you know.

Then there was the neighborhood saloon near my apartment. I hardly ever went into it, but one night I did, just to sort of have a beer and think. You know.

The bartender said, "Hey, aren't you Ralph What's-his-name?" I said, "Yeah, why?"

He leaned an elbow on the bar and looked at me with funny little fish eyes. "Oh, nothin'." Then he moved away.

When I went out, he said, "Hey, Ralph, say hello to Louise, huh? From Butchy."

I said, "Sure, Butchy." He glowered at me.

That was one more thing that made a guy wonder.

ON FRIDAY NIGHT Louise met me outside the hardware plant when I got off work. She was wearing a new dress and shoes and looked pretty good. "You never take me nowhere, Ralph," she said. "How about us going to Manny's Hofbrau for dinner?"

I said, looking at her new stuff, "I can't afford it."

She sniffed. "Jeez, Ralph, you sure are a cheapskate."

Well, I took her, and it cost me fourteen bucks this time. She went for the Wiener-something-or-other and two martinis. Man, *did* she sop up the gin!

I had just about done all my thinking by then. I don't go off half-cocked or anything.

It was dark when we got out of the cafe and strolled back across the bridge. There wasn't any traffic at all, so I threw her over the railing into the river and went on home.

Hand in Glove

James Holding

TWIST ENDING II

Raymond Chandler points out in The Simple Art of Murder *that "the detective story, even in its most conventional form, is difficult to write well. Good specimens of the art are much rarer than good serious novels." If we grant this, and further grant that the short-short story is perhaps the most exacting form of fiction, then we arrive at the proposition that the mystery short-short probably is the most difficult fictional form there is, approaching the sonnet in its logical complexity as an art form. All of which has not a little to do with "Hand in Glove," which makes the difficult not only look easy, but entertaining as well. Florida-based James Holding has never published a novel (at least not as far as your editors know); but during the past fifteen years, several hundred of his short stories have appeared in almost every conceivable magazine and journal both here and abroad. J.G.*

"THE MAN WAS A BLACKMAILER," said Inspector Graves, wrinkling his nose in distaste. "There's nothing nastier. Therefore, in my opinion, the person who killed him deserves a vote of thanks, not censure and a possible prison term."

Golightly, standing with his back to the fireplace and jingling his change in his trousers pocket, looked at the inspector with surprise. "A blackmailer," he inquired. "The newspaper report of the murder made no mention of that."

"Naturally not," said the inspector, "since it was one of the few clues we had to work with in the case. Releasing it to the press would have complicated matters enormously."

"I can understand that," said Golightly. Then, curiously, "What I *can't* understand is how you concluded Clifford was a blackmailer."

The inspector said, "Quite simple, really. We found a list of his victims in a wall safe behind a painting in his bedroom—with the amount of blackmail each one had paid to Clifford, and at what intervals. It was a very revealing document."

"I daresay." Golightly nodded agreement. "It also answers a question that has puzzled me ever since you knocked at my door a few moments ago, Inspector."

"Why I am here, you mean? Yes, Mr. Golightly, your name is on Clifford's list. He was into you for a rather staggering amount, wasn't he?"

"You could say so." Golightly looked bleakly about his once luxurious flat. Everything had a slightly shabby and uncared-for look now. "I make no secret of the fact that Clifford's murder made me a happy man."

"As it did every other victim on his list," acknowledged the inspector. "And all have admitted it readily, once they realized we were onto Clifford's dirty work. We have, of course, contacted them all. They comprise a ready-made list of suspects, as you will appreciate."

"But you have not been able to discover the murderer?"

"Each of Clifford's other blackmail victims has an unshakable alibi for the evening of Clifford's murder, as it happens," said the inspector sadly. He gave Golightly an expectant glance. "Are you also provided with one, Mr. Golightly?"

Golightly seemed taken aback. "For last Saturday evening?"

"Friday evening. From ten to midnight, approximately."

"Friday, yes, let me see." Golightly frowned in the act of memory, then smiled. "As it happens, I, too, have an alibi, Inspector. I would prefer, however, not to give you her name except in the ultimate extremity. She is what Clifford's blackmail demands on me were all about. I can tell you this much: she is a lady of high station—and thus far—unblemished reputation. Do you see my dilemma?"

The inspector sighed. "Perfectly," he said. "Yet if our other line of investigation proves a dead end, we may very well come to your ultimate extremity, Mr. Golightly. It is only fair to warn you."

"Thank you." Golightly bowed. "You do have other clues, then?"

"Only one. A full set of bloody fingerprints on the sill of the rear window by which the killer made his exit from Clifford's home."

"Bloody fingerprints, you say?"

"Yes. As the newspapers reported, Clifford was stabbed with a paper knife, a letter opener. There was a great deal of blood about."

Golightly looked baffled. "Perhaps I am dull," he said, "but if you have a set of fingerprints to work with... Aren't they infallible in establishing identity?"

The inspector nodded. "If they are clear and unsmudged, they are infallible. But our bloody fingerprints were far from clear, I regret to say. They were badly smeared. Even without the smearing, they presented certain difficulties."

"What difficulties, Inspector, may I ask?"

"Whoever left bloody fingerprints on Clifford's windowsill was wearing gloves."

Golightly started. "Gloves! Then no wonder it was impossible to learn anything from the prints."

"I said difficult, not impossible," murmured the inspector. "As a matter of fact, I was able to deduce certain basic information from the prints, even though the fingers that made them were gloved."

"I shall never cease being astonished at police technology," said Golightly. "What could you possibly deduce from prints made by gloved fingers?"

The inspector ticked off his points on his own fingers. "One, I deduced that the gloves worn by Clifford's murderer were of a type that would be very expensive. Under high magnification, the prints showed that the gloves worn by the killer had been string gloves—you know, the woven or knitted type. And not just knitted of the ordinary kind of cotton, but of fine silken thread. Two, some seam stitching showed quite plainly in one of the glove prints, and it was so fine and so carefully contrived that our laboratory had no hesitation in pronouncing that the gloves had been handmade; custom-made, if you prefer. And by a very expensive glove-maker."

"You astound me, Inspector."

"I sometimes astound myself," the inspector said comfortably. "In any event, these and other characteristics of the glove smudges indicated to us that they might provide a feasible, even a fertile, field of inquiry."

"And you followed it up?"

"Just so. I, myself, after a city-wide search, unearthed a custom glover in a byway off Baker Street, Mr. Golightly, who admitted to producing gloves of this particular kind. His testimony is available if needed."

"He must have made such gloves for scores of clients," Golightly suggested.

Inspector Graves shook his head. "Such was not the case. This glover had made only a single pair of gloves like the ones I described to him. One pair only. Several years ago. Yet by great good luck, his records still contained the name and address of that client."

"Indeed?" said Golightly. "That *was* good luck, Inspector. For you, if not for me." He shrugged his shoulders. "I suppose," he went on with a wry smile, "that your investigation's success now depends rather heavily upon a show of hands, does it not?"

Inspector Graves nodded regretfully. "If you please, Mr. Golightly."

Golightly stopped jingling his coins. Slowly he withdrew his bands from his trouser pockets and held them out for Graves' inspection.

His right hand had six fingers on it.

The Silver Curtain

John Dickson Carr

THE FORMAL MYSTERY

What can be said about John Dickson Carr that has not already been said hundreds of times before? He is one of the three or four acknowledged masters of the formal mystery story, a positive genius at concocting "impossible crime" situations, an MWA Grand Master Award winner in 1962, and the recipient of an MWA Anniversary Award in 1970 commemorating his fortieth year of professional writing. These are just a few highlights of a most distinguished career—a career which continues today with an occasional novel and a monthly column of mystery-book reviews for Ellery Queen's Mystery Magazine. "The Silver Curtain," one of his early stories featuring The Department of Queer Complaints, is a typical Carr story: ingenious, baffling, plausible, and very well-written indeed. - B.P.

THE CROUPIER'S wrist moved with such fluent ease as to seem boneless. Over the green baize its snaky activity never hesitated, never wavered, never was still. His rake, like an enormous butter-pat, attracted the cards, flicked them up, juggled them, and slid them in a steady stream through the slot of the table.

No voice was raised in the Casino at La Bandelette. There was much casualness; hardly any laughter. The tall red curtains and the padded red floors closed in a sort of idle concentration at a dozen tables. And out of it, at table number six, the croupier's monotone droned on.

"*Six mille. Banco? Six mille. Banco? Banco?*"

"*Banco,*" said the young Englishman across the table. The cards, white and grey, slipped smoothly from the shoe. And the young man lost again.

The croupier hadn't time to notice much. The people round him, moving in hundreds through the season, were hardly human beings at all. There was a calculating machine inside his head; he heard its clicks, he watched the run of its numbers, and it was all he had time for. Yet so acutely were his senses developed that he could tell almost within a hundred francs how much money the players at his table still retained. The young man opposite was nearly broke.

(Best be careful. This perhaps means trouble.)

Casually, the croupier glanced round his table. There were five players, all English, as was to be expected. There was the fair-haired girl with the elderly man, obviously her father, who had a bald head and looked ill; he breathed behind his hand. There was the very heavy, military-looking man whom someone had addressed as Colonel March. There was the fat, sleek, swarthy young man with the twisty eyebrows (dubious English?), whose complacency had grown with his run of luck and whose wallet stuffed with *mille* notes lay at his elbow. Finally, there was the young man who lost so much.

The young man got up from his chair.

He had no poker face. The atmosphere about him was so desperately embarrassed that the fair-haired girl spoke.

"Leaving, Mr. Winton?" she asked.

"Er—yes," said Mr. Winton. He seemed grateful for that little help thrown into his disquiet. He seized at it; he smiled back at her. "No luck yet. Time to get a drink and offer up prayers for the next session."

(*Look here,* thought Jerry Winton, *why stand here explaining? It's not serious. You'll get out of it, even if it does mean a nasty bit of trouble. They all know you're broke. Stop standing here laughing like a gawk, and get away from the table.* He looked into the eyes of the fair-haired girl and wished he hadn't been such an ass.)

"Get a drink," he repeated.

He strode away from the table with (imagined) laughter following him. The sleek young man had lifted a moon-face and merely looked at him in a way that roused Jerry Winton's wrath.

Curse La Bandelette and *baccara* and everything else.

"There," reflected the croupier, "is a young man who will have trouble with his hotel. *Banco? Six mille. Banco?*"

In the bar, which adjoined the casino rooms, Jerry Winton crawled up on one of the high stools, called for an Armagnac, and pushed his last hundred-franc note across the counter. His head was full of a row of figures written in the spidery style of France. His hotel bill for a week would come to-what? Four, five, six thousand francs? It would be presented tomorrow, and all he had was his return ticket to London by plane.

In the big mirror behind the bar a new image emerged from the crowd. It was that of the fat, sleek, oily-faced young man who had cleaned up such a packet at the table, and who was even now fingering his wallet lovingly before he put it away. He climbed up on a stool beside Jerry. He called for mineral water: how shrewd and finicky-crafty these expert gamblers were! He relighted the stump of a cigar in one comer of his mouth.

Then he spoke.

"Broke?" he inquired off-handedly.

Jerry Winton glared at his reflection in the mirror. "I don't see," he said, with a slow and murderous choosing of words, "that that's anybody's business except mine."

"Oh, that's all right," said the stranger, in the same unpleasantly off-handed tone. He took several puffs at his cigar; he drank a little mineral water. He added: "I expect it's pretty serious, though? Eh?"

"If the matter," said Jerry, turning round, "is of so much interest to you: no, it's not serious. I have plenty of money back home. The trouble is that this is Friday night, and I can't get in touch with the bank until Monday." Though this was quite true, he saw the other's fishy expression grow broader. "It's a damned nuisance, because they don't know me the hotel. But a nuisance is all it is. If you think I'm liable to go out in the garden and shoot myself, stop thinking it."

The other smiled sadly and fishily, and shook his head. "You don't say? I can't believe that, now can I?"

"I don't care what you believe."

"You should care," said his companion, unruffled. As Jerry slid down from the stool, he reached out and tapped Jerry on the arm.

"Don't be in such a rush. You say you're a boy Croesus. All right: you're a boy Croesus. *I* won't argue with you. But tell me: how's your nerve?"

"My what?"

"Your nerve. Your courage," explained his companion, with something like a sneer.

Jerry Winton looked back at the bland, self-assured face poised above the mineral water. His companion's feet were entangled with the legs of the bar stool; his short upper lip was lifted with acute self-confidence; and a blank eye jeered down.

"I thought I'd ask," he pursued. "My name is Davos, Ferdie Davos. Everybody knows me." He swept his hand towards the crowd. "How'd you like to make ten thousand francs?"

"I'd like it a whole lot. But I don't know whether I'd like to make it out of any business of yours."

Davos was unruffled. "It's no good trying to be on your dignity with me. It don't impress me and it won't help you. I still ask: how would you like to make ten thousand francs? That would more than cover what you owe or are likely to owe, wouldn't it? I thought so. Do you or don't you want to make ten thousand francs?"

"Yes, I do," Jerry snarled back.

"All right. See a doctor."

"*What?*"

"See a doctor," Davos repeated coolly. "A nerve tonic is what you want: pills. No, I'm not wise-cracking." He looked at the clock, whose hands stood at five minutes to eleven. "Go to this address—listen carefully while I tell you—and there'll be ten thousand in it for you. Go to this address in about an hour. No sooner, no later. Do your job properly, and there may be even more than ten thousand in it for you. Number two, Square St Jean, Avenue des Phares, in about an hour. We'll see how your nerve is then."

La Bandelette, "the fillet," that strip of silver beach along the channel, is full of flat-roofed and queerly painted houses which give it the look of a town in a Walt Disney film. But the town itself is of secondary consideration. The English colony, which is of a frantic fashionableness, lies among great trees behind. Close to the Casino de la Forêt are three great hotels, gay with awning and piling sham

Gothic turrets into the sky. The air is aromatic; open carriages clop and jingle along broad avenues; and the art of extracting money from guests has become so perfected that we find our hands going to our pockets even in sleep.

This sleep is taken by day. By night, when La Bandelette is sealed up except for the Casino, the beam of the great island lighthouse sweeps the streets. It dazzles and then dies, once every twenty seconds. And, as Jerry Winton strode under the trees towards the Avenue of the Lighthouses, its beam was beginning to be blurred by rain.

Square St. Jean, Avenue des Phares. Where? And why?

If Davos had approached him in any other way, Jerry admitted to himself, he would have paid no attention to it. But he was annoyed and curious. Besides, unless there were a trick in it, he could use ten thousand francs. There was probably a trick in it. But who cared?

It was the rain that made him hesitate. He heard it patter in the trees, and deepen to a heavy rustling, as he saw the signboard pointing to the Avenue des Phares. He was without hat or coat. But by this time, he meant to see the thing through.

Ahead of him was a street of fashionable villas, lighted by mere sparks of gas. An infernally dark street. Something queer, and more than queer, about this. Total strangers didn't ask you how strong your nerves were, and then offer you ten thousand francs on top of it, for any purpose that would pass the customs. Which was all the more reason why...

Then he saw Davos.

Davos did not see him. Davos was ahead of him, walking fast and with little short steps along the dim street. The white beam of the lighthouse shone out overhead, turning the rain to silver; and Jerry could see the gleam of his polished black hair and the light tan topcoat he was now wearing.

Pulling up the collar of his dinner jacket, Jerry followed.

A few yards farther on, Davos slackened his pace. He peered round and up. On his left was the entrance to a courtyard, evidently the Square St. Jean. But to call it a "square" was a noble overstatement; it was only a cul-de-sac some twenty feet wide by forty feet deep.

Two of its three sides were merely tall, blank brick walls. The third side, on the right, was formed of a tall flat house all of whose windows were closely shuttered. But there was at least a sign of life about the house. Over its door burned a dim white globe, showing that there was a doctor's brass nameplate beside the door. A sedate house with blue-painted shutters in the bare cul-de-sac—and Davos was making for it.

All this Jerry saw at a glance. Then he moved back from the cul-de-sac. The rain was sluicing down on him, blurring the dim white globe with shadow and gleam. Davos had almost reached the doctor's door. He had paused, as though to consider or look at something; and then...

Jerry Winton later swore that he had taken his eyes off Davos only for a second. This was true. Jerry had, in fact, glanced back along the Avenue des Phares behind him, and was heartened to see the figure of a policeman some distance away. What made him look quickly back again was a noise from the cul-de-sac, a noise that was something between a cough and a scream, bubbling up horribly under the rain; and afterwards the thud of a body on asphalt.

One moment Davos had been on his feet. The next moment he was lying on his side on the pavement, and kicking.

Overhead, the beam of the lighthouse wheeled again. Jerry, reaching Davos in a run of half a dozen long strides, saw the whole scene picked out by that momentary light. Davos's fingers still clutched, or tried to clutch, the well-filled wallet Jerry had last seen at the casino. His tan topcoat was now dark with rain. His heels scraped on the pavement, for he had been stabbed through the back of the neck with a heavy knife whose polished-metal handle projected four inches. Then the wallet slipped out of his fingers, and splashed into a puddle, for the man died.

JERRY WINTON LOOKED, and did not believe his own eyes. Mechanically he reached down and picked up the wallet out of the puddle, shaking it. He backed away as he heard running footfalls pound into the cul-de-sac, and he saw the flying waterproof of a policeman.

'Halt there!' the law shouted in French. The policeman, a dim shape under the waterproof, pulled up short and stared. After seeing what was on the pavement, he made a noise like a man hit in the stomach.

Jerry pulled his wits together and conned over his French for the proper phrases.

"His—this wallet," said Jerry, extending it.

"So I see."

"He is dead."

"That would appear obvious," agreed the other, with a kind of snort. "Well! Give it to me. Quick, quick, quick! His wallet."

The policeman extended his hand, snapping the fingers. He added: "No stupidities, if you please! I am prepared for you."

"But I didn't kill him."

"That remains to be seen."

"Man, you don't think—?"

He broke off. The trouble was that it had happened too rapidly. Jerry's feeling was that of one who meets a super-salesman and under whirlwind tactics is persuaded to buy some huge and useless article before he realizes what the talk is all about.

For here was a minor miracle. He had seen the man Davos stabbed under his eyes. Davos had been stabbed by a straight blow from behind, the heavy knife entering in a straight line sloping a little upward, as though the blow had been struck from the direction of the pavement. Yet at the same time Davos had been alone in an empty cul-de-sac as bare as a biscuit-box.

"It is not my business to think," said the policeman curtly. "I make my notes and I report to my *commissaire*. Now!" He withdrew into the shelter of the dimly lit doorway, his wary eye fixed on Jerry, and whipped out his notebook. "Let us have no nonsense. You killed this man and attempted to rob him. I saw you."

"No!"

"You were alone with him in this court. I saw as much myself."

"Yes, that is true."

"Good; he admits it! You saw no one else in the court?"

"No."

"*Justement.* Could any assassin have approached without being seen?"

Jerry, even as he saw the bleak eye grow bleaker, had to admit that this was impossible. On two sides were blank brick walls; on the third side was a house whose door or windows, he could swear, had not opened a crack. In the second's space of time while he looked away, no murderer could have approached, stabbed Davos, and got back to cover again. There was no cover. This was so apparent that Jerry could not even think of a reasonable lie. He merely stuttered.

"I do not know what happened," he insisted. "One minute he was there, and then he fell. I saw nobody." Then a light opened in his mind. "Wait! That knife there—it must have been thrown at him."

Rich and sardonic humor stared at him from the doorway. "Thrown, you say? Thrown from where?"

"I don't know," admitted Jerry. The light went out. Again he stared at blank brick walls, and at the house from whose sealed front no knife could have been thrown.

"Consider," pursued his companion, in an agony of logic, "the position of the knife. This gentleman was walking with his back to you?"

"Yes."

"Good; we progress." He pointed. "The knife enters the back of his neck in a straight line. It enters from the direction where you were standing. Could it have been thrown past you from the entrance to the court?"

"No. Impossible."

"No. That is evident," blared his companion. "I cannot listen to any more stupidities. I indulge you because you are English, and we have orders to indulge the English. But this goes beyond reason! You will go with me to the Hotel de Ville. Look at the notecase in his hand. Does be offer it to you and say: 'Monsieur, honor me by accepting my notecase'?"

"No. He had it in his own hand."

"He had it in his own hand, say you. Why?"

"I don't know."

Jerry broke off, both because the story of his losses at the Casino must now come out with deadly significance, and because they heard the rattle of a door being unlocked. The door of the doctor's house opened; and out stepped the fair-haired girl whom Jerry had last seen at the Casino.

Beside the door the brass name-plate read *Dr. Edouard Hébert*, with consulting hours inscribed underneath, and an aggressive *Speaks English*. Behind the girl, craning his neck, stood a bristly middle-aged man of immense dignity. His truculent eyeglasses had a broad black ribbon which seemed to form a kind of electrical circuit with the ends of his brushed-up moustache.

But Jerry Winton was not looking at Dr. Hébert. He was looking at the girl. In addition to a light fur coat, she now wore a cream-colored scarf drawn over her hair; she had in one hand a tiny box, wrapped in white paper. Her smooth, worried face, her long, pale-blue eyes, seemed to reflect the expression of the dead man staring back at her from the pavement.

She jerked back, bumping into the policeman. She put her hand on Dr. Hébert's arm. With her other hand she pointed sharply to Davos. "That's the man!" she cried.

M. GORON, prefect of Police, was a comfortable man, a round, catlike amiable sort of man, famous for his manners. Crime, rare in La Bandelette, distressed him. But he was also an able man. At one o'clock in the morning, he sat in his office at the town hall examining his fingernails and creaking back and forth in a squeaky swivel chair whose noise had begun to get on Jerry Winton's nerves.

The girl, who for the tenth time had given her name as Eleanor Hood, was insistent.

"M. Goron!"

"*Mademoiselle?*" said the prefect politely, and seemed to wake out of a dream.

Eleanor Hood turned round and gave Jerry Winton a despairing look.

"I only wish to know," she urged, in excellent French, "why we are here, Dr. Hébert and I. And Mr. Winton too, if it comes to that." This time the look she gave Jerry was one of smiling companionship: a human sort of look, which warmed that miscreant "But as for us—why? It is not as though we were witnesses. I have told you why I was at Dr. Hébert's house."

"*Mademoiselle's* father," murmured M. Goron.

"Yes. He is ill. Dr. Hébert has been treating him for several days, and he had another attack at the Casino tonight. Mr. Winton will confirm that."

Jerry nodded. The old boy at the table, he reflected, had certainly looked ill.

"I took my father back to our hotel, the Brittany, at half past eleven," the girl went on, speaking with great intensity. "I tried to communicate with Dr. Hébert by telephone. I could not reach him. So I went to his house; it is only a short distance from the hotel. On the way I kept seeing that man—the man you call Davos. I thought he was following me. He seemed to be looking at me from behind every tree. That is why I said, 'That's the man,' when I saw him lying on the pavement with his eyes open. His eyes did not even blink when the rain struck them. It was a horrible sight. I was upset. Do you blame me?"

M. Goron made a sympathetic noise.

"I reached Dr. Hébert's house at perhaps twenty minutes to twelve. Dr. Hébert had retired, but he consented to go with me. I waited while he dressed. We went out, and on the door step we found—what you know. Please believe that is all I know about it."

She had a singularly expressive voice and personality. She was either all anxiety or all persuasiveness, fashioning the clipped syllables. When she turned her wrist, you saw Davos lying in the rain and the searchlight wheeling overhead.

Then she added abruptly in English, looking at Jerry: "He was a nasty little beast; but I don't for a moment believe you killed him."

"Thanks. But why?"

"I don't know," said Eleanor simply. "You just couldn't have!"

"Now there is logic!" cried M. Goron, giving his desk an admiring whack.

M. Goron's swivel chair creaked with pleasure. There were many lights in his office, which smelt of creosote. On the desk in front of him lay Davos's sodden wallet and (curiously) the tiny round box, wrapped in a spill of paper, which Eleanor Hood had been carrying.

M. Goron never spoke to Jerry, never looked at him; ignored him as completely and blandly as though he were not there.

"But," he continued, growing very sober again, "you will forgive me, *mademoiselle*, if I pursue this matter further. You say that Dr. Hébert has been treating your father?"

"Yes."

M. Goron pointed to the small box on the table. "With pills, perhaps?"

"Ah, my God!" said Dr. Hébert, and slapped his forehead tragically.

For several minutes, Jerry had been afraid that the good doctor would have an apoplectic stroke. Dr. Hébert had indicated his distinguished position in the community. He had pointed out that physicians do not go out in the middle of the night on errands of mercy, and then get dragged off to police stations; it is bad for business. His truculent eyeglasses and moustache bristling, he left off his stiff pacing of the room only to go and look the prefect in the eye.

"I *will* speak," he said coldly, from deep in his throat.

"As *monsieur* pleases."

"Well, it is as this lady says! Why are we here? Why? We are not witnesses." He broke off and slapped at the shoulders of his coat as though to rid himself of insects. "This young man here tells us a story which may or may not be true. If it is true, I do not see why the man Davos should have given him *my* address. I do not see why Davos should have been knifed on my doorstep. I did not know the man Davos, except as a patient of mine."

"Ah!" said the prefect. "You gave him pills, perhaps?"

Dr. Hébert sat down.

"Are you mad on the subject of pills?" he inquired, with restraint. "Because this young man—" again he looked with disfavor at Jerry, "— tells you that Davos made some drunken mention of 'pills' at the Casino tonight, is that why you pursue the subject?"

"It is possible."

"It is ridiculous," said Dr. Hébert. "Do you even question my pills on the desk there? They are for Miss Hood's father. They are ordinary tablets, with digitalin for the heart. Do you think they contain poison? If so, why not test them?"

"It is an idea," conceded M. Goron.

He picked up the box and removed the paper.

The box contained half a dozen sugar-coated pellets. With great seriousness M. Goran put one of the tablets into his mouth, tasted it, bit it, and finally appeared to swallow it.

"No poison?" asked the doctor.

"No poison," agreed M. Goron. The telephone on his desk rang. He picked it up, listened for a moment with a dreamy smile, and replaced it. "Now this is really excellent!" He beamed, rubbing his hands. "My good friend Colonel March, of the English police, has been making investigations. He was sent here when a certain form of activity in La Bandelette became intolerable both to the French and English authorities. You perhaps noticed him at the casino tonight, all of you?"

"I remember," said Jerry suddenly. "Very large bloke, quiet as sin."

"An apt description," said the prefect.

"But—" began Dr. Hébert.

"I said 'all of you,' Dr. Hébert," repeated the prefect. "One small question is permitted? I thank you. When *mademoiselle* telephoned to your house at eleven-thirty tonight, you were not there. You were at the casino, perhaps?"

Dr. Hébert stared at him.

"It is possible. But—"

"You saw M. Davos there, perhaps?"

"It is possible." Still Dr. Hebert stared at him with hideous perplexity. "But, M. Goron, will you have the goodness to explain this? You surely do not suspect either *mademoiselle* or myself of having any concern with this business? You do not think that either *mademoiselle* or I left the house at the time of the murder?"

"I am certain you did not."

"You do not think either *mademoiselle* or myself went near a door or a window to get at this accursed Davos?"

"I am certain you did not," beamed the prefect.

"Well, then?"

"But there, you see," argued M. Goron, lifting one finger for emphasis, "we encounter a difficulty. We are among thorns. For this would mean that M. Winton must have committed the murder. And that," he added, looking at Jerry, "is absurd. We never for a moment believed that M. Winton had anything to do with this; and my friend Colonel March will tell you why."

Jerry sat back and studied the face of the prefect, wondering if he had heard right. He felt like an emotional punching bag. But with great gravity he returned the prefect's nod as a *sergent de ville* opened the door of the office.

"We will speak English," announced M. Goron, bouncing up. "This is my friend Colonel March."

"Evening," said the colonel. His large, speckled face was as bland as M. Goron's; his fists were on his hips. He looked first at Eleanor, then at Jerry, then at Dr. Hébert. "Sorry you were put to this inconvenience, Miss Hood. But I've seen your father, and it will be all right. As for you, Mr. Winton, I hope they have put you out of your misery?"

"Misery?"

"Told you you're not headed for Devil's Island, or anything of the sort? We had three very good reasons for believing you had nothing to do with this. Here is the first reason."

Reaching into the pocket of his dinner-jacket, he produced an article which he held out to them. It was a black leather notecase, exactly like the one already on M. Goron's desk. But whereas the first was stuffed with *mille* notes, this one had only a few hundred francs in it

"We found this second notecase in Davos's pocket," said Colonel March.

He seemed to wait for a comment, but none came.

"Well, what about it?" Jerry demanded, after a pause.

"Oh, come! Two notecases! Why was Davos carrying two notecases? Why should any man carry two notecases? That is my first reason. Here is my second."

From the inside pocket of his coat, with the air of a conjurer, he drew out the knife with which Davos had been stabbed.

A suggestive sight. Now cleansed of blood, it was a long, thin, heavy blade with a light metal handle and crosspiece. As Colonel March turned it round, glittering in the light, Jerry Winton felt that its glitter struck a chord of familiarity in his mind: that a scene from the past bad almost come back to him: that, for a swift and tantalizing second, he had almost grasped the meaning of the whole problem.

"And now we come to my third reason," said Colonel March. "The third reason is Ferdie Davos. Ferdie was a hotel thief. A great deal too clever for us poor policemen. Eh, Goron? Though I always told him he was a bad judge of men. At the height of the summer season, at hotels like the Brittany and the Donjon, he had rich pickings. He specialized in necklaces; particularly in pearl necklaces. Kindly note that."

A growing look of comprehension had come into Eleanor Hood's face. She opened her mouth to speak, and then checked herself.

"His problem," pursued Colonel March, "was how to smuggle the stolen stuff over to England, where he had a market for it. He couldn't carry it himself. In a little place like La Bandelette, Goron would have had him turned inside out if he had as much as taken a step towards Boulogne. So he had to have accomplices. I mean accomplices picked from among the hordes of unattached young men who come here every season. Find some young fool who's just dropped more than he can afford at the tables; and he may grab at the chance to earn a few thousand francs by a little harmless customs bilking. You follow me, Mr. Winton?"

"You mean I was chosen—?"

"Yes."

"But, good lord, how? I couldn't smuggle a pearl necklace through the customs if my life depended on it."

"You could if you needed a tonic," Colonel March pointed out. "Davos told you so. The necklace would first be taken to pieces for you.

Each pearl would be given a thick sugar-coating, forming a neat medicinal pill. They would then be poured into a neat bottle or box under the prescription of a well-known doctor. At the height of the tourist rush, the customs can't currycomb everybody. They would be looking for a pearl-smuggler: not for an obviously respectable young tourist with stomach trouble."

Eleanor Hood, with sudden realization in her face, looked at the box of pills on M. Goron's desk.

"So *that* is why you tasted my pills!" she said to the prefect of police, who made deprecating noises. "And kept me here for so long. And—"

"*Mademoiselle*, I assure you!" said M. Goron. "We were sure there was nothing wrong with those pills!" He somewhat spoiled the gallant effect of this by adding: "There are not enough of them, for one thing. But, since you received them from Dr. Hébert after office hours, you had to be investigated. The trick is neat, *hein*? I fear the firm of Hebert and Davos have been working it for some time."

They all turned to look at Dr. Hébert.

He was sitting bolt upright, his chin drawn into his collar as though he were going to sing. On his face was a look of what can only be called frightened skepticism. Even his mouth was half-open with this effect, or with unuttered sounds of ridicule.

"We were also obliged to delay you all," pursued M. Goron, "until my men found Madame Fley's pearls, which were stolen a week ago, hidden in Dr. Hébert's surgery. I repeat: it was a neat trick. We might never have seen it if Davos had not incautiously hinted at it to M. Winton. But then Davos was getting a bit above himself." He added: "That, Colonel March thinks, is why Dr. Hébert decided to kill him."

Still, Dr. Hébert said nothing.

It was, in fact, Jerry Winton who spoke. "Sir, I don't hold any brief for this fellow. I should think you were right. But how could he have killed Davos? He couldn't have!"

"You are forgetting," said Colonel March, as cheerfully as though the emotional temperature of the room had not gone up several degrees, "you are forgetting the two notecases. Why was Davos carrying two notecases?"

"Well?"

"He wasn't," said Colonel March, with his eye on Hébert. "Our good doctor here was, of course, the brains of the partnership. He supplied the resources for Ferdie's noble front. When Ferdie played baccara at the Casino, he was playing with Dr. Hébert's money. And, when Dr. Hébert saw Ferdie at the Casino tonight, he very prudently took away the large sum you saw in Ferdie's notecase at the tables. When Ferdie came to the doctor's house at midnight, he had only his few hundred francs commission in his own notecase, which was in his pocket.

"You see, Dr. Hébert needed that large sum of money in his plan to kill Ferdie. He knew what time Ferdie would call at his house. He knew Mr. Winton would be close behind Ferdie. Mr. Winton would, in fact, walk into the murder and get the blame. All Dr. Hébert had to do was take that packet of *mille* notes, stuff them into another notecase just like Ferdie Davos's, and use it as a trap."

"A trap?" repeated Eleanor.

"A trap," said Colonel March.

"Your presence. Miss Hood," he went on, "gave the doctor an unexpected alibi. He left you downstairs in his house. He went upstairs to 'get dressed.' A few minutes before Davos was due to arrive, he went quietly up to the roof of his house—a flat roof, like most of those in La Bandelette. He looked down over the parapet into that cul-de-sac, forty feet below. He saw his own doorstep with the lamp burning over it. He dropped that notecase over the parapet, so that it landed on the pavement before his own doorstep.

"Well?" continued Colonel March. "What would Davos do? What would *you* do, if you walked along a pavement and saw a notecase bulging with thousand-franc notes lying just in front of you?"

Again, Jerry Winton saw that dim cul-de-sac. He heard the rain splashing; he saw it moving and gleaming past the door-lamp, and past the beam of the lighthouse overhead. He saw the jaunty figure of Davos stop short as though to look at something—

"I imagine," Jerry said, "that I'd bend over and pick up the notecase."

"Yes," said Colonel March. "That's the whole sad story. You would bend over so that your body was parallel with the ground. The back of your neck would be a plain target to anybody standing forty feet up above you, with a needle-sharp knife whose blade is much heavier than the handle. The murderer has merely to drop that knife: stretch out his fingers and drop it. Gravity will do the rest.

"My friend, you looked straight at that murder, and you never saw it. You never saw it because a shifting, gleaming wall of rain, a kind of silver curtain, fell across the door-lamp and the beam of the lighthouse.

It hid the fall of a thin, long blade made of bright metal. Behind that curtain moved invisibly our ingenious friend Dr. Hébert, who, if he can be persuaded to speak—"

Dr. Hébert could not be persuaded to speak, even when they took him away. But Eleanor Hood and Jerry Winton walked home through the summer dawn, under a sky colored with a less evil silver; and they had discovered any number of mutual acquaintances by the time they reached the hotel.

Shut the Final Door

Joe L. Hensley

THE RAZOR'S EDGE

TOO OFTEN WE think of the "surprise" or "twist" ending as merely a gimmick, an extended one-liner rather than an exposure of sudden truth. But a blinding flash of truth is exactly what we get from this deeply disturbing exploration into the mind of a crippled black boy poised on the razor's edge of decision in a ghetto which might be in my city...or yours. Joe L. Hensley, well known in science-fiction circles for his short fiction and in mystery circles for his Doubleday Crime Club *novels* (Song of Corpus Juris, The Poison Summer), *is no stranger to disturbing human truths. At the time of submitting this story, he had the sobering responsibility of sitting as trial judge on his first murder case in an Indiana Circuit Court. - J.G.*

THE NIGHT WAS gentle and so Willie sat out on the combination fire escape and screened play area that hung in zigzags from the north side of the government-built, low-rent apartment building. He stayed out there in his wheelchair for a long time watching the world of lights from the other buildings around him. He liked the night. It softened the savage world, so that he could forget the things he saw and did in the day. Those things still existed, but darkness fogged them.

He reached around, fumbling under his shirt, and let his hand touch the long scar where it started. He couldn't reach all of it for it ran the width of his back, a slanting line, raised from the skin. Sometimes it ached and there was a little of that tonight, but it wasn't really bad any more. It was only that he was dead below the scar line, that the upper half of him still lived and felt, but the lower felt nothing, did nothing.

Once they'd called him Willie the Runner and he had been very fast, the running a defense from the cruel world of the apartments, a way out, a thing of which he'd been quite proud. That had been when he was thirteen. Now he was fifteen. The running was gone forever and there was only a scar to remind him of what had been once. But the new gift had come, the one the doctors had hinted about. And those two who'd been responsible for the scar had died.

A cloud passed across the moon and a tiny, soft rain began to fall. He wheeled off the fire escape and into the dirty hall. It was very dark inside. Someone had again removed the light bulbs from their receptacles. Piles of refuse crowded the corners and hungry insects scurried at the vibration of Willie's wheelchair.

In the apartment, his mother sat in front of the television. Her eyes were open, but she wasn't seeing the picture. She was on something new, exotic. He'd found one of the bottles where she'd carefully hidden it. Dilaudin, or something like that. It treated her well. He worked the wheelchair over to the television and turned off the late-night comic, but she still sat there, eyes open and lost, looking intently at the darkened tube. He went on into his own bedroom, got the wheelchair close to the bed, and clumsily levered himself between the dirty sheets.

He slept and sleeping brought the usual dreams of the days of fear and running. In the dream they laughed coldly and caught him in the dark place and he felt the searing pain of the knife. He remembered the kind doctor in the hospital, the one who kept coming back to talk to him, the one who talked about compensation and factors of recovery. The doctor had told him his arms might grow very strong and agile. He'd told him about blind men who'd developed special senses. He'd smiled and been very nice, and Willie had liked him. The gift he'd promised had come. Time passed in the dream, and it became better and Willie smiled.

IN THE MORNING, before his mother left for the weekly ordeal with the people at the welfare office, Willie again had her wheel him down to the screened play area and fire escape. In the hall, with the arrival of day, the smell was stifling, a combination of dirt and urine and cooking odors and garbage. The apartments in the building were almost new, but the people who inhabited the apartments had lived in tenement squalor for so long that they soon wore all newness away. The tenants stole the light bulbs from the hallways, used dark corners as toilets of convenience, discarded the leftovers of living in the quickest, easiest places. And they fought and stole and raped and, sometimes, killed.

Sometimes, Willie had seen a police car pass in the streets outside, but the policemen usually rode with eyes straight ahead and windows rolled up tight. On the few times that police came into the apartment area, they came in squads for their own protection.

Outside, the air was better. Willie could see the other government apartments that made up the complex and if he leaned forward he could, by straining, see the early morning traffic weaving along the expressway by the faraway river.

His mother frowned languidly at the sky, her chocolate-brown face severe. "It'll maybe rain," she said, slurring the words together. "If it rains you get back in, hear?"

"Okay," he said, and then again, because he was never sure she heard him: "Okay!" He looked at her swollen, sullen face, wanting to say more, but no words came. She was so very young. He'd been born almost in her childhood and there was within him the feeling that she resented him, hated caring for him, abominated being tied to him, but did the dreary duty only because there was no one else and because the mother-feeling within warred with all the other wants and drives and sometimes won an occasional victory. Willie remembered no father, and his mother had never spoken of one.

"None of them bad kids bother you up here, do they?" she asked, always suspicious.

He smiled, really amused. "No," he said.

She shook her head tiredly and he noticed the twitch in the side of her dark face. She said: "Some of them's bad enough to bother around a fifteen-year-old boy in a wheelchair. Bad enough to do 'most anything, I guess. When we moved in here, I thought it would be better." She looked up at the sky. "It's worse," she ended softly.

Willie patiently waited out her automatic ministrations, the poking at the blanket around his wasting legs, the peck on the forehead. Finally, she left.

For a while then he was alone and he could crane and watch the expressway and the river and the downtown to the north. He could hear the complex around him come to angry life, the voices raised in argument and strife. Down below, four boys came out of a neighboring building. They were dressed alike, tight jeans, brown jackets, hair long. He saw them gather in front of the building and one of them looked up and saw him watching. That one nudged the others and they all looked up, startled, and they went away like deer, around the far corner of their building at a quick lope. Willie only nodded.

A block away, just within his vision, a tall boy came out of the shadows and engaged another boy in a shouting argument. A small crowd gathered and watched indolently, some yelling advice. Willie watched with interest. When the fight began they rolled out of sight and Willie could only see the edges of the milling crowd and soon lost interest in watching.

The sun came out and the sky lightened, and Willie felt more like facing the day. He looked down at his legs without real sorrow. Regret was an old acquaintance, the feeling between them no longer strong. Willie leaned back in the wheelchair. With trained ears alert to any sudden sound of danger, he dozed lightly.

Memory again became a dream. When he had become sure of the gift, he had followed them to their clubhouse. It was in a ruined building that the city was tearing down to build more of the interminable housing units. He rolled right up to the door and beat on it boldly and they came and he saw the surprise on their faces and their quick looks to see if he'd brought police along.

"Hello, Running Willie, you crippled bastard," the one who'd wielded the knife said. The one who'd held him and watched smiled insolently.

He sat there alone in the chair and looked back at them, hating them with that peculiar, complete intensity, wanting them dead. The sickness came in his stomach and the whirling in his head and he saw them move at him before the sunlit world went dark brown.

Now they were dead.

A DOOR OPENED BELOW, and Willie came warily awake. He looked down and saw Twig Roberts observing the day.

"Okay to come on up, Willie?" Twig asked carefully.

"Sure," Willie said negligently.

Twig came up the stairs slowly and sat down on the top one, looking away into the distance, refusing to meet Willie's eyes. He was a large, dark boy, muscled like a wrestler, with a quick, foxy face. He lived in the apartment below Willie's.

"What we goin' to do today, Willie boy?" Twig asked it softly, his voice a whine. "Where we headin'?" He continued to look out at the empty sky and Willie knew again that Twig feared him. A small part of Willie relished the fear and fed on it and Willie knew that the fear diminished both of them.

Willie thought about the day. Once the trips, the forays, into that wild, jackdaw land below had been an exciting thing, a thing of danger. That had been when the power was unsure and slow, but the trips were as nothing now. Instead of finding fear below, he brought it

He said softly: "We'll do something, Twig." Then he nodded, feeling small malice. "Maybe down at Building Nineteen. You been complaining about Building Nineteen, ain't you?" He smiled, hiding the malice. "You got someone down there for me?"

Twig looked at him for the first time. "You got it wrong, Willie. I got relatives in that building. I never even taken you around there for fear..." He stopped and then went on. "There's nothing wrong with Nineteen." He watched earnestly until Willie let his smile widen. "You were puttin' me on, Willie," Twig said, in careful half-reproach.

"Sure, Twig," Willie said, closing his eyes and leaning back in the wheelchair. "We'll go down and just sort of look around."

THE FAN in the elevator didn't work and hadn't worked for a long time, but at least today the elevator itself worked. The odor in the shaft was almost overpowering, and Willie was glad when they were outside in the bright sun that had eaten away the morning fog.

Twig maneuvered him out the back entrance of the building. Outside, the ground was covered with litter, despite the fact that there were numerous trash receptacles. A rat wheeled and flashed between garbage cans and Willie shivered. The running rat reminded Willie of the days of fear.

They moved on along the sidewalks, Willie in the chair, Twig dutifully behind. Ahead of them, Willie could almost feel the word spread. The cool boys vanished. The gangs hid in trembling fear, their zip guns and knives forgotten. Arguments quieted. In the graveled play yards the rough games suspended. Small children watched in wonder from behind convenient bushes, eyes wide. Willie smiled and waved at them, but no one came out. Once a rock came toward them, but when Willie turned there was no one to be seen.

There was a dead zone where they walked. It was always like that these days.

A queer thought came to Willie as he rode along in solitary patrol. It was an odd thought, shiny and unreal. He wondered if someplace there was a someone with the gift of life, a someone who could set stopped breath to moving again, bring color back to a bloodless face, restart a failed heart, bring thought back to a dead mind. He rather hoped that such a gift existed, but he knew that on these streets such a gift wouldn't last. In this filth, in this world of murderous intent the life-giver would have been torn apart. If the life-giver was Willie—if that had been the gift—they would have jerked him from the moving casket he rode, stomped him, mutilated him. And laughed.

There were other worlds. Willie knew that dimly, without remembrance, without real awareness. There was only a kind of dim longing. He knew that the legs were the things that had saved him from a thousand dangers. He remembered the leering man who'd followed him one day when he was twelve, the one who wanted something, who touched and took. He remembered the angry ones with their knives and bicycle chains, the gangs that banded together to spread, rather than absorb, terror. He looked at his world: the ones who'd roll you for the price of a drink and the ones who'd kill you for a fix. It was the only world he knew. Downtown was a thing of minutes spent. It wasn't life. Life was here.

The legs had been survival. A knife had taken them. The doctor had promised something, and Willie had believed. Survival was still necessary and the world savage.

So was the compensating gift.

Twig pushed on into a narrow alley between trash cans. The sound of their coming disturbed an old white man who was dirtily burrowing in one of the cans. He looked up at them, filthy hands still rooting in the can. His thin, knobby armed body seemed lost in indecision between whether to dig deeper in the muck or take flight. Hunger won.

"What you doin' there, man?" Twig demanded, instantly pugnacious at the sight of the dirty, white face.

The old man stood his ground stubbornly and Willie felt an almost empathy with him, remembering hungry days. The man's old eyes were cunning, the head a turtle's head, scrawnily protruding up from its shell of filthy clothing. Those eyes had run a thousand times from imagined terror, but they could still calculate chances. Those eyes saw only a boy in a wheelchair, a larger boy behind.

The old man reached in his pocket. "Ge' away, you li'l black bassurds. Ge' away fum me." The hand came out and there was a flash of dull metal. A knife.

Willie saw Twig smile triumphantly. Those who stood their ground were hard to find in these days of increasing fear.

"Hate him, Willie," Twig said softly. "Hate him now!"

Willie smiled at the old man and hated him without dislike. He had to concentrate very hard, but finally the wrenching, tearing feeling came in his head and the brownout and the sickness became all. He faded himself into the hate and became one with it and time stopped until there was nothing. When it was done and he was again aware, he opened his eyes.

The old man was gone. There was nothing left to show he'd ever existed, no clothes, no knife.

"Did he run?" Willie asked.

Twig shook his head. "He smoked," he said, smiling hugely. "That was the best one yet. He smoked a kind of brown smoke and there was a big puff of flame and suddenly he ain't there anymore." He cocked his bead and clapped his hands in false exuberance. "That one was good, Willie. It was sure good." He smiled a good smile that failed to reach his eyes.

THE SUN WAS warm and Willie sat there and knew he'd been alone for all fifteen of his years and now, with the gift, that he would remain alone and that he was quite sanely mad.

He looked again at the children playing their rough games in the measured gravel and he knew he could explode them all like toy balloons, but the insanity he owned, he realized, should be worse than that.

The sun remained warm and be contemplated it and thought about it and wondered how far the gift extended. *If I should hate the sun...*

There was another thought. He worked it over in his head for a long time, while his fingers absently reached and stroked the long scar on his back.

There was a way out, a possible escape.

Tomorrow he might try hating himself.

The Counterfeit Conman

Albert F. Nussbaum

"THE STING"

The central gimmick of Al Nussbaum's "The Counterfeit Conman" is one neither of us has ever seen used in crime fiction—and this is rather surprising, considering the simplicity of it. Mr. Nussbaum assures us that it is perfectly credible, and if anyone should know, he is that person: he is currently an inmate of the Federal Penitentiary at Marion, Illinois. In addition to writing excellent "con man" stories such as this one, and other mystery shorts (many of which have been anthologized), Mr. Nussbaum is a nationally syndicated and sagacious book reviewer and an expert on subjects dealing with film. - B.P.

HE WAS A BIG, red-faced man with a nose that was too large and eyes that were too small, and I never heard a grown man whine so much. He sat at the bar, surrounded by flunkies, and didn't shut up for a moment. To hear him tell it, and no one in the lounge of the Buena Vista Casino heard much else that afternoon, he hadn't made a nickel's profit in years. Taxes had left him with nothing.

He might have convinced the Internal Revenue Service, but he didn't convince me. His hundred-dollar English leather shoes, four-hundred-dollar hand-tailored suit, and thousand-dollar wafer-thin wrist watch all said he was a liar. So did the large diamond he wore on the little finger of his right hand—the hand he gestured with—and the thick roll of currency he carried.

From where I sat, with my back to the wall, I had a good view of both the bar and the entrance arch. I watched Benny Krotz nervously make his way across the casino floor, past the crap tables, twenty-one dealers, and roulette wheels. He paused in the entrance for a moment, blinking his eyes rapidly to adjust them to the reduced illumination. When he spotted me, he came over and dropped lightly into the seat beside me. Benny was a gambler who believed in flying saucers and luck, but he'd never seen either one. A loser if I'd ever seen one, not that my white hair and conservative clothes made me look like a world beater.

I nodded toward the big mouth at the bar. "Is that the mark?" I asked.

Benny hesitated, afraid of giving away the only thing he had to sell. Finally, he acknowledged, "Yeah, that's the guy. How'd you make him so fast?" His expression was glum.

"I'd have to be deaf, blind, and have a cold to miss him," I said quietly.

"A cold?"

"Even if I couldn't hear him or see him, his smell would give him away." I allowed myself a brief smile. "He smells like money."

Benny brightened. "He looks good to you, huh?"

"He looks almost perfect. He's a liar who lives well, so he's probably dishonest and greedy. There's no better target for a con game. There's only one trouble."

"One trouble?" Benny echoed.

"Uh-huh—this town is crawling with hustlers. If I can spot that guy in less time than it takes to light a cigarette, others have done it too. He's probably been propositioned more times than the chorus line at Radio City Music Hall. And, considering the type of person he is, he's probably already fallen for more than one con game, and is extra cautious now. That's right, isn't it?"

"Yeah," Benny admitted. "That's right. He's been burned."

"Badly?"

"Yeah, pretty bad. He's been taken in card games, crap games, and a bunch of con games already."

I finished my drink and signaled for the waitress. When she had taken our order and left, I turned back to Benny. "What kind of con games?" I asked.

"All the usual: phony stock, underwater real estate, cheap stolen goods that turned out to be perfectly legitimate factory rejects. And Red Harris took him for twenty thousand about six months ago with a counterfeit-money swindle. Red gave him fifty brand-new twenties, telling him they were samples of the stuff he had for sale. He let him try them out all over town, then sold him a wrapped-up telephone book and made a nineteen-grand profit."

I laughed and looked over to where the mark was sitting. "That must have hurt his pride," I said. "How about his wallet? What kind of shape is that in?"

"Good shape. Very good shape. That's Big Jim Thompson, the drilling contractor. He has about half a hundred rigs working throughout the Southwest, and he gets paid whether they hit anything or not."

"That's fine," I said, smiling again. "It would ruin my Robin Hood image to take money from a poor man."

The waitress brought our drinks, and I paid for them while Benny fumbled politely in his empty pockets. Because my money clip was already out, I removed three one-hundred-dollar bills and passed them to Benny. "For your help," I said.

"You're satisfied with him?" Benny asked, snatching up the money. He couldn't conceal his surprise. "He's gonna be mighty cautious."

I shrugged. "I don't think that will be a problem. Can you introduce us?"

"Yeah, sure." Benny started to push his chair back. "What's your name?"

Benny had been recommended to me as a source of information. Since he was in the business of selling what he knew about people, I hadn't given him any more about me than he needed to know, which was nothing. I had been in the game too long to make that kind of mistake.

Now I gave him a name. "William Henk," I said, but I didn't move to get up. "There's no hurry, Benny. Finish your drink, then we'll go over."

Benny could have had ten more drinks; it wouldn't have mattered. Big Jim Thompson was firmly ensconced at the bar. He was still holding court over his followers when we walked over to them a few minutes later, and he gave every impression of being there for hours to come. He glanced contemptuously at Benny, then he noticed me, and his small eyes narrowed.

"Mr. Thompson," Benny said, "my friend William Henk wants to meetcha."

Thompson swung around on his stool, but he didn't extend his hand, and I didn't offer mine. "Why?" he challenged.

"Because I've been hearing a lot about you," I said.

"What have you been hearing?"

"That you're a real sucker for a con game." I answered, and Benny looked as though someone had just kicked him in the stomach.

Thompson's face started to go from red to purple. "What business is it of yours?"

"I might have a deal for you."

"*Might* have?" Thompson snorted disdainfully.

"Okay, *will* have. Tomorrow. Meet me here at this time and I'll tell you about it."

"What makes you think I'll be interested in any deal of yours?"

"It will give you a chance to get even for your losses. Maybe get a little ahead. You'd like that, right?"

"So why wait till tomorrow?"

I nodded pleasantly at all his friends. "The audience is too big, and I have someone waiting for me. There's no rush. This is no con game," I said, then turned on my heel and walked away. I could feel their eyes on me, but I didn't look back. I had sunk the hook into Thompson. Now all I had to do was reel him in. Carefully.

I bought a stack of out-of-town newspapers, then drove back toward the hotel where I was staying. I made a lot of unnecessary turns to be sure I wasn't being followed, and put the rented car in a lot a block away.

I could hear the shower running when I opened the door of the suite, and my wife Margie's soft voice floated out to me. She was singing an old folk song, but she'd forgotten most of the words. I slipped out of my suit coat, kicked off my shoes, and sprawled across the bed with the newspapers. I read all the crime news I could find. Doctors read medical journals; I study newspapers. Both of us are keeping abreast of the changes in our professions.

Margie came out of the bathroom wrapped in her yellow terrycloth robe. Her long chestnut hair was freshly brushed and shiny. She sat on the edge of the bed and kissed me.

"Anything new in the papers?" she asked. I'd married Margie because she was beautiful and young and made me feel young, too. Later I noticed I had received a bonus—no one ever looked at me when we were together.

"Not much," I answered. "A couple of bank robberies in New York City—amateurs; a jewel robbery in Miami that has the police excited; and the Los Angeles cops are still hunting for the four men who held up the armored car three days ago."

"Do you think they'll catch them?"

"Probably. Men who have to make their livings with guns in their fists will never win any prize for brains," I said.

Margie stood up and started to unpack more of our clothes. I stopped her. "Don't bother," I said. "We won't be here as long as I figured. I've found a live one."

"Are you going to tell me about it?"

"When it's over. I'm still working it out in my head," I said.

THE NEXT AFTERNOON, Thompson was waiting for me in the lounge of the Buena Vista Casino when I arrived. He was alone and seemed smaller. He was one of those people who needs an audience before he can come alive.

"What've you got to sell?" he asked, bypassing all small-talk preliminaries.

"Counterfeit," I answered, handing him a single bill.

Thompson stood up without another word and headed for the entrance. I followed him through the arch, across the casino floor, and into the coffee shop. The place was all stainless steel and white Formica, and long rows of fluorescent lights hung from the ceiling. There were a couple of customers at the counter, but that was all. Thompson went to the last booth along the wall and sat down, waving away a waitress who started toward him. I took the seat opposite his and waited.

He pulled a ten-power jeweler's loupe out of his pocket, screwed it into his right eye, and examined the fifty-dollar bill I had given him. I knew he was studying the portrait of Grant, the scrollwork along the borders, and the sharpness of the points on the Treasury seal. And he was finding everything perfect.

"You must think I'm a real fool," he said with a nasty smile. "This ain't counterfeit."

"You don't think so, huh?" I handed him another fifty-dollar bill. "What about this?"

He was a little faster this time, but his verdict was the same. "It's real."

"And this one?"

A look, a feel, a snap. "Good as gold."

"Nope." I shook my head. "Counterfeit."

He pointed a blunt finger at the center of my chest. "Listen, punk, I know genuine money when I see it. Whatever you're planning ain't gonna work, so forget it."

"You can be sure of one thing."

"What's that?"

I gave him a nasty smile. "I won't try to sell you a twenty-thousand-dollar telephone book."

His jaw tightened.

"Instead," I continued, "I'm going to give you the chance of a life-time. Those bills *are* counterfeit. In fact, these samples have one major flaw that the rest of my stock doesn't have."

I took the three bills out of his hand and lined them up on the table between us. Then I added three more fifties to the row. "Unlike genuine currency," I told him, "all six of these bills have the same serial numbers."

Thompson's eyes jerked back to the bills, and he snatched up two of them. He held them up to the light and studied them, frowning. After that he compared two more, and sat staring at the six identical Federal Reserve notes.

"Do you still think they're real?" I taunted.

"I've never seen anything like this," he said in an awed tone. "These bills are perfect."

"*Almost* perfect," I corrected. "But I'll deliver brand-new, absolutely perfect bills."

He started to scoop up the money from the table, but I put my hand over his. "Where do you think you're going with that?" I asked.

He gestured toward the gaming tables. "Out into the casino to test some of this."

"Not without paying for it first. I don't give free samples, mister. I don't have to. I've got the best queer there is, and I get fifty cents on the dollar for *every* dollar. That three hundred will cost you one-fifty."

"That's pretty steep for counterfeit, isn't it?"

"You said yourself, you've never seen anything like it. I've been in business for five years and not one bill has ever been questioned, let alone detected. It's not every day you get a chance to double your money."

Thompson gave me a hundred and fifty from the roll he carried, then took my six identical bills into the casino. I ordered a cup of coffee and a hamburger, and settled down to wait for him. I was drinking my second cup of coffee when he returned.

He looked a little stunned by his success. "Not one dealer so much as blinked an eye. I've had 'em look closer at good money," he said.

I didn't have to give him any more of my sales pitch. He was selling himself. I sat back and sipped my coffee.

He didn't keep me waiting long. "Tell you what, I'll take twenty-five-thousand worth."

I shook my head.

"That too much?" he asked.

"Too little. You've seen the last samples you ever will. From now on I sell nothing smaller than hundred-thousand-dollar lots."

He did some mental arithmetic. "That's fifty thousand to me, right?"

"No. The hundred thousand is what *you* pay. In exchange, I give you two hundred thousand in crisp, new tens, twenties, and fifties. Each bill with a *different* serial number."

He didn't say anything right away. I gave him two full minutes to think about it, then slid out of the booth and stood up. "Hell, I thought you were big time," I said disdainfully, then started to walk away.

Thompson called me back, as I knew he would. He was as predictable as a fixed race. "Okay," he said. "You've got a deal, but you better not be planning a rip-off."

"How can there be a rip-off? You're going to examine every bill before you pay me, and you can bring all the help you think you'll need. And I'm not worried about being hijacked by you because I'll tell some friends who I'll be doing business with. If anything happened to me, you wouldn't be hard to find."

"So we understand each other," he said. "Okay, when can we complete the deal?"

"The sooner the better," I said. "The sooner the better."

FOUR HOURS LATER, Margie and I were on our way out of town with Thompson's hundred grand. We were in the rented car because I figured we'd better leave before there was any chance of Thompson getting wise to how I'd tricked him. I could return the car to the agency's office in L.A. or Frisco.

"You're really something," Margie said, hugging my arm while I drove. "When you bought the loot from the armored-car robbery in Los Angeles, you paid ten cents on the dollar because all the money was new, and the numbers had been recorded. You said it was so hot you'd be lucky to get fifteen or twenty cents on the dollar, and then only after you located the right buyer."

"That's what I thought until I met Thompson."

"Didn't he know the money was stolen?"

"No. He thought it was counterfeit. I showed him six perfect fifties, all with the same serial numbers." I told her what had happened in the coffee shop.

"Where did you get counterfeit money?" she demanded.

"I didn't. It was good. Part of the armored-car loot, in fact."

"You must think I'm stupid," Margie said. "I know good money doesn't have the same serial numbers."

I stopped for a traffic light, then got the car rolling again after it changed. "It does if you take half a dozen consecutively numbered bills and erase the last digit."

Margie's mouth opened in surprise. "You can do that? You can erase the numbers?"

"Easier than you'd think," I said, smiling. "And without leaving a trace, either."

My Sister and I

Jean L. Backus

SIBLING RIVALRY

One of the most persistent themes in the world's literatures is that of twins whose identical appearance leads to mistaken identities, substitutions, and farcical or tragic human interplays. Castor and Pollux, the twin sons of Jupiter and Leda, moved from Roman mythology to wheel overhead as the constellation Gemini. And in Twelfth Night, Shakespeare turns his plot on the identical twins Viola and Sebastian. "My Sister and I," in turn, plays a remarkable new variation on this ancient theme which is as compelling as it is unexpected. Jean L. Backus has been a professional writer most of her adult life and a teacher of writing for the past several years. She writes mainstream novels (Dusha) under her own name, and spy-thrillers (Troika, Fellow-Traveller, Traitor's Wife) under the pen name of David Montross. - J.G.

Some twins are truly identical and some are not; some are early friends and grow into jealous enmity at a later date. And then consider my sister Celia and me, two girls so mutually dependent we hardly ever thought of ourselves as individuals. Naturally there were some differences, mostly of temperament, for Celia was imaginative, while I had a better mind. But in most respects we got along well enough. Nobody ever made mental demands on either of us, and certainly we had everything material with which to be comfortable and happy.

Our situation was privileged because of family standing and wealth, and we grew up with servants and a gardener to care for the great park that surrounded the old Mason house on the city's edge. Because we had each other and Father, plus constant attention from Eleanor, our nurse and governess, we hardly missed the pleasures of going to school and making friends.

Father was a dear man. I could imagine him before our mother died when we were born. At that time he would have been about twenty-eight, a young and vigorous veteran of the Korean War, a member of various social and fraternal organizations, and a senior partner in Mason and Heathly because our grandfather had founded the profitable investment firm. Probably our parents had entertained a good deal. He was the only surviving member of the socially attractive Mason family, and she, although an orphan, came from people as acceptable if not as wealthy. But all that changed nineteen years ago when we were born, and he was left a widower with a pair of daughters on his hands and no relatives to help him out.

Apparently his loss was greater than the compensation he might have found in us. He hired Eleanor who was a registered nurse, and he resigned his active partnership, though the business continued to bear his name and pay him a handsome income. He might have traveled, but instead his vitality must have diminished for he became something of a recluse, only leaving the house once a week after lunch when he would drive into the city to dine with friends. Or at least Celia and I assumed that's what he did. He never came home and told us what a good dinner he'd had, or how nice it had been to see this or that old acquaintance.

Otherwise he spent a good deal of his time in the study, writing letters abroad for church and public records to be used in the compilation of the Mason family history.

I don't mean to say he isolated himself entirely, not at all. We ate our meals together, and on fine days he would drive us around the grounds in a pony cart; when it rained he would often read aloud to us. We never expressed a desire for a toy or book or dress that he didn't supply it, and last year when Eleanor suggested it might be time for her to move on, we were terrified and begged so hard to have him make her stay that he doubled her salary. She positively bloomed after that, while he seemed both relieved and more content. Consequently, it never occurred to me that he might have grown restive under his own restraints until Celia called it to my attention a month ago.

"Clara," she asked, "have you noticed how preoccupied Father always is after his day out on Thursday?"

"Yes. What about it?"

"It's Eleanor's day off too."

"What of it? She goes away in a taxi as she always has, and he drives off alone."

"Well, I don't like it," Celia said. "I'm sure they meet later."

"What if they do? If he thought of it, he'd invite her to ride into the city with him. Why shouldn't he? What are you getting at?"

"I think she proposes to marry him. I think she's just recently told him."

I was shocked into silence. Eleanor had been with us since before I could remember, first as our nurse, then governess, and since last year as our housekeeper-companion. As far as I was concerned, she was our mother. She wasn't a woman to give her own feelings away, but underneath her quiet manner was the reliable assurance that whatever happened, she was ready to hand out punishment or affection with such tactful justice that neither of us had ever complained of partiality. She dressed quietly, moved unobtrusively about the house on various domestic errands, and never forgot the exact nature of her relationship to us or to Father.

Now I realized that being stupid, self-centered little beasts, we knew almost nothing about her, where she'd come from, or who her family was, or what she did on her days off. Maybe her parents were still alive, maybe she visited relatives or friends, or went shopping or alone to a movie. I'd never thought about what she did, only how uneventful Thursday always was because she wasn't there to make it interesting.

Then on that Thursday night a month ago, Celia added, "Remember when Eleanor told us about marriage and all that stuff? Clara, she said something then I'll never forget."

"What did she say?"

Being a clever mimic, my sister went on in Eleanor's normal tones: "Marriage and the family are changing institutions, girls, but there will always be certain women who hold out for legal status. Illicit affairs may be good enough when a woman is young, but there comes a time when she can't keep it up. And then she demands marriage, if only for children of her own and security in her old age."

As soon as Celia said the words, I could see Eleanor's face twisting as she spoke that day, her hands twining one about the other in her lap. Now I knew she'd been describing herself, letting her secret desires for once overcome her reticence. Because of course she wasn't anybody's wife, and she wasn't anybody's mother.

Celia's suspicion upset me. I didn't often think of marriage because it was one more experience we'd have to forego, and since nothing could change us, there was no use worrying about it. Now, thinking about Eleanor's lecture that day, and the book she'd handed us in answer to our questions, and thinking about her with Father, I grew hot and anxious, even disgusted.

Celia said, "They've been having an affair, they've been making love together for at least a year, Clara, I'm sure of it."

"How can you be?"

"Because of how she tried to leave us. Remember she said certain women get too old for an affair and demand marriage? Well, she's not getting any younger. Pretty soon she'll be too old for babies."

"Oh, Celia, don't talk like that. It's horrible."

"But we have to be realistic. I don't understand why you're so shocked. When men and women are in love, they want to sleep together. There's nothing horrible about it. Don't tell me you haven't thought about making love."

I wouldn't answer that. I said, "How did you guess about Father and Eleanor?"

"Oh, Clara, whatever is wrong with you? I didn't guess. We overheard them in the lower hall just before lunch today. Weren't you listening? You know how the stairwell acts as a sound conductor. Didn't you hear her say, 'I'll meet you at the motel as usual, darling'?"

"She didn't!"

"She did too. I heard her."

"I heard their voices," I said, thinking back. "I didn't pay any attention to the words. And they didn't come home together."

"They're being clever," Celia said. "But I'm convinced she's given him an ultimatum. I wonder how we can break it up."

I had to stop and think before I answered. Why should we break it up? Eleanor was attractive, Father was charming, and we loved them both. What would change? What difference would their marriage make to us?

"I ask you, Clara, how can we break them up? Short of murder."

"That's a terrible thing to say. Would it be so awful if they married?"

"Awful," Celia said into the darkness of our bedroom. "She's still young enough to have babies, and we don't want anyone else to share whatever money's left when Father dies. Do we?"

I thought about that for a minute and said slowly, "No, I guess not."

"You'd better guess not," she said. "And we'd better do something before it's too late. Start thinking, Clara, and I will too."

I did try, but it wasn't easy. Always before when we wanted something we'd gone to Father. This time we couldn't. Not possibly. The best I could come up with was a plan to drive Eleanor away, make it so unhappy for her she'd give up and leave of her own accord.

Celia hooted when I reluctantly offered my plan. "You are stupid," she said. "She's paid to accept whatever we do, no matter how bad it is. Anyway, she'd twist Father until he'd desert us before he did her."

"I don't believe it. Celia, you're a beast. I'm back to thinking there's no truth in what you suspect. I don't believe they're in love at all. And I don't care if they are."

"We may both be stupid," my sister said, "but you're worse than I am."

I wanted to hit her for insisting without any more proof than what she claimed to have overheard. Instead, I proposed we listen at the stairwell whenever Eleanor went down. And for three weeks we sneaked around and spied and discussed the problem. We got nowhere, having heard not one word that wasn't perfectly normal and innocuous.

Another week went by, and today being Thursday we were on the job early, making ourselves conspicuous, apparently, because at lunch Eleanor asked if we weren't feeling well.

"I wonder if I ought to go out this afternoon," she said. "You girls have been jumpy and unsettled for the past month. Is anything wrong?"

"What's that?" Father looked up from his lemon pie. "What's wrong?"

"It's an uneasy feeling I have, Mr. Mason. The girls have been unlike themselves for days now, and I'm worried." Eleanor's expression was as concerned as I'd seen it hundreds of times when she treated us for a cold or gave us a pill for cramps or to make us sleep. And her manner was as formal with Father, as if she'd never mentioned a motel to him or called him darling in Celia's hearing if not in mine.

Father's hair had been gray for years although he wasn't fifty yet, but his lined, pale face was very sad and old at the moment. "You must do as you think best, Eleanor," he said without looking at her. "Although it seems a shame for you to miss your day off." Then he looked at us, which we always accepted as painful for him. "Is something wrong, Clara?"

"No, Father," I mumbled, looking at my plate because his expression hurt me, although I sympathized. My sister and I took care never to look directly at each other either if we could help it.

"Celia?"

"Not a thing, Father." She stared at him defiantly. "I can't imagine what's got into Eleanor, making a fuss about nothing. We're fine."

Eleanor sighed. "All right then, but I'm going to give you both a tranquilizer, and in the future I want you to promise to tell me if anything bothers you."

"We will," Celia and I said together.

Eleanor went up from lunch to the medicine cabinet in her bathroom where she kept all the salves and ointments and pills we might need, and she stood over us while we swallowed the capsules she handed out.

"That should do it," she said. "You'll settle down quietly for a nap, and when I come home tonight, I'll give you a sleeping pill if you need it."

Then she closed the cabinet and got her things and went off in a taxi. An hour or so later Father waved to us as he drove down to the gates in the wall around our grounds.

I was already more tranquil than I'd been for the past month, and I told Celia what I'd decided. "This uncertainty is too much for me," I said. "Tomorrow we're going to Father and ask him if he wants to marry Eleanor. He'll tell us if it's true. He's always been honest with us."

Inadvertently I met her eyes and looked away. I had always felt Father had been too honest about our prospects. Now I wondered if that same resentment was driving Celia to make trouble.

"He wouldn't be honest about this," she replied. "It's too disgusting."

"Well, I don't care. I don't like spying. I don't like being upset. I don't like what you're doing. And even if we got a lie from him, I'd feel better. Wouldn't you? Really?"

"No, I wouldn't," she said. "Because he'd either marry Eleanor at once or he'd send her away, whatever he told us. Then we'd be in for a miserable time."

"But I'm miserable now. Anyway, I want her to stay. I want them to be happy. I love Eleanor."

"As a stepmother?" Celia asked with scorn. "Having babies to dilute whatever fortune Father will leave?"

"I don't care about the fortune. Or the babies either. Anyway, there isn't anything else we can do. We just have to shut up and see what happens."

"I won't do that," she said. "If I knew where to get some poison, I'd give it to her. If I knew where to get a gun, I'd shoot her."

I caught my breath. "That's terrible! You shouldn't say things like that. You shouldn't even think them."

"I'll think what I please," Celia said. "I'll do what has to be done. Nobody's going to take Father away from me. Not Eleanor, not you, not anybody. He's mine, and I won't ever let him go."

I moved compulsively, wondering at my blindness. Celia didn't care about the stepmother bit, she didn't care about the babies or the diluted fortune. Celia was insanely jealous of Eleanor, she was insanely in love with Father.

Horror filled me, and for the first time, loathing. Always before I'd accepted the fact that we were too close to each other, and always I'd ignored it. But I couldn't any longer, I simply could not. Eleanor's safety, her life, depended on whatever I did now. And of course there was no way for me to do anything. Nothing at all.

Unless...

Murder and suicide. And the quicker the better, before I thought it over, although I doubted I'd change my mind. I was only nineteen, and in addition to Eleanor's danger, there were still many barren and hopeless years stretching ahead.

"Come along, Celia," I said, lightheaded already. "Let's go explore Eleanor's medicine cabinet."

"Yes, let's," she agreed. "I knew you'd see it my way."

Sleeping pills, I was thinking to myself, a whole handful taken in secret as a distracted Celia hunted eagerly for a bottle of poison.

Poor Father. He'd never understand. Or maybe he would. Anyway, he and Eleanor would console each other.

Linked eternally by our common circulatory system, my sister and I moved steadily up the stairs and along the hall—with equal determination, if on different errands...

Goodbye, Cora

Richard Ellington

"BLACK MASK" SCHOOL

Both of us are admitted and dedicated aficionados (not to mention sometime writers) of the "Black Mask," or "hardboiled," school of suspense fiction, and so naturally we wanted to use a representative example of this type of story herein. Richard Ellington's "Goodbye, Cora" was one of the earliest submissions we received, and after reading it we knew we had to look no further. As well as being a genuine McGuffin, it is realistic, sensitive, relentless, violent, and ultimately quite moving—all the qualities of the "hardboiled" school at its very best. Mr. Ellington is the author of five novels featuring private eye Steve Drake, all of which appeared in the late 1940s and early 1950s, and numerous radio scripts and short stories; at present he lives in the Virgin Islands, the setting of this story. - B.P.

THE MAN WAS FAT, over three-hundred pounds. He wore khaki trousers and a short-sleeved, open-at-the-throat shirt of the same material. The back of the shirt was soggy and dark with perspiration. He leaned forward on the bench, put his elbows on the table, and said in a worried voice, "You don't look so good, Carter. You sick, man?" His accent was faintly West Indian.

Carter sat down slowly on a bench across the table. He was tall and lean and his shoulders were slightly stooped. His tanned face was heavily lined. He wore a flowered sports shirt, white linen slacks, and a wide-brimmed, expensive Panama hat.

He took off the Panama, put it on the bench beside him, and nodded. "I've been drunk for three days. This morning I got your message and decided I'd better come out of it. It's not easy." He drew cigarettes from the pocket of his sports shirt and lit one with trembling fingers. Sweat broke out on his forehead. He dabbed at it with a hand-kerchief and grinned painfully. "I'm a damned fool, Tommy. I always think it'll help, but it never does."

Behind them, a jukebox came to life. A native woman came out of the pavilion carrying a tray with a bottle of champagne on it. She crossed the open cement terrace and put the champagne on the table. The woman went back into the pavilion. The fat man poured cham-pagne into one of the glasses. He picked it up, made a little gesture toward Carter, and said, "Well, first today." He drank half a glassful and put the glass down on the table in front of him.

Carter watched him, and more sweat crept onto his forehead. He inhaled his cigarette and blew smoke upward. A light breeze trailed it off toward the water. Carter followed the smoke with his eyes and let them come to rest on the town of Charlotte Amalie across the bay. The juke box stopped moaning, and the faint tooting of automobile horns floated across the harbor. Otherwise it was quiet and still.

Tommy leaned forward again.

"What's the matter, Carter?" he asked in a gently worried voice.

Carter kept his eyes on the town. His mouth tightened and one of his face muscles jerked. He said in a low, tight voice, "Cora's not coming back, Tommy. She's left me."

Amazement came over the fat man's face. "But Christ, man! After all these years."

Carter nodded and said dully, "Twenty-two."

"But I don't understand. What happened?"

"I don't know exactly. I've been noticing a change in her for the last year or so, and I had a funny feeling about things when she went up to visit her sister in the States last month. She wrote a couple of times, sort of half-interested letters. And then this one came four days ago. She just said it was all over."

"Is there another man?"

"I don't think so. No, I guess she just got tired of it. All this." Carter gestured wearily toward the town. "The boat, the heat, the drinking, the people, the tropics, and me. Mostly I guess it was me. She never understood about me, and she never understood about the Islands. I don't think she ever knew or cared how much I loved her, how much I depended on her."

"I'm sorry, Carter."

"Yeah."

"You'll get used to it in time."

"Uh-uh." Carter shook his head again. "You don't understand, Tommy. If she left me after a month or even a year or two years, it wouldn't have mattered so much. I wouldn't have known her so well then or loved her so much. It—it's like losing your arms or your legs or your eyes."

Tommy said kindly, "People lose those things every day, Carter, and they go on and make the best of it."

Carter swung his bloodshot eyes back on the fat man. "Not all of them," he said, "not the ones like me. The others have something I don't have. Maybe it's character or strength or just plain guts. I don't know. Maybe that's why Cora left me. I wasn't ever what she really wanted anyway. She really wanted security, a husband who had a steady job, and a home in the suburbs of some city up north. But I was picturesque when she met me. Picturesque!" He laughed a short, bitter little laugh. "You're not picturesque when you're no better than a beach-combing bum at forty-five."

"You're no beachcomber." Carter didn't seem to hear him.

"These last three days have been hell, Tommy, hell. I never left the boat and I saw her everywhere, some dresses hanging over a bunk, that old robe I know so well, some hairpins and powder in a drawer. I tell you, Tommy, I—"

"Stop it, Carter!" The fat man's deep voice was sharp, almost angry.

Carter had half-risen from the bench with both hands flat on the table in front of him. Finally, he sank slowly down on the bench.

"Sure, Tommy. I almost forgot you sent me that message. What did you want to see me about?"

The fat man leaned toward Carter and lowered his voice. "It's Greg. Some men are going to kill him."

The impact of the fat man's words stopped Carter's train of thought completely. He stared for a second or two at his friend and then said in an incredulous voice, "Kill him?"

"Yes."

"Why? What's Greg done?"

"I don't know the whole story. It happened in the States. That's why he came back here to St. Thomas a month ago. You knew he was back?"

"No. I had no idea he was in St. Thomas."

"I guess nobody knows it but Mom and me and—these men who are going to kill him."

"They know he's here on the Island?"

"Yes. When Greg got here last month I could tell right away that something was wrong. He wouldn't go out and didn't want to see anybody. He told Mom he was sick, but I knew better. I finally got it out of him. He didn't tell me what he'd done, but I think he got mixed up with that crime syndicate. Maybe he double-crossed them in some way, or maybe he got paid for something he couldn't deliver."

"He's out at your mother's place?"

"Yes." The fat man finished his champagne and refilled the glass. He stared down at the drink and said bitterly, "Greg's a no-good louse, but you know that Mom thinks he's Jesus' own shadow. She worships him. It'd kill her if she found out the truth, if anything happened to him." He sipped his champagne, and then added, "And he *is* my kid brother. I've got to save him, Carter. That's why I sent for you. I thought maybe you could think of something, help me."

Carter shook his head slowly. "When those boys send a killer to do a job, he usually does it."

"Yes, I know. But there must be some way."

"You said they knew Greg was here in St. Thomas. What makes you think so?"

"A private plane from Miami landed at the airport last night. There were two men aboard: one was the pilot; the other man didn't look like a wealthy businessman or a tourist. They each carried one small suitcase and they registered at the Grand Hotel. The pilot gave his name as William Leary, and the other man signed in as Ancil Dolph."

Carter shrugged his shoulders. "Why, hell, Tommy, that may not mean anything. They could be here for a dozen reasons."

"Uh-uh." The fat man wiped perspiration off his forehead with a handkerchief. "I've had a good check on the airport ever since Greg told me about his trouble. These men asked in the coffee shop where Gregory Braun could be reached. The counter-boy said he didn't know, said he'd never heard of him. I don't think they did any more inquiring." Tommy glanced at his wrist watch. "They were still in their room at the Grand half an hour ago."

Carter spoke slowly in a tired voice. "I guess the police are out."

"I guess they are."

"No chance of just keeping Greg hidden until these fellows give up and go away?"

"What do *you* think?"

Slight annoyance crept over Carter's face. "You know I'd like to help, Tommy. You're my best friend. You're like a brother to me. But just what the hell can I do? What did you think *I* could do?"

The fat man spread his hands helplessly. "I don't know," he said. "I—I just thought that maybe—well, that you'd know about these things, know what to do."

Carter lit another cigarette. "I ran rum and whisky at twenty-nine and thirty. Today I'll run brandy if the price is right. I've made my share of petty payoffs, and I've thrown shots twice and never hit anything. Once I took a slug in the shoulder and had an all-night swim for my trouble. That was a long time ago. No, Tommy, these boys are way out of my class. I don't see how I can help."

Disappointment showed in the fat man's kind eyes. "Well," he said, "I guess that's that. Maybe Greg can make a run for it again." Carter turned and looked out across the bay. A large white yacht was unfurling her sails and moving slowly across the harbor toward the open sea. He watched it without really seeing it. "It won't do any good," he said. "If they want him, they'll find him."

"Yeah," Tommy said.

Carter's eyes were on the red roofs of the town. They stayed there for ten more seconds. Then very slowly he turned and looked at Tommy. The faint trace of a smile played around his lips.

"Hell," he said, "I wonder—"

There was a pause. The fat man frowned and asked, "You wonder what?"

"If it's possible." The smile spread a little.

"What? Something about Cora?"

"No. Cora's finished, but Greg may not be."

"I don't understand."

Carter stood up. The smile had gone from his face but there was still a hint of excitement in his eyes. "I just had an idea. If it's any good, maybe we can save Greg after all."

"How? What are you going to do?"

"First, I've got to find out if it'll work. You'll hear from me if it does. Just keep Greg out of the way and don't tell him anything about any of this."

"All right. But don't you need help?"

"No." Carter picked up his Panama and put it on. He held out his hand. "Sit tight until you hear from me." The fat man nodded uneasily, and they shook hands.

Carter crossed the terrace, went through the pavilion and out to the road leading to the airport. An empty cab was just passing. He flagged it down, got in, and told the driver to take him to the Grand Hotel.

The road led around the bay and into Cha Cha Town, the old French quarter of Charlotte Amalie. The cab swung around a corner and the Normandie Bar came into view. Carter looked at the Normandie, shrugged wearily, and said, "The hell with it."

The driver slowed the car and half-turned in his seat. "What?" he asked. Carter told him to stop and wait for him. He got out of the cab, entered the Normandie Bar, and ordered a double shot of rum. The bartender said, "Hello, Carter," but Carter didn't hear him. He was thinking of other times in the Normandie Bar, other times when she had been with him. There was that night during the war when the big Marine had made the pass at her. He looked down at his knuckles. The scars were still there. Later that night, she'd laid her head on his shoulder and cried and told him how much she loved him.

Carter lifted his glass, closed his eyes, drank the double shot of rum in one gulp. Then he paid for the drink and returned to the waiting cab. They passed the ancient walled cemetery, circled the market, and finally reached the square at the end of Charlotte Amalie's main street. It was a "boat day" and one of the bigger cruise ships was in port. Crowds of eager-eyed, pale tourists filled the sidewalks, gawking, taking pictures, and shopping.

When Carter's cab reached the Post Office, he told the driver to circle the square and stop near the steps of the Grand Hotel. The driver was lucky enough to find a parking place. Carter got out, paid his fare, and then asked the driver if he wanted to earn ten dollars. The driver's eyes said he did. Carter told him to wait.

The Grand Hotel is one of the oldest in the West Indies, a large rambling building that covers half a block. Various shops and offices line the ground floor, and the lobby is up one flight of worn steps. Carter went up the stairs and entered the big shadowy room.

The rum had sent a pleasant warm glow through him and now, as the ten-degree cooler temperature of the lobby hit him, the drink began to take effect. Coming on an empty stomach, it gave him a feeling of remote numbness. His nerves suddenly seemed to relax, and he noticed that he'd stopped perspiring.

He stopped at the desk and coughed. The dozing clerk opened his eyes, yawned, and stood up. Carter asked him if Mr. Dolph and Mr. Leary were still in their room. The clerk looked at the row of mailboxes, nodded, and gave Carter the number of the room.

Carter thanked him and asked if he sold stamps. The clerk yawned and nodded again. Carter bought two stamps, an airmail and a first-class.

There were two writing desks in the lobby. Carter crossed over to one of them, sat down, and hurriedly wrote two notes. He put them in envelopes, sealed them, and put the air mail stamp on one and the first-class stamp on the other. Then he went down the steps to the street. The taxi was still waiting for him. He took ten dollars from his pocket and handed it to the driver. Then he gave him the two letters he'd written. "Now listen carefully," he said. The driver put on a frown of concentration. Carter spoke very slowly.

The driver repeated the instructions. It satisfied Carter. He went up the steps to the lobby of the hotel, walked the length of it, and entered a dim, musty corridor. Rooms opened off each side of it, and all the doors were closed.

At the end of the long hallway Carter turned to the right, climbed a flight of stairs, and found the number he was looking for. He stopped in front of the door, listened a second, and knocked.

There was a pause, and then from inside the room a hoarse voice with a Brooklyn accent said, "Yeah? Who is it?"

Carter said very distinctly, "It's Gregory Braun."

Nothing happened for nearly five seconds, and then the door

swung open. A heavy set, stocky man with thick, black hair and a swarthy face stood framed in the doorway. His eyes were hard and expressionless. He wore only his underwear and he held a towel in his hand. There was a trace of shaving soap under his left ear.

Behind him Carter saw a slim, blond young man sitting on the edge of the bed. He was fully dressed except for one shoe. He held the shoe in his hand and stared at Carter. His silky hair was thinning at the front, and he wore glasses.

The dark haired, stocky man squinted, looked up at Carter, and said, "What did you say your name was?"

"Gregory Braun."

"So?"

"I heard you were asking where to find me, out at the airport last night. I wondered why."

A sneer spread over the swarthy face and the stocky man's head tilted several degrees to one side. His voice had velvet wrapped around it. "Don't you know?"

Carter's lean body seemed to sag a little. He nodded, and said in a tired voice, "Yeah, I guess I do."

The dark man stepped aside and motioned Carter into the room with his head. Carter moved through the doorway, toward the only chair in the room. When he was still four feet from it, the man behind him said, "Far enough! Freeze it right there." Carter stopped and stared at the wall in front of him.

The thin blond put his shoe on and got up off the bed. He went over to Carter and quickly searched him. "He's clean," he said. He had a friendly voice with no particular accent. He went back and sat down on the edge of the bed again.

"Okay," the stocky man said, "you can relax, Braun." Carter turned around. The stocky man had a .45 automatic in his hand. He let it hang loosely at his side.

The blond man laughed and shook his head. "You're sure making it easy, Buster."

Carter looked bleakly at him. "I got tired of running." He shifted his eyes to the other man. "Can I square it?"

"Not with us. We've already been paid to do a job."

The blond man said almost absently, "I fly planes, Ancil. Remember?"

"I don't mean you guys," Carter said. "I mean the boys up north. Can I square it with them?"

Ancil shrugged. "It musta been a big chunk, very big."

"It was," Carter said, "and I've still got it."

Ancil's eyebrows lifted in surprise. "Not on you."

"Hell, no."

"But you can lay hands on it?"

"Yes. I'll give it back to them if they'll forget it."

Ancil looked at the blond. "What do you think, Bill?"

"We might give it a whirl. Everybody likes to get their money back."

"Right." Ancil turned his eyes on Carter again. "Okay, Braun, where is it?"

"Hidden on a boat I've been living on."

"Where's the boat?"

"It's anchored out at Nazareth Bay at the other end of the Island."

"You got a car?"

"No, we'll have to rent one or hire a cab."

Ancil turned to the blond. "Go hire a car, Bill."

Bill got up, crossed to the door and went out. Ancil started putting on his clothes, and Carter sat down on the only chair in the room.

It wasn't really such a long ride, but it seemed to Carter as if it would last forever. Bill did the driving and Carter sat beside him on the front seat. Ancil sat in the rear. He'd removed his coat, opened his vest, and rolled up his sleeves. The coat lay loosely across his knees and Carter knew the .45 was under it. There was little conversation, but once when a speeding taxi narrowly missed them, Bill grunted angrily, "God damn this driving on the left."

Ancil said, "Yeah." Otherwise they rode in silence.

Carter sat stiffly and watched the town drop away beneath them as they circled upward on the Red Hook road. He let his eyes run lingeringly over the familiar scenes below. The boats in the harbor looked like toys, and the still, blue water resembled glass. People on the streets were moving specks, and cars were no bigger than crawling ants.

The car reached the summit of the mountain and dropped off sharply in the direction of St. John. The low, deep moan of an incoming freighter sounded faintly above the motor of the car as the town disappeared from sight.

Occasionally the car passed dilapidated shacks with their strangely contrasting profusion of tropical plants and flowers. There was no traffic; and except for wandering goats and cows, they had the winding road to themselves. Five more minutes passed and the entrance to a dirt road came into view ahead of them. Carter indicated it with his head.

Bill slowed, swung the car into the deep ruts, and they crawled and bounced upward through deep jungle-like growth. The road leveled off when they reached the top of the hill and far below a wide panorama of islands stretched out before them. Three miles away, directly in front of them, the bright, green mountains of St. John rose majestically toward the sky. White beaches lined the water's edge and sparkled brightly in the hot morning sun.

Ancil said, "How much further is it?"

"Another mile or so," Carter told him. "The bay is just beyond the end of the road."

He was thinking about the beaches of St. John. His eyes were closed, and he was remembering moonlight nights, the feel of hot sand against his back, the gentle roll of a boat riding at anchor, and, most of all, Cora.

THE BUMPY, dirt road ended on a bluff a couple of hundred feet above the water. The three men left the car and walked down a path until they came out on the beach. There was very little breeze, and it was hot. All three were sweating profusely.

The bay was ringed with palms and sea-grapes, and the white beach lay like a ribbon in front of them. The beach was empty except for a dinghy drawn up on the sand. About three hundred feet out in the bay a two-masted sixty-foot motor sailor rode at anchor. Otherwise there was no sign of human habitation. The only sound was the occasional cry of a sea gull and the gentle slap of water on the beach.

Ancil pointed to the boat. "Is that it?"

"Yes." Carter indicated the dinghy. "We'll have to row out."

Bill and Carter dragged the dinghy down to the water and the three men got in. Bill sat in the bow. Carter did the rowing, and Ancil sat in the stern facing Carter. He took his heavy automatic out of his pocket and held it on his knees.

When they reached the boat, Bill got out first and climbed aboard. Ancil handed him the automatic and went up the ladder. Once on deck he took the pistol again and covered Carter as he climbed aboard and made the dinghy fast.

Carter led the way through a companionway, and they entered a large, roomy cabin. It was musty and dimly lit. Dirty dishes filled the small sink in the galley and there were three or four empty whisky bottles scattered around. A woman's dress hung on a hanger just inside the companionway leading forward. The door to the head was open, and it swung lazily back and forth with the even roll of the boat. An open letter and envelope lay on the deck near a small secured table with drawers in it.

Ancil motioned vaguely with his automatic. "Okay, Braun, where's the dough?"

Carter's bloodshot eyes seemed to stare through Ancil. He seemed to be looking at something a long way off. "It's there in the drawer," he said. He turned and took two steps toward the table with the drawers in it.

Ancil lifted his automatic and squeezed the trigger. The pistol roared and jumped in his hand.

The bullet hit Carter just left of center in the middle of his back. The impact knocked him forward against the bulkhead. He hit it hard, face-on, with both arms outstretched. His knees buckled, and he slid down into a kneeling position. It was as if he were praying to the bulkhead.

He made no sound and stayed in the bent-over kneeling position for five or six seconds. A dark stain of blood was spreading over the back of the flowered sports shirt. It spread incredibly fast. A little gurgling noise came from his mouth, and he toppled sideways onto the deck. He didn't move again.

The thin blond man's face had turned the color of cigar ash. He stared at the man on the floor and said, "Christ, Ancil!"

Nothing had happened to Ancil's face. He jerked his head toward the small table. "See if there's any dough in there."

Bill nodded and walked stiff-legged to the table with his eyes still fixed on Carter's body. There were three drawers. He opened all of them and looked inside. He shook his head. "Nothing in here."

He looked bewildered and a little sick.

"I don't get it. What was he trying to pull? That talk about the money and—"

"Hell," Ancil said, "he was just stalling, that's all."

"You mean you knew it and let him bring us all the way out here?"

"Can you think of a better place?" Ancil ran his eyes around the cabin in a business-like manner. "Can you run this tub?"

Bill said, as if he were thinking of something else, "Yeah, I guess so."

"Good. Let's haul the anchor and get sloggin'."

"Why? Where to?"

Ancil pointed a stubby finger at the dead man on the deck. "Straight out to sea for a couple of miles, and back here again. The sharks oughta go for all that blood."

"Oh," Bill said.

THE NEXT MORNING Tommy Braun received a letter. It read as follows:

Dear Tommy,

Everything worked out okay. Greg is squared and the lead throwers are leaving the Island. Just make sure Greg sticks around and behaves himself.

As for me, I'm leaving the islands. I guess you know why. I don't yet know where I'm going, but I have a hunch I'll be okay.

Don't worry about the boat. She was mortgaged to the hilt so I'm just leaving it for Kempers to take over.

Take care of yourself.

Carter

TWO DAYS LATER, a woman in Reading, Pennsylvania, also received a letter. She was sitting on the front porch of her sister's home when the mailman brought it. Her sister was sitting in a swing beside her. The woman tore the letter open and read it. When she finished, she smiled and shook her head. Her sister said, "From Carter?"

"Yes," the woman said. "He hasn't changed any."

"What did he say?"

"Not much. He'll miss me, but he'll get along all right. He's going to try his luck somewhere in South America."

"Didn't he say anything else?"

The woman looked down at the open letter again. Then she started absently tearing it into small pieces. "Yes," she replied. "He said, 'Goodbye, Cora.'"

Multiples

Bill Pronzini and Barry N. Malzberg

?

One of the logics behind this anthology was our desire to present as many variations as possible on the theme mysterium. Ergo, such headings as HOWDUNIT, THE IMPOSSIBLE CRIME, THE FORMAL MYSTERY, and the like. At the head of this page, however, you will note a simple "?" Why? Because my co-editor and his collaborator have created a story which defies classification. The events occurred—or did they? The man is mad—or is he? The wife is dead—or is she? It is a nest of Chinese boxes, each answer only creating a new and more puzzling question. Writing alone, Mr. Pronzini has carved himself an enviable niche as a suspense writer (Snowbound, Panic!), and Mr. Malzberg as a science-fiction writer (Beyond Apollo). Writing in tandem, they have startled mainstream readers with The Running of Beasts and will absolutely stun them with the forthcoming Justice. - J.G.

KENNER MURDERED his wife for the tenth time on the evening of July 28, in the kitchen of their New York apartment. Or perhaps it was July 29. One day is much the same as another, and I cannot seem to keep dates clearly delineated in my head. He did it for the usual reasons: because she had dominated him for fourteen years of marriage (fifteen? sixteen?), and openly and regularly ridiculed him, and sapped all his energy and drive, and, oh I simply could not stand it anymore. He did not try to be elaborately clever as to method and execution. The simpler the better-that was the way he liked to do it. So he poisoned her with ten capsules of potassium, I mean nitrous oxide, disguised as saccharine tablets, which he neatly placed in her coffee with a twist of the wrist like a kiss. Nothing amiss.

She assumed almost at once the characteristic attitude of oxide poisoning, turning a faint green as she bent into the crockery on the table. A cigarette still smoldered unevenly beside her. She drank twenty cups of coffee every day and smoked approximately four packages of cigarettes, despite repeated warnings from her doctor. Kenner found it amusing to think that her last sensations were composed of acridity, need, and lung-filling inhalation. It was even possible that she believed, as death majestically overtook her, that the *cigarette* had done her in.

Kenner, a forty-five-year-old social worker of mundane background, few friends, and full civil service tenure (but nevertheless in grave trouble with his superiors, who had recently found him to be "insufficiently motivated"), then made all efforts to arrange the scene in what he thought to be a natural manner: adjusting the corpse in a comfortable position, cleaning the unused pellets of cyanide from the table, letting the damned cat out, and so forth. Immediately afterward, he went to a movie theater; that is, he went immediately after shutting off all the lights and locking all the doors. Windows were left open in the kitchen, however, to better disperse what he thought of as "the stench of death."

What Kenner did at the movie theater was to sit through a double feature. The price he paid for admission and what films he saw or did not really see are not known at the time of this writing. Furthermore, what he hoped to gain by leaving the scene of the crime only to reenter at a "safer" time remains in doubt. I must have been crazy. Also, Kenner's usual punctiliousness and sense of order did not control his actions during this tragic series of events. I was too excited.

After emerging from the theater, Kenner purchased an ice cream cone from a nearby stand and ate it slowly while walking back to his apartment. As be turned in a westerly direction, he was accosted by two co-workers at the Welfare Unit where he was employed. They greeted him and asked the whereabouts of his wife. Kenner responded that she had had a severe headache and, since she suffered from a mild heart condition complicated by diabetes, wanted to restrain her activities to the minimum. I suppose Kenner was attempting with this tactic to lay the groundwork for a "death by natural causes" verdict, but I'm not quite sure. I do know that one of the coworkers, commenting on Kenner's appearance, said that he looked "ghastly."

Once parted from his colleagues, Kenner continued west and eventually re-entered his apartment at 10:51 P.M. It was frightening in the dark. Turning on the lights, be went into the living room and found his wife waiting there for him-sitting under a small lamp, reading and drinking coffee and smoking five cigarettes in various stages of completion. Much perturbed, he was unable to account for the fact that she was still alive. I felt as if I were dreaming.

There was a brief exchange of dialogue between Kenner and his wife, the substance of which I cannot recall, and then he proceeded to his own room. He wanted to lock the door behind him but could not, owing to the fact that his wife—saying that separate bedrooms or not, she wanted to know what the "little fool" was doing at all times—had forbidden him a bolt. On the way, he noticed that the plates had been removed from the kitchen table and heaped as always to fester in the sink, and that there was no sign of the violence he was *sure* had taken place earlier.

Immediately after closing his door, Kenner seized his journal and began to record the evening's curious events in his usual style. I could have been a published writer if only I had worked at it. He was hopeful that the documentation would help him to understand matters, but I was wrong, this was never the answer.

He was interrupted midway through his writing by his wife's customarily unannounced entrance into his room. She told him that his strange state of excitation this evening had upset even her, and therefore agitated her mild heart condition (she had one, all right, although she did not have diabetes). She said she thought I was "breaking down," and went on to say that she knew the "impulse to murder her" had long been uppermost in Kenner's mind, but he "didn't have the guts to do it." She further stated that Kenner was no doubt "dreaming all the time of ways and means and you probably fill that damned journal of yours with all your raving imaginations; I've never cared enough to bother reading it, but it's sure to be *full* of lunatic fantasies."

Kenner responded that he was a mature person and thus not prey to hostile thoughts. He begged her to leave the room so that he could continue his entries. I told her I was writing a novel, but she didn't believe me. She knows everything.

She laughed at him and dared him to make her leave the room. Kenner stared at her mutely, whereupon she laughed again and said if looks could kill, she'd certainly be dead right now. Then she said, "But if I were dead, you'd be completely lost; you'd fall apart altogether. You need me and you don't *really* want me dead, you know, even though as I'm talking to you you're probably filling up pages with more vicious fantasies. I'll bet I even know what you're writing this very minute. You're imagining me dead, aren't you? You're writing down right this minute that I'm dead."

She's dead.

She's dead.

She-is-dead!

KENNER MURDERED his wife for the eleventh time on July 29 or July 30, in her bedroom in their New York apartment He did it for the usual reasons, and he did not attempt to be elaborately clever as to method and execution. In fact, he chose to repeat the procedure of the previous evening. While she lounged in bed as was her custom on weekends (this was either Saturday or Sunday), I made her breakfast and poisoned her coffee with eleven capsules of nitrous oxide.

When Kenner took the tray into her bedroom, she was sitting up in bed and there were three cigarettes burning on the nightstand. She smiled at him maliciously as she lifted her cup and asked if he had "put in a few drops of arsenic or something to sweeten the taste." After which she laughed in her diabolical way and drank some of the coffee.

With clinical curiosity, Kenner watched the cup slip from her fingers and spill the rest of the liquid over the bedclothes; watched her expression alter and her face and body once more assume the characteristic attitude of oxide poisoning as she fell back against the headboard. The faint green color looked quite well on her, he concluded.

This time Kenner did not arrange the scene in what he thought to be a natural manner. He also did not open the windows. He simply left the apartment and took a subway to Times Square, where he consumed a breakfast of indeterminate nature in a restaurant or perhaps a cafeteria. Once finished he browsed through a bookstore, purchased a candy bar, and finally took the subway home again. Upon entering his apartment, I think the time was 10:51 A.M., he proceeded directly to his wife's bedroom.

She was still lying in bed, and she was still quite surprisingly dead. The scene, however, had after all been changed in certain ways. The coffee which he was *sure* had been spilled across the bedclothes had not been spilled at all; the cup, in point of fact, rested empty on the breakfast tray. Her color was not greenish, but rather a violent purple. The three cigarettes had become four, and each had burned down to skeletal fingers of gray ash. Her hands were clutched somewhat pathetically at her breast.

Kenner stared at her for a long time, after which scrutiny be went to his room and attempted to write in his journal. I could not seem to think, I knew I would have to wait until later. Returning to his wife's bedroom once more, he paused to study the empty coffee cup and the remains of the cigarettes. It was then that he understood the truth.

The *cigarettes* and the *coffee,* not Kenner, had done her in.

What he did next is not clear. Very little is clear even now, many hours later. He does seem to have telephoned his wife's doctor, since the physician arrived eventually and pronounced her dead of a heart attack. Two or three interns also came with a stretcher and took her away. As I write this, I can still smell the after-shave lotion one of them was wearing.

One thing, therefore, is quite clear: she's dead.

Damn her, she really is dead and gone forever.

What am I going to do *now?*

KENNER MURDERED his dead wife for the first time on August 1, or possibly August 6, in the bathroom of their New York apartment...

The Deveraux Monster

Jack Ritchie

TONGUE-IN-CHEEK

In writing to Jack Ritchie's agent for permission to reprint "The Deveraux Monster," the undersigned editor said that "no anthology is complete without a Ritchie story." This is by no means an isolated opinion. Anthony Boucher and Donald Westlake, among a host of others, have spoken glowingly of Mr. Ritchie's abundant talents, the most notable of which is his amazing ability to put more plot and more characterization into fewer words than any crime writer past or present "The Deveraux Monster" is a consummate illustration of this talent (and of his unique brand of tongue-in-cheek humor)—a 6,000-word mini-novel loaded with enough twists and turns to fill a 60,000-word book. Mr. Ritchie is the author of over 200 stories and one collection, The New Leaf and Other Stories; he resides quietly in Wisconsin, where, 'tis devoutly to be wish'd, he will write several hundred more. - B.P.

"HAVE *YOU* EVER SEEN THE MONSTER?" my fiancée, Diana Munson, asked.

"No," I said. But I had. A number of times. I smiled. "However, everyone seems to agree that the Deveraux monster rather resembles the Abominable Snowman, but with a coloring more suitable to a temperate climate. Dark brown or black, I believe."

"I wouldn't take this at all lightly, Gerald," Diana said. "After all, my father *did* see your family beast last night."

"Actually, it was dusk," Colonel Munson said. "I'd just completed a stroll and was about to turn into the gate when I looked back. The fog was about, nevertheless I clearly saw the creature at a distance of approximately sixty feet. It glared at me, and I immediately rushed toward the house for my shotgun."

Freddie Hawkins summoned the energy to look attentive. "You took a shot at it?"

Colonel Munson flushed. "No. I slipped and fell. Knocked myself unconscious." He glared at us. "I did not faint. I definitely did not faint."

"Of course not, sir," I said.

Colonel Munson, recently retired, and his daughter Diana came to our district some eight months ago and purchased a house at the edge of the village.

Fresh from Sandhurst and bursting for a good show, he joined his regiment on November 12, 1918, and that initiated a remarkably consistent career. In the Second World War he sat in England during Monty's North African campaign. When he finally wrangled a transfer to that continent, he arrived three days after Rommel's command disintegrated. He fretted under the African sun during the invasion of Europe and when at last he breathlessly reached France, the fighting had moved to Belgium. He still fumed at a training depot near Cannes when our forces joined the Russians in Germany. In the 1950's he set foot in Korea just as the cease fire was announced and during the Suez incident he was firmly stationed at Gibraltar. It is rumored that his last regiment's junior officers—in secret assembly—formally nominated him for the Nobel Peace Prize.

Freddie sighed. "All I have at my place is a ghostly cavalier who scoots about shouting for his sword and cursing Cromwell. Rather common, don't you think? Haven't seen him myself yet, but I'm still hoping."

Diana frowned in thought. "Who else, besides Father, has seen the Deveraux monster recently?"

"Norm Wakins did a few nights ago," Freddie said.

I smiled. "Ah."

Freddie nodded. "I know. Norm hasn't gone to bed sober since he discovered alcohol. However, he has always managed to walk home under his own power. As a matter of fact, on Friday evening he was quite capable of running. Norm left the village at his usual time—when his favorite pub closed—and his journey was routine until just north of the Worly Cairn when 'something made me look up.' And there he saw it—crouching and glaring down at him from one of those huge boulders strewn about. His description of the animal is a bit vague—he did not linger in the area long—but from what I was able to piece together, it was somewhat apelike, with dangling arms, a hideous face, and glowing yellow eyes. He claims that it was fanged and that it howled as it pursued him to his very cottage door."

"I shall have to carry a revolver loaded with silver bullets," I murmured.

"Only effective against werewolves." Freddie stretched lazily. "During the last ninety years the monster has been seen dozens of times."

Diana turned to me. "Gerald, just how did your family *acquire* this monster?"

"There are dark rumors. But I assure you, there is *no* Deveraux monster."

Freddie scratched an ear. "Gerald's grandfather had a brother. Leslie. Well, Leslie was always a bit wild and just before he disappeared..."

"He went to India," I said. "And eventually died there."

"...just before he *disappeared*, Leslie seemed to grow a bit *hairy*."

I remembered a few paragraphs of the letter my grandfather had left to his son—a letter which had been passed on to me by my father.

"I FIRST BECAME aware of what was happening when I accidentally came across Leslie at the Red Boar. It is not my usual pub—when I do go to pubs—but I was in the vicinity after seeing my tailor, and thirsty for a pint.

When I entered, I recognized my brother's back at the bar. I also noticed that the other patrons seemed to shy away from him and that the barmaid, in fact, appeared rather pale.

When Leslie turned at my approach, I stopped in shock. His eyebrows had grown thick and shaggy, his hairline was almost down to his eyes, and his complexion had turned a dark brown. He leered when he saw me, revealing stained yellow teeth.

I had seen him less than two hours before, but now I scarcely knew him!"

"ACCORDING TO LEGEND," Freddie continued, "Gerald's great uncle never did go to Africa, or India, or some beastly place like that. His brother was finally forced to keep him confined. In the east room on the third floor, wasn't it, Gerald?"

"Someplace about the house," I said. "Though if you have a monster, I should think that a more logical place to keep him might be in one of the cellars."

"Too damp," Freddie said. "And you must remember that your grandfather was rather fond of his brother—monster or not."

Diana's eyes widened. "You don't mean that...?"

"Oh, yes," Freddie said. "Leslie is supposed to have turned into the Deveraux monster."

"How ghastly," Diana said dutifully. "But *why?*"

Freddie shrugged. "Heredity, possibly. The monster eventually escaped. Bit through his chains, I believe. The Deverauxs always had good teeth." He looked at me. "Either that or he was let out periodically for a constitutional?"

"My grandfather would never release a monster," I said firmly. "Matter of honor."

Freddie calculated. "If this monster is human...I mean solidly animal, then it would be about ninety years old—considering Leslie's age at the time of his metamorphosis. Rather decrepit by now, I should think. Did you happen to notice its condition, Colonel?"

Colonel Munson glowered at the floor. "Seemed spry enough to me."

"I know that people have *seen* the monster," Diana said. "But is it dangerous?"

Freddie smiled faintly. "Eighty-five years ago, a Sam Garvis was found dead on the moors. He was frightfully mangled."

"Packs of wild dogs roamed this area in those days," I said. "Garvis was unfortunate enough to meet one of them."

"Possibly. But fifteen years later your grandfather was found dead at the base of a cliff."

"He fell," I said. "Broke his neck."

"Probably he fell because he was being pursued by the monster,"

Freddie said. "It had been seen just before he died. And then there was your father. Died of fright practically at his front door."

"I did not *faint*," Colonel Munson muttered.

"Father did not die of fright," I said. "Weak heart plus too much exercise." I glanced at my watch and rose. "I'll have to be running along, Diana."

Freddie got up too. "Mother's expecting me. Besides, Gerald needs an escort across the moors. Someone fearless."

The colonel saw us to the door. He was a short, broad-shouldered man with a military mustache in gray prime. "I'm going to hunt the beast."

"Best of luck," I said.

"I'll need it," he said morosely. "Hunted tigers in Malaya, leopard in Kenya, grizzly in Canada. Never got a blasted one."

Freddie and I said our goodbyes, adjusted our collars against the late afternoon's chilly mist, and began walking.

"I rather envy you," Freddie said.

"I'm perfectly willing to give you the monster."

"I mean Diana."

"Quite different."

Freddie brooded. "Of course, I can't court her now. You do have some kind of a definite arrangement, don't you?"

"We're getting married in June."

He sighed. "My only hope is that the monster might slaughter you before then."

"No assists, please."

"Wouldn't think of it. After all, we've known each other since time began, so to speak. Served in the same regiment. I saved your life."

"Barely."

"I'm fumble-fingers with bandages and the like. Besides, I couldn't remember where the pressure points were supposed to be."

We walked silently for a while and then he said, "You don't really believe there is a monster, do you?"

"Of course not."

We parted at the branch in the path and I went on toward Stonecroft.

I made my way among the lichen-covered boulders and paused for a moment at the remains of the huts. They were low roofless circles of stones now, but once they had been the dwellings of a forgotten, unwritten race. Perhaps they were men erect, but I have always had a feeling that they might have been shaggy and that they crawled and scuttled by preference.

I wondered again what had happened to them. Were they all really dead and dust or did their blood linger in our veins?

The moor wind died, and I glanced up at a faint rustle. A dark figure moved slowly toward me in the swirling wisps of fog.

When it was within twenty feet of me, I recognized Verdie Tibbs.

Verdie is simple. Actually quite simple, and he likes to roam the moors.

I thought he seemed a little disappointed when he saw me, but he smiled as I said, "Hello, Verdie."

"I thought it was my friend," Verdie said.

"Your friend?"

Verdie frowned. "But he always runs away."

"Who does?"

Verdie smiled again. "He has fur."

"Who has fur?"

"My friend. But he always runs away." Verdie shook his head and wandered back into the dusk.

I reached Stonecroft ten minutes later. No one seems to know just how old my home is. It had begun existence as a modest stone building in a distant time, but generations of Deverauxs had added to it, the last substantial addition being in 1720. My contribution has been the installation of plumbing, electricity, and the telephone. At the present time, I occupy only the central portion of the three-story structure, and very little of that.

When I reached the studded front door, I heard the great key in the lock and the bolt being drawn. The massive door opened. "Well, Jarman," I said. "Taken to locking the doors?"

He smiled faintly. "It's my wife who insists, sir. She feels that it would be wiser at the present time."

"I've never heard that the monster enters buildings."

"There's always a first time, sir."

Jarman, his wife, and their twenty-year-old son Albert, are my only servants at present. I could perhaps do without Albert, but it is family history that the Deverauxs and the Jarmans stepped over the threshold of Stonecroft at approximately the same moment. Turning out a

Jarman would be equivalent to removing one of the cornerstones or snatching away the foundation of Stonecroft.

AT LATE BREAKFAST the next morning, I noticed that Jarman seemed worried and preoccupied. When he brought the coffee, I said, "Is there something troubling you, Jarman?"

He nodded. "It's Albert, sir. Yesterday evening he went to the village. He wasn't back by ten-thirty, but my wife and I thought nothing of it and retired. This morning we found that he hadn't slept in his bed."

"Probably spent the night with one of his friends."

"Yes, sir. But he should at least have phoned."

Freddie Hawkins wandered in from the garden and took a seat at the table. "Thought I'd drop over and see if you're tired." He helped himself to bacon. "Sleep well last night?"

"Like a top."

"No sleep walking?"

"Never in my life."

"You look a bit hairy, Gerald."

"I need a haircut and I haven't shaved yet. Bachelor's privilege."

"Do you mind if I examine the bottoms of your shoes?"

"Too personal. Besides, if I roamed the moors last night as the monster, I wouldn't have worn shoes."

"There is the possibility that you are a monster only from the ankles up, Gerald." He took some scrambled eggs. "I suppose you'll be dropping in at the Munsons?"

"Of course."

"Mind if I toddle along?"

"You're frightfully infatuated, aren't you?"

"Fatally. We male Hawkinses are invariably lanky, tired, and muddle-headed, but we are always attracted to the brisk, practical woman. The moment I saw Diana and learned that she had once taken a course in accounting, I experienced an immense electrical reaction. You couldn't step out of the picture, could you, Gerald? For an old comrade-in-arms?"

"Not the thing to do."

"Of course," he said glumly. "Not gentlemanly. It's the woman's prerogative to break up things like this." He seemed to have something else on his mind and after a while he spoke again. "Gerald, last night Diana saw the monster."

I frowned. "How do *you* know?"

"She phoned my mother," Freddie said. "They get along rather well." He put down his coffee cup. "Just after she retired, Diana thought she heard a noise outside. She went to the window and there in the moonlit garden she saw the monster. By the time she roused the colonel and he found his shotgun, the creature had scampered away."

I lit a cigar and took several thoughtful puffs.

Freddie watched me. "I don't know what to make of it either."

After I shaved, we walked to the Munson house.

Diana met us at the door. "Gerald, I'd like to talk to you alone for a few moments, please."

Freddie waved a languid goodbye. "I'll go on to the village. The Red Boar, if anyone needs me desperately."

When we were alone, Diana turned to me. "Really, Gerald, I cannot accept a monster."

"But Freddie is really very—"

"I mean the Deveraux monster."

"Diana, if the animal exists, I believe that it is actually benign."

"Benign, my foot! That thing is dangerous."

"Even if it is, Diana, it seems that only the male Deverauxs have anything to fear."

"Gerald, I am looking at this from the practical point of view. I simply cannot have you murdered after our marriage, especially if we have children. Do you realize that the death duties these days would force me to sell Stonecroft? I might even have to go to London to find some employment. And I do not believe in working mothers."

"But, Diana..."

"I'm sorry, Gerald, but I've been thinking this whole thing over. Especially since last night. I'm afraid I'll have to call off our engagement."

"Diana," I said—and winced. "Is there...is there someone else?"

She thought for a moment. "I'll be frank with you, Gerald. I've been examining Freddie. He does seem to need management. I've met his mother and we seem to have a lot in common."

"Freddie has his ghost too," I pointed out. "That cavalier who runs about looking for his horse."

"His sword. But he is entirely harmless. He's tramped about the grounds since 1643, and has never yet harmed anyone."

"Suppose he finds his sword?"

"We will cross that bridge when we come to it."

I went to the window. "That cursed monster."

"It's your own fault," Diana said. "You Deverauxs should have watched your genetics and things like that."

I left her for the village and stopped at the Red Boar. Freddie was rather pale. "I just heard," he said. "Jarman's son, Albert, was found dead on the moor a half an hour ago. Head bashed in. Quite a messy business."

"Good Lord! Who did it?"

"No one knows yet, Gerald. But I'm afraid that people are talking about the Deveraux monster." He smiled faintly. "Gerald, I'm afraid that I've given you a rather hard time about that. I just want to say that I really believe that you only need a haircut and that's all."

I returned immediately to Stonecroft, but the Jarmans had evidently gone on to the village.

I went upstairs to the east room and unlocked the chest. I removed the envelope and re-read my grandfather's letter.

"I BELIEVE that the expression on my face gave Leslie considerable pleasure. I pulled myself together and was about to ask for some explanation, but Leslie took my arm and led me outside. "Later," he said.

We mounted our horses and rode out of the village. After half a mile, Leslie pulled up and dismounted. He removed his hat and then I watched a transformation. He pulled at his forehead and the coarse hair forming his low hairline came away in his fingers. His bushy eyebrows disappeared in the same manner. "And, my dear brother," he said, "my complexion can be washed away, and a good tooth brushing will remove the stain from my teeth."

"Leslie," I demanded sternly. "What is the meaning of this?"

He grinned. "I'm creating a monster. The Deveraux monster."

He put his hand on my shoulder. "Bradley, we Deverauxs have been here since the dawn of history. We were here before the Norman invasion. Deveraux is not French, it is simply a corruption of some pre-historic grunts applied to one of our ancestors. And yet, Bradley, do you realize that we are not haunted by anything or anyone?"

He waved an arm at the horizon. "The Hawkins family has its blasted cavalier. The Trentons have their weeping maid waiting for Johnny to come home from the fair, or some such thing. And even the Barleys, nouveau riche, have their bally butler drifting through the house looking for the fish forks. But what do we have? I'll tell you. Nothing."

"But, Leslie," I said. "These are authentic apparitions."

"Authentic, my Aunt Marcy! They were all invented by someone with imagination to add to the midnight charm of the homeplace. People are not really repelled by ghosts. They want them. And so, when they do not tell outright lies about seeing them, they eventually convince themselves that they have.

"Bradley," Leslie continued. "I am creating a Deveraux monster. And what better way than this? The villagers actually see me gradually turning into an apelike creature. And in a week or so, I, the human Leslie Deveraux, will disappear."

I blinked. "Disappear?"

"Bradley, I'm the younger son. I cannot possibly remain at Stonecroft the rest of my life waiting for your demise. You seem remarkably healthy. I suppose I could poison you, but I'm really fond of you. Therefore, the only course left is for me to go abroad to seek fame, fortune, and all that rot. But before I go—as a parting present, so to speak—I am leaving you the Deveraux monster. I will be seen wandering the moors—in full costume— and pursuing a passerby here and there. I have had a complete suit constructed, Bradley. It is locked in a chest in the east room, and I will don it for my midnight forays."

I immediately and vigorously launched into argument condemning his scheme as absolutely ridiculous and insane, and, at the time, I thought I had succeeded in convincing him to give up the entire thing. But I should have known Leslie and that half-smile when he finally nodded in agreement.

He wandered the moors in his Deveraux monster suit the next week— though I did not learn about it until later. It seems that people were reluctant to bring the creature's existence to my attention, since there was a general feeling that Leslie was undergoing a transformation.

And then Leslie disappeared.

It was not until a year later that Leslie wrote me from India, but in the meantime I had no answer to those of our friends who cautiously inquired about his disappearance. In a fit of pique one day, I declared that actually I kept Leslie chained in the east room. It was an unfortunate remark, and my words were eagerly taken at face value by a number of people who should *have known better. I might have exposed the Deveraux myth when Leslie's letter finally came, if, in the meantime, this district had not enacted the mantrap laws.*

I have never scattered mantraps about my grounds. I feel that their jaws are quite capable of severing a poacher's leg. But I have nourished the impression in the countryside and at the village that I was quite liberal in strewing them about my property. That was quite sufficient to keep most of the poachers off my land.

But then, as I mentioned, the mantraps were outlawed, and if I have a reputation for anything, it is obeying the law and the poachers know that. They immediately descended upon me with their snares and traps, causing untold depredations to the American quail and partridge I had introduced on the moor.

I tried everything to stop them, of course. I appealed to the authorities, I hired a gamekeeper, and I even personally threatened to thrash any poacher I apprehended on my property.

But nothing availed.

It was in a moment of total desperation that a wild idea descended upon me. I gathered up the house keys and went up to the east room. I opened the chest Leslie had left behind and the Deveraux monster costume was inside.

It fit me perfectly.

I believe I have never since enjoyed myself as much as I did in the next few weeks. At night I would don the costume and wander about I tell you, my son, it was with the most delicious pleasure that I pursued-with blood-chilling howls—the elder Garvis to the very door of his cottage.

The elder Garvis did not poach again—to my knowledge—but it is unfortunate that his experience, or his relation of that experience, did not make an impression upon his son. He persisted in poaching, and eventually toppled off a cliff and broke his neck.

It is widely believed that his demise occurred while the monster pursued him. That is not true. I never met Sam, Jr. on the moors. But I have done nothing to discourage the legend. As a matter of fact, the monster has been "seen" a number of times when I did not leave the house.

And so, my son, when I depart, I leave you the Deveraux monster. Perhaps you too will find some use for him.

Your loving father,
Bradley Deveraux

· · ·

MY OWN FATHER had added a note.

GERALD, it is remarkable how persistent the Garvis family is. Each Garvis, apparently, must learn about the monster from first-hand experience before he refrains from poaching.

I PULLED the costume from the chest and slipped into it. At the mirror I gazed at the monster once again.

Yes, he was indeed frightening, and the good colonel *had* fainted. Norm Wakins had seen the Deveraux monster, and simple Verdie Tibbs, and Diana.

But Albert Jarman? No.

After I let Diana catch a glimpse of me, I had returned directly home. I had met no one on the way and I had gone directly to bed. And slept soundly. Except for the dream.

I removed the head of my costume and stared at my reflection. Did I need a shave again?

AT DUSK, I saw the Jarmans returning to Stonecroft and let them in the front door.

Mrs. Jarman was a spare woman with dark eyes, and she stared at me as though she was thinking something she didn't want to believe.

"Mrs. Jarman," I said. "I'd like to extend my most sincere..."

She walked by me and disappeared into the back hall.

Jarman frowned. "Mrs. Jarman is very upset, sir. We all are."

"Of course."

Jarman was about to pass me, but I stopped him. "Jarman, do the authorities have any idea who might have killed your son?"

"No, sir."

"Is there any...any talk?"

"Yes, sir," Jarman said. "There is talk about the Deveraux monster." He sighed. "Excuse me, sir. I should go to my wife."

Before turning in for the night, I opened the bedroom windows for air. The rolling hills of the moor were bright with the moon and in the distance a dog howled. I felt the drift of the cool wind.

A movement in the shadows below caught my eye. I watched the spot until I made out a crouching figure. It moved again and stepped into the light. It was Verdie Tibbs. He glanced back at the house for a moment, and then disappeared into the darkness.

That night I dreamed again. I dreamed that I left the house and roamed across the moors until I found the circle of stones. I remained there waiting. For anyone.

Albert Jarman's funeral took place on Thursday and I, of course, attended. It was a dark day, and at the graveside the mist turned to light rain. Most of the countryside seemed to be in attendance, and I was conscious that a great many of the eyes found me with a covert glance.

Freddie Hawkins came to Stonecroft the next morning, while Jarman and I were going over the household accounts.

He sat down. "Frank Garvis was found dead in his garden this morning. Strangled. He had several tufts of hair...or fur...clutched in his fingers. Definitely not human, according to the inspector."

Jarman looked up, but said nothing.

I rubbed my neck. "Freddie, just what do *you* make of all this?"

"I don't know. Perhaps some ape has escaped from a circus or something of the sort?"

"The papers would have carried a notice."

He shrugged. "Could there actually *be* a Deveraux monster?" He looked at Jarman. "What do you think?"

"I have no opinion, sir."

Freddie grinned. "Perhaps Gerald rises in the middle of the night, gripped by some mysterious force, and goes loping about the moors searching for a victim." He shook his head. "But I guess that's out too. I hardly think that he would grow fur just for the occasion. Or does he slip into a monkey suit of some kind?"

Freddie looked at me for a few moments and then changed the subject. "My mother told me about your break with Diana. Dreadful sorry, Gerald."

"I think she rather fancies you," I said.

He flushed. "Really?"

"No doubt. She's impressed by your intelligence and drive."

He smiled. "No need to get nasty."

After he left, I went upstairs to the east room and unlocked the chest. I pulled out the Deveraux monster. Tufts of hair had been torn from both of the arms.

THAT EVENING I was in my study with a half-empty bottle of whiskey when Jarman entered.

"Will that be all for today, sir?" he asked.

"Yes."

He glanced at the bottle and then turned to go.

"Jarman."

"Yes, sir."

"How is Mrs. Jarman?"

"She is...adjusting, sir."

I wanted to pour another glass, but not while Jarman was watching. "Do the authorities still have no suspects for your son's murder?"

"No, sir. No suspects."

"Do *you* have any...ideas?" His eyes flickered. "No, sir."

I decided to pour the glass. "Does your *wife* have any ideas? Does she think that the Deveraux...?" I found myself unable to go on.

I drank the whiskey, and my next words came suddenly, and were undoubtedly inspired by the drink. "Jarman, I want you to lock me in my bedroom tonight."

"Sir?"

"Lock me in my bedroom," I snapped.

He studied me and there was worry in his eyes.

I took a deep breath and came to a decision. "Jarman, follow me. I have something to show you."

I led him to the east room, unlocked the chest, and put the envelope in his hands. "Read this."

I waited impatiently until he finished and looked up.

"You see," I said. "There is *no* actual Deveraux monster."

"No, sir."

"Jarman, I wouldn't tell you what I am now going to if it weren't for the present circumstances. I must have your word of honor that you will not repeat my words to a soul. To no one at all, do you understand?"

"You have my word, sir."

I paced the room. "First of all, you know that the poachers have been plaguing us again?"

He nodded.

"Well, Jarman, I have been wearing the Deveraux monster. I am the one responsible for chasing Norm Wakins to his door. I am the one who met poor simple Verdie. Accidentally, I assure you. He is not a poacher. He actually tried to make friends with me, and I was forced to flee." I stopped pacing. "My only intention was to frighten away poachers."

Jarman smiled faintly. "Is Colonel Munson a poacher?"

I felt myself flushing. "That was a spur of the moment thing. A lark."

He raised an eyebrow ever so slightly. "A lark, sir?"

I decided that I might as well be embarrassingly candid. "Jarman, you are aware that the colonel and Diana Munson came here about eight months ago? And that within two months I found myself engaged?"

"Yes, sir. Rather sudden."

I agreed and cleared my throat. "I was committed, and I am a gentleman. A man of my word, but still..."

The comers of Jarman's mouth turned slightly. "You found yourself not quite as happy as you thought you should be?"

I flushed again. "I happened to see Colonel Munson while I was in the monster suit and suddenly it occurred to me that if the colonel, and perhaps Diana herself, should see the monster, they might not be so eager for me to..." I wished I were downstairs with the bottle.

"I understand, sir," Jarman said. "And I am sure that Miss Munson will be quite satisfied with Mr. Hawkins."

"Jarman," I said. "I have frightened a number of people, but I have injured no one. I am...positive...that I did not kill your son." I stared down at the Deveraux monster in the chest and at the bare spots on the arms.

Jarman's voice was quiet. "Do you still want to be locked up for the night, sir?"

There was silence in the room and when I looked up, I saw that he was watching me.

Finally, Jarman said, "I *know* you didn't kill Albert."

"You *know*?"

"Yes, sir. Two nights ago, Verdie Tibbs came to the back door and spoke to me. He saw Albert killed. He saw the murder from a distance, too far away to give aid to Albert...and the crime was over in an instant."

Jarman looked tired. "Albert was returning from the village and apparently he came across a set of poacher's snares or nets. According to Verdie, Albert was bending over them and he seemed to be tearing them apart, when suddenly someone leaped behind him and struck him with a rock."

"Who was it?" I demanded.

Jarman closed his eyes for a moment. "Frank Garvis, sir."

"But why didn't Verdie go to the authorities?"

"Verdie was afraid, sir. He's heard talk that he might be sent to an institution, and he wants nothing to do with any public officials. But even if he had gone to the authorities, what good would that have done, sir? It would have been the word of simple Verdie against that of Frank Garvis."

"But then *who* killed Garvis last night?" I looked down at the chest again and wondered if I had only been dreaming when...

"Sir," Jarman said quietly. "The Jarmans and the Deverauxs have been together ever since the beginning. There are no secrets a Deveraux can keep from a Jarman—not for long." He smiled faintly. "My grandfather also left a letter to his son, and, in turn, to me."

He took a key out of his vest pocket. "This unlocks the chest too, sir, and the Deveraux monster fits me—as it did my grandfather and my father whenever they wished to wear it."

Jarman sighed. "I would have preferred to remain silent on the whole matter and let it pass. But I could see that you were beginning to fear that you were responsible, and so I had to speak. Now that you know, I will put my affairs in order, and then go to the police with a full confession."

"What have you told your wife?"

"Nothing but that Garvis killed Albert. I did not want her to think what the villagers are thinking."

I rubbed my neck. "Jarman, I fail to see that any...good...can come of your going to the police."

"Sir?"

"The Deveraux monster murdered Garvis," I said. "I think that it is much, much better if we leave it that way."

After a while, Jarman spoke faintly. "Thank you, sir."

I pulled the Deveraux monster out of the chest. "However, I believe that we should destroy this, don't you, Jarman? After all, someone might manage to compare it with the tufts of hair Garvis had in his fingers."

Jarman put the monster over his arm. "Yes, sir. I'll burn it." At the door he looked back. "Is the Deveraux monster dead, sir?"

A sudden gust of moor wind whispered around the shutters.

"Yes," I said. "The Deveraux monster is dead."

When he was gone, I happened to glance at the mirror.

Strange. I rather needed a shave again.

Afterword

We at Mystery Writers of America hope you enjoyed this collection of stories from our great writers. *Tricks and Treats*, edited by Joe Gores and Bill Pronzini, is the latest in a series of classic crime collections in our new program, Mystery Writers of America Classics.

Since 1945, MWA has been America's premiere organization for professional mystery writers, a group dedicated to learning from each other, helping new members, and sharing our successes and good times. One way we celebrate our talent is through the production of original, themed anthologies, published more or less yearly since 1946, in which one remarkable writer invites others to his or her collection.

Read more about our anthology program, both the new ones and classic re-issues, on our web page: https://mysterywriters.org

And watch for future editions of Mystery Writers of America Classics. To receive notifications, please subscribe here: http://mysterywriters.org/mwa-anthologies/classics-newsletter/

The Mystery Writers of America Presents Classic Anthology Series

1. *A Hot and Sultry Night for Crime*, Edited by Jeffery Deaver
2. *Woman's Wiles*, Edited by Michele Slung
3. *Blood on Their Hands*, Edited by Lawrence Block
4. *The Lethal Sex*, Edited by John D. MacDonald
5. *Merchants of Menace*, Edited by Hilary Waugh
6. *Tricks and Treats*, Edited by Joe Gores and Bill Pronzini

Story Copyrights

Made in the USA
Middletown, DE
16 February 2021